AMNESIA

Michael Ridpath spent eight years as a bond trader in the City, before giving up his job to write full time. He lives in North London with his wife and three children.

Visit his website at
www.michaelridpath.com.

AMNESIA

Michael Ridpath

CORVUS

First published in trade paperback in Great Britain in 2017 by Corvus,
an imprint of Atlantic Books Ltd. This paperback edition published
in 2018 by Corvus.

10 9 8 7 6 5 4 3 2 1

A CIP catalogue record for this book is available from the British Library.

Paperback ISBN: 978 1 78239 758 8
E-book ISBN: 978 1 78239 757 1

Printed in Great Britain by CPI Group (UK) Ltd, Croydon CR0 4YY

Corvus
An imprint of Atlantic Books Ltd
Ormond House
26–27 Boswell Street
London
WC1N 3JZ

www.corvus-books.co.uk

In memory of my late uncle, Michael Ridpath, ornithologist,
of Mundaring, Western Australia

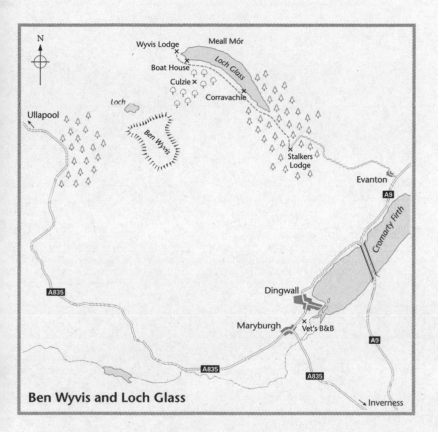

Ben Wyvis and Loch Glass

PART ONE

PROLOGUE

Friday 5 March 1999, Wyvis, Scotland

He heard a cry, almost a scream, cut short. Then the rapid tap of feet on floorboards.

'Jesus Christ! What happened to you? How long have you been there like that? Oh, you poor wee man!'

The voice was Scottish, female, concern verging on panic.

He was lying on something hard. He was cold. And his head hurt like hell. He tried to open his eyes but he couldn't.

He felt a gentle nudge on his arm. And then a hand on his cheek. Warmth.

'You're so cold! Are you alive, pet? Wake up! Open your eyes!'

His eyelids felt as if they were zipped shut, but he wanted to re-assure the woman before panic overwhelmed her.

He forced them open. He saw a pair of tight blue jeans. And a concerned, lined face beneath short blond hair. A tattoo of a Chinese character in green ink on a collarbone.

'Thank Christ! You *are* alive!'

He tried to say 'yes', but all he could manage was a groan.

His head hurt. A herd of elephants wearing stilettoes was performing a dance at the back of his brain.

'You're freezing. Stay there! I'll call an ambulance.'

The woman disappeared from view, and he heard her voice on a telephone.

He was lying on a wooden floor. He lifted his cheek. It was sticky. Blood – he could smell it, the tang of iron, of rust.

He tried to haul himself upright, but he couldn't. He tried harder. Somehow he pulled himself up onto his elbows, dragged himself a couple of feet across the floor, and twisted round so that his back was resting against the wall.

He was in a hallway. Above him, a steep, spiral wooden staircase, shiny with wear, curved into darkness. Next to him, a patch of dry brown spread across the floorboards. He raised his hand to his cheek, and then to the back of his skull. His head was caked in the stuff. The elephants were still dancing.

The woman returned, and squatted on the bottom step of the staircase staring at him. She was tall, long-limbed, about forty. Kind blue eyes. 'Don't worry. They're on their way.'

He tried to say something. He couldn't. He tried harder.

'Who are you?' he managed to croak.

The woman's eyebrows shot up in surprise. 'Och, you know who I am! I'm Sheila. Sheila MacInnes? From the Stalker's Lodge?'

'I don't know who you are,' he said.

Then another, more worrying question occurred to him.

'Who am I?'

1

Clémence huddled deep into her coat against the wind threading its way through the university buildings from the North Sea, only a quarter of a mile away. One day into the spring vacation, the town was already almost empty of students. Clémence was staying on: she lived in Hong Kong, and for one reason or another, she couldn't go back there for the holiday. She had just dropped her friend Livvie off at Edinburgh Airport to join a university ski trip somewhere in Austria. Livvie had said Clémence could borrow her car while she was away, provided Clémence picked her up the following week.

It was very nice of her – the car was a cute yellow Clio, brand new – but where would you drive to in Scotland alone in the middle of March?

She had also dropped off her boyfriend Callum, who was taking the bus back to Glasgow, where he was going to be working in a pub to earn much-needed spending money. They had only been going out three weeks, but Clémence would miss him. The university discouraged students from staying on in the vacation, and she would be virtually alone in St Andrews. She had considered asking Callum whether she could stay with him, but it was too early in their relationship for that. Maybe she would visit him for a couple of days over the weekend.

She had moped in her room in halls for an hour, and then set off for the university library. If she was going to be stuck in St Andrews, she may as well use the time productively. She had fallen behind with her work: a bit too much socializing, a bit too much drinking, way too much faffing about. Callum. Nothing drastic, nothing that a couple of weeks in the library wouldn't sort out.

St Andrews was an ancient university of beautiful buildings, but its library looked like a car park built in the 1960s. Yet it was familiar, it was welcoming, and it was out of the wind.

She was walking through the entrance to the entry gates, when her phone buzzed. She checked the number and grinned. An American international dialling code. New York.

'Tante Madeleine!' she said. 'How are you?'

Tante Madeleine was actually a great-aunt, the sister of Clémence's long-dead French grandmother. It was Aunt Madeleine who had paid for Clémence to go to boarding school in England, and who was now paying for St Andrews. Clémence's own parents were teachers, divorced from each other, and earning little money. More importantly, it was Aunt Madeleine who cared about her.

They spoke in French. 'Oh, Clémence, darling, I am so worried. I need to ask you a favour, a very great favour. I hope you can help me?'

'Of course,' said Clémence, more worried herself by how long the favour would take to explain than what it actually was. International calls from Aunt Madeleine ate up her phone credit.

'There is an old friend of mine, of your grandparents, called Alastair Cunningham. Have you heard of him?'

'Maybe,' said Clémence. 'I think he visited us in Morocco when I was little.'

'That's right. Well, he knew your grandfather at university, then became a doctor and emigrated to Australia. Anyway, he came back to Britain last year and now he lives in the highlands of Scotland in a little cottage somewhere.'

'Do you want me to visit him?' said Clémence. 'I can. It's the spring vacation and I can borrow a car.'

'It's more than that,' said Madeleine. 'Last week he fell down the stairs and hit his head. It is serious: so serious he has lost almost all of his memory. He's in Inverness Hospital, and he has no relatives still alive in this country, nor friends for that matter.'

'Poor man!'

'Exactly. Somehow the hospital got hold of my number, and I am planning to fly over to Scotland to organize things for him. But could you fetch him from the hospital in Inverness and take him back to his cottage and look after him? It will only be for a few days. I remember you saying that you volunteered at the old people's home?'

'All I do is read to them,' said Clémence. 'I don't know how to look after them.'

'The hospital say he is ready to go home,' said Madeleine. 'I don't think it will be too difficult.' She paused. 'I know it is a lot to ask, Clémence, and I would understand if you said no. I can probably employ a nurse to stay with him, but I feel so bad for the poor man.'

Clémence did too. She had a reputation for being a bit of a ditz, partially justified, and she wasn't confident of her ability to take care of a sick old person. But her Aunt Madeleine rarely asked her for anything – *never* asked her for anything – and Clémence owed the old lady so much.

Besides which, St Andrews, a town she normally loved, was already beginning to depress her.

'All right, Aunt Madeleine. I will go and pick him up tomorrow.'

They discussed details and then Clémence hung up, a little worried about what the next few days would bring, but pleased she still had some phone credit left.

Sunday 14 March 1999, Raigmore Hospital, Inverness

'Who the hell are you?'

The old man's brown eyes stared up at her, shrewd, angry but also unsure. Vulnerable.

'Clémence,' she answered, in as encouraging a tone as she could muster.

'Do I know you?'

'No. I mean yes. Sort of. We met when I was little. In Morocco. But not since then.'

The old man took in the information from his position propped up in the hospital bed. He looked a tough old bird: firm wrinkles, a square jaw with a cleft chiselled at its centre, a thinning grey buzz-cut mocked by dense shaggy eyebrows. His eyes were sharp. Demanding. But unsure.

'Are we related?'

'No,' said Clémence. 'I'm Madeleine's niece, or rather great-niece. Madeleine Giannelli? A French lady? An old friend of yours?'

'I know who Madeleine Giannelli is,' said the old man, with a flash of irritation.

The nurse, an Irish woman who had been hovering behind Clémence's shoulder, leaned forward. 'Be nice to the girl, Alastair. She doesn't know what you can remember and what you can't.'

The irritation switched from Clémence to the nurse. Then the old man grunted. 'They tell me Madeleine is an old friend,' he said. 'I have to believe them. So far she is the only friend of mine they have discovered. I have no family, apparently.'

Clémence glanced at one end of a neat scar, the stitch marks still visible, that sneaked up the side of the old man's skull from his pillow.

'She'll be here as soon as she can,' said Clémence. 'She lives in America. I'll bring you home and take care of you until she arrives.'

The old man looked Clémence up and down doubtfully and grunted. The nurse clucked her disapproval.

Clémence thought the old man had a point.

'Ah, here's Dr Stenhouse,' the nurse said.

Clémence turned to see a small dark-haired woman in a white coat moving towards her briskly.

'Are you here to take Dr Cunningham home?'

It took a moment for Clémence to realize that the doctor was talking about the old man, not one of her colleagues. 'Er, yes,' she said.

'Can I have a word before you go?'

'Of course,' said Clémence.

'I'll get Alastair ready,' said the nurse.

Clémence followed the doctor away from the beds to a quiet corner beyond the nurses' station.

'I'm very glad you can do this,' said the doctor. 'It's not just that we need the bed. Dr Cunningham may be eighty-three, but he was a very fit man when he came in here, and if we keep him in too long, his muscles will atrophy and we'll never get him out of bed.'

'Has he recovered fully?' Clémence asked.

'Physically, yes,' said the doctor. 'He fell on the stairs and the trauma was quite severe. He was unconscious for several hours and, as you can see, he has suffered severe memory loss. He had a subdural haematoma which we had to drain surgically. An MRI showed that he had sustained at least two previous head injuries in the past; your aunt says he used to play rugby, which might have been responsible. He was admitted nine days ago, but he hasn't complained of a head-ache for three days.'

'What about the wound?'

'It's healing nicely. Bring him back next week and we'll take the stitches out.'

'Can he remember anything at all?' Clémence asked.

'He has retrograde amnesia, which means he has lost the ability to recall events in his past dating back to his childhood. He can remember his parents, but not his late wife, for example. But he can remember everything required for day-to-day life. He could probably drive a car, although I don't recommend you try that one out. He doesn't remember going to medical school or being a GP, but he has a detailed knowledge of medicine.'

'Could it be Alzheimer's?' Clémence asked.

'No, it's definitely trauma. Alzheimer's doesn't show up in scans, but Mrs Giannelli said he was alert mentally the last time she spoke to him, and showed no sign of memory loss. Although, if he did have incipient Alzheimer's, then a head injury could easily make things worse.'

'Will he get any of these memories back?'

'Probably. That's where you come in. Jogging his memory is the best way to encourage recall, but that's difficult when there seems to be no one in this country who knows him. But do the best you can. That's why it's important to take him back to his home. He moved into a cottage on the Wyvis Estate up by Loch Glass last year and shut himself away. The stalker's wife up there, Sheila MacInnes, is responsible for renting out the cottage and cleaned it for him once a week. Fortunately, she pops in almost every day to check on him, and she discovered him at the bottom of the stairs.'

'That is lucky.'

'She says there are plenty of papers there and photos; she found your aunt's address on a letter on his desk. Try to talk through those with him. Do you know much about him?'

'Almost nothing,' Clémence said. 'Only the little bit my great-aunt has told me.'

'Well, phone her and find out what you can. When your aunt gets over here in a few days, I'm sure she will be able to help a lot. Now, make an appointment with me back here for early next week, and we will see what progress he has made and take care of those stitches. The district nurse will check in on you to make sure he's all right, but I don't anticipate any problems.'

She might not, but Clémence did. Stuck in a cottage with a grumpy old man who could barely remember his own name suddenly seemed like a big responsibility for a twenty-year-old. It scared her. Maybe this wasn't such a good idea after all.

The doctor seemed to sense her doubts. 'Mrs Giannelli said you had experience working with old people?'

'Oh, yes,' said Clémence, smiling. 'Yes, I do.' Reading to them. Not feeding them or wiping their bums or washing them.

No. This wasn't going to work. 'Look. Can't he just stay here for a few days until Madeleine arrives?' Clémence said. 'It might be better for him in the long run.'

Dr Stenhouse's lips pursed. 'When fit and healthy old people have severe injuries one of two things can happen. Either we and they give up and they spend the rest of their life in a bed in a home somewhere, or we pull our fingers out and help them and they recover. I've seen people take the easy option too often, not just doctors, but relatives and the patients themselves. You can never be sure in these cases, but in my judgement, there is a chance that if you take Dr Cunningham back to his home and talk to him and jog his memory, he might recover. That's not certain by any means, but it's a possibility. He's a brave man, not the kind of person to take the easy way out. But if you leave him here to rot, he will do just that. That is for sure.'

Pull yourself together, girl, the doctor was saying. Fair enough, thought Clémence. She didn't know the old man, but he needed her help and she should give it.

'OK,' she said. 'I'll do it. Let's go back and get him.'

2

Clémence drove north out of Inverness, the old man silent beside her. They were soon on the high modern bridge crossing the Moray Firth, with the jumble of the port of Inverness beneath them on one side, and an oil rig lurking in the firth on the other. In the distance, to the north-west, stood a broad-shouldered, white-caped, mountain.

'Is that Ben Wyvis?' Clémence asked.

'How should I know?' said the old man. 'I didn't even know I was in Scotland till they told me.'

'Take a look at the map,' said Clémence. 'It's on the back seat.'

The old man hesitated, and for a moment Clémence thought he would refuse, then he twisted around, retrieved the map and examined it. She suddenly had an awful thought that his reluctance might be because he had forgotten how to map read.

He hadn't. 'We're on the A9, aren't we?' he said.

'I hope so,' said Clémence.

'Yes, that's Ben Wyvis.'

'Your cottage is on the other side of that, by Loch Glass.'

'I see it. On the map, it looks like it's in the middle of nowhere.'

'It does, doesn't it? Is that coming our way?'

Behind the mountain, large dark clouds were gathering.

'I think it is.'

Great, thought Clémence. She wasn't a confident driver, and navigating narrow mountain roads in a storm with a grouchy old man beside her didn't sound like much fun.

They were on the north side of the Moray Firth now, on the Black Isle, the peninsula of rich farmland between the Moray and the

Cromarty firths: low rolling hills, fields of green and brown, scattered whitewashed buildings with grey roofs.

'So what do you know about yourself?' Clémence asked.

'Nothing,' said the old man. 'Absolutely nothing.'

'Oh come on,' said Clémence. 'You must know something. We have to start somewhere. Did you speak to Aunt Madeleine?'

'No,' said the old man. Clémence waited.

The old man sighed. 'She told the nurses I was born in 1916, grew up in Yorkshire, went to Oxford University, became a GP back in Yorkshire, and then I emigrated to Western Australia in the nineteen sixties. I got married and then divorced. No children. And then for some reason I came back here last year and rented a cottage at this place called Wyvis. Why I suddenly did that I have no idea.'

'Sometimes people want to go back to their roots, don't they?'

'Yes, but I never lived in Scotland! Or at least I assume I didn't. I don't know, do I? I don't know anything!'

The frustration burned in his voice.

'But you remember Yorkshire?'

'Yes,' said the old man. 'Or at least the Yorkshire of my childhood.'

'Well?'

'Well what?'

'How was that? The Yorkshire of your childhood? Where did you live?'

The old man looked at Clémence sharply. 'You don't know what it's like, do you? You're just a child. You can't possibly know what it's like – to have forgotten everything.' The bitterness oozed from his voice. 'I don't see how they think you can help me. This is just a waste of time.'

Clémence realized that unless she did something about the old man's attitude soon, the next week was going to be a nightmare. They were passing a turn-off to a small village. She swerved off the main road and followed a narrow lane for fifty yards, until she came to a gate, where she pulled over. Two shaggy red cows with long sharp horns looked up to study the car from beneath unkempt fringes.

'Hey! What are you doing?'

Clémence switched the engine off and turned towards the old man.

She kept her voice calm but firm. 'Dr Cunningham. You're quite right, I can have no idea what it's like to be you. But remember what the doctor at the hospital said? It would be easy for all of us to give up on you. You spend the rest of your life in a hospital bed, watching *Countdown* on TV, without knowing who you really are. You forget how to walk, how to look after yourself, and everyone loses interest in your life. You lose interest in your life. So at some point it stops and everyone just gets on without you. Do you want that?'

The old man had raised his bushy eyebrows. Now he lowered them. But he didn't answer her question.

'Because if you do, I can take you back to the hospital right now. But if you don't . . .' She smiled, and softened her voice. 'I'll help you. I'll help you get better. I'll help you remember.'

The old man glared at her.

'Now. Shall I take you back to hospital?'

For a moment Clémence thought the old man was going to say yes. Then he closed his eyes. He sighed. 'No,' he whispered.

'Say that again. Louder.'

'No,' the old man repeated, looking at Clémence. There was anger in his eyes, but there was also need. He did need her help.

'So when I get back on the main road and ask you questions about your life, you will have a go at answering them?'

The old man nodded slowly. 'All right. I will.'

Clémence examined his face to check whether he meant what he said. He seemed sincere.

'OK. Let's go.' She executed a five-point turn in the lane, and within a minute they were back on the main road heading north.

'All right. So tell me about Yorkshire.'

The old man said nothing. Frustrated, Clémence took her eyes off the road to shoot him a quick glance. But he seemed preoccupied, thinking. She decided to let him.

Eventually, he spoke. 'We lived in a little town called Pateley Bridge on the River Nidd. My father was a doctor there. We had a grey stone house with ivy growing up the outside to my bedroom window. I can remember that clearly. I can remember my little sister Joyce.' He paused, but this time Clémence sensed not reluctance, but pleasure at the memory. 'I can remember her giggle; she used to giggle constantly. I loved to make her laugh. I used to do impressions of her friends, or the teachers at the school. Even politicians on the wireless. I could do a good Ramsay MacDonald, I remember.'

'Go on.'

'What?'

'Go on. Do your Ramsay MacDonald.'

The old man hesitated and then cleared his throat. He spoke in prim, clipped Scottish tones: '"My friends, we are beginning a contest which will be one of the most historical in the story of our country."'

'Very good!'

'How do you know? Do you even know who Ramsay MacDonald was?'

'I certainly do,' said Clémence. 'Prime minister before the war. Labour? No, Liberal.'

'Labour and then the National Government. Bit of a twit, quite frankly. Born working class, did his best to die a toff.'

'Do you know who the current prime minister is?' Clémence asked.

'I do, as a matter of fact, but only because the doctors told me. Some chap called Tony Blair. But I do remember the one before him, or maybe it was two before him. Margaret Thatcher. And James Callaghan before her, and Harold Wilson and Edward Heath.'

'Not bad,' said Clémence.

'And I know who won the 1966 election in Australia. Harold Holt for the Liberals beat Arthur Calwell for Labor. Now isn't it strange that I can remember that, but I can't remember the name of my own wife?'

'Yeah. That's seriously weird.'

'The wiring in my brain is a complete mess. I need a good electrician. Do you think you're a good electrician, Clémence?'

'An expert,' she said, knowing she wasn't.

They drove on. Then he smiled. 'There is so much I remember of my childhood. I have been going over it all in my mind in bed in the hospital. I went away to boarding school. I played rugger, I was good at it, I played centre three-quarter for the first XV. Then . . .'

He sighed. 'Then it just disappears. The doctors think I might have had a concussion at school, which is when the wiring in my brain first became damaged. Who knows? I certainly don't.'

'We'll get it back,' said Clémence.

The old man frowned. 'I hope so,' he said. 'I really hope so.'

They drove on, the light grey of the sky darkening. Soon rain was splattering the windscreen.

'This last week has been very odd,' said the old man, staring straight ahead at the rain. 'Without memories, you don't know who you are. I have to accept who other people say I am. They say I'm a doctor. I know medical things, I know that the metacarpals are fixed to the distal carpal bones, so I must be a doctor. They say I have spent much of my life in Australia. I know that the Mundaring librarian is called Jeanette, so I must have lived in Australia.'

'It must be weird,' said Clémence. 'But maybe we can figure out where Mundaring is, why you know the library. Then we can piece together that part of your life. And then another part, and another, until it all makes sense.'

The old man smiled. 'Thank you for your help, Clémence. I'm sorry I was so ungrateful back there. It is actually good to have someone from my old life – my real life – with me. But sometimes it just seems too difficult. And it's frightening. I mean, why don't I have any friends in this country? And if that's the case, why am I here? What sort of person am I? Am I kind? Am I generous? Am I mean? I know I'm bad-tempered, but maybe that's just the frustration of my situation. And why did my wife leave me? Was I unbearable to live with? Or was she? Did I have an affair? Did she? Am I trustworthy? Can I trust myself?'

'God, I see what you mean,' said Clémence.

'And what happened to Joyce? She was younger than me; is she dead? I hope not.'

She must be, thought Clémence, or someone would have found her. As must be his parents, obviously.

'If I were a young man, perhaps I could start a new life, a new personality. But I'm eighty-three! Or so they say. Far too old to start a new life. And barely enough time to recover the old.'

Clémence looked across at the old man. He met her glance. His eyes were uncertain. How would she feel if she were him? Lost. Afraid. Alone.

They drove on in silence, the rain turning to sleet. They came to the long, low bridge over the Cromarty Firth, with the town of Dingwall only just visible through the murk. She had an idea.

'Who was your best friend at school?' she said.

'Why do you want to know?'

'We've got to start somewhere. Let's begin with what you do know.'

The old man nodded. 'All right,' he said, smiling. 'I know the answer to that. Porky Bakewell. His real name was Dennis, but we called him Porky because he was so thin.'

And he told her all about Porky, and what they used to do together. Damming a beck on Greenhow Hill, exploring the forbidden disused lead mines, drawing endless maps of an invented tropical island, getting in trouble for trying to lasso Mr Heptonstall's bullocks. As the old man relaxed, his voice became a warm rumble. And actually, the adventures of Porky Bakewell and the young Alastair Cunningham were entertaining, at least to Clémence. One of her skills was that she was easily amused. Lucky that.

They turned off the main road at the village of Evanton, and climbed a steep wooded glen, the sleet turning to snow. After five miles or so, they reached a wooden bridge over what the map told them was the River Glass. The bridge was guarded by the Stalker's Lodge and a high white metal gate bearing the sign *Wyvis Estate. Private Road.*

The words 'Wyvis Estate' were familiar to Clémence. She wondered if this was the mythical Scottish estate that had once been in her grandfather's family. Maybe she was making false connections, but on the other hand that might explain why the old man had decided to ensconce himself there.

It was a beautiful spot. The snow had stopped. Soft white flakes clung to the needles of the pine trees that surrounded the lodge, and the road was slick with a damp film of it, cut with neatly spaced wheel tracks. The low late-afternoon sun slunk beneath the clouds retreating to the east, and glistened on the drops of water already being squeezed from the thawing snowfall.

Clémence left the old man in the car and, as she approached the lodge, she spotted an envelope on the doorstep bearing an approximation of her name, *CLEMENTS*, printed in large letters. Inside was a note from Sheila MacInnes, enclosing a key and giving directions to the old man's cottage. Mrs MacInnes had stocked the place up with essentials and she promised she would drop by that evening if she could, or else the following morning. She had parked the old man's car in a shed at the lodge to keep it safe.

They followed the track from the Stalker's Lodge and drove through woods beside the stream. According to Mrs MacInnes's directions, they would reach Loch Glass in a mile. Clémence drove carefully; Livvie's Clio was new, and the last thing she wanted to do was to slide off the snow-covered road into a ditch or a tree.

The old man was silent, preoccupied.

'Does any of this seem familiar?' Clémence asked.

'No,' said the old man. 'It's just . . .'

'Just what?'

The old man looked away. 'I'm not sure now I do want to remember my old life.'

'Why not?'

'I don't know,' said the old man. The smile had gone and the wrinkles were firmly set in a frown.

They emerged from the woods and a long curved loch appeared in front of them, a deep royal blue. Loch Glass. On the far side of the loch was a wall of almost vertical rock. Above them, on their side of the water, rose the massive dome of Ben Wyvis, a pure white hump against the pale-blue sky. The sun was low in the sky now, and the great mountain cast a shadow over the top end of the loch, which took on a darker grey colour.

'It's beautiful,' said Clémence. 'No wonder you chose to come up here.'

They drove along the shore of the loch, which seemed to be uninhabited, except for a white cottage on a little spit of land. Smoke was rising from its chimney.

The track was in good condition, luckily for the Clio, which had no trouble gripping through the thin layer of snow. After a couple of miles, the water curved around to the left, and a handsome house came into view at the head of the loch a mile or so ahead. It was large but fell short of meriting the term 'castle'; in fact the gables and stockbroker Tudor timbering gave it a home counties feel. Beside it rose a stand of tall Scots pines, and in front squatted two small square buildings, also of stockbroker Tudor.

'That's not it, is it?' Clémence said, slowing to consult her directions.

'No,' said the old man.

Clémence glanced at him. 'You remember?'

'It's hardly the kind of cottage that an eighty-three-year-old man would live in alone, is it?' he said, with a grin.

'I suppose not,' said Clémence, feeling a little stupid. Indeed, the directions called upon her to turn left up the slope from the loch through a wood.

The wood was a tangle of deciduous trees, clambering up the rock-strewn hill from the loch shore. Their trunks were silver grey, and they were twisted and heavily laden with thick green moss and white scoops of snow. Their branches ended in a mass of tangled fingers. The track rose steeply for a couple of hundred yards, until it emerged into a clearing, in the centre of which stood a square, trim stone cottage in a simple garden protected by a wooden picket fence. A weather-beaten sign board announced *Culzie* in faded black lettering.

3

Clémence unlocked the front door to the cottage. The old man shuffled along behind her.

The cottage immediately charmed her. A flagstoned hallway led through to a cosy sitting room, panelled in wood with a large stone fireplace. Prints of highland scenes lined the walls, and the floorboards were covered in ancient threadbare rugs. A steep wooden spiral staircase, with rope acting as a banister, led up to the bedrooms. The kitchen seemed both quaintly old-fashioned and useful, with modern appliances and a microwave, Clémence was glad to see. Mrs MacInnes had been busy: everything was tidy, and there was a faint smell of polish.

'This is lovely!' she exclaimed.

The old man looked around him, with a slight frown. Clémence had the impression that memories were stirring, but she didn't want to ask him right away for fear of irritating him.

He helped her carry in the shopping she had bought at a Tesco's on the way from St Andrews to Inverness, and his own small suitcase. He seemed to know immediately which of the three bedrooms upstairs was his. Mrs MacInnes had set up one of the others for Clémence, and the third was a small study with a desk.

Clémence unpacked the groceries, paid for with the promise of a five-hundred-pound transfer into her bank account by Aunt Madeleine for expenses. Given what Mrs MacInnes had already supplied, the cottage was now well stocked. Then she went into the sitting room and studied the fireplace. She squatted and began to stack the wood in a neat pile in the grate.

'Do you want some help?' The old man was watching her.

'Not much call for wood fires in Hong Kong,' said Clémence, embarrassed by her ignorance.

'Oh, don't worry about it,' said the old man, unstacking the wood and rolling the sheets of newspaper by the fire up into complicated shapes. 'It's good there's something useful that I can actually remember how to do. Here, let me show you.'

He soon had it lit, and they stood back to admire his work.

'Why aren't you back there now?' the old man asked. 'In Hong Kong? I suppose it's too far to go just for a couple of weeks?'

'That's right,' said Clémence. 'It's just too expensive.' But she knew she was looking shifty as she said it – Aunt Madeleine had always paid for flights home in the school holidays and would be happy to pay for them while Clémence was at university. Clémence had never been a good liar, and from the way the old man was looking at her, she was pretty sure he knew she wasn't telling the truth.

She fled to the kitchen and set about preparing an early supper. Her cooking skills were limited, her repertoire cheap-and-easy student food, but she was good with pasta. While she was cooking, she was aware of the old man pacing around the house, picking things up and putting them down again. He went outside for a few minutes, to walk around the tiny garden and stare through the trees to the loch below.

Mrs MacInnes had left a bottle of red wine, and Clémence opened that, even though she had brought her own supply. She and the old man sat down.

'Are you hungry, Dr Cunningham?' she said, as she served him.

'I am, actually,' he said. 'And call me Alastair. Everyone seems to think that's my name, and so I must take that on trust.'

'You must know that's your name,' said Clémence. 'Isn't there some recognition?'

'Yes, there is now,' said Alastair. 'And some of this is familiar. I know that the corkscrew came from that drawer, for example,' he said, pointing to the second drawer down.

'You know, I think my grandfather might have owned this estate. Or my great-grandfather,' said Clémence. 'I recognize the name, Wyvis.'

'But you can't remember?' said the old man with a grin.

Clémence laughed. 'No. But I can ask Grandpa. He's still alive. He lives in London.'

'That's Madeleine's brother-in-law?' said Alastair.

'That's right.' For a second Clémence assumed that he had remembered something, but then realized that it was just what the doctors and she had told him. At least it showed his short-term memory for new things was working well.

'I'm surprised they didn't send him up here,' said Alastair.

'He's pretty old,' said Clémence.

'So is Madeleine, presumably.'

'That's true,' said Clémence. 'And her husband died last year, run over in Arizona, it was horrible. But she is a terrific organizer, whereas no one expects very much from Grandpa. I think he's an alcoholic? Or used to be. I don't know him very well. But I will give him a call tomorrow and ask him about you.'

'So his wife was Madeleine's sister?' said the old man.

'Exactly. My grandmother. I never knew her; she died long before I was born. Drowned on holiday. No one likes to talk about it.'

'She was French,' said the old man frowning, fighting for memory.

'Yes,' said Clémence. They were still on information the old man had been given or could deduce.

He looked up at Clémence, his eyes shining. 'She was very beautiful. Wasn't she?'

Clémence remembered a black-and-white portrait of her grandmother that her father kept in his bedroom. 'Yes, she was.'

'She looked like you.'

'Did she?' She glanced at the old man, who flashed a grin of unexpected warmth, even charm. She felt herself blush. 'I thought she had blond hair?' Clémence's was dark.

'She did. But she had your eyes. And your chin. And there is something about the way you move that reminds me of her.'

'That's fantastic, Alastair!' said Clémence. 'You remember her!'

He smiled. 'Yes, I remember her. I don't remember your grandfather, or this Madeleine woman, but I do remember her.'

'Perhaps if I describe Grandpa, you might remember him,' Clémence said. 'His name is Stephen. Stephen Trickett-Smith.'

'No, Clémence. I'm tired. Let's start on all that tomorrow.'

'OK,' said Clémence. 'The doctor said that we should go through your papers and photos to see whether that might jog anything. Do you mind if I look at them? I feel bad about going through your private stuff.'

Alastair didn't answer. The smile had disappeared. For a brief moment his face seemed stricken with something close to horror, and then his jaw set.

'What is it, Alastair? If you don't want me to look through your papers, I won't. We can just talk.'

He finished his pasta and put down his knife and fork. 'The truth is, I'm scared of what you might find. What I might find.'

'You mean some horrible secret?' Clémence had said this with an attempt at humour, but as soon as the words were out of her mouth she regretted them.

'Yes,' said the old man. 'That's exactly what I mean. We all have secrets. But I have a feeling I have a particularly unpleasant one.'

'OK, that's fine. I have no desire to learn your unpleasant secrets,' said Clémence. And she didn't, she really didn't. 'Why don't you go through your papers yourself and you decide what you want to talk to me about?'

The old man frowned. Then he seemed to shake himself, and he smiled at Clémence. She liked his smile. The wrinkles in his face, the deep valleys and the canyons, rearranged themselves in a lacework of smaller, narrower lines, radiating across his cheeks. It was a shame he wasn't someone's grandfather. 'That was a very good supper,

Clémence,' he said. 'I really appreciate you staying with me, and helping me with this, and I'm sorry I was so difficult earlier.'

'That's OK,' said Clémence.

'And now, I know it's early, but if you don't mind, I'd like to go to bed.'

Clémence cleared the table as the old man climbed the stairs to his room. He was slow, but he seemed to have no real trouble. Nor had there been any discussion about Clémence needing to help him get to bed. That was a relief. She would go up and check on him in half an hour or so, just to make sure.

She was looking forward to helping him try to recover his life. Clémence had a tendency to feel sorry for people, and she definitely felt sorry for the old man. It was bad enough to be an old person alone without family or friends – she had met enough of them at the nursing home – but the idea of lacking memories as well appalled her. No wonder he had appeared frustrated and scared; she wasn't sure how she would cope if she was in his position. The loneliness must be almost total. She remembered the pleasure he had shown at recalling his sister, how he had warmed to his memories of Porky and his childhood.

And the rest of his life? All gone. Erased as if it had never existed.

She could forgive his grumpiness, but she was very glad she had had the courage to stand up to him. She could help him. She was patient, she was a good listener, she was easily entertained. She *would* help him.

It was dark now outside the cottage, and she heard the quavering hoot of an owl from somewhere among the twisted trees. She felt very alone here, she and the old man in a little house miles from anywhere. And it *was* miles from anywhere. Three miles to the Stalker's Lodge and five miles beyond that to the village of Evanton and the Cromarty Firth. It felt both creepy and exciting at the same time. For a girl brought up in overcrowded Hong Kong, the emptiness and desolation of the Scottish Highlands had a lot going for it. It was one of the reasons she had chosen to go to St Andrews, about as far removed from a big-city university as you could get.

But then St Andrews was also a long way from her parents, which seemed to suit them very well. Not for the first time she wondered, if they had lived in Scotland rather than Hong Kong, would she be going to university in New Zealand?

She stuck the plates in the dishwasher, tidied the kitchen and went up to her room to fetch a book. The light was on under the old man's door, and she could hear him moving around inside there. She thought of knocking on his door and asking if he was OK, but decided not to in case it irritated him.

She peeked in to the study. It was a small room containing a desk, a chair, a bookcase and a tatty armchair. An Ordnance Survey map showing Loch Glass hung on one wall, and a print of a golden eagle on another. She examined the books on the theory that you can tell a lot about a man from his bookshelf. There weren't many of them: half were about birds, although there were one or two novels – William Boyd and Ken Follett – and some history – *Stalingrad*, a book on the Norman Conquest and another on the Crusades. A couple were on local subjects.

A blue air-mail envelope lay in the middle of the old man's desk. It was addressed to Dr Alastair Cunningham at Culzie, Loch Glass and it had been opened. Clémence recognized the handwriting. She flipped it over, and sure enough, the sender's address was that of her Aunt Madeleine in New York City; it must have been the letter Mrs MacInnes had found. Clémence was about to slip out the couple of sheets of paper inside it, when she stopped herself, remembering her promise not to look through the old man's private papers.

Despite what Mrs MacInnes had said, Clémence couldn't see much evidence of private papers or photos in the study, but she resolved not to look too closely. All that would be up to Alastair to check. So she went back to her own room, pulled out a copy of *Le Cid* by Corneille, a set text for her French Literature course, and took it down to the sitting room, noticing on the way a darker stain of brown peeking out under a rug at the foot of the stairs.

She shuddered. Blood. Alastair's blood.

There was no TV, of course, although there was a telephone in the hallway. She knew she should telephone Aunt Madeleine in the States, and possibly also her grandfather, but she thought she would leave that until the next day. She also wanted to ring Callum, but she knew he would be working. She couldn't even text him – although she had brought her mobile phone with her, there was no reception. So she put some more wood on the fire and curled up on the sofa.

Le Cid was hard going. It wasn't just that the French was archaic, the plot didn't inspire her. All that courtly love and self-denial in the name of honour was just dumb, in her opinion. Not for the first time she wondered why she hadn't chosen the module on twentieth-century existentialism.

She put the book down and stoked the fire. The house was quiet, perhaps the old man had put himself to bed. As she replaced the poker, she saw a neat pile of paper on the floor next to the old leather armchair.

She examined it. The paper was yellowing, and slightly dirty. It was a manuscript, in spiky black Biro handwriting. The title page proclaimed *Death At Wyvis* by Alastair Cunningham and a date: 23rd May 1973.

No one had mentioned anything about Alastair writing a novel. Presumably it hadn't been published. But Clémence's interest was far more piqued by the manuscript than *Le Cid.*

A novel couldn't be private, could it? Perhaps it could. She hesitated. If it turned out to be steamy, or really bad, she would just pretend she hadn't read it.

She carefully shifted the manuscript to the sofa and began to read.

She read the first sentence and let out a small cry, her hand flying to her mouth.

It was a warm, still night and the cry of a tawny owl swirled through the birch trees by the loch, when I killed the only woman I have ever loved.

Clémence sat bolt upright, the sheet of spiky writing shaking in her hand. But wait a sec. She was letting the cottage's isolation, the owl, the dark, the old man's fear get to her. If the old man had written a novel called *Death At Wyvis*, then of course it might start with a murder.

She had to read on.

The first page of the novel was a brief prologue. It continued:

We had made love on the bare wooden boards of the floor of the boathouse, out of sight of the others, with the water lapping against the pilings beneath us.

Afterwards, as she lay in my arms, I had asked her to leave her husband. She refused. I remonstrated. We argued. Our whispers became muffled shouts.

I left her naked in the boathouse and climbed up the path back towards the cottage. I was angry, I was drunk and I just couldn't accept her decision. Without her, my life would mean nothing.

I stopped. An owl somewhere in the woods mocked my indecision. I couldn't just give up on her that easily, so I turned back. I would make her do what I wanted. The anger closed around me in a mist of black and red.

The stalker found her the next day, face-down in the loch, caught up in the gnarled fingers of a fallen tree. At first they thought she had drowned, but when the police came and examined her properly they found finger marks on her throat; she had been strangled.

I have thought of that night every day of my life since then. It's a story I was too much of a coward to tell. But now I must.

28

What she had just read couldn't be the truth, could it? Alastair Cunningham couldn't have killed someone, murdered someone? Surely this manuscript must be a novel rather than a memoir? A killing he had imagined, rather than experienced.

But it sounded like a memoir. It sounded like the frail old man upstairs had murdered someone right here at Wyvis. Clémence hadn't seen a boathouse on the drive up to the cottage, but there could easily be one on the shore by the woods. She would check first thing in the morning.

That would explain the dreadful secret he didn't want to remember.

And if, in fact, Alastair had murdered someone, she knew who it must be.

Sophie. Her grandmother, whom everyone had said had drowned, but who had actually been killed by the old man upstairs. And when the 'I' in the manuscript had begged the nameless woman to leave her nameless husband, what he had really been doing was telling Clémence's grandmother to leave her grandfather.

If the Wyvis Estate had in fact been in her grandfather's family, they could easily have gone there on holiday. And if her grandmother had indeed been murdered, and they wanted to lie to a little girl about it, they might have claimed she had drowned. They would have claimed she had drowned.

Had the old man upstairs murdered her grandmother?

No. No, she didn't know that. She was jumping to premature conclusions. It must be a novel, after all, perhaps written after Alastair had visited her grandparents at Wyvis. She had no proof it was a memoir. It just . . . it just *felt* like one.

She had to find out, right away. Clémence crept up to her room, determined not to alert the old man, and dug out her address book. She picked up the phone in the hallway and dialled Aunt Madeleine's number in New York. It was mid-afternoon New York time. Clémence had no idea of Aunt Madeleine's routine, she just hoped she was in.

The phone switched to the answer machine, and Aunt Madeleine's thick French accent asking the caller to leave a message.

Clémence left one, in French.

'Aunt Madeleine. It's Clémence. I have Alastair and I have taken him back to the cottage at Wyvis. But I need you to call me as soon as you get this message. It's urgent!' Then she read off the phone number from the label on the face of the phone.

What now? She could hardly ask the old man if his manuscript was true. Her question might shock him into remembering: more likely it would throw him into confusion. But she *had* to know.

Wait a moment. She recalled something she had spotted earlier that evening. She climbed the stairs and turned on the light in the study. She checked the little bookshelf. There, next to *Stalingrad*, stood a slim hardback book with a blue jacket, bearing the words *Death At Wyvis* on the spine. The author was Angus Culzie.

This cottage was called Culzie. The name had to be a pseudonym.

She pulled the book off the shelf. The cover showed a stag on a moor looking down at a generic loch. She carried it downstairs and opened it.

© 1974 Angus Culzie. The publisher was Woodrow and Shippe, a firm Clémence vaguely recognized.

The first page, the prologue, was identical to the manuscript.

She turned the page to the first chapter and read the first couple of paragraphs. She then checked back with the manuscript. They were identical, except that the narrator had been transformed from Alastair into Angus.

She read the rest of the chapter, and then put it down.

Never mind the Alastair and the Angus. There were other names in there she recognized. Stephen Trickett-Smith. Madeleine de Parzac, and her sister Sophie.

It *was* a memoir. The old man upstairs was a murderer. And he had murdered her grandmother, her beautiful grandmother!

Her heart was beating rapidly and the book was shaking in her hands. She closed her eyes. Oh, God, what should she do now? What the hell should she do now?

She was alone in an isolated cottage with a murderer. She should just leave: take the book and drive off. Call the police. Call Madeleine. Leave the old man to fend for himself.

But. But the novel or memoir or whatever it was had been published. People would have read it. Aunt Madeleine would have read it, Grandpa, the police. This was all news to her, but not to everyone else.

Yet it would be news to the old man upstairs. He didn't know he was a killer. Or at least not yet.

She had an idea; she knew what she would do.

4

The old man opened his eyes. Sunshine was leaking into his bedroom through a gap in the curtain, and the birds outside were making a racket.

He stood up, pulled back the curtain, and looked over the trees to the bare hillside of Ben Wyvis above him, still covered with snow. He scanned the ridge closest to the cottage, looking for movement, and spotted some. He grabbed the pair of binoculars he kept at the ready and focused on a small group of hinds making their way up the hill towards the high tops.

That wide expanse of moorland was known as Wyvis Forest, although there was not a tree standing up there.

He pulled back the curtain of the other window, the one facing down towards Loch Glass, a ruffled grey in the breeze. The loch was rarely smooth like a looking glass, but was often grey, for *glas* was the Gaelic word for grey-green. Over the top of the birch trees, and on the other side of the loch, he saw the rocky face of Meall Mòr, smeared with streaks of snow. He scanned the sky for eagles, but couldn't see any.

But there was movement right below his bedroom window. He saw Sophie setting off down the narrow footpath into the woods.

Sophie?

It couldn't be Sophie. Of course it wasn't Sophie. It was that girl Clémence, Sophie's granddaughter, and the great-niece of that woman called Madeleine.

32

And he didn't know who the hell he was.

Except for a minute there, he had. He had woken up, recognized the room as his bedroom in Culzie Cottage, known his name was Alastair Cunningham, remembered the details of the surrounding landscape and . . .

And what else? He knew about Sophie. Sophie as a nineteen-year-old, about Clémence's age. Seeing her by a harbour somewhere in France. Her laughing.

Then something else. Something unknown. There was something very bad about Sophie, about remembering Sophie. Dread. Cold dread clutched at his chest.

What was it?

He needed to pee.

He went into the bathroom, peed, washed his face and shaved. He noticed Clémence's washing bag on the bathroom cabinet.

He liked her. He liked that she had an aura of familiarity, that she had a link, however tenuous, to his real life. He touched the scar on the back of his skull. It was barely sore any more.

And Clémence was absolutely right; if he was going to get over his injury, he would have to remember who the hell he was. And here, in the almost-familiar surroundings of Culzie, he felt he could do it, with her help. If there were indeed nasty secrets, then he would just have to share them with her. The embarrassment or shame would be worth it, worth getting his life back.

He stuck his head into the study. He almost knew what was in there. Together he and Clémence would attack it. After breakfast.

He dressed and went downstairs to the kitchen, boiled water, found the cafetière straight away and filled it with coffee, and laid the table for breakfast.

He saw her return up the narrow path through the woods, wearing a baggy green jumper and leggings. She looked grim.

'Good morning!' he greeted her, with a smile, as she came into the kitchen.

She looked at him in surprise, and then at the table in more surprise.

'Breakfast?' said the old man. 'I can make you some bacon and eggs if you want.'

'Oh, no, thank you,' said Clémence with an attempt at brightness. 'I'll just make myself a piece of toast.'

'Did you go down to the boathouse?'

Clémence looked at the old man sharply. 'Yes. How did you know there was a boathouse down there? We didn't see it from the road on the way here.'

'I suppose I must have remembered it.'

The old man tried to catch Clémence's eye, pleased with his small success, but she turned away from him to pop some bread in a toaster. They stared at it in silence. Some of Clémence's warmth of the day before had left her.

That was understandable. Here she was, a young woman trapped in the middle of nowhere with an old git she didn't know from Adam. Actually, he didn't know her from Eve.

She did remind him of Sophie, although she was pleasant-looking, rather than beautiful. She was tall, a little on the plump side, with very straight dark hair, big blue eyes and clear skin. He smiled to himself as he noticed a few large freckles on the end of her nose. He counted them. Four. Sophie had had three.

'Clémence is a nice name,' he said. 'Does it have something to do with your grandmother?'

'Not really,' said Clémence. 'My father is half-French, as you know now, but then my mother is French also. They met in Morocco. He teaches English and she teaches French. So I suppose I am three-quarters French.'

'You don't have a French accent.'

'No. I'm perfectly bilingual. My parents moved to Vietnam when I was small and then to Hong Kong. They split up three years ago; my mother is still there but my father moved back to Vietnam. I was sent to boarding school in England and then St Andrews University. I don't know whether I am French or English or what I am.'

'In that case your surname would be Trickett-Smith like your grandfather?'

'Just Smith. My father dropped the Trickett. He dropped just about everything. He left England and became a hippie in the sixties. He still is one, really. Rupert Trickett-Smith isn't a cool name for a hippie.'

'I suppose not,' said the old man. 'I'm sorry about your parents splitting up.'

Clémence shrugged. She looked away, studying the orange rubbish bin in the corner of the kitchen. Despite her ostentatious lack of interest, he sensed she actually wanted to say more, and he was tempted to ask her, but it was none of his business.

He put the bacon and eggs back in the fridge, poured himself a bowl of cereal and sat down to eat. He wanted to find out more about her, and searched for a safer subject. 'What are you studying at St Andrews?'

'French mostly. Some English Literature, some Philosophy. But I think I am going to do my honours in French.'

'I read history at university,' the old man said.

Clémence was buttering her toast and looked up sharply. 'The doctor said you studied medicine.'

'Yes,' said the old man, frowning. He grinned. 'Who knows?'

Clémence bit into her toast. They ate in silence.

'You know I'd like to take you up on your offer to help me recall my life,' said the old man. 'We can go up to the study after breakfast, if you like.'

'Actually, I've got an idea about that,' said Clémence. 'Wait a sec.'

She disappeared from the kitchen and the old man heard her running up the stairs to her bedroom. She reappeared a minute later carrying a thin hardback book.

'Do you recognize this?' she asked him.

He read the title. *Death At Wyvis* by Angus Culzie. 'No.'

'Do you know who Angus Culzie is?'

The old man paused and thought. Nothing. Somehow he thought he *should* know who Angus Culzie was, but nothing. It was so frustrating. 'I've no idea. Except that this cottage is called Culzie, isn't it? It must be a pen name. Either that or it's an amazing coincidence.'

'Well, this book is all about you,' Clémence said.

'About me?' The old man stared at the book, confusion boiling up inside him. 'How can that be? Who *is* Angus Culzie? How does he know about me? Are you sure?'

'All good questions, Alastair. But I thought we could read the book together. Then perhaps you will remember.'

'What about the death in the title? What's that? I mean, it happens here, does it? The death.'

'I don't know, I presume so,' said Clémence. 'Let's read the book and find out.'

'Have you read it?'

'Only the first chapter. It's definitely about you, but for some reason you are called Angus not Alastair. My grandfather Stephen is in it. And Madeleine. And Sophie.'

The old man's confusion turned to panic. Fear. 'I don't know,' he said.

'What don't you know?' said Clémence. 'Are you afraid of the truth?'

'Yes,' replied the old man, honestly. 'Yes, I am.'

'And do you know what that truth is?' asked Clémence. She was watching him closely, with those big blue eyes.

'No, I don't. I'm not sure I want to.'

Clémence tossed the book down between them. 'Well, it's entirely up to you. But if you don't want to find out who you really are, I will leave now. It's clear you can look after yourself and you don't need me.'

The old man stared at the book, and then at Clémence. Her expression was firm. She meant what she said.

There was something bad in that book, he knew it. But he had to face up to it. At the age of eighty-three he couldn't pretend to himself that he could start a new life with a blank slate.

He needed to find out who he really was. And, whoever that man turned out to be, to learn to live with him.

And he really didn't want Clémence to leave him.

'All right,' he said. 'Let's read it.'

They carried their coffee into the cosy sitting room. The old man sat in the armchair and Clémence lit the fire. She picked up the book and it seemed to him that she skipped over the first couple of pages. But then she began to read.

CHAPTER I

A Paris Adventure

Northern France, August 1935

I WATCHED THE FIELDS of Picardy pass by the train window. I was fascinated; the countryside might be flat but it wasn't dull, at least not to my eyes. The long, straight little roads lined with plane trees, the occasional glimpse of oxen in the fields, the field patterns themselves – ordered, rectangular, often hedgeless – all proclaimed that I was not looking at England's green and pleasant land. It was the first time I had been abroad, and I was excited.

I glanced back into the compartment at my two travelling companions, whose eyes were focused on their books rather than the scenery. Both of them were much better travelled than me: Stephen Trickett-Smith had a mother who lived a debauched life in Antibes, one which she was eager to share with her nineteen-year-old son, and Nathan Giannelli was American, so his existence in the carriage testified to travel over much larger distances than merely the English Channel.

We made an odd trio. The trip had been planned three months earlier, during Trinity term of our first year at Oxford. Stephen was in my rooms, polishing off a bottle of hock while I was dipping in and out of F.W. Maitland's book on the Domesday Book, when Nathan barged in.

Nathan Giannelli was a Rhodes Scholar from Pennsylvania, who had made friends with me in our first term. He was small and dark, with neat features and quick brown eyes; his family owned an oil company. Nathan made much of his wealth, although he lacked the polish and the expensive clothes of some of his compatriots at Oxford. He was energetic and intelligent and unlike some other first-year undergraduates, I was willing to take his American friendliness at face value, rather than a sign of superficiality.

'Hey, Angus, do you have any plans over the summer?'

'Not really,' I said. 'I'll go home to Yorkshire, I suppose. See my mother.'

'Would you like to come with me to Paris?' Nathan waved a letter in front of my face. 'My Uncle Alden has invited me there for a couple of weeks, and asked me to bring one or two friends. I figured you might like to come along.'

I was surprised by the invitation, but intrigued. 'That's kind of you to think of me, Nathan. But I'm not sure I can scrape the finances together.'

'Of course you can! All you need to cover is the train fare – Uncle Alden will pay for everything else. He's loaded, and generous. You'll like him. He may be my uncle, but he's actually only ten years older than me, and he acts much younger.'

I had always wanted to travel to Europe, and Paris in particular. Frankly, this might be my best opportunity, especially if I had somewhere to stay for free, and Nathan would be an amusing travelling companion. I would beg or steal the train fare, somehow. 'All right. Yes. Thanks very much, Nathan.'

Nathan turned to Stephen, who had been watching all this with mild amusement. 'What about you, Trickett-Smith? Will you come?' Nathan seemed nervous as he asked the question.

As well he might. Stephen Trickett-Smith was not only one of the wealthiest undergraduates in college, he had also attended the country's most prestigious public school. He was tall, with floppy fair hair, a long aquiline nose, and wide, thin lips. He had an arrogant, lazy charm, which bewitched women. And men.

He and his set looked down on the likes of middle-American parvenus like Nathan, just as they looked down on boys from northern minor public schools, like me.

'It's very kind of you, old man, but I am planning to drive around Italy with Maurice in August. Then off to Salzburg to meet Tutton.'

Maurice Bellincourt was an old school friend of Stephen's, in fact Stephen's best friend. Clever, pale, a wicked gossip who revelled in giving and taking offence, he and I did not get on, despite the fact that he was the cause of Stephen and me becoming friends. Or maybe because of it. Dr Tutton was a young Classics tutor of independent means who liked to suck up to the more glamorous undergraduates; Stephen had him under his spell.

The disappointment on Nathan's face was obvious, and the suspicion germinated in my mind that I myself had only been asked as a way of persuading the more socially impressive Stephen to come too.

Nathan did his best to get Stephen to change his mind over the next couple of weeks, persisting to the point of rudeness, but without success. Until, that is, just before the end of term, when Stephen and Maurice quarrelled. I wasn't quite sure what was the cause, but it seemed to be something Stephen had said to a cherubic Organ Scholar called Perrin with whom Maurice had developed an obsession. So Stephen was looking for an excuse to avoid spending August with his old school friend and Nathan's invitation suddenly appeared much more attractive.

So now here we all were, on a train to Paris.

Nathan's uncle, Alden O. Burns Jr, was waiting for us at the station. Nathan was right: Alden didn't look much older than him, although he was a couple of inches taller, and glimpses of his forehead could be seen through his brushed-back red hair. But he seemed to have just as much energy as his nephew as he shook Nathan's hand and clapped him on the back. Nathan introduced Stephen first, and then me. Alden's smile was all charm and welcome.

'I've got to apologize right away,' he said. 'I can't fit all of you into my apartment. My niece Elaine is staying with us for a month or so. But don't worry, I've gotten you rooms at the little hotel down the street. It's small, but very comfortable, and they know me there. I'll take care of the bill.'

'Thank you, Mr Burns,' said Stephen. 'I'm sure we can cover it ourselves.'

I felt a moment of panic as I heard Stephen's polite offer. Stephen might be able to cover a two-week hotel bill in Paris, but I was quite sure I couldn't.

To my embarrassment, Alden caught my eye and smiled. 'Absolutely not. I insist. While you are here, you are my guests. It's wonderful to have Nathan over in Europe and I want to take as much advantage of it as I can.'

We climbed into Alden's powerful Hispano-Suiza, parked close to the station, and he guided us through Paris's jammed streets, with the top down. It was a warm, stuffy afternoon, but as long as the car was moving, the air kept us cool.

I looked around me in wonder. To me, London was glamorous, I had scarcely visited the capital more than three times in my life, but Paris was on a completely different plane: the brightly coloured awnings of the *boulangeries* and the *pâtisseries*, the elaborately decorated buildings, the boulevards, the trees and the people – men and women alike, exquisitely dressed, stylish, poised, purposeful. The old Paris clichés had come alive and were promenading in front of me: dachshunds and poodles trotted along next to slender ankles above high heels; street vendors wearing berets and full, dark moustaches pushed handcarts; slim men strolled and strutted, bearing smaller, trimmer moustaches, striped blazers and canes; gendarmes with their white batons and high kepis conducted it all. The sounds of accordion music swirled through the horns, the gear-grinding and the chuntering of the slow-moving traffic. Posters on the newspaper kiosks advertised the latest shows at the Moulin Rouge or the Casino de Paris. And everywhere the elegant swirl of the word '*Métropolitaine*' promised modernity and style, even underground.

Alden lived on the left bank, so the Hispano-Suiza battled its way around the place de la Concorde and across the Seine, the Eiffel Tower rising on one side and Notre-Dame on the other. Alden's apartment was in the rue du Bac, an elegant residential street stretching south from the river near the glamorous Gare D'Orsay. The buildings were made of a stone that glimmered yellow in the hazy afternoon sun, each high window skirted by balconies of elaborate iron lace. Alden dropped us at our hotel, with instructions for us to join him at his apartment for cocktails at seven.

At Stephen's gentle suggestion, we arrived at a quarter past, rather than seven on the dot, which had been Nathan's initial idea. We passed the concierge at the entrance to the building, climbed a broad stone staircase to the first floor, and were greeted at the door of Alden's apartment by an English butler. Alden was sitting sipping cocktails with three women and leaped to his feet to welcome his guests.

'This is my wife, Madeleine, and her sister Sophie, and this is Elaine, whom you know, of course, Nathan.'

'*Enchanté, Madame,*' I said to the stunningly beautiful woman who was Alden's wife. I was pretty good at French, I could read it well and speak it passably, and I was eager to try it out.

Madame Burns smiled at me, her brown eyes amused. She was dark, with wide cheekbones and full red lips that pouted and pursed. She wore a sleek black dress, which showed off a figure that would excite any red-blooded nineteen-year-old. Her neck was adorned with a thin pearl necklace, and delicate sapphires glinted beneath her ears. A complicated jewel of diamonds and a large emerald drew my attention to her chest, which is where it would have been drawn anyway. A hint of the scent of a warm summer garden drifted around her.

'And I am very pleased to meet you,' she said in heavily accented English. 'It's OK, I think we will speak English this evening. Elaine is supposed to be learning French, but I am sure she will enjoy the interruption.'

'I sure will,' said Elaine, who was a pretty girl of perhaps sixteen or seventeen with a small red mouth, dark curly hair and a pert upturned nose. She smiled at me, looked me up and down, wasn't impressed, and turned towards Stephen.

The third woman was Sophie de Parzac, Mrs Burns's younger but taller sister. Her hair was short and fair, her eyes large and blue, with a slightly lost look that I found extremely appealing.

'Have you ever been to Paris before, Mr Culzie?' Mrs Burns asked me.

'Er . . .' I said.

Madeleine Burns raised her eyebrows.

I wanted to try to convey how excited I was to be in Paris, how I had dreamed of visiting the city, how different it was to the Dales, how grateful I was that Nathan's uncle had extended his invitation to his friends. 'No,' I said.

'And you, Mr Trickett-Smith?' She looked up at Stephen, her eyes seeming to linger on his face, in a way they hadn't on mine.

'Oh, yes, I love Paris,' said Stephen with enthusiasm. 'My mother often meets me here during the vacs. We spend a couple of days in the city before heading down to Antibes.'

'Oh? And where do you stay?'

'Mother likes the Meurice.'

I had never heard of the place, but Madeleine clearly had. 'Ah, I am sorry that our little hotel down the street must seem a little simple compared to that.'

'Oh, no, not at all!' said Stephen. 'You can't imagine how nice it is to see the real Paris with real Parisians.' Stephen flashed a wide smile. 'And when Nathan said we were going to stay with his old aunt, I never thought he meant someone as charming as you.'

Stephen's eyes glinted. Somehow he managed to combine a polite schoolboy innocence with something altogether more dangerous, more thrilling. There was silence for a moment as Madeleine caught those blue eyes. Under her make-up she flushed and her throat reddened.

If I had said something like that, Madeleine would either have slapped me or laughed at me. Not for the first time, I thought that it wasn't what Stephen said that made such an impression, it was who he was and how he said it.

She composed herself. 'Thank you, Mr Trickett-Smith. I do hope you enjoy your stay with us.'

As Stephen and Nathan's Uncle Alden and the others chatted and charmed, I couldn't help feeling out of my depth. Whereas Stephen was able to match a witty remark with a wittier one, I was struck down into polite submission by any attempt to speak to me. Nathan was doing his best, and was helped by the obvious pleasure that his uncle had in seeing him.

The room was a large one, with high ceilings and tall windows looking out on to the street on one side and a court-yard on the other. My eyes were drawn to the paintings around the wall. I knew a little about modern art, and thought I recognized a Matisse and a Chagall. There were also three rather odd paintings that appeared to portray rotting vegetables in a Paris street.

'Do you like them, Angus?' asked Alden, noticing where my eyes were wandering.

'I don't know. They are certainly interesting. I'm trying to work out what they are.'

'Trash. Garbage. The alleyways of Paris as they truly are.'

'That's what I thought,' I said, feeling slightly pleased with myself.

'They are painted by a friend of mine. Tony Volstead. American. I hope you'll meet him. They are a sound investment. You wait, in ten years he will be the next big thing. Five years. You should buy one yourself.'

'And is that a Chagall?' I asked, nodding to a bright picture of a harbour and some boats. I regretted the words as soon as they passed out of my mouth: it was a bit of a stupid question because the artist's signature was clearly visible.

'It is. I like to dabble in art. Some established painters, some less so, like Tony. This is the city to buy art. You can't do it from the States.'

'How long have you been in Paris, Mr Burns?'

'Alden. I told you, you got to call me Alden! Nearly three years now. I came to Paris the first time in 1929 and then again in 1931. I loved it. So when my father died, I came back to live here.'

'I'm sorry,' I said. 'About your father.' My own father had died the previous autumn; something that I wanted to admit to the friendly American, but couldn't quite bring myself to.

But Alden's smile showed he appreciated the genuineness of my sympathy. 'Thank you. I loved the old guy, although he spent his whole life devoted to Wakefield Oil. That's the family company. It ate him up: it killed him in the end. I'm not going to let it kill me. I've gotten other people running it back in New York and Texas. I can lead a much more civilized life here.'

'I can see that. Is your mother still alive?'

Alden's enthusiasm flickered. 'No. She died when I was eleven. That's how I got to know Nathan. His mother is my elder sister, Peggy. My father moved Wakefield Oil's headquarters to New York over twenty years ago, but Peggy stayed on back in Pennsylvania, in the city of Wakefield. She had just gotten married to a new young lawyer in town, Giannelli. My father couldn't stand the fact that Giannelli was a Catholic, and an Italian, and he had tried to stop the marriage. But there was no stopping Peggy, she didn't care if he cut her off.

'After Mother died, Father relented and allowed me to visit Peggy in the summers. Nathan and his little sister Lucy were born. They were ten years younger than me, but I guess we grew up together. I was so pleased when he went to Yale; that's my alma mater. And to Oxford, of course.'

Hearing this, I suspected that Alden was paying for more than just Nathan's trip to France; I would bet that he had paid for Nathan's education too.

'So Elaine isn't Nathan's sister?'

'Oh, no. They are cousins. Elaine's mother came between Peggy and me. She married a banker from Pittsburgh, much more to Father's liking.'

We went through to the dining room, and we were served the best dinner of my life. Foie gras, soft tender duck, soft cheeses like I had never tasted before, and a pear tart. I was no expert on wine, but even I could appreciate the claret. I was sitting next to the American girl, Elaine, who ignored me, and Stephen, who was charming Sophie sitting on his other side. Nathan was showing off to Madeleine about his life at Oxford, and she was egging him on. Despite this slight awkwardness, the food and the wine and the sophistication got to me; I was enjoying myself. The wine flowed. Elaine clearly wasn't used to it and began to giggle in all the wrong places.

Eventually, at close to midnight, Alden turned to his nephew. 'Why don't I show you and your friends what Paris is like at night. Do you like jazz?'

'Sure,' said Nathan. 'What do you think, Stephen?'

'Rather,' said Stephen smiling. I knew the idea of a night out in Paris would appeal to him.

So we set off, hailing a taxi out in the street and leaving Madeleine to look after Elaine, who was most put out that she wasn't invited. Sophie left for home: she was working the following day.

Alden took us to a small smoky nightclub, where a black American woman sang songs of low mellow sadness, joined by a saxophonist whose notes swam through the thick smoky atmosphere to tug at her listeners' hearts. I had never heard such music so close before, and I was lost on its melancholy richness. I was also quite drunk.

I had no idea how much time had passed before I noticed that the others were leaving and beckoning me to follow. Alden and Nathan were laughing with each other, but Stephen had a purposeful gleam in his eye. We crammed into another cab, twisted through some narrow streets and ended up at another club, the Panier Fleuri. This place charged an entrance fee, which Alden paid, and he ordered glasses of cognac at a small bar. There were half a dozen men at the bar, but more women, who were wearing open cotton gowns, and who stared at the four of us as we sat down.

Stephen saw my face and smiled. He leaned over. 'Angus, old man. You know what this place is?'

'Er. Yes.' Shock, confusion and lust hit me hard, all at the same time. A small girl with naughty dark eyes looked sideways at me. One of the *fleurs* of the flower basket, no doubt.

'Don't worry, Angus,' said Alden. 'This is Paris. Men do this kind of thing all the time. They even come here with their wives. I would have brought Madeleine along, if she didn't need to look after Elaine.'

It was true: a well-dressed couple sat in a corner, a man and a woman in their forties, talking to one of the girls. All three stood up and left the bar, the woman holding the girl's hand.

The girl who had made eyes at me approached us, followed by three of her colleagues. I panicked. I was tempted to stay, but I was also scared that I might do something I would regret later. Or savour. I put down my cognac.

'Do you mind if I leave you to it?' I said. 'I need some air. I'll walk back to the hotel.'

'It's a long way,' said Alden. 'You should stay here. You might learn something.' He chuckled.

'Yes, stay, Angus,' said Nathan.

'Let him go,' said Stephen with a laugh. 'Angus's innocence is too tiresome to do battle with.'

So I escaped into the warm night, and began the long walk back to our hotel. I had no idea in which direction I should go, but within a few moments I was stopped by a helpful-looking young woman of about my own age who seemed to want to spend half an hour with me. This time I had no trouble refusing, but she did point me towards the rue de Bac.

My pride couldn't accept the idea of allowing a stranger to pay for me to have sexual relations with another stranger. I was still a virgin, and I rather hoped that the first time would be with some girl whom I loved. Did that make me a romantic? Or was I just a stuffy provincial afraid of breaking the rules? Was it pride, or was it cowardice?

Oddly, despite his own eagerness to break all rules, especially where sex was concerned, Stephen had seemed to understand me. I was grateful for my friend's help in making my escape. Pleasantly drunk, and grinning at the memory of my first evening in Paris, I eventually found myself at the rue de Bac and our hotel, and put myself to bed, trying not to allow my thoughts to dwell too much upon what the others were up to.

CHAPTER II

A Sojourn in Normandy

S TEPHEN, NATHAN AND I spent the next couple of days sitting in cafés chatting, reading and drinking, interspersed with the odd stroll around a church or the Louvre. I would have liked to have spent a little more time in the Louvre, and I did my best to hide my impatience, but actually it was very pleasant just sitting, idling. I had brought *À la Recherche du Temps Perdu* with me to France, which I was reading extremely slowly, but that was fine. Stephen and Nathan seemed to get on much better than I had feared. Nathan was highly intelligent, and although it was his first time in France and his language skills were poor, he was quick to observe the ways of the natives and to exchange these observations with Stephen. The night spent at the Panier Fleuri seemed to have created a bond between them.

We passed the evenings at Alden's apartment, arriving for cocktails after a day's steady drinking already half intoxicated. Neither Alden nor Madeleine seemed to mind. There were no more nocturnal excursions; instead we stayed up until the small hours, talking, drinking Alden's excellent brandy and playing backgammon. Elaine, who spent the day at drawing classes, joined us, doing her best to flirt with Stephen, but not making much impression.

Alden had taken a villa at Deauville for the summer, and it was decided to go down there for four days. There was a big horse race on, apparently, and Alden wanted to show Nathan the town.

Alden's friend, Tony Volstead, the painter of the rotten vege-tables, was to join us.

Despite its size, there wasn't enough room for everyone to fit in Alden's Hispano-Suiza for the trip, so it was decided that I would travel down with Tony in Tony's car. This turned out to be a sporty Amilcar convertible. Tony Volstead did not look much like a struggling artist: big and bluff, with ruddy cheeks and a pencil-thin moustache, he wore a striped blazer and a broad grin. He slung my bag in the back and me in the front seat next to him, and we were off.

The idea was that we were supposed to be following the Hispano-Suiza, but once we were outside Paris, the convoy turned into a race. The Hispano was clearly much more powerful, but the Amilcar was nimble, and Tony was willing to take risks with it. Tearing through the French countryside, with a maniac at the wheel and lesser cars ducking out of the way, was bloody marvellous.

'Ever been horse racing, Angus?' Tony asked, as he settled in to a winding stretch of road where even he couldn't overtake.

'A couple of times. At Ripon. It's a local course near where I live.'

'Win anything?'

'Gambled half a crown and lost it all.'

'I can give you a few tips, if you like,' Tony said. 'I know people. You have to know the right people.'

'That's all right,' I said. 'I'll just watch.'

'Oh, don't worry about that,' said Tony. 'I'm sure Alden will front you some stake money.'

'I couldn't possibly. I've taken far too much of his hospitality as it is.'

'He won't mind. Alden's a stand-up guy. Smart too. He's been a big supporter of my paintings.'

I asked him about the pictures I had seen in Alden's drawing room. Despite his outward impression, Tony took his art desperately seriously and was happy to explain why he thought his paintings of discarded food in Parisian alleyways symbolized the decay of twentieth-century Europe. It made some sort of sense to me, and I couldn't deny that it was genuinely expressed. Whether Tony was as good a painter as he clearly thought he was, I had no idea. But I did like the man.

After luncheon with the others in Rouen, we arrived at Deauville, a seaside resort of smart people, smart shops and flowers wherever you looked. The villa Alden had taken was a large house on the edge of the town, at the foot of a wooded hillside. It was tall and square with high steep roofs, two or three fairy-tale turrets and a timbered cream façade, set in a large garden of fruit trees and roses. Inside, suits of armour guarded the hallways, and swords, halberds and arquebuses hung from the walls.

'The owner is an antiquarian nutcase,' Alden explained. 'English. Just your cup of tea, Angus.'

Alden had joined in Stephen and Nathan's gentle teasing of my interest in all things medieval. And indeed I enjoyed studying the armour and the prints of old French maps and charters.

We went to the races the following day, a Friday, and for the first time on the trip, my English dowdiness made me feel uncomfortable. It was August and it was hot, and I felt sweaty in my crumpled Hepworth's worsted suit bought at Allen's in Harrogate. This was one of the great weeks in the French social calendar and half of Paris had descended on Normandy. It was not just that the clothes were so elegant and expensive, it was that they were worn with such style. Madeleine looked gorgeous in a dress of polka dots and a broad summer hat, and she and Elaine had been shopping at Schiaparelli for a light-blue dress that transformed the seventeen-year-old from American schoolgirl into a pretty Parisian woman. Stephen was every inch the young elegant English gentleman, and Tony and Alden sported blazers and boaters.

I refused to accept stake money from Alden, and in doing so managed to offend my host for the first time. I had no moral objection to gambling, but my pride wouldn't let me keep my winnings and expect Alden to cover my losses. Just like it seemed wrong to expect Alden to pay a woman to have sex with me. The others all bet. Tony won one race, Madeleine another, and Elaine was terribly excited when her fifteen-to-one outsider came in first at the last race.

Sophie joined us for dinner that evening, having taken the train down from Paris. Unlike everyone else at the table, she seemed to have a job that involved her going into work on weekdays.

There was great enthusiasm for the next day's racing. Elaine was eager to repeat her success, vowing to stick with outsiders. Tony seemed in high spirits but nervous, and he and Alden exchanged some knowing comments about a horse called Fantastic, which they pronounced the French way. I had the feeling that there was a big bet about to be placed, if it hadn't been placed already.

After we had polished off a delicious clafoutis, made with cherries from the villa's own garden, Alden turned to me. 'Racing isn't really your thing, is it, old man?'

I was about to protest politely, but actually I regretted rebuffing Alden's offer of stake money earlier. I liked our host and decided it was best to give him a straight answer. 'Not really. Sorry.'

'Have you heard of Honfleur?' Alden said. 'It's only a few miles from here.'

'Where Henry V led his men once more into the breach?'

'I think so,' said Alden. 'It's a pretty place. Old. Real old. French painters love it. Why don't you go there tomorrow instead of the races? Sophie will take you, won't you, Sophie? She hates racing too.'

'I'd be happy to,' said Sophie, smiling at me politely.

Flustered by the prospect of spending a day with Alden's beautiful sister-in-law and not wishing to offend my host again, I hesitated. 'Er . . .'

'Don't worry,' Alden said. 'You will be doing Sophie a favour. Is it OK if they borrow your car, Tony?'

'Sure,' said Tony.

The realization dawned on me that actually Alden preferred to go to the racecourse without his scruffy, non-gambling English guest.

Embarrassed and a little humiliated, I agreed. 'That's very kind. Thank you, Sophie, it will be interesting.'

I was enchanted by Honfleur; I was also enchanted by Sophie. We were sitting outside one of the restaurants around the little town's old harbour. The air in Normandy was fresher than in Paris, and the afternoon was pleasantly warm rather than unbearably hot. A breeze from an unseen English Channel squeezed its way through the ancient buildings into the harbour. The basin was packed with yachts and the odd fishing boat, and surrounded by tall tottering houses of cream and orange and yellow, most of them skirted with red or gold awnings shading pavement cafés. It seemed appropriate to order fish, and Sophie had chosen a delicious crisp wine from Sancerre, which was apparently near where she came from. The meal would bust my budget, but it was worth it.

We had spent the morning in the town's art galleries, the remarkable wooden church of Saint Catherine, and two old salt barns: quantities of salt were vital for the long-distance fisherman harvesting cod from the Grand Banks of Newfoundland. Sophie was a knowledgeable guide, pointing out where Eugène Boudin had painted, as well as Monet and Courbet.

She was polite and not unfriendly, but I had the impression that she thought she had been lumbered with an awkward young student, and was making the best of a bad job. Not unreasonable, really. Her blue dress was simple, yet elegant, and she wore a scarf around her neck with casual sophistication. Her large eyes fascinated me: at one moment they would be absent-mindedly drifting off into the distance, and then they would focus on me and whatever I was saying, large pools of intelligence. Three freckles danced playfully on the end of her nose. At any moment I was expecting one of the many wealthy Parisian men loafing around the harbour to elbow me out of the way and take over. And who could blame them, or her for responding?

'What are we doing this afternoon?' I said.

'If you have the energy we can walk up to the chapel of Notre-Dame de Grâce. There's a lovely view of the town from there.'

'What about the walls? Can we see them?'

'I think they've been demolished.'

'That's a shame,' I said. 'I'd like to see where Henry V broke through. You know Shakespeare wrote a play about him, and one of the big scenes takes place in Honfleur?'

Sophie didn't answer. She looked as if she was about to laugh, but covered it up by looking out over the harbour.

'What is it, Sophie?' I was aware I had said something stupid; I just wasn't aware what it was.

'It is nothing,' said Sophie. But her lips were twitching, and her blue eyes shining. *"Once more unto the breach, dear friends, once more,"* you mean that one?'

'I see you know your Shakespeare.'

'I do. And it's Harfleur, not Honfleur.'

'Ah.' I realized that I had, in fact, made a fool of myself. 'They are not the same place?'

'No,' said Sophie. 'Harfleur is on the other side of the Seine estuary.'

I winced. 'Oh Lord. What an idiot! I'm supposed to know my medieval English history. Are you sure?'

Sophie nodded. 'I am French. I have been to both places. I'm pretty sure I am right.'

'I can see that.'

Sophie laughed. It was a kind laugh, at least.

'Do you know much about the Hundred Years War?' I said.

'Yes. I enjoy history. Even English history. The Norman Conquest. The Battle of Hastings. The Siege of Calais. And from here raiders set out to attack the Sussex coast.'

'All right, all right. In that case, what I don't understand is why you don't all speak English? We are taught all about the big battles of the war: Poitiers, Crécy, Agincourt. We won them all. But we don't seem to have won the war, do we? I suspect they are not telling us something.'

Sophie laughed. 'I see what you mean. Have you forgotten Jeanne d'Arc, or don't they teach you about her?'

'They do. In fact, I've seen the play – *Saint Joan*. But didn't we burn her in the end?'

'You did. Not very gentlemanly, not cricket at all. But after Jeanne it was all over for you. You lost. Sorry.'

'It's probably for the best. It wouldn't be quite the same if the waiter had a Brummie accent and we were drinking tea and eating jellied eels.'

Sophie shuddered.

'Not an Anglophile, then?'

'Actually, I am. I like reading English historical novels. And Scottish. Robert Louis Stephenson. Walter Scott.'

'No wonder your English is so good.'

'Thank you,' she said with a small smile of pleasure. 'You are studying history at university?'

Despite my Harfleur–Honfleur error, I did know quite a lot about medieval history, but so, it turned out, did Sophie. We talked at length and with great enthusiasm about the Black Death and its effects on medieval English and French society. I badly wanted to regale her with my theories on bastard feudalism, but I thought that might be pushing my luck.

'Would you have liked to have studied history at university yourself?' I asked.

The enthusiasm left Sophie. 'My father wouldn't let me.'

'Oh. That's a shame.'

'He is very traditional. My whole family is very traditional, very Catholic. I'm not even sure he would let Hector go to university. He's my younger brother, but he will inherit the estate and Papa never wanted him to be distracted by too much education. He's at Saint-Cyr, the military college.'

I realized I had no idea how old Sophie was, or her older sister Madeleine. Twenty-five and twenty-seven, I guessed.

'So what are you supposed to do?'

'Go to Paris. Find a husband. Marry him.'

'Oh. And how long have you been doing that for?' As soon as I said it, I realized how ridiculous it sounded. Sophie burst out laughing.

'Almost a year, now.'

'Any luck?'

'Not yet.'

'I'm surprised.'

'Why, thank you.'

'Wait a moment,' I said. 'How old are you?'

'Nineteen.'

'But that's my age!' I protested.

'When's your birthday?'

'March.'

'Well mine is September. Which means I am significantly older than you.'

I examined the beautiful creature sitting opposite me. There was no chance that she had been sent to Paris to find someone like me, which took a lot of the pressure off. She was fun to talk to.

'Do you have a job?'

'Yes. I am working for my uncle in an insurance office. He arranges insurance for unusual shipments; it sounds dull, but it is actually quite interesting. I use my English: I speak it much better than my uncle. I have learned a lot, business is booming, I was doing more and more for him, developing business with English-speaking insurers, in fact things were going so well that he employed an English-speaking man to do my work. Now I'm back to filing.'

'That's rotten!'

'It is,' said Sophie, two spots of angry pink on her pale cheeks.

'Did you say anything to him?'

'I did. It hadn't even occurred to him that I could do the job, or that I *was* doing the job. I also got the impression that he was afraid of what my parents would say if he gave it to me.'

A brave seagull dived for Sophie's bread, but I batted it away just in time. The bird hovered a few feet above us, squawking. I glared at it and it swooped down to the harbour.

Sophie popped the bread in her mouth. 'I do envy you. Getting to read all that history.'

'Actually, I think I'm going to give it up.'

'Really? Why? You clearly love it.'

'I'm planning to switch to medicine when I get back in October.'

'Can you do that?'

'It's tricky, but possible. I need to pass some science tests. I've been working at it over the summer.'

Sophie looked disappointed. 'Why are you changing? I know medicine is a noble profession, but . . .'

'It is. My father was a doctor, and he was determined that I should become one too. But I am just as stubborn as he, so I did what *I* wanted to do. History.'

'Was? Is he—'

'He died in my first term at the university. Eight months ago. Nine months next Tuesday.'

'I'm sorry.'

I shrugged. An English shrug, not a French shrug. A shrug pretending it was nothing to worry about, that I was untouched, that my life would carry on regardless. When plainly it wouldn't.

I glanced at Sophie. She understood the shrug and the lie it represented.

'He was a wonderful man,' I said. 'That was so clear at his funeral. I have been to hardly any funerals, thank God, but they give you a view of a person's life, their whole life. And many viewpoints. To his family, him being a doctor was just a job, albeit a job that meant everyone in our town knew him. But doctors make a difference to lots of people; for some they mean the difference of life and death. For others it is just comfort, psychological as much as physical. But it's a life worth leading. I know it's obvious, but I only really realized that about my father after he had gone.'

'So now you are doing what he wanted you to do when he was alive?'

'Yes, I suppose I do.'

'Are you sure that's what *you* want to do?'

I was surprised by the question. 'Yes. Yes, of course it is. I have thought hard about it.'

Sophie looked at me closely, and I felt a sudden fear that she was going to question my decision. Why be afraid of that? She didn't know me at all; I didn't need her approval.

But she let it drop. 'Let's go and see this chapel.'

I paid the bill and we walked around the harbour, the rigging of the fishing boats clattering in the breeze. We passed a man in front of an easel painting the boats and the harbour, and the tall old houses behind them. I spotted the restaurant we had just eaten in; Sophie was immortalized as a dab of blue, I was an indistinct grey.

'Not bad,' I said.

'No,' said Sophie. 'But I think that view has been done before.'

'If Tony Volstead was here he'd be *behind* the houses painting their rubbish.'

Sophie giggled. 'You're right. I can see the painting now. Part of an exhibition. *The Trash of Honfleur.*'

'It's an interesting idea,' I said. 'At least Tony thinks it is. I can't believe he will really start a whole artistic movement.'

'He does think it's interesting,' said Sophie. 'But he's the only one. He and Alden. He's been trying to get Gertrude Stein to buy one of his paintings, but she takes no notice of them or him. The problem is, he's not very good at the painting bit. Did you look at his pictures closely? He paints an aubergine spilled on the street, and it looks like a hole in the pavement.'

'But Alden supports him?'

'Alden likes having an artist as a best friend. He is also very loyal.'

'I like Alden,' I said. 'He's very generous. Very friendly. He made us feel at home right away. And he loves France.'

'Do you know why he loves France so much?' Sophie asked.

'The people? The art? Because Paris is so beautiful?'

'Because of the sex.'

'Er . . .' I wasn't sure what to say.

'Alden likes sex. Lots of it.'

'Right,' I said uncomfortably. 'And does your sister?'

'Oh, yes. But that's not enough for him. Is it?' We had left the harbour and were walking uphill along a narrow street of stooped houses.

'Isn't it?' I said, swallowing.

'He took you to the Panier Fleuri the other night, didn't he?'

For a moment, I considered lying. But then I remembered what

Alden had said about Madeleine. How he would have brought her along if she hadn't had to look after Elaine.

'Yes. He did. But he said he brings Madeleine to places like that.'

'*Bof.*' Sophie snorted. '*Quel idiot!* He asked her to go and she refused. Alden has the idea that all Frenchwomen are happy for their husbands to have mistresses or to go to brothels whenever they feel like it. It might be true for some people, but I tell you it is not true for my sister. She *hates* it.'

'Has she told him?'

'But of course! He doesn't listen. He doesn't want to believe it. You heard him say she approved of it. It's a real problem.'

'Is she going to leave him?'

Sophie shrugged. A French shrug. 'I think she will. I hope she does.'

I shook my head. 'And I thought they had a perfect marriage.'

'She loves him, that's her problem,' Sophie said. 'And he just takes advantage of that.'

'You are right, he is an idiot. If I were married to your sister, I wouldn't spend my nights in brothels.'

'Quite right,' said Sophie. Then she looked at me slyly. 'Did you enjoy it? Your night at the Panier Fleuri?'

'I left early,' I confessed. I wasn't sure how she would take this, pleased that I had not sinned, or dismissive that I wasn't man enough to take my pleasure.

She laughed. She had this way of laughing at me that I was growing to like.

'Angus?' she said. 'Have you ever . . .?'

'What?' I asked, shocked and embarrassed by the question.

Sophie shrugged, a half smile on her lips.

'No,' I said. And then, emboldened. 'Have you?'

She shook her head. 'Madeleine is always encouraging me to. She says I won't know I have found the right man until I know

60

what the wrong man is like. But that doesn't seem to have worked for her.'

We walked in silence, our breath coming heavily as we climbed the steep hill, I reflecting on the extraordinary turns the conversation had taken with this extraordinary girl. The truth was, I had not really spoken to many girls. Joyce, my younger sister, and some of her friends, of course, but very few during my all-male schooldays or at my all-male college. I rather liked talking to this one.

We reached the top of the hill and a bulbous old stone chapel, besides which a fine set of ancient bells hung from a large wooden rack. Just past it, a dramatic view emerged over the town, the Seine estuary and the industrial port of Le Havre.

'Harfleur is over there somewhere,' said Sophie. 'It has been swallowed up by Le Havre now.'

We sat on a bench, birds shouting loudly behind us from the trees and bushes surrounding the chapel. I imagined Henry V's fleet hove to in front of what was now the docks of Le Havre. Or perhaps the coastline was further inland in the Middle Ages, and the English ships would actually have anchored where the warehouses now stood?

A lizard, surprised, darted under a stone.

'Angus?'

'Yes?'

'When Alden took you to the Panier Fleuri, did Stephen stay?'

CHAPTER III

A Death in Deauville

TONY HAD WON, and he was ecstatic. Fantastic had come through in the final furlong of the Grand Prix to win by a head, with a pile of Tony's money riding with him.

They all arrived back at the villa in Deauville with a case of champagne. Several bottles were drunk by the time dinner was served. Alden had given his English butler the weekend off; Monsieur and Madame Lemoine, who took care of the villa, would cook and wait on us. The dinner was lamb cutlets, and the champagne gave way to red wine. Tony had big plans; he announced that now he could stay on in Europe he would travel down to Italy for a month, staying in either Florence or maybe Capri to paint in peace.

'He must have put a serious amount on that horse,' I said to Stephen, who was sitting next to me. 'And he must not be quite as rich as he seems.'

'He did. Actually, my guess is Alden gave him the stake money. In theory Alden had a thousand-franc bet on Fantastic, but from the way he watched the race it seemed like a lot more.'

'How did you do?'

Stephen winced. 'Lost every race. It was a painful day for me.' For Stephen to wince like that he must have bet a considerable sum. I had no idea how wealthy Stephen was apart from that he had more than enough to meet his needs; I had never yet seen him in a position where the cost of anything had been a consideration.

'I thought I knew what I was doing, but I should have followed Elaine,' Stephen said. 'She backed two outsiders. Luck seems to be smiling on her.'

Elaine, on the other side of the table, was basking in her good fortune, and in the good champagne.

'I think she would rather have you smiling on her,' I said.

'Far too young for me,' said Stephen. 'Are you interested?'

'I don't think I'm her type, somehow,' I said. She was only a couple of years younger than Stephen and me, about the same age as Joyce.

'How did you get on with Sophie today?'

'It was terrific. Honfleur is gorgeous.'

'As is Sophie.'

'She's only nineteen, you know? Much too young for you.'

Stephen had a penchant for older women, and they had a penchant for him. His mother, who was only thirty-eight, had shared him around some of her friends in the Riviera. It was just one of the countless ways that Stephen's life was different from mine.

'Only nineteen?' said Stephen. 'I'm not sure whether I'm disappointed or intrigued.'

'Forget it,' I said, trying and failing to keep the irritation out of my voice. 'Not your type.'

Although I had no illusions about his chances with Sophie, the idea of Stephen having his way with her appalled me. She was better than that.

After dinner we went through to the drawing room. Here the English owner had outdone himself, although I rather liked the result. Huge tapestries showing knights and maidens hung on the walls, vying for attention with a boar's head and two pairs of swords. A cuirassier's breastplate and helmet stood beside the large fireplace and an arquebus rested above it. Several heavy dark wooden chests lurked on the floor. The chairs and sofas were covered in embroidered fabric of a deep red, but they were comfortable.

More champagne was opened. Alden, Tony and Elaine were really quite drunk now. Elaine was giggling, Tony was beaming at everyone and everything and Alden's words were losing clarity and gaining volume. The rest of us were quite merry too, and my head was swimming pleasantly.

'You wait till we get back to Paris, Tony!' Alden exclaimed. 'We'll celebrate properly then.'

'We will, we will!' said Tony raising his glass.

'We will!' said Elaine raising her glass too and knocking back the contents.

'Oh, Alden!' said Madeleine. There was more than frustration with her husband in her voice, there was anger.

'Oh come on, my darling,' Alden said, smiling. 'You can come too. You will enjoy it.'

'Enjoy it? Enjoy it?' Madame Burns's face was reddening under her make-up. 'Who do you think I am?' She had switched to French, but her words were loud and clear, so that I could easily understand them and so could her husband. 'You don't understand me at all! I forbid you to go to those places. I forbid it!'

For a moment fury danced in Alden's eyes, fury and danger. The room was silent. The genial host had disappeared and someone else had taken his place.

Alden looked at his guests, and smiled. The fury was gone, the danger had passed. 'Of course, my darling,' he said in English. 'Would you like some more champagne?'

'No,' said Madeleine. 'I'm going to bed now. I have a headache.'

She jumped up from her chair. Sophie stood up to follow her sister.

'You stay, Sophie,' Madeleine said in French. 'Stay!'

It was a command, and Sophie stayed.

'But you should be in bed, Elaine,' Madeleine said.

For a second Elaine looked as if she was going to argue, but then she latched on to a better strategy. 'Of course, I will go in just a moment.'

'See that she does,' said Madeleine to her husband and left the room.

Alden grinned at his guests, winked at Tony and refilled glasses. I glanced at Sophie. She caught my eye – see what I mean? I did. Did Alden just not understand his wife, or by pretending not to, did he hope he could get his way? I was very glad now I hadn't stayed on at the Panier Fleuri.

A damp blanket of silence settled on the room, like mist on a meadow, but like a mist it was soon melted away by the champagne and by the excitement of the afternoon's winnings. Tony asked me about the paintings I had seen in Honfleur's galleries. Elaine lingered, perching on the armrest of Tony's chair. Stephen was sitting next to Sophie and gently got her to loosen up. Nathan chatted to his uncle, trying to recover the mood.

Even when drunk, Tony Volstead's enthusiasm for art was infectious. Elaine seemed to like it, she had slipped off the armrest of the chair into his lap. Alden had joined Stephen and Sophie on one of the sofas; everyone always seemed to drift towards Stephen. Nathan was slumped on the other sofa, staring at his champagne glass.

'Get off me, Alden!'

I turned to see Sophie pushing Alden away from her. Her voice was sharp, but Alden was now very drunk. He rocked backwards, and then pursing his lips in a ludicrous pucker leaned forward again.

'I said, get off me!' Sophie repeated.

I leaped to my feet and grabbed Alden's shoulder. 'I say, steady on. You'd better leave her alone, don't you think?'

'But she's so beautiful,' said Alden. 'Madeleine won't mind.'

God, this is going to be embarrassing in the morning, I

thought. 'I think she will,' I said quietly. 'But more to the point, Sophie minds.'

Alden opened his mouth, but before he could say anything I heard a swish of steel through air.

'En garde!' Stephen had taken down one of the swords from the wall. 'Unhand that wench!'

'Stephen, put that down!' I protested.

Alden smiled. 'Ha!' he cried, unhanded Sophie and leaped for the other sword.

He slashed two or three times in front of his body, with remarkable speed for one so drunk.

'Come on, chaps, put them down,' I said. I considered stepping forward to intervene, but the points of those blades looked sharp. They weren't fencing swords; they were the real things, manufactured a few centuries before for killing people.

Stephen took up a dramatic pose, no doubt imagining himself as some kind of d'Artagnan. Alden slipped into something altogether more professional; this man had fenced before.

'Show him, Alden!' Tony yelled. 'One for all and all for one! No. All for one and one for all!'

Stephen slashed his sword at least a couple of feet away from Alden's face.

Alden lunged, parried and nicked Stephen's sleeve. He then stood up and grinned. 'The wench is mine!'

To my relief, Stephen lowered his sword and turned away. Alden also turned to bend low to Sophie to claim his prize. Sophie looked distinctly unhappy and then her eyes widened.

Stephen had been feinting. He swivelled and swung his sword clumsily over Alden's head. At that moment, Alden lurched upwards, thrusting his face into the path of Stephen's blade.

'Aargh!' he cried, clutching his face. Blood was springing out of his jaw.

'Christ!' said Stephen, lowering his weapon. 'Why did you move like that? Oh, God! I'm sorry.'

Alden stood upright, wincing and grabbed his jaw. Then he examined his fingers. There was a lot of blood.

With a roar, he charged at Stephen, who didn't resist. He knocked him on to the ground, his eyes blazing with the fury we had all glimpsed earlier. He held his sword over Stephen, the tip inches above his throat. Stephen's eyes were wide with terror. 'Die!'

For a moment it looked as if Alden was actually going to kill him. Then Alden stiffened. His eyes opened wide in surprise, he dropped his weapon and crumpled face-down on to the floor, a sword rising straight up out of his back.

Nathan stood, mouth open in disbelief, staring at his uncle on the floor at his feet.

CHAPTER IV

Clearing Up

FOR A COUPLE of seconds, nobody did anything.
Then Elaine let out a shriek. 'Is he dead?'

I was the doctor's son, so I leaped to Alden's side to check. The American's eyes were open, lifeless. He couldn't have died so quickly, could he? I grabbed his wrist to look for a pulse, but I couldn't immediately feel anything and so I felt Alden's neck instead. Despite what my father had done and what I intended to do, I had no clue. But those eyes were staring.

'I think he is,' I said. 'The sword must have pierced his heart.' Actually, I had no idea whether that was the case, but it seemed plausible.

'Fuck,' said Nathan. 'Fuck.'

'Why did you do that?' said Tony. 'Why did you kill him?'

'I thought he was going to slit Stephen's throat. I didn't mean to kill him. I just meant to distract him. Fuck.'

Stephen had rolled over out of the way of Alden, and was now on all fours, staring at the body. 'If it's any comfort, I thought he was going to kill me too.'

'Is he really dead?' Horror had ripped apart Elaine's soft young face, and she began to cry.

We all stared. After the drink, the laughter, the warmth, the body didn't seem real. It was as if only Elaine had appreciated the reality, the rest of us were still stunned.

Someone had to do something. 'We've got to get help,' I said. 'An ambulance.'

'There's no point in ringing for an ambulance if he's dead,' said Stephen.

'The police,' said Sophie.

They all looked at Tony. He was the oldest amongst us, the only real adult.

His face was pale. 'Don't look at me,' he said. 'I have nothing to do with this.'

Elaine's sobs turned into a wail. Sophie moved over to comfort her.

'We can't call the police,' said Stephen. 'Nathan will be done for murder.'

'Fuck,' said Nathan.

'We can explain what happened,' I said.

'What happened was he killed Alden and we all saw it,' said Stephen.

Nathan fell back on to the sofa and put his head in his hands.

'We have to, I don't know, change things,' said Stephen. 'Make out it was self-defence. Or suicide.'

'He ran himself through with his own sword? In the back?' I said.

'All right, all right. I know,' said Stephen. 'But Nathan didn't mean to kill him. And he thought he was saving my life. Unless we do something, we all do something . . .' A pointed look at Tony. '. . . Nathan will spend the rest of his life in a French prison. They might even hang him. That's not fair. It's not just.'

'I appreciate the thought, Stephen, but what can we say?' said Nathan, distraught.

Although I had drunk an awful lot of champagne, my brain cleared. I came to a decision; someone had to.

'We all went back to our rooms,' I said. 'Alden stayed up here, drinking. Someone broke in. A burglar. Alden surprised him. There was a fight and Alden was killed. The burglar ran away.'

There was silence.

'Will that work?' said Nathan.

'Yes,' said Stephen. 'It's brilliant!'

'But we all need to go along with it,' I said. I stared at Tony, Alden's best friend. If there was a weak link, it was Tony.

Tony looked at his friend, lying dead on the floor. He looked at Nathan. He sighed. A tear appeared on his cheek and he wiped it away.

'It was an accident,' he said. 'It was your fault, Stephen, for playing with those swords, and Alden's for playing too seriously. But no one really meant to kill anyone.' He stared at Nathan. 'Stephen's right; you will go to gaol and you don't deserve that. So, I'll go along with it.'

'Thank you, Tony,' said Nathan.

'What about Madeleine?' said Sophie. 'We have to tell Madeleine.'

My brain was working fast now, very fast, and I had already thought of that. 'We can't tell Madeleine. She needs to discover it herself; that way her reaction will be genuine. Credible.'

'I can't lie to my sister about this,' said Sophie. 'She is Alden's wife. She must know what happened.'

Sophie was right. They were all looking at me. 'Yes, you have to tell her, but not right away. Tell her, I don't know, in a day or so. After the initial questioning, but before the police investigation is closed. Make it her choice. She decides whether Nathan goes to gaol or not. That's only fair.'

Nathan swallowed and nodded. But he was very pale; he looked as if he was about to be sick.

'If she decides that we should tell the police Nathan killed him, won't we be in trouble for lying to them?' Tony asked.

'We might,' I said. 'But if it's we who tell them, not Madeleine, I don't think that's likely. You're right, though, it *is* a risk we are taking.'

I looked around the group. They were silent, thoughtful. They almost looked sober.

I turned to Sophie. 'I hope you will persuade your sister that she should go along with the rest of us.'

'I think we should go to the police,' she said. 'We should explain what happened. That it was an accident.'

'If you believe Nathan should spend the rest of his life in prison, then you should tell them,' I said. 'If you are not certain of that, then leave it to Madeleine to decide.'

Sophie closed her eyes. 'We still use the guillotine in France.'

I had assumed that with the extenuating circumstances, they wouldn't execute Nathan, but I didn't know what the French judicial system would decide. I could only guess.

'Well, Sophie?'

She took a deep breath. 'All right. So what do we do?'

'OK,' I said. 'I will organize this. The story for the rest of you needs to be very simple so you don't contradict each other.' I checked my watch. 'It's now a quarter to twelve. I have just said I am going to bed. You all agree. But you all leave before me – you can't remember in what order. So it's just me and Alden here when you go. That's all you need to know. Everything, do you understand? And everyone get up late tomorrow.'

'Who will discover Alden's body?'

'That's not your concern,' I said. 'You'll find out tomorrow.'

'What about Madeleine?' Sophie said.

'She will find out too,' I replied.

'But she will know Alden didn't come to bed with her.'

Damn. Sophie was right. I hadn't thought of that. How could I hope to think of everything? I could only try.

'That's true. But don't worry about it. Just go to bed, everyone.'

Elaine stood up, wiped her tears, and headed out of the door. Tony stared at his friend, hesitated, glanced at me and followed her, as did the others. Soon I was alone in the room with Alden.

First I felt for a pulse. There definitely wasn't one. Alden was definitely dead.

For a moment the enormity of what had happened almost overwhelmed me; that a man had been killed right in front of me. But I crammed a lid on those feelings. I sat down on the sofa and forced myself to think. I thought hard and I thought quickly.

I had never been involved in a real-life murder, or indeed had any dealings with the police, although I had read three or four Agatha Christies, a Dashiell Hammett and a Maigret. That would have to do.

So what was involved in a detective investigation? Motive? Alden's friends had none, the unnamed burglar did. Good. Interviews. Everyone had a simple story; I would need to think through mine. Alibis? In a way, we all had alibis for each other, until the moment we all went to bed. But the police might believe that any one of us could have sneaked back and killed Nathan. Not much I could do about that. Time of death? Middle of the night. Discovery of the body? Ideally, the French couple, when they woke up to make breakfast and tidy up. Possibly Madeleine, if she got up to look for Alden in the middle of the night. She might assume he decided to sleep elsewhere. Signs of a break-in? Footprints? Fingerprints? List of stolen property? Anyone hear anything in the night?

With the questions came answers thick and fast, but I forced myself to sit tight and think things through. Then I went to work.

The house was woken at a few minutes after seven by a scream from Madame Lemoine, who had discovered Alden Burns's body in the drawing room, with a sword sticking out of his back. The police were called. The investigation, led by an Inspector Pasquier, established that Alden had last been seen by me at about midnight. The others had all gone to bed, and I had left Alden a few minutes later, finishing a bottle of champagne alone in the drawing room.

A window was broken, and earth from the flower beds was scattered underneath it, although outside in the beds themselves footprints were scuffed; the ground was hard from several days without rain. Alden's wallet was missing, as was a small medieval silver goblet that Madame Lemoine said had stood on top of a chest next to the window. The hilt of the sword in Alden's back had been wiped clean of fingerprints. Another sword lay on the floor by his body, this one sporting Alden's own prints. The room itself was full of prints, but these could all be matched with the house guests. The area around the window had been wiped clean.

No one had heard anything, apart from me, who told the police I had heard a whisper in French outside in the garden in the middle of the night. I wasn't sure of the time, but I guessed it was quite soon after I had gone to sleep. To my regret, I did not investigate. Mme Burns had heard nothing. She too had woken up in the middle of the night – she didn't know what time – to find the space next to her in bed empty. She had argued with her husband earlier in the evening, and assumed that either he had stayed up all night drinking, or he had fallen asleep on the sofa. No one in the street leading up to the house had seen anything. Local suspects had been interviewed with no result. But since it was the weekend of the Grand Prix de Deauville, the town was a magnet for thieves from far and wide.

The investigation continued. For a day or so, Inspector Pasquier considered the possibility that Madame Burns had murdered her husband. He had been unfaithful to her, and she was very angry about it. But the inspector knew that such a quotidian situation was not proof in and of itself of murder. His instinct told him strongly that she was innocent and no evidence emerged to suggest otherwise.

So, after three days, the houseguests were allowed to return to Paris and to England. Then there was a breakthrough: a known burglar from Paris was discovered to have been at Deauville for the races. He was interviewed and his alibi was weak, drinking with fellow riff-raff in bar in town. But he was a pro. He denied all knowledge of the murder and despite all Inspector Pasquier's stratagems, he made no slip-ups. Eventually the inspector had to let him go. The investigation continued for several weeks but was then reluctantly closed. Reluctantly, because the inspector was still convinced that the Parisian burglar was his man.

Alden Burns's murder remained unsolved.

5

Clémence closed the book, marking her place with the flap of the dust jacket. The killing of Alden had shocked her. It wasn't just its suddenness, or the fact that it was the dreadful consequence of a bunch of students her age having too much fun. Nor was it only that they had colluded to hide the truth from the police, and that amongst those who had colluded were her grandfather, her grandmother and the man sitting opposite her. She had been expecting, dreading, a different death. That would come, she was sure, but there was a long way to go yet.

The old man was staring at her under those bushy eyebrows, his chin resting on one hand, in total concentration.

'Well?' she said.

He didn't answer.

She pressed. 'Do you remember any of that?'

'I do,' said the old man. 'I remember that afternoon in Honfleur when I met Sophie. I remember the train coming out of Calais. And then . . .'

'What?'

The old man just shook his head.

'Do you remember Nathan killing his uncle?'

'No. I don't,' said the old man. 'I don't remember Alden at all.'

'What about Nathan? And Stephen, my grandfather?'

'Almost.'

'Almost?' said Clémence in frustration. 'How can you almost remember something?'

The old man wrinkled his brows in concentration, ignoring Clémence's irritation. 'It's as if you are looking into a room, which you know is full of people, but there are blank spaces where the people should be. You know they are there, you know you know them, but you can't see them, and just for the moment you can't remember who they are. It's most odd. Do you think it's true? About Alden? It can't be, can it?'

He looked at her, his brown eyes vulnerable, seeking assurance. Clémence was not in the mood to give assurance to her grandmother's murderer.

'I think it probably is. When Aunt Madeleine gets here, I'll ask her. She should know; she was there. But until then, we can assume it is true: you and your friends covered up a murder.'

'Manslaughter, surely? It sounded like an accident.'

'Whatever.' A man had died. Clémence agreed with Sophie: they should have come clean to the police. She was disappointed that Sophie hadn't stood her ground. 'Can you remember what happens next?'

The old man shook his head. 'No. No, I can't. You know yesterday I was sure there was something bad I didn't want to remember? Killing Alden must have been it.'

He looked relieved as he spoke. The old man's part in Alden's killing was bad, but not the stuff of eternal shame.

Not like strangling another man's wife.

'I'll make lunch,' said Clémence.

'Shall I help?' said the old man.

'No. You stay here,' said Clémence sharply. 'I'll give you a shout when it's ready.'

She went into the kitchen, put some soup on the hob, and dug some Brie out of the fridge.

She was revolted by Alastair. The bones of what had happened were already clear. He had fallen in love with Sophie when they had first met. But then she had married someone else, her grandfather

Stephen, and some time later Angus/Alastair had strangled her. She wasn't sure exactly when her grandmother had died, but it was obviously after her father was born, and she knew that was 1948.

So what now?

She felt like getting into Livvie's Clio and just driving off, leaving the old man to his own devices. He could probably survive until Aunt Madeleine arrived. And he could read the damn book himself and find out what an evil monster he really was.

And yet. While Clémence often visited her French mother's family in Rheims, she knew virtually nothing about her family on her father's side. Apart from a couple of visits on her way to boarding school, she had been kept away from her grandfather Stephen. She was aware there were cousins – children of her father's sister whose name she thought was Beatrice – but she had never met them. She got the impression that Stephen's family had once been wealthy, with an estate in England and one in Scotland as well, but the feckless Stephen had frittered it all away. She was vaguely aware that Stephen himself had been briefly famous as an actor in the forties, but now nobody had heard of him, and according to her mother his films weren't any good anyway. Then there had been some kind of scandal: her mother muttered darkly about drink. Her father said nothing at all.

There was Aunt Madeleine, her fairy godmother, and Uncle Nathan, whom she occasionally saw, and of course that framed black-and-white photograph of her beautiful grandmother Sophie. And that was it.

No one had told her the truth about her grandmother's death. They hadn't even told her Alden Burns existed, let alone he had been killed and they had all connived at covering it up. Who might have told her? Grandpa? She didn't have that kind of relationship with him. Her father? He never spoke about his own family. Aunt Madeleine? Clémence certainly had some questions for Aunt Madeleine now.

Because now she wanted to find out more. She needed to find out more. Without the knowledge of what had happened back then, her family didn't make sense. And that meant *she* didn't make sense.

There was so much she had never questioned: how her grandmother had died, why her grandfather was a broken-down old man. Why her father had dropped out and gone to Morocco when he was in his early twenties.

And all that determined who she was. Half-French, half-English, living in Hong Kong, educated in Britain, with parents who had never really got the hippie out of their systems. Or at least her father hadn't. He was ten years older than her mother, and although he had eventually become a career teacher at a private school in Hong Kong, he had never reconciled himself to his own father. And then he had walked out on his wife and daughter, and left the island to get a job in Vietnam. After a few months, Clémence's mother had moved into a nice apartment in Mid-Levels with an Australian fund manager called Patrick. It was only recently that Clémence had begun to suspect that Patrick was the cause, not the result, of her father's departure.

It was why last Christmas had been so horrible. Why she never wanted to go back to Hong Kong. Ever.

All this, everything that had happened to her in her first twenty years, had causes, had roots.

Those roots were in that book. And Dr Alastair Cunningham, of whom she had barely heard, and whom she had met only once before, knew about them. More than that, he had had an active part in planting them.

Despite herself, part of her couldn't bring herself to abandon him, at least until she was absolutely sure what he had done. Those brown eyes, firm, intelligent, yet vulnerable tugged at her. He needed her help. Clémence liked it when people needed her help.

She heard the old man make his way up the steep spiral stairs to his room. The soup was bubbling, so she turned the gas down. A car came up the drive to the cottage, a Suzuki four-wheel-drive. A very tall woman with broad shoulders, long legs in tight blue jeans and short blond hair got out and waved to Clémence through the kitchen window.

Clémence opened the front door.

'Hi, I'm Sheila,' said the woman. 'Sheila MacInnes.' She held out her hand, and Clémence shook it briefly. The voice was soft and friendly and very Scottish. For some reason, Clémence had expected someone much smaller and a little older – Sheila was about forty, she guessed.

'Oh, hi, come in. I'm just making some lunch. Do you want some?'

'Och, no. I'll pop back in later, if you like?'

'No, no, no,' said Clémence. 'Please stay. It's only soup, it can wait. I'll turn it off for now. Have a coffee.'

'That would be very nice. I'm so sorry I wasn't here last night. My mother's poorly and she lives all the way over in Ullapool, I had to check on her. How's Dr Cunningham? Is he here?'

'Oh, yes. He's upstairs. I can call him if you like. But actually it would be nice if I could ask you a couple of things first.'

'Of course, pet. How is he?'

'Physically, he's not bad at all,' Clémence said, putting the kettle on. 'Mentally he's quite sharp. And he seems to know his way around the cottage. But he can remember next to nothing about his life.'

'Aye, I know. It's right weird. But at least he's still alive. When I found him, I thought he was a goner, if you see what I mean.' She shuddered. 'He was right at the bottom of those stairs. They're very steep, you tell him to watch himself on them. He was out cold, and there was a pool of blood by his head. You can still see a wee patch on the floorboards; I couldn't get rid of it no matter how much I scrubbed.'

'Can you tell me anything about him?' Clémence said. 'Did you speak to him at all? Before the accident.'

'Aye, I did,' the woman laughed. 'But I suppose I did most of the talking. That's the way it is with me, if you see what I mean. But he told me a wee bit about himself.'

'How long had he been here?'

'He wrote to me last year asking about renting the cottage for the winter. Usually, that would have been a problem, but we've had some difficulties with the owners recently, so it made sense. And when I spoke to him on the phone, he sounded awful nice. He had just come back to England from Australia. He was staying in a hotel somewhere in Yorkshire, but decided he wanted somewhere a bit more remote.'

'Did he say he had been here before?'

'Aye, he did. Just the once and that was a long time ago. He was very curious about the estate. I told him what I could – Terry and I only came here ten years ago. We are both from Ullapool, Terry was a stalker at an estate over there.'

'Who owns the Wyvis Estate?'

'A Dutchman, Mr de Bruijn. He's a lovely man, but he's getting old, too old for the stalking. He used to come for months at a time, and bring lots of his friends with him, but we hardly see him now. That's why we rented out this cottage and Corravachie down by the loch. You might have passed it on the way up?'

Clémence remembered the smoke she had seen rising up from the white building on a spit of land.

'What about the big house at the head of the lake?'

'That's Wyvis Lodge, where Mr de Bruijn lives when he comes. We're thinking about renting that out as well. We should get a fair wee bit for it. But it's empty at the moment. I keep it clean and we make sure the grounds are tidy.'

The kettle boiled and Clémence spooned instant coffee into cups. 'Thanks for getting the food and coffee,' she said.

'Och, it's no bother. I'm glad you could come and look after him.'

They sat down opposite each other at the kitchen table. Clémence noticed that Sheila had a small tattoo of a Chinese character under her T-shirt by her collar bone, though it was not one of the few that Clémence recognized. Clémence liked her: she seemed competent and willing, and Clémence might need her help in the next few days.

'This may sound odd, but did a family called Trickett-Smith ever own the estate?'

'Yes, they did. Dr Cunningham asked all about them. But they sold up in the nineteen seventies.'

'That was my grandfather's family,' said Clémence. 'I thought I had heard it mentioned.'

'A hundred years ago the estate was bought by a man who owned a big furniture store in London. Bought it for the deer stalking, of course. Then the Trickett-Smiths owned it, and then a German and now Mr de Bruijn. Mind you, the local history society says that a couple of hundred years ago, there were dozens of Scottish families up here farming. Before the clearances.'

'The clearances?' Clémence had a feeling she had vaguely heard of them. She feared they were bad.

'Aye. When the rich landowners turfed out all the folk because you could make more money out the sheep than out the crofters.'

She was right; it was bad. 'Oh,' she said.

Sheila smiled. 'That was a wee while ago. And we can hardly complain. Terry's job needs people who want to spend a lot of money stalking deer, if you see what I mean.'

Clémence had yet to see a deer at Wyvis. She assumed stalking meant sneaking up on them and shooting them. Memories of the *Bambi* video she had watched over and over again as a kid flooded back; it was scary and it was sad. But she decided not to make any comment.

'Have you ever heard of a book called *Death At Wyvis*?' she asked.

'Aye, I think there's a copy in Dr Cunningham's study. It's an old book.'

'Have you ever read it?'

'No, pet. But I know some of the locals around here did when it came out. I think it's about a murder.'

'I think it is,' said Clémence. 'I have started to read it to Dr Cunningham. Do you know if it's true?'

'Well, I can't be sure, because I haven't read it, see, but there was a murder just down the loch thirty years ago, something like that. A woman was found, drowned, I think.'

'Did they find who did it?' Clémence asked. She realized she was holding her breath as she waited for an answer.

Sheila thought for a moment. 'I can't just mind, if I ever knew. The old stalker's wife still lives in Dingwall, Pauline Ferguson. You could ask her.'

'Maybe I will,' said Clémence.

Just then she heard the sound of slow, uneven footsteps on the stairs.

'Dr Cunningham!' Sheila exclaimed as the old man entered the kitchen. 'It's lovely to see you out the hospital, pet.'

The old man smiled. It was clear that he recognized her, but then Clémence realized that she had probably visited him in hospital.

Sheila fussed over him for a few minutes and then left them to the soup, promising to pop in again at least once a day to make sure they were all right.

Clémence was alone again with her grandmother's killer.

6

They ate lunch. Clémence wasn't in the mood to talk, unlike the old man.

'Nice woman, Mrs MacInnes,' he said. 'I'm damned lucky she found me. At the hospital they said I might have died of hypothermia.'

Clémence grunted. She was tempted to say that she wished he had, but she couldn't quite go that far.

'You read very well.'

'I like reading out loud,' Clémence said.

'Even to an old fool who can't remember his name?'

'Even to you.' She winced inwardly: that sounded ruder than she had meant it. But the old man didn't seem to mind.

'Were you impressed by my chat-up lines?'

'Not especially.'

'Medieval land reform doesn't do it for you, eh?' The old man chuckled to himself. 'Sophie must have been very patient. I sounded so *young*, don't you think? Your friends aren't that innocent, are they?'

'I don't think many of them have been to Parisian brothels. At least I like to think they haven't.'

'That's a point. I'm curious to hear what happens next, aren't you?'

'Yes,' said Clémence, as unenthusiastically as possible, although in truth she *was* curious. At last, her terse replies had the desired effect: the old man gave up and they ate the rest of the meal in silence. But just as she was clearing the soup bowls, he grabbed her hand.

She tugged it away from him.

'No. Let me look. At that mark.'

She knew immediately what he meant. The ragged red spot on her wrist. Reluctantly, she offered him her hand.

His fingers were firm as he examined it. 'You should get that checked,' the old man said. 'Soon. And while they are at it, get them to check the rest of your skin.'

'Is it skin cancer?'

'Almost certainly,' the old man said. She felt a jolt run through her body. His eyes met hers. Strong. Comforting. 'Don't worry, it's basal cell carcinoma, the least serious, and we've caught it early. It's practically harmless. But it will need to be cut out.'

'Are you sure it's not going to kill me?' she said.

'I've seen hundreds of these in Australia,' he said.

Clémence raised her eyebrows. 'You remember Australia?'

The old man smiled. 'I don't know how, but I do know I have seen them before. You said you lived in Hong Kong. Have you spent a lot of time out in the sun?'

'Yes. When I was little we lived in Morocco and then Vietnam. Maman tried to put sun cream on me, but she didn't do a very good job.'

'Did you burn?'

Clémence remembered wriggling in her sheets when she was small, her shoulders itching. 'Yes. I did.' She looked at the old man in panic. 'Will I get more of these?'

'Probably, in time,' he said. 'Just be very careful from now on with the sunscreen.'

He patted her wrist and let go of it. 'Don't worry. But make an appointment as soon as you can. You'll be OK.'

Clémence wanted to believe him. It was only a tiny spot. She *would* be OK. 'You are sure it won't spread?'

'Quite sure.'

She took a deep breath and cleared the rest of the table. The old man moved to help her with the little bit of washing up.

She couldn't stand him hovering over her shoulder. She felt a sudden urge to leave the cottage. 'Look. I'm going out for a walk. When I get back, we'll read some more of the book.' It was a command, not a suggestion.

The old man nodded. 'All right. I'll see you later.'

The sky was blue and the sun had some warmth to it. The snow had completely melted off the branches of the trees, and was slipping away from the heather. It almost felt warm, although the temperature was certainly below ten degrees.

She walked down the path through the woods and soon reached the loch. She headed along the shore towards the Stalker's Lodge.

The loch was a dark Prussian blue in the sunshine. Two swans drifted across its surface. She wondered if you could tell how deep it was just by looking at it. It seemed to her that it must be very deep. Was there a Loch Glass monster down there?

Was there a monster in the cottage?

He was just an old man. Whatever he had done had been done decades ago when he was younger, a different person. Was he a different person? She didn't know. *He* didn't even know. Why hadn't Aunt Madeleine told her about this?

She was alone in an isolated cottage with a murderer. Should she be frightened? The old man was in his eighties, but he was still a couple of inches taller than her. He had a stoop, but his shoulders were square and he was fit. She had no idea whether she could overcome him in a fight. Or he might take her unawares – there were knives in the kitchen.

But she just wasn't scared of him. Those soft brown vulnerable eyes. She felt safe with him – not just safe from him, but protected. She was supposed to be looking after him, but despite his age, she also felt he was looking after her. She was still angry with him, though.

She broke out of the woods. Above her skylarks were twittering away, fluttering vertically up into the sky and then diving down again into the snow-patched heather.

The white tops of Ben Wyvis soared high above her. But there was a ridge about halfway up, and she thought she saw some movement on the skyline. She stopped and stared. Yes! A deer, silhouetted against the snowy slopes above. And another, grazing. And then one of them lifted its head and she could see the antlers. They were a long way away, but it was a magnificent sight.

She walked on, fast, relishing the exercise and the fresh air. She rounded the curve of the loch and the white cottage on the spit of land came into view. Once again, smoke rose in a twisted column from the chimney. A new blue Peugeot was parked on a gravel apron by the front door.

As she approached along the track, she thought she heard music: a guitar and some singing. A man in a blue parka was sitting on a stone right on the shore of the loch, holding a guitar and staring out at the rocky wall opposite.

Clémence hesitated and then approached. The man knew what he was doing. The voice had a kind of gravelly clarity. She was only a few feet away from the figure and she stopped. He hadn't noticed her, but she didn't want to interrupt him, partly because it was rude, and partly because she wanted to hear the rest of the song, which she didn't recognize.

But then he stopped mid verse, and stared at his guitar, thoughtfully.

She coughed.

The man whipped round. He was thin, tall with a short neat grey beard, very short grey hair and blue eyes surrounded by crows' feet.

'Whoa! You scared me!' he said. 'This isn't the kind of place you expect an audience.'

'Well you've got one,' said Clémence. 'So don't let me stop you. Play something else.'

He shrugged. 'OK.' He started playing a few chords that Clémence instantly recognized: 'My Woman Wept For Me', a folk song from the seventies by Don Ahern. He played it more slowly than she remembered it.

She perched on the other end of the rock a few feet away from him and listened. The music, and the loch, and the sunshine on her face, and the cool crisp air, made her heart sing. Clémence wasn't good at being grumpy. This was just what she needed.

'That was lovely,' she said, when the man had finished.

'You recognize it?' the man said. He had an American accent.

'My parents played it all the time. It reminds me of growing up.'

The man smiled and nodded to himself, clearly pleased.

An absurd thought hit Clémence. 'You're not Don Ahern?' From what she could remember of Don Ahern he was small with long dark curly hair, but maybe she had got that wrong.

'Don died ten years ago,' said the man. 'But I did write this song.'

'Wow!' said Clémence. 'Are you really famous?'

The man chuckled. 'No, sadly not. Don's producer heard me play it in 1971 and contacted me a year later, asking me if Don could use it. I guess he did a better job. But I still prefer it my way.'

'Have you written any other hits?' Clémence asked.

'A few near misses, a bunch of advertising jingles, but that's the only one. So far. That's why I came here. I live in California, but I needed to get away to try something new. Way way away.' He leaned over towards her and held out his hand. 'Jerry. Jerry Ranger.'

'Clémence Smith,' said Clémence shaking it.

'Are you staying up at Culzie?'

'Yes. I'm looking after Dr Cunningham.'

'Is he OK? Sheila told me he had taken a tumble.'

'I think he's OK. But he's lost his memory. It's the weirdest thing, amnesia.'

'He can't remember anything?'

'Absolutely nothing. Or nothing important. He couldn't remember who he is, they had to tell him. That's part of what I am doing. Most of it. Trying to jog his memory.'

'Is it working?' Jerry asked.

'I think so. Slowly.'

'Well, tell him I wish him a quick recovery,' said Jerry. 'I've been here for three weeks now; we've spoken a few times, had a couple of drinks together. Nice guy, once you get to talk to him.'

'I will tell him, if you like, but I doubt very much if he will remember who you are.'

'Oh, yes, of course,' said Jerry. He frowned. 'That's a shame.'

'Do you want to drop by and help me?' Clémence asked. 'He might remember something more easily that's more recent. And I don't know very much about his past, which makes it difficult.'

'Neither do I,' said Jerry. 'Although he did talk about Australia some. He used to live in the hills near Perth before he came here. And he did some stuff with eagles there, capturing them and counting them. He got all excited about the pair of golden eagles up the other end of the loch. They nest in the cliffs of Meall Mòr.' He smiled at Clémence. 'But sure, I'll drop by.'

'Great,' Clémence said. 'Play something else. And then I had better get back.'

She had been away nearly two hours by the time she returned to the cottage. The old man was out – he must have gone for his own walk. This troubled Clémence; she wasn't sure whether he was fit enough to go out on his own. She considered looking for him, but then she decided to take advantage of his absence to make some phone calls first.

She called Callum on his mobile. He sounded as pleased to hear her voice as she was to hear his.

'Hey, Clemmie, how are you?'

'I'm OK, I suppose, but the weirdest thing is happening here. Tell me if I sound mental, but I've found this book in the old guy's house. I think he killed my grandmother!'

She explained it all to Callum, who listened carefully. 'Are you sure you should be there with him alone?' Callum asked when she had finished.

'Yeah, it's OK. He doesn't seem dangerous, and my aunt wouldn't let me stay here if it was a problem.'

'I don't know, Clemmie,' said Callum.

That pulled Clémence up a bit. Callum might be a year younger than her, but he was one of the most sensible guys she knew. If he was worried, maybe she should be.

'I'm sure I'll be OK,' she said. Then she had an idea. 'Do you want to come here and keep me company?'

'Maybe I should. I am a bit worried about you.'

Clémence's heart leaped. They hadn't been going out very long, but Clémence really really liked him, and what was cool was the more she got to know him, the more that liking grew. She had the strong impression he felt the same way about her.

'It's beautiful up here. You could bring your bike – there's a good track beside the loch. Maybe you could take it on the train and ride it up here? Or I could pick you up in Livvie's car, although I don't think we could fit the bike in the boot.'

'Thinking about it, I'd better not,' said Callum. 'I've only just started at the pub, and I can't take shifts off right away. Plus I need the money.'

'I understand,' said Clémence. She was disappointed, but on the other hand she was pleased with his concern, and she could tell from his voice that he genuinely wanted to come. 'I'll call you tomorrow.'

'Look after yourself, Clemmie.'

'I will.'

Next was Aunt Madeleine in New York. Her phone was answered on the fourth ring by a woman with a Hispanic accent, a maid presumably. She said that Mrs Giannelli had said that Clémence might call and that Mrs Giannelli expected to be in Scotland the following day. She was flying to Heathrow overnight and then to Edinburgh and taking a train from there to Dingwall. She would get a taxi to Dr Cunningham's address.

All this was clearly read out from a note left by Aunt Madeleine, and that was all the maid knew.

Clémence was frustrated she couldn't ask Aunt Madeleine the questions she wanted right away, but there was only twenty-four hours to wait.

In the meantime there was one more person she could call.

7

Stephen paused for breath as he made his way up Campden Hill. Either the hill was getting steeper or he was getting older. What had a few years before been a pleasant twenty-minute stroll to the pub from his flat, was now a major excursion.

He was getting older.

But at least his pint of Guinness would taste good when he eventually got there.

And it did. The Windsor Castle was an old pub split into a number of bars by wooden screens. The smallest, the Sherry Bar, was his favourite, and he usually got there early enough to grab his favourite seat. Maitland, a tiny crooked man who looked ninety, but who was in fact only seventy-seven, was already there with the *Telegraph* crossword open in front of him.

'How many have you done?' Stephen asked.

'Four. It's tricky today.'

Stephen eased himself onto the wooden bench with a harrumph, and took his second sip of Guinness. A small sip. The pint, and the crossword, would last him a couple of hours.

'Give me one.'

'"Solution given by Italian who made notes before court." Seven letters.'

'Ah.'

Although they usually finished their pints, Stephen and Maitland never finished the crossword. That was the point.

His ruminations were interrupted by Harry, a recently retired

91

stockbroker, who really needed to find himself another pub. Preferably in Woking or Weybridge or somewhere.

'Morning, gents,' he said, setting his gin and tonic in front of him. 'Lovely day.' He beamed at them from a face of flab and sweat.

Maitland grunted. Stephen ignored him. '"Made notes". Music, do you think?'

'Doing the crossword?' Harry said.

Of course they were bloody doing the crossword. Just like they did every day.

'You two are like the furniture in here,' Harry said. 'How long have you been coming here? Doing the crossword together?'

'1962 we did our first one, don't you think, Stephen?' Maitland answered.

Stephen nodded. 'That sounds about right.'

'But not here,' said Maitland. 'Somewhere else.'

'Did you work together?' asked Harry.

'No.'

'Old school friends?'

Stephen glanced at Maitland. This man had to be dealt with. 'Cell mates.'

Harry laughed. 'Shared an office, eh? Or was it National Service?'

'Wormwood Scrubs.'

'Ah.' Harry sipped his drink uncomfortably.

Stephen waited. Anyone with any decency would let it rest there. But Harry . . .

'What were you in for, if you don't mind me asking?'

Actually Stephen did mind.

'Murder,' said Stephen.

'Murder,' said Maitland.

'You're kidding, right?' said Henry. He tugged at his double chin nervously. 'You're not kidding.'

'They let us out when they thought we were no longer a threat to society,' said Stephen. 'But you know what?' He leaned forward.

'What?' said Harry, distinctly uneasy now.

'When you've killed once, you can always kill again.'

The retired stockbroker drained his glass and left the pub, knocking the table and spilling Stephen's Guinness on the way.

Stephen glanced at Maitland. One side of his friend's lip twitched. Then he returned to business. 'An Italian musical instrument. Piccolo?'

Two hours later, Stephen made the trek back to his flat just on the other side of Notting Hill Gate. He wanted to catch the three-thirty at Newmarket on Channel 4. He had enjoyed dealing with Harry. He and Maitland were a good team. He was a good man, Maitland, even if he had murdered his wife with a cricket bat.

Stephen lived in a tiny basement flat bought for him twenty years before by his sister-in-law for fifteen thousand pounds. The other people in the building were yuppie bankers and solicitors, who had paid twenty times that for theirs. The flat was dark and it was a tip; but Stephen knew where everything was, and he liked it.

He was bursting, so he dived into the lavatory as soon as he got in the front door.

He had just finished when the phone rang.

'All right, all right,' he muttered to himself. Why people bothered him like that, he would never know.

He picked up the receiver. 'Yes.'

'Grandpa?' It was a woman's voice, a young woman.

'I think you've got the wrong number.' Stephen did have a few grandchildren, but they never wanted to speak to him. More to the point, he didn't want to speak to them.

'Is that Mr Trickett-Smith?'

'Yes,' Stephen admitted.

'It's Clémence. Your granddaughter.'

It was true, Clémence was his granddaughter. Rupert's girl. Although Stephen had hardly ever seen her.

'Are you telephoning from Hong Kong?'

'No. Scotland. I go to St Andrews University. You know that.'

'Yes, yes of course,' he said, relieved that she wasn't in London and about to take him out to tea. Although actually from what he remembered of her, he rather liked Clémence.

'But I'm at Wyvis now. Looking after Dr Cunningham. Alastair Cunningham? Your old friend.'

'Wyvis? Alastair?' Stephen had been standing holding the telephone receiver, but now he slumped into an armchair.

'Yes. He fell down the stairs last week and hit his head. Badly. They took him to hospital, but now they've let him out and Aunt Madeleine asked me to look after him until she gets over here.'

Interfering old bat.

Clémence was in full flow. 'Alastair has suffered a brain injury and has forgotten everything, so I am trying to help him remember. Was Wyvis the Scottish estate that was in our family?'

'Yes,' said Stephen. 'We had to sell it in the seventies when my father died. Death duties.'

'I thought so,' said Clémence. 'Alastair's been living in a cottage called Culzie. I found a book in there, which I have been reading to him. *Death At Wyvis*. Have you read it?'

'Yes, I've read it,' said Stephen.

'We've only done a few chapters, but it starts with Alastair killing my grandmother, Sophie. The author calls the protagonist Angus, but it's definitely Alastair, isn't it?'

'I remember the beginning,' said Stephen.

'Well, is it true?'

'Why do you ask?'

'What do you mean, why do I ask?' said Clémence. She was beginning to sound angry now. 'My grandmother was murdered, and no one told me. This old man killed her and Aunt Madeleine makes me stay with him. I want to know what's going on!'

'Listen to me, young lady,' said Stephen. 'There are very good reasons why no one told you what happened to Sophie. It's a bad idea to read that book. If you ask me, Alastair is lucky he has forgotten some things. Put that book back on the bookshelf and leave it alone. Better still, throw it in the loch where it belongs.'

'Grandpa!'

'Now I have something to watch on television. Goodbye, Clémence.'

Stephen put the receiver down. His eyes were drawn to the mantelpiece above the fire, and the photograph of Sophie aged twenty-four, looking at him over her right shoulder, with that quiet smile. By the time he switched on the television he had missed the three-thirty race. And the four o'clock.

It was good to be out in the open, walking again. The old man had listened to the lecture from Dr Stenhouse in the hospital about making sure he got both his mind and his body going again. So he had left the cottage and let his feet take him where they wanted. They led him on to a rough path out of the woods and on to the hillside of heather, dead bracken and peat bog, with Ben Wyvis rising to his left and Loch Glass beneath him on his right. The path made its way diagonally down the hill to the loch, just by Wyvis Lodge.

He couldn't see any deer, but as he scanned the sky, he spotted a large bird wheeling above the stand of pines near the Lodge. It was too far to see its colouration, but he could tell from the splayed 'fingers' at its wingtips that it was a golden eagle.

He stopped and stared at the magnificent bird. He loved eagles.

And then, suddenly, he remembered another eagle a continent away, several continents away. They were in the outback somewhere in WA, three hundred kilometres from Perth. Him and Mike. Mike was a young guy, in his thirties, Alastair's next-door neighbour. He was studying wedge-tailed eagles. He needed to trap them to tag them, and that was very difficult. He and Alastair had discussed the problem one evening over a beer on Alastair's veranda, and Alastair had come up with a solution. The eagles were so big that they needed a run-up to take off. So if you built a wire cage, open at the top, which was big enough for them to swoop down into, but did not give them enough space to take off, you might catch one.

Mike had taken Alastair out to try the idea, and it had worked! They had caught a young male. Problem solved! Mike was overjoyed.

Alastair smiled at the memory. Slowly his life was coming back to him.

When he had woken up in hospital, the realization that he didn't know who he was had scared the hell out of him. As the fuzziness in his brain had receded over the next couple of days, the emptiness that was his life had taken on a kind of awful clarity. Without memory, could there be life? How could he be a person if he didn't know who he was? What was existence – I forget therefore I'm not? How could he remember Descartes when he couldn't even recall his own wife's name?

And then there was the dread. The fear that he didn't want to remember his life, that his memories would horrify him, terrify him. And if his life was too dreadful to remember, perhaps it hadn't been worth living? He had been tempted to withdraw, to curl up in a dark cave of forgetfulness.

But Clémence had come and taken him away from the hospital and slowly, slowly he was getting back in control.

He could remember some things clearly. His childhood: the grey stone house on the edge of Pateley Bridge overlooking the River Nidd; Riggs Moor and Fountains Abbey; his mother and father; his little sister Joyce; Porky Bakewell; his boarding school at the head of another dale many miles away; his school friends Greenhalgh and Murray and Simpson Minor; playing rugger; the exhilaration of scoring a try against Ampleforth.

And now he had remembered Sophie at Honfleur, he remembered Wyvis, he remembered the eagles in Australia. With patience and effort more of it would come back. Perhaps he would even remember his wife – Helen they said her name was. It was very odd not to be able to remember your wife. He assumed she was dead; she must be, otherwise he would have heard from her. How had she died? Had he been heartbroken? Would he be heartbroken again when he eventually recalled it? Or maybe he hated her or she hated him – they had divorced after all. Whose fault was that, his or hers?

The dread had receded, thank God. Alden's death had been bad; they should definitely have reported what had really happened to the police, but it was a long time ago, and he could forgive himself. Especially since it wasn't actually he who had killed the man.

If he was ever going to break out of this limbo, this half life of half memories, he *had* to find out more. He had been tempted to pick up the book while Clémence was out and read the next chapter to himself, but he couldn't find it. She must have hidden it in her room somewhere, and he couldn't bring himself to search her stuff for it. Anyway, he preferred to read the novel with her. It seemed safer to have her company unearthing these lost memories – he didn't want to do it alone. And she had a lovely soft voice; she was a good reader.

Something was wrong, though. She had lost her initial friendliness of the day before. She must disapprove of what he had done, what they all had done, with Alden. It was a shame. She was only young, but Alastair didn't want her disapproval.

He was now down by the loch and Wyvis Lodge. The lodge was large enough for a decent-sized house party. Luxury in the midst of isolation, and all in the name of massacring deer. He turned away and followed the track along the loch. He soon came to a wooden boathouse with a metal roof, which stretched out from the shore on pilings. That he definitely remembered.

Just beyond it, the trees came down to the loch, and a path led up through the woods to Culzie.

He stopped and looked up the boulder-strewn slope, with its twisted grey tree trunks and their tangled branches, fingers in mossy gloves clutching and fidgeting all around him, pointing at him, accusing him. Of what? He was tired, and his right knee was stiffening up. He wasn't sure he had the energy to get up there.

Suddenly, the dread that had released him from its grip clutched at his chest. He turned to the boathouse.

The memories came crashing over his head, like a tidal wave erupting from the loch. Night. Sophie. An owl. Sophie.

'No!

'No, no, no!'

He turned and stumbled up the path, pursued by memories of that other night when he had stumbled up the same path and his life had been changed for ever.

CHAPTER V

The Isle of Goats

Antibes, June 1939

A BLAST OF MID-AFTERNOON Mediterranean heat struck me
as I stepped out on to the unshaded platform. I turned my
face up to the sun, high in a pale-blue sky, savouring the freedom
from countless hours cooped up in railway carriages. I was hot, I
was tired, I was sweaty, but the strong direct sunlight invigorated
my Yorkshire soul.

'Angus!'

I turned to see the tall figure of Stephen ambling towards me
in an open-necked shirt and sunglasses.

'Good to see you, old man! Let me take that.'

Stephen grabbed my scratched suitcase and led me out to his
car, a two-seater electric-blue Railton with the top down.

Stephen had spent nearly two weeks in France already, driving
out from London in his sports car. He had attended the wedding
at the de Parzacs' chateau just south of Orléans, and then driven
down to the Riviera to stay with his mother. The plan was to meet
me there, and then drive through Italy to Tony Volstead's villa on
the island of Capri, where the newly married couple would stay
for the last week of their honeymoon.

The newly married couple were Nathan and Madeleine.

When I had opened Nathan's letter telling me they were
getting engaged, I was so surprised I had had to read it twice.
Nathan and I had corresponded regularly since we had left

Oxford two years before. I was aware that Alden's will had been a mess. Alden had intended to leave his French property to his wife, and his considerable stake in Wakefield Oil to his favourite nephew, Nathan. The trouble was that the will had been drawn up by an American lawyer friend on holiday in Paris, who had failed to take proper account of French inheritance laws. Madeleine's lawyers had taken aim at Nathan's lawyers and war had ensued. However, the more the two principals saw of each other, the less belligerent they became, until, as Nathan put it, he had suggested the perfect solution. And, amazingly, Madeleine had agreed. So now they were married.

Stephen drove me through the lazy palm-lined streets of Antibes with the Mediterranean sparkling over to our left. We would set out for Italy in the morning; in the meantime there were cocktails to be drunk and a pool to be swum in at his mother's villa. This was small and white, but right by the sea, with a terrace overlooking the swimming pool, and beyond that, the Baie des Anges.

It was the first time I had met Stephen's notorious mother, and I was nervous. She must have been about forty, but she looked much younger. She was blonde, tall, with Stephen's long nose, and her smooth legs went on for ever. She insisted that I plunge into the pool right away after my long journey. By six o'clock I was sitting watching the sailing boats in the bay, clutching a Manhattan and thinking life was pretty good.

We set off early the next morning, equipped with hangovers. Mrs Trickett-Smith emerged in her dressing gown to wave us off.

'Angus, promise me something,' Stephen said as the car drifted along the empty esplanade at Antibes. 'If my mother tries to jump on you, please fend her off.'

I laughed. 'She'd never do that.'

'Oh yes, she would,' said Stephen. 'You underestimate yourself. You always have.'

I smiled. 'I seem to be a natural target for the Trickett-Smiths.'

'I shall ignore that,' said Stephen.

'Speaking of which, have you heard from Maurice?'

'He and I have rather lost touch,' said Stephen. 'But he hasn't grown up. He's still at Oxford; the last I heard he was besotted with an undergraduate at New College called Daisy Haughton-Jones who won't acknowledge his existence.'

I laughed. 'Is Daisy Mr Haughton-Jones's real name, do you think?'

'He probably doesn't even know he's called Daisy, poor sod.'

It was Maurice's roving eye that had first brought me to Stephen's attention. Stephen later told me Maurice had considered me rough and handsome, yet innocent, and hence ideal prey. So Maurice had challenged Stephen to seduce me, and Stephen had spent a week good-humouredly trying. I knew what was going on; there had been some homosexuality at my boarding school, although clearly not nearly as much as at Stephen's.

Then one evening Stephen had arrived in my room completely drunk and very upset. He had tried to pour his heart out to me. It had started out as an embarrassing paean to my supposed rough beauty, but it had soon become something else, something more genuine. He had received a letter from his mother saying she was never going to return to his father, but was going to live in Antibes with a French count. Stephen knew that his parents' marriage was a sham, but now he could no longer pretend that the sham was the truth, he felt the ground taken away from underneath him.

I had listened and understood. Stephen had disappeared, returning with two bottles of wine that I helped him polish off late into the night. Stephen explained what it was like being Stephen. The wealth, the popularity, the position in society, the open admiration from boys and women alike. Yet underneath it all, the foundations of his life were cracked. He felt at any moment as if he were going to fall into an abyss of despair.

He didn't fancy me at all, he said, he admired me. He admired my stable family, my ability to work hard, my obvious love for my subject. He didn't want to seduce me, he wanted to be like me. And he had never told anyone any of this.

That was why he and I were friends.

It took us three days to motor from Antibes to Naples. I would have liked to take a week: we passed Genoa, Florence, Siena and Rome on the way, all of which I wanted to explore. The June weather was fabulous – the Tuscan hills were still green and lush, and poppies nodded to us from roadside verges as we swept by.

I had not seen Stephen for a couple of months, and there was a lot to catch up on. After Oxford, I had gone on to Bart's Hospital in the City of London. I loved the life of a medical student – the beer and the rugger as much as the anatomy and the physiology. But once Hitler's troops had stomped into what remained of Czechoslovakia in March, I decided that if a war was coming, I was going to fight in it.

To fight, not to tend the wounded. That proved to be a bit of a problem, because the authorities wanted me either to finish my medical studies or to become a medical orderly. Also, a severe concussion I had suffered in a rugger match in February against Guy's had caused trouble at my physical examination. But I had tried a different angle, with more success. Thanks to an old friend of my father, I was due to join the Green Howards in two weeks as a private.

Stephen too had been busy. He had decided he needed a proper, steady, responsible job after university, and had begun training as an articled clerk with a firm of chartered accountants. He told me he was determined to break away from his family's lackadaisical attitude to money and work. All very admirable, but accountancy was not something to which Stephen was well suited. A friend had introduced him to a film producer, who had fixed him up with a couple of jobs as an extra at Pinewood Studios, and he had just landed his first speaking role, in a film called *A Breeze From the Sea*. He played the bounder from whom the leading lady was trying to escape. It wasn't a big role, but Stephen had enjoyed it and was hoping it would lead to more opportunities. So he had chucked the accountancy before the accountancy had had a chance to chuck him.

There was one subject that I was eager to broach, but felt reluctant to do so. I summoned up the courage, for I needed courage, as we were just finishing off a bottle of red wine after lunch at a restaurant in a tiny town perched on a hill in Umbria. The view was astounding – fields of hay, vines and poppies stretching for miles in every direction, interspersed with steep green domes, most of which were topped with fortified towns. The roofs and bell tower of an abbey nestled in a grove of cypresses in the valley beneath us. It looked just like the background of a portrait by Bellini or Titian.

'Was Sophie at the wedding?'

'Yes, of course. She was a bridesmaid. She looked gorgeous.'

'I'm sure she did,' I said. Then came the tricky question: 'Was she alone?'

'You mean did she have a man in tow?' Stephen asked with a grin.

'Yes,' I admitted.

Stephen's grin disappeared, replaced with the ghost of a frown. He hesitated before replying. 'No. No, she didn't.'

Thank God for that. Sophie was joining us on Capri. I hadn't seen her since Deauville, but I had thought of her many times. It was stupid really, I knew I had no chance, but I couldn't help it.

'She said you had written to her,' said Stephen.

'Yes, once or twice.' I would have written to her every day, if I had allowed myself, but I didn't want to appear overly keen. Actually, what I didn't want to do was provoke rejection. Which was probably going to happen anyway, on Capri. I hadn't admitted my infatuation to Stephen, but I could tell he could see it, and I could tell it troubled him.

'Be careful, old man,' said Stephen. 'Don't set yourself up for a disappointment.'

I felt both crushed and irritated by this comment in equal measure. Stephen was a good friend who rarely looked down his impressive nose at me. But every now and then he could be *so* arrogant and insensitive. Of course Sophie was too good for me, I knew that. But Stephen could be just a little more encouraging; could let me dream.

We finished our wine in silence, paid the bill, and set off southwards once again.

It was a relief to get out of the bustle of Naples and on to the bay. The steamer puffed into a steady breeze from the west. Behind and to the left rose the broken cone of slumbering Vesuvius, with the remains of Pompeii splattered on to its lower slopes. From there the Cape of Sorrento reached out and pointed towards the two hunks of rock that formed Capri. The island appeared dark at first glance against the sparkling blue sea, but as the boat neared, it resolved itself into light-grey cliff and dark-green trees, with a smattering of white houses in the cradle in the middle.

'Do you suppose the Villa Jovis is up there?' I said, looking up at the nearest cliff of bleached grey, soaring hundreds of feet above the sea.

'Villa Jovis?' said Stephen. 'I thought Tony's place was the Villa Amaryllis?'

'Tiberius's palace,' I said. 'There is a spot somewhere up

104

there where he used to chuck people off the cliff to their deaths. The Salto di Tiberio.' On the train south from Calais I had read Suetonius's *Lives of the Caesars*, in particular the chapters on Tiberius, the deranged emperor who had retired to the 'Isle of Goats', as the Romans called it, to spend the last years of his life in an orgy of sex and torture.

'You're going to make us climb all the way up there, aren't you?'

'You bet I am. You can borrow my copy of Suetonius if you like. It's pretty racy.'

'It's not in Latin, is it? Please tell me it's not in Latin.'

'It is,' I admitted. 'You'll manage.'

'I think I'll stick with Dornford Yates, if that's all right with you,' said Stephen. 'In the original English.'

Tony and Nathan were waiting for us on the quay. I hadn't seen Nathan for two years. He looked tanned, relaxed and happy. Tony was a little plumper, a little balder, but his genial smile was intact.

'Congratulations, old man,' I said. 'I'm sorry I couldn't get to the wedding. Exams, you know.'

'That's all right,' said Nathan. 'I'm just pleased you could make it here. I know Madeleine will be happy to see you. And you too, Stephen.'

We jostled on to a funicular railway with the day trippers who had arrived with us on the steamer from Naples. This hauled us up to a small town crammed against the sheer cliff face of a mountain. We emerged on to a piazza, already filling up with tourists, and Tony approached a group of horse carriages. 'Ernesto!'

One of the drivers, a tiny man with a large black moustache, grinned and jumped down to take our suitcases. The four of us climbed on to the small carriage, which set off along a narrow alley, barely wide enough for us to pass through.

'Did you find the garage I told you about in Naples?' Tony asked Stephen.

'Yes. Are you sure the old girl will be all right?'

Stephen had been reluctant, to put it mildly, to leave his beloved Railton at the place Tony had recommended, a ramshackle shed at the heart of a warren of narrow streets.

'Augusto is the only honest garage-owner in the city,' said Tony. 'Or at least he is honest with the expatriates on this island. He has a reputation to preserve.'

Stephen grunted, clearly not convinced. But there had really been no alternative.

The newer houses of Capri were either white or cream, the older ones various shades of faded red, orange and bleached blue, with barrel roofs. Flowers sprang out of their garden walls at all angles: petunias, geraniums, marguerites, and many that I didn't recognize, in a riot of blues and reds and yellows. A delicate white flower that hung from some of the trees suffused the air with the scent of citrus and honey. It took a moment for me to realize it was orange blossom. There wasn't a lot of that back home in Nidderdale. Everywhere, unseen birds were singing.

'How's law school?' I asked.

'Finished!' said Nathan. 'I hopped on to the SS *Normandie* the day after exams to come over here for the wedding.'

'Are you going to practise with your father?' Nathan's father was an attorney in Nathan's home town in Pennsylvania.

'No. I'm going to take an active interest in Wakefield Oil. Shake them up a bit.'

'Do you *know* anything about the oil business?'

'I've learned a lot over the last couple of years. And I am a quick learner.'

'That's true.' I had been impressed by the speed of Nathan's mind in joint history tutorials with him in our first year.

'And what I've learned is that the future for a medium-sized oil company like ours based in New York isn't in Texas, it's overseas.'

'That's not what the management think?'

'Alden handed the management of the company to a Texan named Rodding. All he's comfortable with is fighting for scraps from his cronies in Houston. That's going to change.'

I felt sorry for Mr Rodding. Nathan might still be well short of thirty, but he was determined and, despite his inexperience, I wouldn't have been surprised if his strategy turned out to be the right one.

'Here we are,' said Tony. The carriage drew up outside a high white wall in which was embedded an arch and a wrought-iron gate. Tony paid Ernesto and led us into a small shaded garden of ancient red-brick pathways, lemon trees and a massive wisteria whose thick wooden arms wrestled the house in a headlock. A tiny fountain tinkled in one corner next to a rockery sprouting spikes of orange and scarlet succulents and crimson amaryllis. Tony led us around the side of the house, up some steps to a terrace with a view over the open Mediterranean to the south of the island, and, much closer, the soft pockmarked rock face of the mountain which dominated the centre of Capri – Monte Solaro.

'This is magnificent, Tony!' said Stephen.

'It is,' said Tony. 'And it's all thanks to Alden. He left me several thousand dollars with the injunction to use it to develop my art, and to spend it slowly. So I bought the Villa Amaryllis with half of it, and it's been a great place for me to get away from Paris and work on my painting, without the distraction of people judging it as it develops.'

'How's that going?' Angus asked.

'Real well,' said Tony. 'I'll be ready to exhibit in Paris next year. If the Boches don't flatten the city first.'

The mention of the forthcoming European war hit me with a jolt. For a brief moment I had forgotten it. Out here, in this green paradise of mysterious beauty, my decision to spend the next few months in a barracks in Yorkshire learning how to march and polish uniform buttons was losing some of its allure.

'Where are the girls?' asked Stephen, echoing my thoughts.

'They went for a walk earlier. They'll be back soon,' said Nathan. 'Let me get you a drink. Vermouth is the thing here.'

So we sat on the terrace in the shade of a lemon tree drinking cold vermouth. I knew it was a lemon tree, because huge lemons drooped from its branches, bigger than any I had ever seen before. They were a little disconcerting; it would hurt if one of those landed on your head.

I pulled out my pipe and started to fill it.

'What is that?' said Nathan in horror.

'You should try it,' I said. 'It's good for contemplation.'

'He's training to be a wise old doctor,' Stephen said. 'He's just got a bit ahead of himself. I'll always prefer a fag.'

'Well, I prefer dames, myself,' said Tony.

Nathan laughed.

'Uncouth colonial,' Stephen muttered.

'Limey pervert,' said Tony with a grin.

'I still can't get over you marrying Madeleine, Nathan,' I said. 'You told me in your letter about the legal wrangling, but there has got to be more to it than that.'

'There is,' said Nathan, grinning. 'We think alike, Madeleine and I. She understands me, what I plan to do with Wakefield Oil, my ambition, my dreams. I would never have discovered that chatting to her over a dinner table; but you learn a lot about a woman negotiating with her. She's smart and she's tough.'

He leaned forward over his drink, his eyes shining. 'It's not because she's a beautiful rich widow, it really isn't. It's because she and I make a good partnership. A great team. That suddenly occurred to me when I came to Paris this last winter to sort out the will. We were having dinner at a Russian restaurant, and I said it out loud, really without thinking. She said she agreed. And so I asked her to marry me. Just like that.' He was grinning broadly.

'And she said yes?' said Stephen.

'She did,' said Nathan with pride and pleasure.

Stephen shook his head. 'She can't be that bright, you know.'

Nathan laughed. 'I know. But I'm very lucky.'

I suspected that Madeleine was as smart as Nathan said. Nathan was clever himself, and determined. He was already rich, and he would become a lot richer. He was also a decent man. Quite a catch, even for a wealthy widow.

But there was an obvious question, and I knew Nathan well enough to ask it. 'What about Deauville?'

'You mean what about the fact that I killed her husband?' The smile had left Nathan's face.

'Since you put it like that, yes.'

'She blames Alden, not me,' Nathan said. 'Thank God. She said that Alden was old enough not to play with swords when he was drunk. And Sophie told her about the pass he made at her. I don't think she could forgive him for that. Her sister, for God's sake!'

I knew that Madeleine had decided not to go to the police once Sophie had explained what had happened that night, but I had never known whether she had gone along with the rest of us with reluctance or with willingness.

'I owe her my life,' said Nathan. He rubbed his throat in involuntary acknowledgement of the guillotine. 'What makes it difficult for me, though, is I owe Alden so much. Firstly his stock in Wakefield Oil, and now his wife.'

'Alden was a good man,' said Tony. 'In almost all ways. We all owe him a lot.'

We heard female voices speaking in French around the side of the house, where the gate led in from the street.

My heart leaped. Sophie.

I stumbled clumsily to my feet as the voices came nearer, and then there she was, just as lovely as I remembered her, wearing a yellow dress and a radiant smile.

'Angus!' she exclaimed when she saw me. She rushed up the steps of the terrace and kissed me on both cheeks. 'It's so nice to see you again!'

For a moment, and it was only for a few seconds, I found myself embraced by that special heaven that exists for people who feel their first love returned.

Then she turned to Stephen and looked into his eyes. He had arranged his lips into their most seductive leer. She gave him a small shy smile, stretched up and pecked him on the cheek. 'Hello.'

Heaven shattered. How the hell did that happen?

'Angus?'

I turned to my hostess. Madeleine's smile was friendly and her eyes were shining: the happy bride.

'Congratulations, Madeleine,' I stammered. Out of the corner of my eye, I saw Sophie's fingers brush Stephen's.

CHAPTER VI

The Opium Den

CAPRI WAS HELL, and I built thick stone walls in a vain attempt to keep the hell out. I was polite to everyone. I smiled. I took refuge in my pipe and my Suetonius, sitting alone for hours staring at the same page, ignoring the view. At first people tried to jolly me up, or engage me in medical conversation, but then they let me be, assuming that I was enjoying the island in my own way. I did a good job of looking thoughtful, rather than miserable. I was aware that Nathan was disappointed in the cooling of our friendship, but I hoped that I gave the impression that I had changed in the couple of years since Oxford. Grown up. Become more introspective.

There was some solace in lengthy discussions with Tony about art. Tony showed me his studio – rotting vegetables on the back alleys of Paris had become rotting vegetables in the narrow streets of Capri town. Tony had become much more serious about his art, but it seemed to me that his paintings were getting worse rather than better. Poor Tony seemed on the verge of panic. I stumbled across a stack of canvases of Parisian refuse, which had been scored out heavily in black paint. Tony saw me examine them and just shrugged. He still professed confidence in the exhibition he was planning in Paris for the following spring.

Madeleine was friendly and hospitable, and I was polite in return. She was clearly very much in love with Nathan, and there was a pleasing equality in the way they treated each other.

Nathan seemed to grow in her presence, the nervous ambition he had displayed at Oxford was developing into confidence. More than confidence, power. With his intelligence, his determination, his money and his beautiful wife, Nathan had the conviction and the ability to get what he wanted.

Sophie tried to speak to me a couple of times, but then gave up. I found it impossible to say anything to her.

The hardest, of course, was Stephen. The villa wasn't very big, and so we were sharing a room. When night came, we didn't speak; we lay on our backs in the dark, staring at the ceiling, awake. An intermittent glow flared up from Stephen's bed as he smoked a cigarette.

I was furious. Stephen had always known what an impression Sophie had made on me, how important that day in Honfleur was to me. I knew I had no absolute claim on Sophie; in fact, I remembered with some pain her question about Stephen when we were sitting on the bench by the chapel above Honfleur. But he knew how I felt about her. If there was something going on between him and Sophie, he had had plenty of opportunity to tell me on the drive down through Italy. And he hadn't. Just some arrogant advice about not raising my expectations.

Silence. The bastard still wasn't saying anything, lying over there, smoking. But Stephen knew what I was thinking. Stephen knew *exactly* what I was thinking, how much pain he had caused me.

And how long had it been going on, this whatever-it-was between him and Sophie. Days? Years? Perhaps Stephen had been stopping off in Paris to see her every time he visited his mother in Antibes, and not telling me anything about it.

The anger was like a worm, creeping through every part of my system. I wanted to leap out of bed, jump onto Stephen and ram my fists into his face. He was tall and broad-shouldered, but I had scarcely ever seen him in any physical contact with anyone. He didn't play sport; he avoided trouble, whereas I let my aggression rip every Saturday on the rugger field. I was well known for my hard tackling – if I crashed into you at full speed, you didn't get up. I could beat the shit out of Stephen. I should beat the shit out of Stephen.

All right, perhaps I shouldn't do that. But I *should* tell him how I felt. How my best friend had betrayed me.

I watched the cigarette glow above his pillow. I *knew* Stephen knew what I was thinking, yet somehow I couldn't bring myself to speak it. It was humiliating, too humiliating to admit to aloud. I had fallen for a girl stupid enough to fall for a cad like him; yet fallen so quietly, so feebly, she probably hadn't even noticed. I was a lot stupider than she.

The anger burned. Even when sleep came eventually, the embers glowed.

Alden was there on Capri too. He joined us for breakfast in the morning; he was with us when we visited the Blue Grotto on a boat hired from the Marina Grande. But he was there as our friend, an uncle who was still benevolent.

We wanted him there as a friend, not as an enemy. He was mentioned in conversation frequently: 'Alden would adore the grotto – he'd rush out and buy a painting of it right away'; 'I bet Alden would have bought a villa on Capri if he had ever visited it'; 'Alden would have loved this limoncello – he was always a sucker for sweet liqueurs.' This was especially true of Madeleine and Nathan. It was as if by invoking his spirit as part of the group of friends, they were affirming his approval for their marriage. Tony saw him as his supportive patron still and Stephen and Sophie went along with the others, Sophie possibly to support her sister, and Stephen because he was a heartless bastard.

I, alone, didn't mention Alden's name. The reason was pretty straightforward really: I felt guilty about helping to kill him.

The murder was only mentioned head-on once, at dinner on the second night. As he was pouring some of the delicious soft *caprese* wine from the third bottle of the evening, Nathan reminded us of the couple who had been looking after the Deauville villa.

'I don't think I told you, but I heard from Monsieur Lemoine a couple of years ago. His wife was getting old and unable to do all the cooking and cleaning that they were used to. They wanted to retire, and buy a small cottage in Pont L'Évêque to be near their daughter and grandchildren. They wondered if I could help them.'

'Good God!' said Stephen. 'That's blackmail!'

'It is indeed,' said Nathan. 'But very nicely done. No mention of what they had or hadn't seen. No threat. They were asking for an amount that we could easily afford.'

'Did you give them the money?' said Stephen.

'Yes,' said Nathan. 'They were very grateful.'

'But how can you know whether they really saw anything?' said Tony.

'They saw something,' said Madeleine. 'Or more probably heard something. It's just they were cunning enough to keep quiet during the murder investigation. They wouldn't make a demand like that unless they knew something was amiss.'

'But they'll just come back for more,' said Stephen.

'They already have,' said Nathan. 'Now they live in Pont L'Évêque they need a car. Just a small one.'

'And you paid them?' said Tony.

'Half of what they asked for,' said Madeleine. 'Just to stop them from getting too greedy. We can afford it, and it's worth it.'

'Since we are all here together now, we just thought we should let the rest of you know what we've done,' said Nathan. 'It's the kind of thing you shouldn't put in a letter.'

There was silence around the table. We were not just friends; we were conspirators.

'We were lucky,' said Tony.

'Very lucky,' said Stephen.

'It was all thanks to Angus,' said Nathan. 'I don't know how you thought of so much so quickly. I will always be grateful.'

He raised his glass. 'To Angus.'

'To Angus,' the others repeated.

'It was nothing,' I said, looking around the table at my friends with a stiff smile. It was true: with the exception of Elaine I had been the most innocent, the most naïve of the people in the room that night, yet it had been me who had somehow cobbled together a story that held up against all Inspector Pasquier's probing. And their gratitude seemed sincere, with the exception of Sophie, who looked uncomfortable, as well she might. The others were willing to go along with the fiction that we had dealt sensibly with a ghastly accident. Indeed, it was a lie I had told myself for the last four years to enable me to live with myself. But it *was* a lie. Nathan had killed Alden and the right thing to do would have been to tell the police.

'We are not quite all here,' said Stephen. 'How is Elaine? Where is she?'

'She's a junior at Bryn Mawr,' said Nathan. 'Studying French, I believe.'

'She wrote me that she's coming over to Europe again next month,' said Tony. 'With a friend from college and possibly her aunt as chaperone, although she is trying to lose the aunt. She's planning to stay here for a week.'

'She hasn't said anything about Alden?' Stephen asked.

'We've never mentioned it,' said Nathan.

'I'll make sure she is OK with it,' said Tony. 'But she's a good kid. She won't talk.'

From what I had seen of her four years before, Elaine didn't strike me as a good kid. But she was probably practised at keeping her own misdemeanours quiet.

'None of us has anything to worry about,' said Nathan. 'I guess the French authorities will have something much more important to be concerned about soon. Like the Germans marching over the Maginot Line.'

There then followed a disjointed and ill-informed discussion of likely German and French strategies in a war. But I feared that Nathan was dead wrong when he said that we need not worry about Alden's death. I suspected we would all be worrying about that for the rest of our lives.

And so we should.

We visited the Villa Jovis on the third day. At breakfast, they all asked me about Tiberius. I described the orgies and torture the emperor was supposed to have indulged in on the island: the teams of sexual performers copulating in triple unions in front of him; the 'old goat's garden' where boys and girls dressed up as Paris and nymphs solicited sex; the paintings and sculptures in his palace and his library of erotica always handy in case guidance was needed on the more complicated techniques. I skimmed over some of the more depraved descriptions involving young boys and babies. Tiberius was a monster, at least according to Suetonius, but I was fascinated by how and why the most powerful man in the world should choose to shut himself up on this island for the last twelve years of his life.

The path up to the palace was steadily uphill, and despite a stiff cool breeze, it was hot work. We shooed off the locals trying to tempt us on to donkeys for the climb. Birds serenaded us from lemon trees and vines along the route. I walked with Tony at the head of the group, who of course knew the route, and with Sophie. After a while, we paused for breath beside a drinking fountain. The Bay of Naples had opened up before us, and behind us was Capri town and the stone ramparts of Monte Solaro.

'Just over there is the Villa Fersen,' Tony said, pointing to a path through orchards and vineyards. 'Baron Fersen was a kind of modern-day Tiberius. His villa is one of the most spectacular on the island.'

'Did he throw people off cliffs?' asked Sophie.

'I don't think so, but he's got the right place for it. He was kicked out of Paris at the beginning of the century for organizing orgies for politicians and other notables, so he came here where he would be left alone to amuse himself with the island's young boys. There used to be a lot of that kind of thing on Capri – still is, probably.'

'I think I've heard of him,' said Sophie. 'It was a big scandal. He was heir to a steel fortune, wasn't he?'

'That's right. He was very wealthy, easily the richest man on the island, and he was still in his twenties when he arrived. He built himself a fabulous villa way up here, and spent most of his days with his boyfriend smoking opium and writing bad poetry. But he was too much even for the Capresi. He died here about fifteen years ago – too much drugs and alcohol. They think it was suicide.'

'Have you seen the villa?' Sophie asked.

'Yes. No one lives there now, but a local family looks after it. If you give them a tip, they'll show you around. It's a bit of a mess, the garden is overgrown, but it's in a spectacular position. And there is an extraordinary opium den in the basement.'

'Can we have a look?'

'Maybe on the way back. If we have the energy.'

We continued the climb, until we finally reached the top of the cliffs and the Villa Jovis. Despite having been only recently exca-vated, the villa itself was a bit of a disappointment: it looked less like a luxurious palace and more like an ancient water-gathering system. Massive cisterns were needed to keep the place watered in the summer, and they were what had survived best after two thousand years. And in an act of pious vandalism, someone had built a little church at the highest point to sniff down on the pagan emperor's infamous ruins.

If the villa was disappointing, its situation was not. In an island full of fabulous views, this was the most magnificent. The classic shore of the Bay of Naples stretched in a long curve from the island of Ischia, through Naples and Vesuvius, to the Cape of Sorrento. On the southern side of the cape lay the fabled Amalfi coast and the Gulf of Salerno and, of course, much closer, lurked the rocky green beauty of Capri itself. Just below the peak, a straight shaded avenue led under pine trees to some flimsy wooden railings. I approached gingerly – this was the notorious Salto di Tiberio – and looked over. Hundreds of feet below, deep-blue water swirled and sucked at the rocks at the foot of the cliffs, so bleached they were nearly white. It was a long, long way down.

Capri was an island of beauty, certainly, but it was also an island of evil. Had Tiberius's depravity inspired Baron Fersen? And all those other Northern Europeans who had visited Capri in search of young boys?

Stephen and Sophie joined me. 'It's amazing, isn't it, Angus?' said Sophie.

'It certainly is,' I said, with a touch of polite enthusiasm.

Stephen nodded to me. I smiled back quickly and insincerely.

I drew back; the couple – because that's what they were – leaned on the wooden railings. I stared at their backs: Stephen's broad shoulders, his shirt damp with sweat from the climb; Sophie's lithe body hugged by her white dress in the breeze.

This was an evil island, where evil acts were done, acts which were not tolerated by civilized society. This was the very spot where Tiberius had watched his enemies, real and imagined, being flung to their deaths. On the climb I had almost forgotten my anger, but now it came flooding back through my veins, burning me from the inside. Two steps forward, a lift and a push, and Stephen would tumble down to sea below. What then? I could leap after him into the cool blackness of oblivion. Perhaps I would take Sophie with me. The anger threatened to overwhelm me, so I turned and stumbled down the path away from the cliff edge to the safety of the shade and the water cisterns.

We were on our way back down the via Tiberio towards Capri town, when Sophie stopped by the water fountain. 'Tony! Is this the way to that villa you were talking about?'

'That's it,' said Tony.

'Can we go and have a look?' Sophie asked.

'Let's get back home,' said Stephen. 'I'm parched. I need a drink.'

'There's a water fountain right here.'

'I mean a real drink.'

Nathan and Madeleine murmured their agreement.

'I can go by myself,' said Sophie. 'I'll catch up with you later.'

I watched Tony hesitate; on the one hand he wanted to be a good host to his guests and their desire for sustenance back at his villa, on the other he was reluctant to let Sophie go unaccompanied.

'I'll come with you,' I said.

For a moment, Sophie looked surprised. Then she smiled. 'Thanks, Angus.'

'OK,' said Tony. 'We'll have lunch ready for you when you get down.'

Sophie and I turned off the road and along a path through orchards and a vineyard. It was comfortable to walk alone with her. I felt calmer than I had on the Salto di Tiberio and I told myself to be civil. She smiled at me and pointed out the general loveliness of the flowers, the trees and Capri. I agreed – how could I not?

After a couple of hundred yards we turned uphill along a walled lane through a wood of pines and cypresses. Suddenly we came upon a wrought-iron gate with a bell pull, which I duly tugged three times. Eventually a small, round woman arrived, dressed in black with her grey hair coiled up on top of her head under a scarf. She smiled at us in a friendly way. In broken Italian, Sophie asked if we could see the villa. I pressed some lire into the woman's hand and she opened the gate.

The villa rose large and white in front of us, surrounded by a jungle of overgrown trees and shrubs. To the side, a broad stairway led down to a bronze sculpture of a naked boy preening himself, and beyond that a view of the island and the harbour far down below. The entrance to the villa was a grand portico flanked by Ionic columns, its white plaster flaking. Above the doorway were the Latin words *Amori et dolori sacrum*: 'Sacred to love and sorrow'.

The heat had risen steadily during the morning, but as we stepped inside the villa's hallway, the temperature dropped noticeably. The woman led us up a marble staircase with a wrought-iron balustrade and into a magnificent bedroom. We were drawn immediately to the balcony, with its view over the sea, emerald near the foot of the cliffs rather than blue, towards the Cape of Sorrento and the Amalfi coast. Above and behind the villa, rosemary bushes and limestone boulders sprouted out of the steep slope beneath Tiberius's ruined palace.

The place smelled of damp and dust. There was plaster on the floors, and cracks in the walls.

'It's pretty exposed up here,' I said. 'It must take a battering from the wind and the rain.'

'Yes, but isn't it marvellous?' said Sophie. 'Imagine what it would have been like in its heyday. What a place to have a party!'

The caretaker led us down to a salon on the ground floor, decorated with blue and white tiles, and gold leaf, and then down some more stairs to the *fumatorio*, the opium den. This was a semi-circular room framed by two thick embossed columns. The floor and walls were tiled in orange. Torn tapestries displaying columns of either Chinese or Japanese characters hung between small windows looking out over the garden, and beyond it the Cape of Sorrento. Dusty divans, their cushions richly embroidered, lined the walls. The caretaker withdrew, leaving Sophie and me alone in the room. The irony of her tactful attempt to allow us to enjoy the romance of the place alone bit into me.

Sophie spoke. 'I like you, Angus.'

'I like you too.'

'And you are a good friend of Stephen's.'

'That's true,' I said, although I wasn't at all sure if it still was.

'I'd like it, we'd like it, if you could remain friends with both of us.'

I didn't answer right away. I sat on the curved window seat and looked out over the garden to the Mediterranean glimmering through the jungle.

'How long have you been . . . together?'

'Since Madeleine's wedding,' Sophie said. 'We got on really well that weekend. Stephen drove me back to Paris and we spent a week there together. Then he went down to Antibes to meet you and bring you on here.'

'He didn't tell me!' I said. Sophie had just stoked the embers of my anger.

'Didn't he?' said Sophie. 'You English, you don't talk about anything, do you? Anything important.'

'It appears not.' I turned again to stare out of the window. The fury was building. The bastard! Why hadn't Stephen told me he had spent a week with Sophie? He must have known I would find out eventually.

'I enjoyed that afternoon in Honfleur, Angus,' Sophie said. 'We had an extraordinary conversation. As I said, I like you, I would like to be your friend. But nothing happened. I don't think I did anything to let you think something had happened. Did I? And it *was* four years ago.'

I didn't reply. She was right, of course; I had built her up over the years to mean so much more to me than she really should. Yet foolish though it sounded, I loved her. Not just then, but now. I loved the way she was talking to me, her kindness and awkward sincerity; I loved her big blue wistful eyes; I loved the little freckles on the end of her nose and I loved her body under that white summer dress . . .

An idea came to me. I recognized it as a bad idea immediately; a mean, nasty idea. I knew I should squash it, but I didn't want to. I wanted to speak before sense and reason stopped me.

'Do you know why Stephen and I are friends?'

'You were in the same college at Oxford,' Sophie said.

'Yes. But I went to a school no one has ever heard of and have a Yorkshire accent. Stephen went to Eton and is loaded.'

'So?'

'So at Oxford people like that don't naturally become friends.'

'That is absurd.'

'Shall I tell you what happened?'

Sophie shrugged. She looked doubtful; I went on before she had a chance to stop me.

'Stephen had a friend from Eton named Maurice. I would say his best friend. They were both good-looking – although Maurice was a good deal more feminine than Stephen, dark, exotic, graceful. They were both rich.'

Sophie was frowning. She could see where this was going and she didn't like it. Well that was too bad for her.

'They used to weigh up the relative attractiveness of freshers in college, and bet each other that they could seduce them. They were quite successful. Anyway, Maurice picked on me as a victim for Stephen. Apparently he thought I was handsome and rough. The wager was ten pounds.'

Sophie's frown had deepened. Good.

'I was difficult. Stephen tried hard, he tried damn hard. But he never earned his ten pounds.'

Sophie was staring at me, her expression one of disgust. Very good.

'That doesn't explain how you became friends,' she said.

'No,' I said. 'But it should warn you that Stephen likes men as much as he likes women. More.'

The expression of disgust deepened. Suddenly I realized that Sophie's distaste was aimed at me, not Stephen.

'There is an English word "hateful", is there not?'

I nodded.

Sophie's disgust had turned to anger. There was moisture in her eyes, but also fire. Her cheeks were red. 'That was hateful. You are hateful, Angus!'

She turned on her heel and left the den.

I closed my eyes. My own anger had been flattened by Sophie's. What the hell was I thinking? She was right, of course. She was absolutely right. And I had given her a completely misleading idea of Stephen's and my friendship, which was based on so much more than that initial failed seduction. Yes, I had misled Sophie, and I had earned her contempt. I had earned my own contempt. Yes, Stephen should have told me about Sophie, of course he should. But he hadn't, and I should forgive him. The fact that I couldn't do that was my problem.

I had behaved appallingly badly and I was in danger of ruining everything for everyone. I was ashamed of myself, so ashamed. I had to leave the island right away. Run. So I hurried back to the villa, apologized to Tony and to Nathan and Madeleine, and caught the 4.30 p.m. steamer back to Naples with five minutes to spare.

I had a war to fight. A war in which, perhaps, I might die.

Or perhaps Stephen would.

8

Clémence closed the book and looked up to meet the old man's gaze. His eyes were full of pain.

'I didn't behave very well, did I?' he said.

'Not really, no,' said Clémence.

'I wish I had behaved better.'

'Do you remember any of it at all?'

'Yes,' said the old man. 'Yes, I do. Bits. I remember that opium den in the Villa Fersen. I remember Tiberius's jump. I remember Stephen now, I can see him and Sophie up there.'

'That's something,' said Clémence.

'You know how I described the hole in my memory – like a gap in the centre of a picture?'

'Yes.'

'It's as if I can begin to see vague shapes in the middle of that picture. Disjointed shapes. I don't know, it's like a half-finished jigsaw puzzle where you have done the edges and are making a start at the centre.'

'I think I understand,' said Clémence. 'Can you remember anything about what happens next?'

The pain intensified in the old man's eyes. 'That's the thing. I'm not sure I want to see the picture. The whole picture.'

For a moment Clémence considered reading out the prologue. But the old man would discover what happened to Sophie soon enough; Clémence didn't want to scare him off. They were making progress with the jigsaw. That was her job. And she was fascinated.

Now she knew how her grandmother and grandfather had met. They had obviously loved each other. She supposed everyone's grandfathers and grandmothers must have loved each other at some point, but she felt privileged to see hers on the page. Especially since her family had subsequently blown itself apart.

'Do you remember writing it? Making the jigsaw?'

'I think so. I think I can remember writing that last scene in the opium den. I can remember the shame. I'm sure now it was me who wrote the book. I *am* Angus Culzie. I *am* Angus. The book *is* the truth, it's not a novel.'

Clémence waited for him to say more.

'It's *my* life. I need to become reacquainted with it if I am going to live with it. However unpleasant it will be.'

'So we'll read some more tomorrow?'

'Yes.' He stared hard at the fireplace, as if looking for an answer behind the glowing logs. 'How old are you, Clémence? Nineteen?'

'Twenty.'

'About the same age as I was when I met Sophie. Have you ever loved anyone like that? Or is the world different now?'

Mind your own business, thought Clémence. But his eyes were pleading. Pleading for what? Understanding probably. Besides which, she had just read his innermost thoughts, his obsession.

'I had a thing for a boy in the year above me at school,' she said. 'For a few weeks I would wake up every day and pray he would talk to me. But that passed. He went out with Gaby Porter. Turned out he was a bit of a . . .' She had wanted to use the word 'prick', but hesitated in front of the old man. 'Not-very-nice guy.'

'Poor Gaby Porter.'

'No. She deserved him. I never liked Gaby Porter since she stole my favourite pair of leggings and claimed they were hers.'

'What colour were they?'

'The leggings? Sort of purple, I think. I got them at Topshop. Why?'

'Just want to get the full picture. And now? Is there anyone now?'

Clémence smiled shyly. 'There's a guy called Callum. From uni. We've only been going out three weeks. But I miss him, now. He's gone home to Glasgow to work in a pub.' She looked at the old man guiltily. 'I asked him to come up here and stay with me.'

'Good,' said the old man, with a smile. 'I'd like to meet him.'

For a moment Clémence thought that she would like Callum to meet the old man too. Then she remembered what he had done. 'But no. That's nothing like your obsession for my grandmother.'

'Yes.' The old man put his head in his hands. 'Your grandmother.'

Clémence felt sorry for him, she couldn't help herself. He already knew his obsession was wrong. He had no idea yet how wrong. Or did he? For the first time she wondered if, in fact, he had an inkling.

'It's weird about Grandpa and his mother in Antibes,' she said.

'What do you mean?' said the old man.

'How he felt abandoned by her. And then how he was worried she would jump on Angus. On you.'

'The upper classes led pretty racy lives in those days.'

'Yes,' said Clémence.

The old man looked at her closely. 'That's not what you meant though, was it?'

'No,' said Clémence.

They sat in silence. A comfortable silence. Then the old man spoke. 'You can tell me if you like. I won't tell anyone else. And I'll probably forget it anyway. It might make you feel better, though your family life has nothing to do with me.'

Clémence was about to shake her head, brush him off, take the book back upstairs, shut herself in her room away from him, but something stopped her. It was those brown eyes, the air of calm attention. She didn't know who the hell Alastair Cunningham was, she had barely even heard of him until a few days before, and yet she felt she knew him. It was partly because she had just read out loud his most intimate secrets as a young man, but it was more than that. She felt he was on her side. And she desperately needed someone to be on her side.

Callum was, of course, but she was too ashamed to tell Callum, at least not yet. But the old man? After all the bad stuff she had read about him, it didn't seem wrong to share the shame.

And she felt alone. *So* alone.

The old man waited.

'My parents split up three years ago when I was seventeen. My mother started going out with a banker, an Australian guy called Patrick. After a few months we moved into his place – he had a two-bedroom apartment in Mid-Levels, so there was room for me. Of course I didn't like him at first, he was my mother's boyfriend, after all, but he was always nice to me, and patient. And I have to admit he was quite good-looking, in a tubby kind of way.'

'Tubby?'

'Yeah. He had a bit of a tummy, small and round that peeked over his belt – nothing like Dad, who is as thin as a rake. In fact I gave his stomach a name: Reginald. I used to say: "Hi, Reginald, are you hungry this morning?" every day at breakfast. It was meant to be nasty, and it wound Maman up, but Patrick seemed to like it. Eventually, I began to tolerate him, and then we got on pretty well. He was funny, and he took me seriously in a way neither of my parents had ever really done.'

She paused. Glanced at the old man, who was listening intently, unsure whether to go on.

'You don't have to tell me more if you don't want to,' he said.

'No, that's OK.' She took a deep breath. 'Then, when I was home over Christmas, just this last January, Maman was out somewhere, I was watching a dumb film on TV, in fact it was actually called *Dumb and Dumber*. Have you seen it?'

'How would I know?' said the old man, with a smile.

'Right. I'm guessing you haven't. Anyway, Patrick joined me on the sofa to watch it. He had opened a bottle of wine and he gave me some. We started swapping comments on how stupid the film was, and what with the wine I was laughing pretty hard. And then . . .'

She raised her eyes to the old man, but there was no point in stopping now, he could see what was coming.

'Then he kissed me. I was so surprised, I responded, but only for a second, then I pushed him away, and yelled at him to get off me. He looked angry, for a moment I thought he was going to force himself on me. Then he said: "you shouldn't have led me on like that", and I ran off to my room.

'Well, I didn't know what to do. I shut myself up in my room. Should I tell Maman? Should I just keep quiet? Would he try it again? How could I even live in his flat with him now?

'I thought the best thing was to confront him, and demand an apology. Make him promise not to ever touch me again. Maybe if he was sincerely sorry, if I believed he really would leave me alone, I might be able to forget it had ever happened. But what if he didn't apologize?

'Anyway, I never got the chance to find out. No one said anything at breakfast the next day, and I could tell Maman was very upset. After Patrick had gone to work, Maman sat me down at the kitchen table. "I know what happened yesterday afternoon, Clémence," she began. For a second I felt really relieved: Patrick had told Maman all about it, and Maman was going to take charge. Maybe she would leave him and take me with her. But then I saw her face. She wasn't just upset, there was anger there, and something else. Hatred. Hatred directed at me.

'She said: "I know what you did, Clémence, and I can't believe it. It's not like you're some thirteen-year-old with a crush, you are twenty, for God's sake! And you know I love Patrick and he loves me. What were you thinking?"

'So I said: "What was I thinking? What do you think happened? What has Patrick told you?"

'And she said: "You tried to kiss him. And when he pushed you away you said that you loved him. Didn't you think he would tell me?"

'Of course, I said that that wasn't what had happened at all, that it was Patrick who had jumped on me, but Patrick had anticipated all that. Maman said that he had told her right away, and that he had been sympathetic towards me, talking about schoolgirl crushes, but that she thought I was an adult woman and knew exactly what I was doing. She was going to buy me an air ticket to Scotland that same day, and she didn't want me to come back to Hong Kong at Easter.'

'How dreadful for you!' said the old man.

'I tried to reason with her, but there was no way she was going to believe me rather than Patrick. She was so besotted with him, she couldn't conceive that he might be lying.'

'Whereas she could conceive that her daughter was lying.'

'That's what it looks like. It's not as if I ever lied very much as a kid.'

'Did you tell your father?'

'I tried. But she'd got to him.' Clémence paused. She swallowed. 'She'd told him that I had tried to seduce her boyfriend.'

'And he believed her and not you? Why would he do that?'

'He and I . . .' Clémence hesitated. 'We have our own problems. He wanted to believe her.'

Clémence closed her eyes and shook her head. Her eyes were stinging, but she didn't want to break down in front of the old man. She needed to keep control.

'I'm so sorry,' he said. And he was. She could tell from the tone of his voice that he was. 'Have you told your boyfriend? Callum, was that his name?'

'No!' Clémence said. She found she couldn't look at the old man. 'I can't tell him. What if *he* doesn't believe me? What if he thinks I'm some slut who wants to jump into bed with middle-aged men? What then? I'd lose him!'

'I'm sure he'd believe you.'

Clémence kept her eyes on the corner of the kitchen, where the orange plastic rubbish bin stood.

'Of course he wouldn't. That was what was so clever about what Patrick did. He took the initiative – got his retaliation in early. Everyone will believe him not me.'

'I believe you,' said the old man. 'Look at me, Clémence.'

Clémence kept her eyes on the rubbish bin.

'I said look at me.'

Reluctantly, she did.

'I believe you. Of course I believe you.'

She sniffed. 'You're just saying that.'

'No, I mean it. It's obvious just looking at you, just listening to you, you're an honest girl, Clémence. I'd bet my life on it.'

She looked into his eyes. He *did* mean it. There was something about that calm, steady gaze under those bushy eyebrows, the composure of that craggy face, that suggested reliability, authority, confidence. The reassurance of a wise doctor who spoke from decades of experience and would never deceive you. She smiled.

'I'm glad you told me,' he said.

'So am I.' And it was true, she did feel lighter. 'But you can see how I might sympathize with Grandpa?'

'I can,' said the old man.

They both heard the front door open. 'Hello!' It was a woman's voice.

'They clearly don't believe in ringing doorbells around here,' Clémence muttered to the old man. 'Yes, hello!' she called, getting to her feet and going out to the hallway.

She was met by a small red-haired woman with a long freckled face, wearing a nurse's uniform.

'You must be Clémence,' she said with a smile. 'I'm Rose, the district nurse. I've come to check up on Dr Cunningham.'

'Come through,' said Clémence.

The nurse fussed over the old man and professed herself very happy with what she saw. Physically, he was recovering well, and she was glad that the memory jogging was going well. She checked that Clémence had made an appointment for Dr Cunningham to see Dr Stenhouse at the hospital in Inverness the following Monday, although Clémence hoped that by then Aunt Madeleine would be in charge.

Just as the nurse was leaving, they had another visitor: Jerry Ranger in his small blue Peugeot, hired at an airport, presumably.

He stood awkwardly in the doorway, tall and rangy. Just like his name. Which, it occurred to Clémence, didn't sound like a real name at all; it must have been made up.

'Hi, Alastair,' he said tentatively to the old man. He proffered his hand, and the old man shook it, staring at Jerry hard. 'I'm Jerry, your neighbour from Corravachie, the cottage further down the loch.'

The old man scratched his scalp and shook his head. 'I'm sorry, Jerry. I'm afraid I've had an accident and my memory has gone.'

'You don't remember me at all?'

The old man's eyes betrayed a mixture of sadness and frustration. 'No. Were we friends?'

'Kind of,' said Jerry. 'Good neighbours, certainly. I've only been here three weeks, but we have had a few conversations, a couple of drinks. I come from California? I write songs? You told me a lot about your time in Australia.'

'Eagles,' said the old man. 'Wedge-tailed eagles. I remember those.'

'That's right. And being a doctor out there. And how the weather was much better than here.'

'My wife. I had a wife called Helen. Did I talk about her much?'

Jerry winced. 'A little. She was an ex-wife. To be honest, you didn't seem to like her much. You've been divorced for years. She's passed away now, so you said. Don't you remember her at all?'

The old man shook his head. 'Not in the slightest.'

Clémence made them all a cup of tea and they sat down around the kitchen table. Jerry, with his neatly trimmed beard, his jeans and the white T-shirt peeking out from under his lumberjack shirt, looked very American in this very Scottish cottage. The old man examined his neighbour closely, hungry for information, for memories.

'So you don't remember anything at all from before the accident?'

'I'm beginning to,' said the old man. 'Thanks to Clémence.'

'We've been reading a book together,' she said. 'It's a kind of memoir, written by Alastair. It starts in the nineteen thirties.'

'Oh, really?' said Jerry. 'That sounds fascinating. Can I take a look?'

132

Clémence nipped upstairs to fetch *Death At Wyvis* from her bedroom and handed it to Jerry. 'Angus Culzie, huh? Just like this cottage. And you say that's you, Alastair?'

'It looks like it,' said Clémence.

'Can I read a bit?' said Jerry.

Clémence reached out and grabbed the book out of his hands. She realized she didn't want Jerry to read the first page, at least not in front of the old man. 'Sorry. It's, um, private. You might ask how a published novel can be private, but it is, at least for now. So please don't read it.'

Jerry seemed a bit taken aback, but he shrugged. 'OK.' He glanced at the old man, who looked troubled. 'So you think your memory is coming back?'

'Slowly,' said the old man. 'But it's just scraps of the past from many years back. Although, interestingly, I can remember my child-hood quite well. It all goes very vague when I get to university.'

Jerry smiled. 'I remember our talks together with pleasure,' he said. 'It's a shame you've forgotten them.'

'They might come back,' said Clémence.

'What do the doctors say?'

'That the memories might come back,' said Clémence. 'Or they might not. "Jogging" helps, which is what we have been doing. But they really don't know.'

'Can you tell me a bit about Australia?' asked the old man. 'At least what I told you.'

Jerry told him what he could, but he couldn't remember himself precisely what the old man had said. He had emigrated to Australia in the sixties, got a job in a town in the hills outside Perth – Jerry thought it was called Montgomery, but Clémence and the old man agreed it must have been Mundaring where Jeanette was the librarian. He had become an eager bird watcher and travelled around Australia, looking in particular for eagles. Jerry remembered a couple of stories featuring eccentric patients at his clinic and some barbed comments about Helen not letting him travel as much as he wanted to. There wasn't really very much, but the old man lapped it up. Clémence could see that the dread he seemed to feel when listening to *Death At Wyvis* was banished.

By the time Jerry left, promising to drop in again the following day, the old man was in better spirits.

Jerry drove back to his own cottage. He made himself a cup of coffee and sat in the living room, looking out over the loch. He had had to check out the old man for himself, and he was relieved with what he had seen and heard.

He picked up the phone and dialled.

'It's me, Jerry . . . the stalker's wife was right, he has forgotten everything . . . he doesn't recognize me.'

He listened.

'No . . . no . . . no, we're fine, I'm sure of it. He definitely doesn't remember me pushing him down the stairs.'

9

Tuesday 16 March 1999, Wyvis

The old man woke up early. His brain had had a busy night, dreaming frantically, as if it was trying out a whole series of connections to find one that worked. People from his past, his whole life, had come and gone in a bewildering swirl of locations: Brimham Rocks in Nidderdale, Oxford, Tiberius's villa, Wyvis, a low bungalow amongst tall trees which he assumed must be his house in Australia. Clémence was with him all the way through, except sometimes she changed into Sophie.

He woke up totally disoriented.

He looked out of his window at the loch and the flank of Ben Wyvis, more brown than white now that the snow melted. That was familiar. He decided to get out and go for a walk before breakfast.

Clémence was awake, but not up; he could hear the radio on in her bedroom. He set off along his familiar route: striking out on to the hill and then down to the loch beside Wyvis Lodge.

The fresh air, the exercise and the familiar landscape comforted him. It was cold, the breeze carried a damp chill and clouds were pressing in over the top of Ben Wyvis, promising rain later, or perhaps snow. Over on the other side of the loch, an eagle was soaring to a height just below the cloud base. A group of hinds threaded their way up the hillside from the water. They were only a quarter of a mile away, and it took them a few moments to notice him before they bounded off.

The isolation, the desolation, the emptiness, lifted his heart. Up here on the moor he could see for miles, but in those miles there were only three signs of habitation – the empty Wyvis Lodge at the head of the loch, Culzie, and the cottage of Corravachie further down.

And yet the moorland was teeming with activity. Birds bustled and twittered, melted snow hustled down the hillside in hidden gullies, bogs and unseen burns. The mountain was alive with skylarks and water.

His walk took him down to the shore of the loch and then along the track towards the boathouse, where a pair of swans were calmly floating. He stopped and stared at the wooden structure.

Eventually, Clémence would read about what happened to Sophie there; her death must be the *Death At Wyvis* of the title. And when Clémence read it, she would hate him. He already hated himself; despised himself. Perhaps somehow a still-functioning part of his brain had tried to erase the unpalatable past from the other damaged part. Helped the amnesia along a little. Was that possible? It seemed unlikely, but he would ask the doctors. Although that would mean admitting that he was a murderer to them. He really didn't want that.

He was ashamed to be who he was.

He decided not to walk past the boathouse that morning, but to take a narrow path through the woods directly back up to Culzie. It was hard work, the path fought its way uphill through large boulders and small stones, and leafless branches reached out and tugged at him. Twice he nearly slipped.

He paused and sat on a mossy log, ignoring the dampness on his arse. He could do it. The balance was the tricky bit, and his right knee was stiff, but he was still physically fit for an eighty-three-year-old.

Which was lucky, because dredging his memory was exhausting. Things were coming back. He could visualize that big house in Deauville. And he could almost see Nathan and Alden. Stephen was taking shape. He could hear his voice. He saw a tall young man, grinning in a leather armchair. Oxford. That was his room at Oxford.

Stephen. There was something he had to tell Stephen. Or give Stephen. What the hell was it? It was something really important. It wasn't that he had killed Sophie, but it was something like that. Another matter of life and death.

Of death.

He groaned out loud. What the hell was it?

Frustrated, angry with himself, he set off up the rough path through the woods back to Culzie.

Jerry put down his binoculars when he saw the old man turn off the lochside track before the boathouse and head off up into the woods. The silhouette was familiar – the lopsided gait, the slight stoop. He was a sprightly old guy, Jerry would have to give him that.

Only the roof of Culzie was visible from outside the woods, but Jerry had spotted the old man on the open hillside. He had found a good vantage point behind a boulder by the shore of the loch, from where he could track the old man's movements. But now the old man was in the woods, he would be out of sight all the way back to Culzie.

Jerry stared at the woods, and the rooftop in their midst. What the hell should he do?

Jerry, too, had had a bad night. His initial relief that the old man couldn't remember him at all had subsided. The old man's memory might return. From what the girl had said, the doctors expected at least some of it to come back over time. But how much? And over what period?

There was a library in Dingwall, there must be some books in there about amnesia. Maybe even access to the Internet. He would check, but the most likely result was that he would remain uncertain, that recovery from head injuries was inherently unpredictable.

There seemed to be two options. Wait and see how much the old man remembered, and just hope that he didn't remember anything important. Or act now.

He had acted before, and it had nearly worked. He should have checked the body more carefully; he could have sworn that the old man wasn't breathing as he lay on the floor at the foot of the stairs, blood dribbling out of the back of his head. Why hadn't he banged the old man's head into the floor a couple of times to finish him off as he had originally intended?

Because he didn't want to leave any incriminating forensic evidence if he didn't have to. But that part of the plan had worked perfectly. No one was in the slightest bit suspicious about an old man falling down the stairs and hitting his head. Why should a forensic scene-of-crime technician go anywhere near him?

Perhaps Jerry should try something more certain. There was an axe at Corravachie, which he used for splitting firewood. And the rifle locked in the gun cupboard.

No. Once the police suspected murder, a house-to-house inquiry around Loch Glass would turn up two houses and one suspect. Him. An accident was much better.

Jerry had an idea. He picked up the binoculars and examined the track near the boathouse.

It was a good idea.

Clémence heard the stairs creak as the old man descended them, followed by the slam of the front door. She turned off Zoë Ball – Radio 1 was the only half-decent station she could get – and extricated her hair from the straighteners. She went downstairs to the phone in the hallway. She hesitated before dialling; these international calls would blow a hole in the old man's phone bill. So what? He deserved to pay. She dialled the Vietnam country code and the number in Ho Chi Minh City.

The school secretary took some persuading, but after a wait that seemed like half an hour but was probably only five minutes, she heard the familiar voice of her father.

'What's up, Clémence?' He spoke in English. They used to speak to each other in French, but somehow they had switched to English after he had left Hong Kong. 'Are you all right?'

He sounded worried. He sounded as if he cared. That was nice.

'I'm OK, Dad. But I've got a couple of questions to ask you.'

'Is it urgent?' His voice was sterner now. 'You told the secretary it was urgent.'

'It is. It is. I'm at Culzie cottage on the Wyvis estate. With Alastair. Alastair Cunningham.'

'What! What the hell are you doing there?'

'He fell down the stairs and had an accident. He has lost his memory: retrograde amnesia, they call it. He doesn't have any relatives. Aunt Madeleine asked me to come and look after him until she can get here from America.'

'Why didn't you check with me first, Clémence?'

'Because we never speak to each other.' It was true. They had only spoken twice in the last six months: once in September when she had returned from her disastrous stay with him in Vietnam, and then again when she had looked for sympathy after telling him about Patrick, and had received contempt. He never called her, and whenever she had called him over the last couple of years, he didn't seem at all interested in talking to her. And it cost a fortune. So she had stopped.

'There is a good reason why that man has no friends in England,' her father said. 'I want you to leave there right away. I want you to have nothing to do with the old bastard. Aunt Madeleine should never have sent you.'

'All right, Dad,' said Clémence. 'She's coming this afternoon, so I can hand over to her then. But I've still got a couple of questions to ask you. And they *are* important.'

Her father sighed. 'All right. What are they?'

Clémence swallowed, listening to the long-distance hiss in the pause. She suspected her father wasn't going to like her questions, but she had to ask them.

'We are reading this book together, to help Alastair remember. It's called *Death At Wyvis* by Angus Culzie. Do you know it?'

'Yes, I know it.'

'Was it written by Alastair? And is it true?'

'How far have you got?'

'They've just gone to Capri. Angus has had an argument with Sophie.'

'Well don't read any more, Clémence. Just leave Wyvis right away. There are things in that book that you are better off not knowing.'

'No!' said Clémence. She didn't often defy her father, but she was angry. 'No, Dad. That's exactly what Grandpa said when I asked him about it—'

'You spoke to *Grandpa*?'

'Yes,' said Clémence.

'Jesus. You shouldn't have done that.'

'Well, I did. And he didn't answer my question. It's all true, isn't it? It must be true or else you wouldn't be so worried about me reading it.'

There was silence, or a hiss, for several seconds.

'Yes. It is true.'

'Why didn't you tell me, Dad? Why didn't you tell me that my grandmother was murdered?'

'Because I didn't want to think about it. I didn't want you to think about it. You didn't even know her. She was *my* mother, remember. After she was killed I ran away to Morocco. I have spent a lot of time and effort making sure that you aren't troubled by that mess. So please do as I ask, Clémence. Promise me you won't read any more of that fucking book.'

Clémence never said no to her father. But what he had said made it even clearer than it had been before, that the key to understanding her screwed-up family lay in the pages of that book. And if she didn't understand her family, she didn't understand herself.

'No, Dad. I don't care what you say, I'm going to read the rest of it. I need to know.'

'Clémence—'

But she hung up.

She felt a mixture of anger and guilt. Clémence had mostly been an obedient child, but she was older now and could make her own decisions. It was OK for her father to warn her that she might not want to learn what had happened at Wyvis to her grandmother. But it was her decision; he had no right to stop her.

She'd had a mostly good relationship with her father, until he had walked out on her and her mother. Subtly encouraged by her mother, she had believed that it was all his fault, that he had abandoned his wife and daughter in a fit of selfishness, but now she was pretty certain that Patrick was the reason that her parents had split apart.

She had hoped that when she had gone to visit him in Hoh Chi Minh City over the summer, she would have been able to rebuild the relationship, at least to see things from his point of view. But she had been surprised – shocked – to find that he was living with a girlfriend, Ngoc, of whom she had never even heard. Ngoc was about thirty, slinkily beautiful, with a simpering, insincere smile. For the first couple of days father and daughter had had some good conversations, but as each day passed Ngoc's displeasure at Clémence's presence became clearer, and her father withdrew. Until, by the time she left, she was under the impression that they were both glad to see the back of her.

For years now, Clémence had lived her life alone. She had envied her friends at boarding school whose homes were only twenty miles away, and whose parents loved each other and visited every other weekend to take their daughters out for lunch or to watch them play netball. She had a mother whom she was growing to hate, and a father whom she never saw. The only thing her parents seemed to agree on was that she should live thousands of miles away from them. Everyone else had a family; why couldn't she have one too?

Inevitably, she had blamed herself for this. There was something wrong with her, there must be or why wouldn't her parents care about her? One good thing about reading *Death At Wyvis* with the old man, was that she was beginning to suspect that actually her problems weren't rooted in the present and defects in her personality, but in the past, between the covers of that book.

She considered the people she had been reading about: Angus's friends, or rather Alastair's. She was getting a pretty good idea of them, but she didn't know what they looked like. She wondered whether there were any photos in the old man's study; Sheila MacInnes had suggested that there were.

The old man would probably be out for a while. She nipped up the stairs to the study and opened the desk drawers. There were some letters, an exercise book, a passport, a birth certificate, bank statements, bills. There was an article from *Cognitive Neuropsychology* dated 1997 and entitled 'Confabulation: knowledge and recollective experience'.

And in the bottom drawer was an old leather-bound photograph album, with the dates '1935–1939' written on it in white pencil.

She opened it. There was a picture of a boy with Alastair's cleft chin standing next to a middle-aged couple by a tree near a stream. They were all smiling at the camera; and the older man was clutching a pipe. Beneath it was scrawled in white *Mother, Me, Father*.

Clémence flipped the pages, fascinated. There was a girl called Joyce – Alastair's younger sister. There was his college at Oxford: a group of male students in jackets and ties, including a tall and incredibly handsome Stephen, her grandfather, standing next to Alastair in the quad of a college. Stephen's smile was knowing, warm, yet dangerous. A couple of Alastair playing rugby for the Greyhounds, whoever they were. Each photograph was labelled in neat white writing.

Then Paris – the Eiffel Tower, the Seine. Nathan, short and swarthy, sitting with Stephen at a café. Deauville: a tall half-timbered house with turrets. Two smiling girls – Madeleine and Sophie – one dark, one fair, both beautiful, both wearing scarves around their necks. It was true, Sophie did look a bit like Clémence, although Sophie was blonder and much prettier. No wonder Alastair had fallen for her. But there was Stephen's wicked smile again, and Clémence could see why Sophie had picked him rather than Alastair.

Only two or three photographs of Bart's, a family Christmas in 1938 and then Capri. Towering mountains, sea of shining grey, flowers blooming in monochrome, two or three shots of the friends relaxing around an outside table on a terrace, always including Sophie. Then a ruin that was labelled *Villa Jovis, water cisterns*. Then a more modern façade with peeling plaster, unlabelled but it must be the Villa Fersen. And the ornate but tattered interior of the villa itself, and a semi-circular room with tapestries: the opium den.

And then nothing. Four or five blank black pages.

Clémence turned back to a couple of the photographs of Alastair. There weren't many of them, which wasn't surprising since he was the photographer. They reminded her of someone or something.

Who?

Stephen speeded up as he approached the crossing, but the green man had finished flickering and turned to red by the time he got there. He swore mildly to himself: that particular crossing took an age to turn green again.

Two young women joined him, shoving pushchairs. They were speaking animatedly in French. This seemed to be the new thing in Notting Hill – first it was the English yuppie bankers, then the Americans, and now the French spilling over from Kensington. There were very few people he still recognized from his arrival in Notting Hill in the seventies. Mr Chaudhury, who had just sold him the copy of the *Racing Post* which he was clutching under his arm, being one of those few.

Stephen eavesdropped. The women were discussing one of the fathers at school who always wore very tight trousers. The question was, did he do that on purpose to advertise the size of his manhood? Indeed, was his manhood worth advertising? The women were so engrossed in the problem that they had not noticed Stephen.

They were quite attractive really, especially the small one with the promising chest. Years ago, they would have noticed him. The conversation would have tailed off, there would have been sideways glances, and then whispers when he walked off. But not now. Obviously not now.

He cleared his throat and addressed the smaller woman. He spoke loudly and clearly in his plummy French accent: he had been taught how to project, after all. *'Madame, ces nibards sont magnifiques! Votre fils a beaucoup de chance.'*

One of the women let out a small shriek and the other reddened instantaneously. The light changed to green and the two pushchairs shot across the road, leaving Stephen chuckling to himself.

He got home and opened the *Racing Post* to plan his campaign for the day. A horse he had backed unsuccessfully before was running at Uttoxeter. He still fancied it. Difficult one.

The phone rang. Who the hell was that? Bloody people, never gave a chap a moment's rest.

He picked it up. The phone hissed. 'Dad? It's Rupert.'

What the hell did he want? But actually, Stephen could guess. He grunted.

'I've just had Clémence on the phone. From Wyvis.'

'I know,' said Stephen. 'She rang me yesterday. Whose stupid idea was it to send her up there?'

Stephen and his son spoke for ten minutes, which must have been the longest conversation they had had in years. Things were unsatisfactory. Most unsatisfactory.

As Stephen hung up the phone, he thought of Clémence. By and large he didn't like his grandchildren much, at least the ones he knew, but he had grown fond of Clémence the couple of times he had seen her as a schoolgirl when she had visited him on her way to boarding school. He didn't want her mixed up in the whole Sophie thing; she would only get hurt like the rest of them.

He stared at the *Racing Post* on the kitchen table, but he couldn't concentrate. His eyes were drawn to the half-empty bottle of Scotch he kept in the kitchen. It wasn't even eleven o'clock. He could wait an hour and a bit until his pint at the Windsor Castle.

He was a bad father. An appalling father. It wasn't entirely his fault, but he had lost his own children long ago, when he had gone to prison. Fabrice, the eldest, had disappeared entirely for years – contact with him had been minimal. Beatrice, Fabrice's younger sister, had cut herself off from him, until he had been released. Then she had reintroduced herself. But she was nuts, frankly, and her three children were out of control. She was now in her late fifties and divorced, and who could blame her husband? She lived in Putney somewhere and occasionally took it upon herself to pester her wayward father.

And Rupert, like his older brother, had taken off, but had kept in slightly better touch. Stephen knew Rupert hated him. And he didn't like Rupert either. So Clémence was the best of the bunch.

Madeleine at least had done what she could to help out her sister's children, and grandchildren, paying for their education. She could be an interfering old bat, but she had a good heart. Stephen glanced at the photograph on the mantelpiece. Which was lucky: Sophie deserved someone more capable than Stephen to look after her offspring.

Stephen felt his eyes stinging. Angrily, he picked up the paper and forced himself to concentrate on the 2.40 p.m. at Uttoxeter.

The old man returned from his walk to find Clémence in the sitting room, ready to resume the book.

He sat down, apprehensive.

'All right?' said Clémence. The old man could tell she, too, was nervous about what she might read.

'All right.' The old man nodded.

Clémence opened the book.

CHAPTER VII

Capri Revisited

The Bay of Naples, June 1947

I WAS GLAD TO be out of Naples and on to the sea. The city had been utterly devastated by the war. It had been poor in 1939, but it had been bustling, purposeful, joyful even; ramshackle new buildings had mixed with the faded glory of the older city. But the war had reached down from the north, picked up Naples, and shaken it to pieces. And then, in 1944, Vesuvius had erupted, shaking it some more. Now there was rubble, rubbish and dust, dust everywhere. The people were thin, dejected and dangerous: boys tried to take your money, girls tried to sell their bodies. And the city stank of refuse and sewage.

Nowhere was happy or prosperous after the war, but as the train had left France and headed south through Italy, the poverty intensified. Nothing in Europe was untouched, and certainly not me. My sister had died. Joyce had been wandering through the streets of London, on leave with her boyfriend Tommy, when a doodlebug's engine had cut out high above them. They had run to the precise spot on the Strand where it had landed – both dead.

As for me, I had become a soldier, and a good one. I had been granted a commission, and shipped out to North Africa, where the Green Howards had fought hard and been defeated soundly by the Afrika Korps at Gazala. I had escaped the confusion of battle with two comrades and trekked through the desert back towards Egypt, although one of us, Corporal Binns, hadn't made it the whole way. Back in the line, more fighting and capture this time. I was one of the last Allied POWs to be evacuated from Africa to a stalag in Germany. After a couple of failed attempts, I had escaped and made my way through France where I had remained holed up in a village in the Massif Central until my hosts were liberated.

From there, back to England, but the war had ended before they could thrust me back into the front line for a third time. Yet for all that toing and froing, for all my efforts, I was pretty sure I hadn't actually succeeded in killing a German, or an Italian.

All a bit of a waste of time, really.

Escaping from the British Army had taken longer than escaping from a German POW camp, but eventually I had been demobbed, and returned to St Bartholomew's Hospital Medical College for my final two years. Bart's in 1946 was totally different from Bart's in 1939. There were those fellow students who were just out of school who had missed the war, and who had the boisterous enthusiasm for medicine which must have infected me at their age. And then there were those who had served in one way or another in the armed forces, but even these were younger than me, for I was now in my thirties. Most of my direct contemporaries from pre-war Bart's had been rushed into becoming field medics. Two others had become pilots, both killed. One had joined the navy and was somewhere at the bottom of the Barents Sea.

I still found medicine interesting, I was good at it, and I had taken up rugger again. But I was a different person, there was no doubt of that.

I had received a letter from Nathan asking me to meet him and Madeleine at Tony's house on Capri. Stephen and Sophie would be there, as would Elaine, who was now Tony's wife. I had not seen Stephen since that afternoon in 1939 when I had fled the island, or at least not seen him in the flesh. I had watched him several times on the cinema screen, for his acting career had indeed taken off and he had performed and eventually starred in at least a dozen British films during the war. He had been working hard. He had also married Sophie, in April 1940 at Holy Trinity Brompton in London. They had invited me, but I had politely and curtly refused.

This was the first time that Nathan had visited Europe since the war: he had extended business commitments, but wanted to meet his old friends as well. Capri seemed to him the place to do it.

God knows why. I wasted no time in refusing. They wouldn't miss me.

But Nathan didn't take no for an answer, and he had written a follow-up letter which I had been unable to ignore; in fact I had kept it in the breast pocket of my jacket on the long journey from London.

Dear Angus,

I was disappointed to receive your refusal to join us in Capri this summer, much more disappointed than I expected. Let me explain why.

The war has destroyed so much. Buildings, lives, families, nations. I was fortunate, I have worked damned hard but I avoided serving in the armed forces, for which, I admit, I feel guilty. My younger brother Bobby died at Okinawa. Out of the historians in our year at college, Wardle and Henderson were killed, and Thurston was badly burned. I lost a couple of good friends from Yale. Madeleine's village in France was one of those the Nazis decided to use as an example – thirty inhabitants were executed as a reprisal for resistance sabotage. I'm sure you saw suffering too.

Yet some things remain. Friendship. Love. Family. You and I were good friends before the war, as you were with

*Stephen. My marriage to Madeleine was easily the best
thing that has happened in my life, and Tony and Elaine are
very happy. So you can understand why I want to get us all
together in Capri again.*

*And I want you there, we all want you there. Madeleine,
Sophie, Stephen, even Tony, who says you were the only
person apart from Alden who ever took his art seriously!*

*I realize that you were badly hurt by Stephen and Sophie
falling in love on Capri – as you can imagine, it is something we have discussed at length together. They understand
why you didn't come to their wedding in 1940, and in fact I
understand why you don't want to come to Capri now.*

*But I hope you will; we hope you will. Because friendship
should be stronger and more long-lasting than this darned
war. You are important to all of us. So please come, damn it!*

*By the way, I have subsequently learned about England's
harsh foreign-exchange restrictions for travelers. Please don't
worry about that, I will cover everything. There is money in
oil; too much money.*

*Yours ever,
Nathan*

Nathan was right, Nathan was absolutely right, and I was looking
forward to seeing him.

Once again, Nathan and Tony were there to meet me as the ferry
docked in the Marina Grande. Nathan had become sleeker, Tony
fatter, and Nathan had grown a thin black moustache. They were
both pleased to see me.

We took the funicular up to the Piazzetta where Ernesto was
waiting for us with his carriage. Capri was clean, green and pros-

perous, seemingly untouched by the war. Tony explained that it had been used as a retreat for R & R, first by German officers, and then by their Allied counterparts. Tony had left his villa in the care of a local family in the winter of 1940 and returned to the States. He had spent the war pottering about the Pacific in a minesweeper. Elaine's visit to Capri in the summer of 1939 had made a deep impression on both of them. They had married in Pittsburgh in 1942 and, as soon as Tony had demobbed, returned to Capri, to find their villa had been fixed up under the supervision of the German officers who had stayed there. Tony was painting again.

The others were waiting for me on the terrace: Stephen, Madeleine, Elaine. And Sophie.

Stephen had changed subtly. He was older, obviously, less floppy, stronger. His arrogance was still there, but it was less superficial, more ingrained. His smile was still dangerous, yet thrilling; he had clearly been working on it. But it was good to see him. After the long, damnably horrible war, it was good to see him. I stepped forward and shook his hand, and then we embraced – something we had never done before as friends.

Madeleine smiled broadly and kissed me on both cheeks – in her mid twenties she had looked like a sophisticated beauty of thirty, and she still did. Elaine had changed the most, but then she had been only sixteen the last time I had seen her. She still had the pert schoolgirl nose, but there was a louche air about her, and she had put on a lot of weight. Standing just behind them was Sophie. Her eyes were shining and her smile was one of relief and happiness, no doubt at seeing her husband and me reconciled.

'Hello, Angus,' she said and reached up to kiss me.

'Hello,' I said, grinning back. I was relieved myself to realize that I didn't feel giddy, jealous, embarrassed, humiliated or any of the other reactions I had feared. I was just happy to see her again and pleased that she was married to my former best friend.

Tony broke out the vermouth, and we got down to some serious drinking – the deep blue of the Mediterranean spread out before us. The alcohol, the late-afternoon sunshine and the warmth of old friendship settled upon me like a comfortable blanket. I wasn't a solitary person: I had formed strong friendships with my fellow soldiers during the war, and there were some good chaps among the other medical students. But there was something more durable, more permanent, more important about my friendship with these people. I was glad Nathan had made me come.

As the sun descended behind Monte Solaro, we moved down the hill to the little Piazzetta, where we installed ourselves in the Bar Tiberio, which took up one wall of the island's main church, and spent an hour watching inhabitants and visitors parade in front of us. Eventually, Tony took us to dinner at Gemma's restaurant, which we reached up some steps beside the church, and along a tiny alleyway under arches. Through this gloomy entrance the dining room opened up on to a terrace overlooking the Bay of Naples. The sun had slipped off the broad shoulders of Monte Solaro, and was now a red ball hanging over the gentle peak of Ischia, a golden path leading from it towards us. An enormous American battleship and its two accompanying destroyers loomed black against the silver and the gold. Tony was fussed over by Gemma herself, an energetic lady with a commanding presence for one so small. She liked Tony: everyone liked Tony.

The back wall was lined with paintings of Capri. One, of the cisterns at the Villa Jovis, caught my eye.

'Is that your signature, Tony?'

Tony grinned. 'Yes it is. As are those two.' He pointed to two depictions of the mouth of a cave – presumably one of Capri's several grottos. 'They are for sale.'

They were actually quite good. Much better than their brethren on the wall of the restaurant.

Out of the corner of my eye, I saw Sophie's surreptitious smile. 'What about the vegetables?' I asked. I had to.

'They are history,' said Tony.

'Oh.'

Elaine sniggered.

Tony shrugged. 'I came back from the war and looked at them afresh. I think the idea is good – I still love the idea. But the paintings aren't. But you know, I don't feel bad. This is a beautiful island and I want to paint it. I've started taking lessons from a little old Scottish lady, Mrs Mackenzie, who is really very good. I'm learning a lot from her.' He nodded at the walls. 'And I can get decent money for these.'

'I'm not surprised,' I said. 'If I had any cash, I'd buy one.'

'We've commissioned one of the terrace outside the villa,' said Madeleine. 'Tony is going to ship it to New York.'

Over dinner, as we admired the progress of the slowly descending sun over the bay, I caught up on what everyone had been doing. Stephen had just been offered a starring role by one of the Hollywood studios in *The Beechwood Legacy*. He was flying to California, leaving Sophie and their two children at their home in Twickenham. Sophie had worked at the Free French headquarters in London for a couple of years, until her son had arrived. Sophie was very proud of her children, Fabrice and Beatrice, and looking at their pictures I could see why. They were both strikingly attractive, which wasn't at all surprising given their parents. Little two-year-old Beatrice, in particular, had Sophie's big eyes.

Nathan had had an energetic war. A modern war needed oil, and Nathan had made himself very useful getting the oil to the right places. Although young, he had soon established his reputation for getting things done quickly, for reliability and for trustworthiness. As soon as war had been declared by Britain and France on Germany, he had recognized that even though his country wasn't involved, its oil would be desperately needed. He had arrived at Wakefield Oil's New York headquarters and taken control. Unlike some of his competitors, he never placed his own company's profits ahead of the needs of his country, something that had not gone unnoticed by the US government. Wakefield Oil was a much stronger company after the war than it had been before it, and as a result, more profitable. Now Nathan was focusing on the Middle East, which he predicted would be the big marginal producer of oil for the rest of the century. I knew nothing about the stock market, but I resolved that if I ever did manage to save some money, I would work out how to buy shares in Wakefield Oil.

Madeleine was proud of her husband. Her English had achieved a rapid fluency, although her accent was still strongly French, but now with a definite American tinge. She said she loved living in New York. There were as yet no small Giannellis to be photographed, but she seemed to be just as proud as Sophie of the little Trickett-Smiths.

And Elaine? Elaine drank and smoked and laughed, occasionally snuggling up to Tony.

CHAPTER VIII

Amori et Dolori Sacrum

W E GOT UP in dribs and drabs the following morning. The plan was to have a picnic luncheon at the Villa Damecuta, one of Tiberius's villas on the other side of Monte Solaro, near the village of Anacapri. Tony tried to take the bus, but it turned out that it was years since Nathan and Madeleine had taken a bus anywhere, and they insisted on two of Capri's open taxis. The journey was only two and a half miles, but the taxis took twenty minutes to heave their way up the dramatic winding road, somehow ascending what looked like an impassable rampart of rock. Staring at the soft fissures in the cliff, like wrinkles in an old man's face, I realized that Capri was made of limestone, just like the Dales back home.

I was sitting next to Stephen.

'I have an apology to make, old man,' he said.

'Don't worry about it. It was a long time ago.'

'No, it's important. I promised Sophie I would make it, and I will.'

I listened.

'I don't apologize for marrying Sophie, but I behaved like a cad when we were driving down here that summer. Of course I knew how you felt about her. I should have told you right away. It would have been unpleasant, but you would have found out soon enough. Which of course you did. So – sorry.'

I smiled. 'Apology accepted. Gratefully.'

'Good,' he said. 'Now, does your old mucker Suetonius have anything to say about this place we're going to?'

'No idea. I haven't read Suetonius for a long time.'

'Glad to hear it. He always struck me as a bit fishy. Even in the original Latin.'

Anacapri was much less sophisticated than Capri town, and it was also a couple of degrees cooler. It was a pleasant walk from the village down through farms and smallholdings of vineyards, olive groves, vegetable gardens and lemon trees. The villa itself turned out to be a pattern of low ruined walls in a field of flowers, grasses and thistles, guarded by a round medieval watchtower. Another cliff edge, another stunning view of Ischia.

Tony had brought along bread, cheese, Italian ham and many bottles of light rosé from Ravello. It was a hot day, but the breeze drifting in from the sea made it bearable. I lay back on one of the walls, closed my eyes and pointed my face towards the sun. Birds chirped lazily from the shrubs behind me. Bees murmured as they plundered the flowers. Butterflies hopped and skipped. Conversation drifted around me in a gentle swirl, interspersed with trickles of laughter.

I let my head loll to the side and opened one eye. Sophie was sitting on a low wall opposite talking to Nathan. She might be thirty and a mother of two, but she was still very pretty. As was Madeleine. Girls in summer dresses at picnics were a good idea, I thought.

Sophie wasn't mine, and that was all right. There would be other women. There was a student nurse called Gillian with whom I had been out three times. She was much younger than me, but she made me laugh. Not as pretty as Sophie, though. I would have to learn to live with that; most girls just weren't as pretty as Sophie.

For some reason, just then, she turned quickly to glance at me. She caught my one eye staring at her. I closed it.

'Hello.' It was a voice from behind me. An American voice.

I hauled myself up on my elbows. Elaine had sat down on the wall next to me, with a glass half full of rosé. A cigarette was hanging from her open lips. I realized that was why she had struck me as louche. It was her mouth: her full lips that never quite closed. They were sloppy, uneven, sexy.

She puffed at her cigarette. 'You poor darling,' she said. 'You look quite exhausted.'

'It's the wine. And the sun. And the view.'

'Here, let me get you some more.'

I didn't object and she brought me a glass. We sat in silence looking out over the bay at the mysterious island of Ischia. There was something unsteady about Elaine's silence.

'It must be lovely living here,' I said.

'It is,' said Elaine. A pause. 'It gets a bit dull after a while.'

'What are the people like?'

'The expats are all old. Old queers. Old lesbians. They are quite fun in their way but, like I said, it gets dull.'

'Tony likes it, doesn't he?'

'Tony loves it. And I love Tony.' She sighed. 'It would be nice to go up to the Riviera. Antibes. Juan. Cap Ferrat.'

'That shouldn't be too hard from here.'

'It shouldn't be, should it?' said Elaine. 'But it turns out we don't have enough money. I thought Tony had a lot of money. He doesn't really. And neither do I.'

She didn't sound bitter. Just disappointed.

'Shame Uncle Alden gave all his money to those two.' She nodded at Nathan and Madeleine.

'He gave some to Tony,' I said.

'Yes, he did,' said Elaine. 'But he had other nephews and nieces, not just Nathan. Me for instance. He didn't leave me a bean.'

I didn't reply. My own opinion was that Alden had realized that Nathan would make something of the family company, but it was probably best not to share that thought with Elaine.

'It's ironic really,' said Elaine. 'Considering it was Nathan who killed him.'

'Yes,' I said. 'Yes, I suppose it is.'

'That doesn't seem quite right. That Nathan should have gotten all the dough.'

'It was an accident. You were there.'

'I suppose it was,' said Elaine in a tone that suggested she supposed it wasn't. 'Do I make you uncomfortable?'

'No,' I said, lying.

Elaine slowly turned her gaze towards me. Her brown eyes held mine. Her lips lolled, glistened. 'Are you sure?'

'Yes,' I said, briskly. I pulled out my pipe. 'Do you mind?'

'Go ahead,' said Elaine, turning away from me. 'I was just hoping you would make Capri a little less dull.'

We went to Gemma's again that evening for dinner, and then staggered back to Tony's villa for limoncello, looking out over the moon-striped water far below. Between us, we had put away a lot of alcohol. We were all drunk, all in our different ways.

Madeleine became sleepy. When Elaine began to look ill, she took her up to bed. Or rather to the lavatory. The heave and splatter could be heard down on the terrace, much to Stephen's amusement.

Stephen was becoming aggressive, his drinking taking on a steady determination. 'Can I have another one, old man?' he asked Nathan, after finishing his third or was it fourth limoncello. Nathan poured him a glass. The rest of us refused: Elaine's retching had introduced some wariness of the sweet yellow liquid around the table.

'So what was the war like for you, Angus?' Stephen asked.

'Oh, you know,' I said.

'I've had to play all sort of fellows who have been involved in real fighting,' said Stephen. 'I find it helps to ask them what it was really like.'

'Getting thrashed by Rommel was unpleasant,' I said. I had no intention of ruining my evening by dragging Gazala on to Capri. 'But I seem to have spent much of the war running away. Playing hide-and-seek with the Jerries in the desert and then in Germany and France.'

'Can't you tell us about that?'

'Actually, I plan to put it in a book,' I said. 'When I was in the stalag, I got caught trying to escape in the back of the laundry wagon. They threw me into the cooler for three weeks. I amused myself by trying to write a book in my head, and then memorizing it. I've got quite a lot of it down on paper now; I'm surprised by how much I've enjoyed writing it. But I've no idea if anyone would be interested in reading it.'

'I would,' said Tony.

'Shame you didn't fight, Nathan,' Stephen said. 'In the war.'

'I feel bad about that,' said Nathan. 'But I genuinely thought I could be more help at Wakefield Oil. I think I was probably right.'

'But Angus fought. And Tony.'

'You didn't though, did you, Stephen?' said Sophie.

'I joined up. I did my duty. I wore a uniform. I was ready to fight. It wasn't my fault they put me in front of a camera.'

'Yes, but you didn't get shot at, did you?' said Sophie. 'You were just the same as Nathan, doing your bit for the war effort.'

Stephen glared at his wife. 'No, Sophie, it's entirely different. I was prepared to fight for my country, Nathan wasn't. It's as simple as that.'

I found Stephen's haranguing difficult to listen to. The war had been necessary, but it had been ghastly. It had changed me, damaged me, and millions of others like me, and actually millions totally unlike me: children, mothers, Russians, Germans, Italians. Some had been fortunate never to step over or on to a dead body, never to have been terrified that they were going to be next to die. Nathan seemed to understand that, Stephen didn't, but I didn't want to explain it to either of them.

They had benefitted from the war; the conflict had accelerated their careers, and at thirty both men were already successful, yet I had not yet even qualified in mine. That was another difference between us.

'What about you, Tony?' Stephen said. 'You must have seen some action.'

'I learned to play poker real well for my country. Shall we play now?'

'I'm not bad at poker,' said Nathan.

'I bet you're not,' I said.

'You're a coward, Nathan,' said Stephen, glaring at him.

'Oh, come on, Stephen! This is absurd,' Sophie said. 'Especially coming from you.'

'Oh, be quiet, you stupid woman! I've played heroes. I know exactly what it's like to fight for your country.'

'Let's go to bed,' I said.

Stephen pushed himself to his feet. 'I said you are a coward! What do you say?' He was swaying unsteadily. Nathan was alarmed.

I looked at Stephen. I looked at Nathan. I knew what to do. I swung and landed Stephen a clean blow on the chin, sending him crumpling to the ground.

'Sorry, old man,' I said to Stephen's moaning body. I rubbed my knuckles. 'Let's get you to bed.'

Tony and I carried Stephen up to bed, with Sophie hovering over us. We got him undressed and lay him down.

'I'm so sorry,' said Sophie. 'That was awful behaviour.'

'Dangerous drink, limoncello,' said Tony.

'Are you all right?' I asked.

Sophie nodded. 'I'll look after him.'

Tony and I tidied up the worst of the debris of empty glasses and bottles outside and then went to bed ourselves. I, as the only single in the group, had a bed made up in a tiny box room on the ground floor.

I undressed and lay on my back, listening to the noises of a Mediterranean night outside my open window.

Then I heard footsteps. And a quiet sob.

I listened. Nothing.

Then another sob.

I swung off the little bed, put on a shirt and trousers and let myself out into the garden.

Sophie was sitting on the floor of the terrace, her back resting against the stone pillars of the balustrade, a tear smearing her left cheek.

She looked up at me and smiled. 'Hello,' she said.

'Hello.' I sat down next to her.

'Did I wake you?'

'No. I wasn't asleep.'

'But you heard me?'

'Only just.'

'I'm sorry. I just can't bear to be in the room with him.'

'That's not good,' I said.

They sat in silence for a while. A long while.

'Do you want to go for a walk?' said Sophie.

'Now?'

'It's a lovely night. And we can't just sit here. I'd like to move.'

'All right. Let me fetch some shoes.'

I sneaked noiselessly back into the house and put on my shoes. We crept around the side of the house and out of the gate into the little road.

'Uphill or downhill?' I asked.

'Uphill.' And so we set off up the hill, towards the peak at the end of the island and the Villa Jovis.

It *was* a lovely night. A tiny cloud dallied in front of the moon, which was almost full, scattering its reflection on the sea. The cliff face of Monte Solaro glimmered light grey, its fissures dark slashes. Cypress trees rose tall, black and twisted. The varied unseen scents of blossom from the gardens on either side swirled around us. We were alone, apart from an occasional cat startled on its night hunt.

'I'm glad you came out to find me,' said Sophie.

'You sounded sad.'

'I am. I *wish* he hadn't done that. Bait Nathan. It was *so* unreasonable. I mean both of them did their stuff for the war effort. We needed oil and we needed morale.'

'He's drunk,' I said. 'Really drunk.'

'Did he get like that at Oxford?' Sophie asked. 'When you got drunk? Somehow I suspect that you did get drunk every now and then.'

'We did,' I said, smiling. 'And no, not really. He would usually talk, ramble on. I remember he did get in a fight with an idiot called Richardson once. But that was Richardson's fault. I broke it up.'

'Is that what you do? Break fights up.'

'I suppose it is.'

'That was quite a blow. When you hit Stephen.'

'I know.' I shook my hand. 'It hurts a bit, to be honest.' We walked in silence for a few moments. 'Is he often that aggressive now when he's drunk?'

'Yes. Yes, he is. I don't like it.'

'I'm sure you don't. He doesn't hit you, does he?'

'No! Oh, no,' said Sophie quickly. 'But . . .'

I waited.

'But sometimes these days I think he might. And he does get drunk rather often.'

'You mustn't let him!' I said. 'Hit you, I mean.'

'It doesn't work like that,' said Sophie. 'Have you got a cigarette?'

''Fraid not. I've got my pipe?'

Sophie laughed. 'No thanks.'

A cat missing half of its tail darted out of the shadows in front of us, and squeezed itself under a gate into a garden.

'Stephen was very good when we were first married,' Sophie said. 'He wanted to be a good husband and then a good father. He tried really hard. I knew he was tempted. When I visited him on set I could see the way the girls looked at him, but he only had eyes for me.'

'Stephen's ambition is to be a reliable man with a reliable job, a reliable wife and two reliable children,' I said.

'Yes. That's why he likes you so much. He talks about you a lot, you know.'

'I didn't know,' I said, but I was pleased to hear it. 'I have to say I haven't quite managed the reliable bit yet.'

'You will, though. You will become the local GP that everyone loves.'

'Like my father,' I said. 'Perhaps I will. I hope I will.'

'But not like Stephen,' said Sophie. 'He tried, he really tried, but he couldn't do it.'

'Has he had any affairs?' I wanted to ask, but didn't.

But Sophie heard the unspoken question. 'I know he has been seeing other women. It started when Beatrice was born. One of the make-up ladies, for God's sake! Then there was an actress on one of the war films he was in. Played his sister. That's incest, isn't it? Should be banned.'

'Have you caught him at it?'

'No,' said Sophie. 'I don't want to catch him at it. I don't want to know.' She sighed. 'But I do.'

'I'm sorry.'

We walked on. We were approaching the little drinking fountain halfway up to the Villa Jovis. A cloud covered the moon, and the road became suddenly darker.

'When he goes to Hollywood for this new film, I *know* he's going to start an affair. He won't be able to help himself.'

'Should you go with him?'

'Maybe,' said Sophie. 'The idea is that if it's a success we all move out there. But I don't want to follow him thousands of miles just to keep an eye on him. That's not how marriage should be.'

'I suppose not.'

Sophie laughed.

'What is it?'

'I was remembering your warning. I have to say that homosexuality has never been a problem with Stephen.'

I winced. 'I was rather hoping you had forgotten that.'

'That's a difficult one to forget.' She touched my hand. 'But I can forgive you.'

'Thanks,' I said.

They reached the little fountain and paused for breath. 'Which way now?' I said. But I knew what her answer would be.

'Do you think we can get in to the Villa Fersen?'

'You mean break in?'

Sophie nodded.

'We can try.'

It was difficult making our way along the lane through the darkness, especially the last stretch through the pine wood. Sophie took my hand. In a few minutes we reached the big iron gate, which had a big steel padlock on it. To the right, the high garden wall ran steeply upwards: it had deteriorated significantly since our last visit. Sophie peered up and spied a tree growing just a foot or so away from it. 'Let's try that.'

It was easy to hop over the wall into the garden: it looked as if we were taking a route that others had followed before. The villa loomed a bluish white in front of us. Several of the windows were broken and a couple were open. We climbed in. The place was a ruin: plaster had fallen from the ceiling and another decade of dust had accumulated. We looked out from the salon at the bay, now moonlit again. Then Sophie led me down to the opium den.

'I've got my pipe,' I whispered. 'But St Bruno Flake isn't quite the same, is it?'

Sophie didn't answer. She reached out and pulled me to her. We kissed.

'Are you sure you want to do this?' I said.

'Quite sure. Aren't you?'

The moonlight streamed through the window of the den. I knew this was a moment I would remember for ever.

'I'm sure.'

Afterwards, as we lay on one of the oriental divans in the den and I was running a single finger over Sophie's naked body, pale and striped in the moonlight, she smiled up at me.

'I have a request. It's a completely unfair request. But I hope you will agree to it. I think you might.'

'What is it?'

'Promise me we won't do this again?'

'What do you mean?'

'I mean never again.' She touched my chest. 'I wanted to do this so badly, ever since I saw you when you arrived yesterday. It seemed, I don't know, inevitable. But I don't want to ruin my marriage. I don't want to hurt my children. I don't even want to lose Stephen.' She hesitated. 'I'm still a Catholic, although obviously not a very good one. I don't want to sin irrevocably. Leaving Stephen would be irrevocable.'

'I see,' I said. And I did, sort of. Although the sinning Catholic bit confused me.

'It's dreadful of me,' Sophie said. 'And it's very unfair on you. It's as if I'm using you. Except—'

'Except what?'

'Except I don't *feel* that I am. Somehow I think you understand me.'

And I did. I wanted her all to myself, of course I did, but I wanted her to be happy, or at least no more unhappy than she had to be. Years ago I would have leaped at this chance, pleaded, cajoled, pestered her to leave Stephen so she could be mine.

But now?

I had had this night. I didn't want to ruin her life, my life, Stephen's life, their children's lives.

'I understand,' I said. 'I promise.'

Sophie smiled. 'Are you sure?'

'Quite sure.'

'And you're not going to run away tomorrow morning?'

'No,' I shook my head. 'I'm not going to run away.'

'And you're not going to beat up Stephen over breakfast?'

'I won't do that either.'

Her smile broadened. I felt myself stir. She reached up to me. 'Come here.'

10

The old man watched Clémence shutting the book.

'What are you smiling at?' she demanded.

'It turns out I'm a war hero,' the old man said. 'I had absolutely no idea. One of those great British escapees who would run away from anywhere for their country.'

'Do you remember Capri at all?'

The old man nodded. 'I do. I can almost see Nathan. And Tony. And I know what the Villa Damecuta looked like.'

'And the Villa Fersen? Do you remember Sophie in the Villa Fersen?'

'I do,' said the old man. He smiled again. That was an evening worth remembering.

'You know that was my grandpa's wife you were shagging?'

Anger blazed in Clémence's big eyes. The pleasure evaporated. If she was angry about that, how much angrier would she be when she discovered that he had killed Sophie in the boathouse? The memory that had struck him as he walked by it the day before had been frighteningly vivid. It must be real. And it must be recorded in a book with the title *Death At Wyvis*.

'I'm sorry,' he said. 'It must be difficult for you to learn all this.'

'It is,' said Clémence. She glanced at the book closed on her lap. 'But I'm glad we are reading it. These are things about my family that I want to know, that they should have told me.'

'Does the next chapter take place at Wyvis?'

Clémence opened the book and flicked forward a couple of pages from where she had saved her place. 'Yes,' she said. 'We're getting near the end.'

The old man nodded.

'Do you remember what happens next?' she asked.

'We'll see,' he said, with a sigh. She was staring hard at him, those large blue eyes painfully focused. Despite her anger, the old man liked Clémence. Perhaps it was because she looked a bit like Sophie – those four little freckles on the end of her nose – perhaps it was her youth, her kindness in helping him. He didn't want to hurt her. To anger her more. But that was unavoidable if she was to read the rest of the book to him. And that was something they both needed to do.

He was alone in the world. She was the only person in his new life whom he knew, or whom he could remember knowing. He didn't want to lose her.

A memory struck him. 'I took you for a ride on a camel.'

'A camel?' Clémence frowned. 'I remember that. I was only little.'

'Very little,' said the old man. 'It was in Morocco, wasn't it? By a beach.'

'Essaouira,' said Clémence. 'We used to go there sometimes when we lived in Marrakech. You came with us once. We played on the beach. I remember that.'

'And a man came with a camel. You wanted a ride. So we rode on it together. It was very high up for such a little girl. You were very brave.'

'There were a lot of camel rides in Morocco, not surprisingly,' Clémence said. 'I remember we dug a big long ditch together, to channel the water when the tide came in. Or went out.'

'Your father was there,' said the old man. 'Rupert. And maybe your mother, but I can't remember her.'

'Tall. Very long dark hair, down to her bum. I loved my mother's hair,' said Clémence. 'But she cut it off three years ago. When Patrick moved in. Now she looks like a banker's wife.'

'You can't be a hippie all your life.'

'I suppose not,' said Clémence. 'It's good you are remembering things that are not in the book.'

'Yes. But I can't remember why I was there. On holiday, I suppose?'

'I would have been about five,' Clémence said. 'So that's 1984.'

'When I was living in Australia. I still have no memory of that, apart from the eagles and the Mundaring library. Do I know your parents? I must do, if I went out to see them.'

'I rang my dad earlier this morning, but he didn't want to talk to you,' said Clémence. 'Or about you. Neither did my grandpa.'

Her words hurt the old man. Just when he was fumbling towards some sort of normal past life, more signs popped up that his old friends didn't like him. Didn't want to have anything to do with him. And that they had good reason.

He was alone.

A thought flitted at the edge of his consciousness, like a bat glimpsed at dusk. 'I have something to discuss with your grandfather. Something important, something I need to show him.' He frowned and then struck his forehead three times. This was *so* frustrating! 'Madeleine will be here this afternoon, you say?'

'Yes. I don't know when. She'll know more about your life than you and me combined.'

'Yes,' said the old man.

'You're scared, aren't you?' said Clémence. There was still anger in her voice, but it was tempered with kindness.

'I'm scared of the unknown. Or rather, I know there are bad things still to uncover in my life, I just don't know exactly what they are.'

Clémence stood up and peered out of the window. 'I'm going for a walk before Aunt Madeleine gets here. I need the fresh air. I'll make us some lunch when I get back.'

The old man considered asking whether he could join her, but he had the feeling that part of what she wanted to do was to escape him. Besides which, he would slow her down. 'All right,' he said. 'See you later.'

*

Clémence strode down the track through the woods to the loch. There was no sign of the sun that morning, and the waters of the loch were shades of grey – slate under the rock face of Meall Mòr, mercury in the middle, and near black under the trees by the shore. On the far side of the loch, clouds heavy with moisture, or perhaps snow, clustered around the screes on the upper slopes of the hills. A cold, damp breeze bit at her cheeks, but that felt good after the stuffy sitting room in the cottage. She had found the description of Angus seducing her grandmother, a woman she had never known, unsettling. Even more unsettling when she admitted to herself that it was Sophie who had seduced Angus. Or Alastair. And that her grandfather was hardly a paragon of marital fidelity either.

Her earlier enthusiasm for Madeleine's arrival was tinged with apprehension. Madeleine would no doubt bring explanations, but also more secrets. She hoped Madeleine was strong enough to take care of the old man herself. An awful thought dawned on her: maybe she would have to take care of both of them.

She wanted someone to take care of her! Or at least show some interest in her. She had thought after her years at boarding school she had become independent, self-reliant. But then she had believed she had a home to go back to, parents who loved her. Turned out that was crap. She didn't. They didn't. Welcome to adulthood.

The loneliness made her feel sick, unsteady, as if the ground she was standing on was slowly crumbling away and she was about to pitch into an abyss that was so deep she couldn't see the bottom.

God she missed Callum! She would have another go at persuading him to come; the old man had said he would be happy to have him staying in the cottage. Of course, they would have to finesse the sleeping arrangements.

She wished she didn't have to hang around waiting for Madeleine; she felt like driving into a village and buying a pint of milk, just for someone to speak to. Or going into a café. The old man must have gone barmy living all alone up here.

As she reached the shore of the loch, Sheila MacInnes's white Suzuki approached her coming the other way. Sheila slowed and wound down her window. 'Hi. What's the crack today?' Sheila said.

Clémence wasn't entirely sure what the crack was. 'Yeah. Er . . . yeah,' she said.

'How's it going with Alastair?'

'Good, I think,' said Clémence. 'I've been reading that book to him. *Death At Wyvis*.'

'Is it working?'

'I think so,' said Clémence. 'He's definitely remembering stuff. But it's a bit difficult for both of us.'

'I'm glad I've caught you alone,' said Sheila, conspiratorially. 'I went to see Pauline Ferguson yesterday afternoon. You mind I tellt you about her – she was the old stalker's wife? I explained about Dr Cunningham's head injury and his amnesia, and how the doctor at the hospital said we should try and jog his memory. She said Dr Cunningham had been to see her a few months ago, asking about that murder in that book you're reading. She had quite a lot to tell him – something about her son getting a job in America – I didn't understand it. But she said she'd be happy to talk to him if he wants, if you see what I mean.'

'Perhaps we should go and see her,' said Clémence. 'Maybe tomorrow. My Aunt Madeleine is coming this afternoon. I'm sure she will be able to tell us a lot.'

'All right, then. Pauline is at Ashwood House nursing home. It's in Dingwall, just on this side of town. Now, I'm just away up to Culzie and tidy up a bit for you.'

'Oh, don't worry about that,' said Clémence. 'I can do it.'

'Och, it's no trouble, pet. Enjoy your walk.' With that Sheila drove off up the track through the woods to the cottage.

Clémence rounded the curve in the loch and Corravachie came into view. Jerry Ranger's blue car was parked outside, and there was smoke coming out of the chimney. Jerry himself seemed to be examining the loch with his binoculars – bird watching, presumably, although he seemed to be ignoring the exotically plumaged ducks that were dabbling right in front of him. Clémence considered turning round, but then she thought it would be nice to chat to someone. Americans were usually friendly, and his song-writing intrigued her.

Jerry must have felt the same way, because he spotted her walking along the track and came out to meet her. 'Would you like a cup of coffee? I still have some of my stock of Peet's left.'

'Peat?' Clémence was confused. Was peat coffee some new Scottish delicacy? They said fried Mars bars were a myth, but Clémence believed in them. 'How do you use peat in coffee?'

'Not peat, Peet's,' said Jerry with a grin. 'Best coffee in California. At least *I* think so. There are folks who would argue with me.' He smiled to himself. 'There's always folks who want to argue with me.'

'OK,' said Clémence. 'I'll try some.'

Jerry's kitchen was well equipped with food and coffee. He put on the kettle to boil and set about grinding beans. 'Have you ever had Oreos? I got a stash of those as well. For special occasions.'

'I don't think so,' said Clémence. 'I've never been to America.'

'You should go. Go out west. See the national parks. Yosemite. Zion – that's in Utah. I think that's my favourite. Too many people just go to the cities in the States: New York or Washington. I wouldn't live in LA myself unless I had to to get work. I much prefer it out here.'

'Don't you get lonely?' Clémence said. 'I've only been here two days and it's getting to me already.'

'Loneliness. Solitude. All depends how you look at it. Alastair knows. He likes it up here.'

'Does he?' said Clémence. 'I suppose he does remember Loch Glass and Wyvis. And he likes to walk around.'

'You got to admit it's beautiful.'

'I admit it.'

'How's his memory coming along?'

'Very well,' Clémence said. 'I mean, he still has a long way to go, but it's coming back fast. We have been reading that book I showed you together, and he's remembering stuff in that. And just now he remembered visiting us when I was a little girl in Morocco. That came out of the blue.'

'That's good,' said Jerry.

'My aunt is coming to see us this afternoon. She knew him throughout his life. I expect that will help a lot.'

'Good. Why don't you go through to the living room?' said Jerry. 'Sorry it's a bit of a mess in there. I'll bring the coffee through in a moment. Here, take these.'

He handed Clémence a plate of round dark sandwich biscuits, and a small jug of milk, and she went through to the sitting room.

There was an old sofa, an armchair and all kinds of electronic music-making equipment, including an acoustic guitar and a keyboard. A computer nestling in pages of notes rested on the desk by the window overlooking the loch. A landscape of a Scottish castle hung from one wall, and a bookcase stood against the other. It was sparsely populated: a guide to Scottish birds, a John Grisham thriller, a rhyming dictionary, a French novel by Pascale Roze, and then a very familiar cover. *Death At Wyvis*. What the hell was that doing there? Maybe it came with the cottage.

But Jerry had acted as if he hadn't recognized her copy the day before.

She took the book down off the shelf; it had been read. She flipped open the pages. Passages were underlined with little notes scribbled in the margin. Had Jerry written those? Or had they been inscribed by a previous occupant of the cottage?

Just then Jerry bustled in with two mugs of coffee. He raised his eyebrows when he saw the book in Clémence's hand. She could feel herself blush. She tried to stop herself, but you can't do that – her face just felt hotter.

She tried to brazen it out. 'This is the book I've been reading to Alastair,' she said.

'Oh. I should take a look. Here's the coffee.'

'Mmm. Smells delicious.' She took a sip. 'Tastes good too.' Was that Jerry's handwriting? Clémence had an idea. She drifted over to his desk and picked up one of the sheets. 'Is this a new song?' she asked.

It *was* his handwriting!

'Yeah, it's coming on nicely. I think I'm going to come up with some really cool material while I'm here.'

'*The Wyvis Album*?' said Clémence, replacing the sheet.

Jerry smiled. 'Hey! That's not a bad title.'

'Shit!'

Jerry watched Clémence walking back to Culzie, his earlier complacency shattered.

Alastair Cunningham was remembering fast. And there was a lot he knew that Jerry could not afford to come to light.

He poured himself the rest of the coffee and took it outside to the rock by the shore of the loch. It was cold, but he didn't care. He needed to make a decision. Fast.

All right. There was a chance that Alastair would remember Jerry visiting him the week before. Remember being pushed down the stairs. But then again, there was a chance that would never come back. Jerry couldn't be sure what the old guy would remember and what was gone for ever. And even if he did remember, it would be difficult to prove murder in court. The forensic evidence would be messed up by now. Jerry could claim he had visited Alastair the day before he fell, and that Alastair was confused. It would be Jerry's word against Alastair's, a befuddled old man with a head injury.

But then Jerry's own criminal record would come to light. Would that matter? Because Jerry had already spent time in jail, for manslaughter. It had happened in 1973 in the dive in Echo Park he shared with his girlfriend. He and Wendy were fighting, as usual. Then they had patched it up in the usual way, with heroin. Except she had somehow taken it twice. Or, rather, Jerry had given it to her twice. Or maybe three times. That was what he thought, and that was what he had stupidly told the police. The DA had offered manslaughter and Jerry's dumb lawyer had persuaded him to plead guilty. But sentencing hadn't gone as planned: the judge didn't like long-haired song-writing drug addicts and thought Los Angeles would be better off without Jerry for a while. A long while. He hadn't gotten out of the state penitentiary until 1984.

He had gotten to know a lot of other manslaughterers inside. And murderers. Some of them were evil, many of them weren't. It was surprising how many men you met who had shot their wives with the gun kept in the bedside drawer and then regretted it for ever afterwards. Those were the kind of guys Jerry liked to hang out with inside. That was the kind of guy he was.

He really didn't want to go through all that again.

OK. So there was a chance that he might avoid a murder rap for the fall on the stairs. But then there was all the other stuff that Alastair knew. That he might want to tell the police about. There was a lot a diligent Scottish detective could discover if he put his mind to it. And Jerry hadn't liked the look on the girl's face when she had been leafing through that book. She would soon start putting two and two together herself.

The previous fall, Jerry had decided to take action. He couldn't back out now. There was a job to finish. And to finish quickly before it was too late, preferably before the aunt arrived.

There was the rifle locked in the gun cupboard at Culzie. Since Jerry didn't have a British firearms certificate, in theory he was only supposed to use it under the supervision of Terry, the stalker. And if he did use it to kill Alastair, it wouldn't take a Sherlock MacHolmes very long to figure out who was responsible.

That was a last resort. There was still his other idea that might work if he was lucky. But he would have to be quick.

He checked his watch. It was about twenty minutes since

Clémence had left – she should be almost back to Culzie now, so he wouldn't pass her. He made a quick phone call, then grabbed his binoculars, jumped in his car and drove to the spot he had occupied earlier that morning.

The clouds were building ominously above Ben Wyvis. Alastair liked to walk – he usually ventured outside at least twice a day – but snow would stop him. Jerry just had to hope that the old man decided to get a walk in before it started to snow.

11

Stephen rewound the video and pressed 'Play' for the third time. On the screen Sophie smiled at him, and little Rupert waved at Daddy. Then he ran across the lawn kicking a blue football, Sophie walking along after him. Then came the moment that hurt most. She turned and smiled at him. Just at him, the man holding the camera.

God, she was beautiful. And she loved him. How could he ever have lost her?

Of course, it wasn't directly his fault, which was something he had always known even if no one else had. But there were things he could have done. He should have treated her better. He should have dealt with Alastair. He should never have suggested that they all went to Wyvis. So many things he should have done differently.

The tears ran down his cheeks. These phone calls the last couple of days from Clémence and from Rupert had opened up old wounds.

But if Madeleine and Clémence and Alastair were all reading that damned book together, there would be trouble. Perhaps he should face it. Perhaps he should go up to Scotland and face it – face them.

No, damn them! They didn't need him, and he didn't need them. Sophie was just a set of images on a VHS tape transferred from old eight-millimetre film. She was gone. In a few years, maybe only a couple of years, he would be gone too.

In the meantime there was a crossword to be done.

Half an hour later, he was sipping his Guinness in the Sherry Bar at the Windsor Castle.

'Will you bloody concentrate, Stephen?' Maitland said. 'Three across. "Bachelor girl in Spanish-speaking country". Seven letters. I thought "senorita" but that's eight. Is it an anagram of somewhere in South America?'

'Sorry, Maitland,' said Stephen. 'My mind was wandering. I think I'm going to get on a train to Scotland.'

'What the hell do you want to do that for?' said Maitland. 'It's March. The weather is abominable in Scotland in March.'

'Bloody children,' said Stephen. 'And grandchildren. And interfering sisters-in-law.'

'Sod the lot of them,' said Maitland. 'In the meantime, what about this senorita?'

Sheila had been and gone by the time Clémence got back to Culzie. In that time she had cleaned the kitchen and bathroom and put some soup on the hob. Clémence felt grateful, embarrassed and irritated in equal measure – she had fancied a ham-and-cheese toastie for lunch.

'What's it like out?' the old man asked.

'Cold,' said Clémence. 'I think it might rain. Or maybe snow.'

'Did you see anything?'

'What do you mean?'

'I don't know. Deer? An eagle, perhaps?'

'I saw your neighbour, Jerry Ranger.'

'How is he?'

'Fine.'

Clémence wasn't sure what to think about Jerry, but she didn't want to discuss him with the old man. There was something not right about the American. Who was he? And why was he interested in *Death At Wyvis*? And, most importantly, why hadn't he admitted his interest when Clémence had shown him the book the day before?

A lot of what he said did add up. Although Jerry Ranger sounded like a fake name, it sounded like the kind of fake name someone would pick if they wanted to become a singer. Kind of like Johnny

Cash, although maybe that was a real name? Anyway, Jerry clearly was a real song writer – she had seen his scribblings and heard him sing – and he had got to know the old man over the couple of weeks before his fall. But now Clémence came to think of it, Jerry's questions about how much the old man had forgotten seemed to be driven by a little more than just curiosity or concern.

She thought about asking the old man about him, but there was no point. He wouldn't have a clue, and she wasn't in the mood for an awkward conversation. Next time she saw Sheila, she would ask her. She'd know something, and she was always happy to talk.

'By the way,' she said, 'did Sheila say anything to you about Pauline Ferguson, the woman who used to work on the estate?'

'Yes, she did,' said the old man. 'Apparently I spoke to her quite recently.'

'Do you want to see her? We could go to Dingwall tomorrow morning.' It would be good to see civilization again, Clémence thought.

'Yes, thank you,' said the old man. 'I would like to do that.' His gratitude was endearing but also irritating.

Clémence went back to her soup. The old man cleared his throat. 'I've been thinking about what you said about your mother and that man Patrick.'

'Oh, yes?' Part of Clémence wished that she hadn't mentioned it to the old man. But part of her was glad she had, glad that someone was interested.

'Yes. It's appalling. Completely unfair. I suppose I can see why your mother might believe the toad, but I don't understand your father.'

Clémence was just about to spoon some soup into her mouth as he said this. Suddenly she couldn't swallow, and she felt a tear leak down her cheek. It took her by surprise. Clémence hardly ever cried; one of the things you learned at boarding school was how not to cry.

'Oh, I'm sorry,' said the old man. 'I didn't mean to upset you, I really didn't.'

'I know you didn't,' said Clémence.

'I'd say don't cry,' said the old man, in a soft voice. 'But, actually, maybe you should.'

Clémence tried to smile, almost succeeded, but then the tears came, flowing strongly.

Slowly, carefully, the old man reached his hand over the table. Clémence moved hers towards him and he held it.

She sobbed. 'I'm sorry.'

'Don't be sorry, Clémence.'

'The trouble is, Dad has this new girlfriend in Vietnam, and she doesn't want me around. I visited them last summer and it was a disaster.' Clémence sniffed. 'So I can't go there either. And that's why Dad won't listen to me.'

'You poor girl!' The old man gripped her hand. 'Look. Why don't we fly over to Hong Kong together, and I'll sort this bastard Patrick out? And his accomplice Reginald.'

'How are you going to do that?'

'I'll go armed. Walking stick or Zimmer frame? Can't decide. I'll take out Reginald first and then deal with Patrick. He won't be expecting it – he'll think I'm a feeble old man.'

Clémence smiled. 'Aren't you a feeble old man?'

'Certainly not! I remember scoring a try against Ampleforth as though it was yesterday. I'm sure I can take him down.'

Clémence grinned, sniffed and wiped her eyes. 'It's very good of you to offer, but it is a long way to go for a fight that you probably wouldn't win.'

'I can go,' said the old man. 'Seriously. I don't have anything else to do. May as well go to Hong Kong. And someone needs to stand up for you if your parents won't.'

'What about money? How would you pay?'

'I've got a wallet with three credit cards in it. We could see how they work.' He leaned forward. 'You know, Clémence. It's a ridiculous thing to say, but you are the person I know best in the world. At least

180

you are the only person I know that I can remember. So certainly I'll fly to Hong Kong to beat up your mother's boyfriend.'

Clémence shook her head. She believed that the old man might actually do it. She was also sure it would be a total waste of time.

'Maybe we should talk to your Aunt Madeleine about it?' he said. 'Maybe she can persuade them you are telling the truth. She sounds like a capable woman.'

'She certainly is,' said Clémence. 'And she's quite capable of bossing my parents around. I'm just not sure they would listen. And—'

'And what?'

'I'd be ashamed to tell her.'

'You have nothing to be ashamed of, Clémence. Do you understand me? Nothing.'

He was right. The old man was right. And Aunt Madeleine was always on her side. 'Yes.' She nodded. 'Yes, I do understand.'

'Good,' said the old man. 'Now how about some Scrabble? I used to be very good at Scrabble. Who knows now? But I'd like to find out. We could treat it as a memory exercise.'

'I'm not bad at Scrabble myself,' said Clémence. 'But do we have a board?'

'In the cupboard in the sitting room.'

'You remember?'

'I remember.'

So they left the washing up and got the Scrabble out. The old man was indeed good, his memory for words seemed not to be damaged one jot, and he took an early lead. Clémence played well and managed to stay in contention. But as they were getting down to the last tiles, she was still forty-two points behind, with only seven low-scoring letters left. Then she suddenly spotted it: ATELIER. Fifty-point bonus for seven letters! She placed the tiles with a flourish.

'I've won!'

'Atelier?' the old man drew his bushy eyebrows together. 'That's a French word.'

'No it's not.'

'Of course it is. The English word is "workshop". You're just confused because you're French.'

'Hah! I've just won because I'm French you mean. Haven't you heard of the atelier tradition?'

'You mean *la tradition atelier?*'

'No, I mean the atelier tradition! It's a way of teaching art. I've won and you know it!'

'All right,' said the old man. 'You won. But I'll get my revenge.'

They put the game back in its box and then the old man pulled himself to his feet. 'Do you mind if I go out myself, before we start on the book again?'

'Go ahead,' said Clémence. 'I'll clear up the kitchen.' She looked outside. 'It still looks like it's going to rain or snow or something. Don't go too far.'

'I'll be OK,' said the old man. He put on his coat and stomped out of the door.

As Clémence loaded the dishwasher, she was grinning to herself over her Scrabble victory. She couldn't wait to tell Callum – he was a keen Scrabble player.

The grin disappeared as she remembered what they had to read together that afternoon. Maybe the old man was as nervous as she was, playing for time by suggesting Scrabble and going out for a walk. But the book had to be finished.

She thought about those last couple of chapters that took place in Capri; maybe she would go there some day. With Callum this summer perhaps, by Interrail, if their relationship lasted that long. She hoped it would.

Then she froze. A thought had struck her, a ridiculous thought, a thought she wanted to ignore, to destroy, to unthink.

But she couldn't.

She ran up the stairs to the old man's study, pulled out the album and stared at the photograph.

There was no doubt. Clémence was not who she thought she was at all.

She had no idea how long she sat on the study floor, cross-legged, with the old album open in front of her, before she heard the sound of a car drawing up outside.

She left the album and ran down the stairs. It was a taxi with a Dingwall phone number emblazoned on its side.

She flung open the front door and saw a small old lady, with black hair and a walking stick, being helped out of the back seat by the driver.

'Tante Madeleine!' she cried, and threw herself into the old lady's arms.

'Clémence, my dear!' Madeleine exclaimed as she hugged her great-niece. 'My, that was a welcome!' she said in French as they eventually broke away.

Clémence hadn't seen her aunt for a couple of years. She looked a little older, a little frailer with the walking stick. But she still had the big friendly brown eyes, and the wide smile. Under a fur-lined coat, she was dressed in trousers, a plaid waistcoat and her trademark Hermès scarf around her neck. Discreet jewels glimmered from her ears and on her fingers and the myriad of wrinkles across her face were softened with careful make-up.

'Shall I tell Davie here to come back and fetch me at five?' Madeleine asked.

'Do you want to stay here? We have room.'

'Oh, no,' said Madeleine, shuddering at the thought. 'I'll be much better in a hotel in Dingwall. I've already checked in.'

'Then five will be fine.'

Madeleine gave instructions to the taxi driver, who seemed happy to do anything his passenger asked, sensing that he would be making a lot more than whatever was on the meter from the afternoon's work.

'Let me show you the cottage,' said Clémence.

Madeleine admired Culzie's warmth and cosiness, Clémence put another log on the fire, and they sat in the sitting room.

'Where is Alastair?' Madeleine asked.

'He's gone for a walk. He should be back in half an hour or so.'

'That's good he can go walking. How is he?'

'Physically, he is fine. He just needs some stitches out of the back of his head. And his memory is coming back. Slowly.'

'So he really has forgotten everything? The poor man!'

'Yes,' said Clémence. 'The poor guy doesn't know who he really is. But, as I said, it's beginning to return.' She picked up the book by her chair. 'We've been reading this.'

Madeleine's hand flew to her mouth. 'Oh, my dear! What a place to start! That is a horrible book!'

Clémence had been pinning her hopes on Madeleine arriving, taking over from her, and making everything all right. But for the first time the reality of Madeleine's role in the story they had been reading became clear. Sophie was Clémence's grandmother, whom she had never met. She was also Madeleine's little sister, with whom Madeleine had grown up.

Oh, God. Two old people who were going to flip.

Clémence thought she had better explain. 'I found a manuscript in this room written by Alastair. It was written in the first person, and the title was *Death At Wyvis*. Then I found this published book on the bookshelf, written by an Angus Culzie. Same book, but the protagonist is a man called Angus. But that's Alastair, isn't it?'

'Yes, it's him,' said Madeleine. 'How much of it have you read?'

'I've read the prologue. Where Sophie . . . your sister . . . gets killed. By Angus. Or Alastair. Or whoever he is. But I have only read to Alastair from the beginning of chapter one, which takes place in Paris. He doesn't know about the murder, or at least I think he doesn't.'

'Have you got to the last section. In Wyvis?'

'Just about to read it. This afternoon.'

'Oh, my poor Clémence! When I sent you to look after him, I didn't mean that you should have to go through all this.'

'Is it true?' said Clémence.

Madeleine nodded.

'All of it?'

'Yes.'

'Then Alastair killed your sister?'

Madeleine hesitated, and then nodded again.

Clémence sighed. 'It has been very hard this last couple of days knowing that Alastair is a killer. He seems like a sweet old man.'

'I'm sure,' said Madeleine. 'But—'

'I am learning a lot about my family. My grandmother. And grandfather for that matter. And you.'

'Not all of it good, I'm afraid.'

'Why didn't any of you tell me anything? I knew nothing!'

Madeleine's big brown eyes were full of sympathy. 'Your father forbade me to. As did your grandfather.' She winced. 'When you read the rest of the book, perhaps you will understand.'

'It gets worse?'

'It does.'

Clémence blew air through her cheeks. The book scared her, but at least now she had an ally in her aunt. 'Do you hate Alastair? For killing your sister?'

Madeleine reached for the scarf at her neck and twisted it. 'I used to. I probably still do. Maybe I have forgiven him, I don't know. When the hospital called and said he had no one, I thought I should come over and help. And thank you for doing what you have been doing yourself, my dear.'

'When did you last see him?'

'Last autumn. He visited us in New York.' She hesitated. 'It was a painful visit. It upset Nathan.'

'I'm sorry about Uncle Nathan,' Clémence said.

'Thank you.' Madeleine smiled quickly. 'We were married a long time. He was a wonderful man. Life is different without him.'

'Aunt Madeleine? Before Alastair comes back, can I show you something?'

'Certainly, my dear,' said her aunt, grateful for the change of subject.

Clémence nipped upstairs and grabbed the photograph album. She brought it back downstairs and opened it at the picture of Alastair and Stephen in a quadrangle in Oxford. 'Who does that remind you of?'

Yes! He had been waiting and watching for over an hour, but then Jerry saw the old man emerge from the woods and strike out across the hillside. Immediately, Jerry set out on foot along the loch towards the woods, clutching his binoculars as alibi. A beaten-up Land Rover drove past and Jerry waved to its occupant, Terry MacInnes, the stalker, on his way to Wyvis Lodge at the head of the loch.

Slow down. Jerry had to time this accurately. He followed the smaller track that branched uphill from the loch towards Culzie, but a hundred yards or so before the cottage he broke off into the woods and cut across the slope. It was hard work – the slope was steep, there were stones and boulders everywhere and every surface was covered in a variety of mosses and lichens in shades of green ranging from grey to bright yellow. Jerry had to cling on to branches to prevent himself from slipping.

Good.

He passed the first path directly down to the boathouse from the cottage, but fought his way through the wood to a second narrower route, which Jerry knew the old man liked to take. Having read *Death At Wyvis* many times, it didn't surprise Jerry that Alastair wanted to avoid the boathouse.

When he reached the second path, he scrambled up it for a few yards until he arrived at a slightly flatter point, just above some rocks. Perfect.

He sat on a fallen trunk, took out his field glasses, focused on a non-existent woodpecker and waited.

After about twenty minutes he heard the sound of boots on rock and heavy breathing below him. He peered down and saw the top of the old man's head making its way slowly up the slope, the scar clearly visible through his close-cropped white hair. The old man was finding it difficult, but he was determined. He slipped and swore, then continued his climb until he was almost upon Jerry. The old man was concentrating so much on where he was putting his feet that he hadn't noticed him.

'Alastair! Hi! That's some climb you're doing there.'

The old man looked up, saw Jerry and smiled. He continued the last few steps, panting heavily, and joined Jerry.

'Whew!' he said. 'That's not easy at my age.'

'I'm impressed!' said Jerry. 'I'll be happy if I am half as fit as you when I'm eighty.'

'What were you looking at?' the old man said, nodding to the binoculars.

'Woodpecker. Great spotted, I think.'

'I didn't hear him.'

'Didn't you?' said Jerry, realizing he had made a minor mistake. But it didn't really matter what he said to the old man, because this time he would make quite sure that the old man would never get the chance to repeat it.

The slope below was perfect. One push and the old man would tumble ten to fifteen feet down the path, banging his head on several likely rocks on the way. This time Jerry would follow him down to make sure he was dead, and not just unconscious.

And then he would raise the alarm, probably by running up to Culzie. A thorough forensic analysis was highly unlikely – who wouldn't believe that the old man had slipped and fallen on such difficult terrain? – but there were bound to be traces of Jerry's presence, a presence that could best be explained by him discovering the body.

The trouble was that the old man had moved a couple of feet away from the path and was resting against a tree trunk. From that position, Jerry could probably lift him bodily and fling him down the slope. But the old man might cling to his sleeve, or start yelling, or create some signs of a struggle. A clean push would be much better. Which meant the old man would have to be persuaded to budge a foot or two.

Jerry whipped his binoculars up to his eyes and pointed them at a tree lower down. 'Yes! Look! Down there!'

'What is it?' The old man was still panting, reluctant to move.

Jerry almost said 'woodpecker', but something more was needed. 'A golden eagle. Man, is he beautiful! Here. Take a look.'

He held the binoculars out for the old man to come and get.

Just then he heard a car heading up the track above the pathway towards Culzie.

The old man took the glasses. Jerry took a step back.

The car stopped. The engine cut out. Jerry heard a car door slam.

Now! If he pushed now, the old man would hurtle down the slope. He might cry out, which would alert whoever was on the track above. That would be OK – the sound of someone slipping and falling. But Jerry wouldn't get the chance to finish off the old man if he had to.

Better wait for whoever it was to walk off, wherever he was planning to go.

The old man was scanning the trees. 'I don't see anything.'

Above them, Jerry could clearly hear the sound of someone descending the path. In a few moments Terry MacInnes appeared.

'Ah, it's you two!' he said. 'I didn't know who it was in the woods.'

'Hey there, Terry!' said Jerry, hiding a flash of frustration. Come on – did the guy really think they were poachers?

'Jerry.' The stalker nodded at him and then approached the old man, who put down his binoculars. 'Dr Cunningham. It's good to see you up and about.'

The old man smiled. 'I'm sorry, I'm afraid I have no memory of who you are. But my guess is you are Sheila's husband, the stalker?'

'Aye, that's me. Sheila told me all about your amnesia.'

The moment was lost. Jerry was furious; it was all he could do to restrain himself from tossing them both down the path. He bade them goodbye and set off down through the trees towards the loch. He hurried back to the car and his own cottage as soon as he could.

He went straight to the gun cupboard and unlocked it. He took down the rifle and the box of ammunition.

No more pissing about. He needed to be certain and he needed to be fast.

'Hello!'

Clémence put the photograph album down beside the sofa. 'Hi!'

'It's crowded out there,' the old man called from the hallway. 'I saw Jerry, and then Terry MacInnes, Sheila's husband. Nice chap, really, but a bit taciturn—'

He came into the sitting room and saw their guest. He smiled.

'Madeleine! How good it is to see you! Thank you for coming all this way.'

Madeleine hesitated and then kissed him on both cheeks. 'Hello, Alastair,' she said. 'I am glad to see you looking so well.'

Madeleine's accent when speaking English – heavy French with American vowels – took Clémence by surprise. Suddenly she seemed like a foreigner, whereas while they had both been speaking French they had seemed very much of the same family.

'And thank you for persuading Clémence to look after me,' said the old man. 'She has been fantastic.'

He stood there, his grey hair dishevelled by the wind, his craggy cheeks ruddy from the cold, smiling at both of them. Clémence couldn't help thinking he looked adorable.

'She is fantastic,' said Madeleine smiling at Clémence. 'I have heard you are making good progress. Do you recognize me?'

'No. But we have been reading *Death At Wyvis;* I'm sure you have read it. But it means that I feel I know you. I've heard all about you, and I can remember you as a young woman. So you are almost a familiar face. And you have no idea how nice that is.'

Madeleine smiled, but without her habitual warmth. 'Yes, I have read that book.'

'I'm sure there is a lot you can tell me about the mystery that is my life,' said the old man. 'But perhaps we ought to finish the book first. Would you like to join us?'

'Oh, no,' said Madeleine. 'I couldn't bear it.'

'Oh, I'm sorry,' said the old man. 'Of course not. You have travelled thousands of miles to get here. We can read it later. Tonight perhaps, or tomorrow?' He glanced at Clémence.

Or never, perhaps, thought Clémence. She was scared of what was in there.

Madeleine looked at the old man and the young woman. And she sighed.

'No. I think you are right. We cannot have a proper conversation until you both know what is in that book. I suggest Clémence reads it now. And I will stay and listen.'

Clémence and the old man exchanged glances. Like her, he seemed to know that whatever was in that book was bad. And, like her, he couldn't hide from it.

'All right,' said Clémence, picking up the novel and taking her place in the armchair.

She opened the book, and began to read.

CHAPTER IX

Wyvis

Knaresborough, West Riding of Yorkshire, June 1959

IT WAS ONLY a brisk ten-minute walk from the surgery on the high street to my little house overlooking the river and under-looking the railway viaduct. I liked to nip back home for lunch, believing the break from the surgery did me good. I felt a glow of satisfaction from my last patient of the morning, a four-year-old boy who had made a complete recovery from meningitis. When I had been called out to the boy's home two weeks before, I had been sure I was going to lose him.

There were two envelopes on the mat, a missive from the RAC and a letter from New York. Nathan and I had kept up a steady correspondence for many years now, writing back and forth every couple of months. They were long letters, which mixed anecdote and gossip with more profound thoughts on the direction our lives were taking, and the choices we were making. We had taken to discussing our work: I described interesting patients or awkward problems with my partners at the practice, and Nathan wrestled with the opportunities and risks of the swiftly growing oil business. I derived a deep pleasure from the correspondence, and I knew that Nathan did too.

I made myself a ham-and-cheese sandwich with Mrs Clapham's home-made piccalilli and opened the letter. It was uncharacter-istically short.

Dear Angus,

*I am visiting Scotland in August on business and thought I
would bring Madeleine with me. We will go on to visit her
family in France afterward. I don't know if you have heard,
but Stephen and Sophie are returning to England next month
– frankly I think his career in Hollywood is finished. Did you
see* Partners in Grime? *It was dire. Anyway, we have been
discussing some kind of vacation for all of us, plus Tony if
he will come. Apparently, Stephen's father has inherited an
estate in the Highlands, and Stephen suggested we could all
stay there. It's a place called Wyvis, and it's not far from
Inverness. The dates would be August 18–24.*

*What do you think? I hope you will just say yes right away
this time and I won't have to persuade you. But, if necessary,
I will!*

Let me know, so Stephen can organize things.

Yours,
Nathan

Why not? I usually didn't take time off in the school holidays;
my two partners had school-aged children and I was happy to let
them have first choice of dates, but I was pretty sure they should
both be back at work by the middle of August.

I had seen Nathan the year before, when I had travelled down
to London to meet him on one of his business trips, and we had
lunched at the Savoy. And Madeleine and Nathan had stayed
with me in Knaresborough in 1955. But I hadn't seen Stephen
since Capri.

Nor Sophie.

I had been tempted to visit Sophie in 1947 right after Capri.

Stephen was in Hollywood, and she was in Twickenham with the children. I had been so tempted.

But I had promised. If I had tried to see her then, and she had let me, her family would have been blown apart. I would have had Sophie for myself, but I had promised, and after the fool I had made of myself before the war, I wanted to keep that promise. I had gone to great lengths to do so, even becoming engaged to Gillian, the student nurse at Bart's. Fortunately for both of us, I had eventually realized that avoiding the temptation of another woman was a really bad reason for marriage, and the engagement had fizzled out.

But now, twelve years later, it would be safe to meet. Sophie would be forty-three now: fat probably, matronly. Stephen, I knew, was still handsome, but in his last film his dangerous charm had changed subtly to aggressive smarm. It would be good to see them, and Tony, whom a bored Elaine had left three years before. No mention of her.

I grabbed pen and writing paper and dashed off a quick reply. Yes, I would love to come.

I took the sleeper up to Inverness and then on to the little station of Novar, which was actually in the village of Evanton. There I was pleased to see Nathan and a chubby Tony waiting for me.

'Thought we'd both come down and get you,' said Nathan, pumping my hand. 'Like the last time.' He was tanned, his neat dark hair was flecked with grey at the edges, although his moustache was still black and his brown eyes as sharp as ever. He was wearing a light tweed suit but with plus fours, not a kilt, thank God; I wasn't sure I could have stood Nathan in a kilt. Tony was wearing slacks, an old cotton shirt and a big grin.

Nathan carried my bag to an old Bentley parked in the small station car park.

'This is very grand,' I said. 'Is it yours?' I could see Nathan owning a Bentley, but I didn't see how he could have got a car to Britain.

'No, it comes with the estate. It belongs to Stephen's father. One of the ghillies doubles as a chauffeur, but I persuaded him to let me drive it.'

'I don't remember Stephen talking about a Scottish estate.' Stephen's family had made its fortune in the previous century out of polish and related cleaning goods. This had bought them a manor house in Wiltshire and Stephen his education at Eton and Oxford, but he hadn't mentioned any visits to the Highlands.

'His father inherited it ten years ago from Stephen's great-uncle. I think Stephen has only been there a couple of times.'

'It was good of his father to let us have it.'

'Oh, I'm renting it for the week,' said Nathan. I raised my eyebrows; that seemed a touch mercenary on the part of Stephen's family.

'Don't worry – it's fine,' said Nathan. 'In fact, I think it's a great idea. And the estate staff are pleased as punch to have the English laird's film-star son here. We plan to go stalking tomorrow. Do they do that kind of thing in Yorkshire?'

'No. Massacring birds is their thing,' I said.

Nathan piloted the Bentley through Evanton, and up a steep wooded glen. 'That's the River Glass down there,' he said. 'It flows down from Loch Glass and Wyvis Lodge.'

'What on earth are you doing in Scotland?' I asked. 'There's no oil up here, is there?'

'There may well be. In the North Sea. And there's definitely gas. It might be the next bonanza, if we can figure out how to get it out. I've been talking to geologists, trying to decide whether Wakefield Oil should get involved.'

'Bit of a risk, isn't it?'

Nathan grinned. 'Absolutely. But, like I'm always telling you, the oil business is all about risk: if you don't take risk, you don't make money. The trick is to take the right risks, and to make sure they don't bankrupt you if they go wrong.'

Wakefield Oil was not going bankrupt. Five years before, I had found a way of investing five hundred pounds of my savings in the stock of the company quoted on the New York Stock Exchange, since when it had quadrupled. I wasn't planning to sell; I would stick with Nathan.

'How's Capri, Tony?' I asked. 'I hope you are still painting?'

'Definitely. But it's quite a while since I painted a rotten eggplant. I'm selling a bunch of pictures to the tourists. They pay top dollar, especially the Germans.'

'I'm sorry to hear about Elaine.'

'I'm not,' said Tony. 'She gave me an ultimatum. Get a proper job and leave Capri, or she would walk out. Wasn't a difficult decision, really. Now she's making some other sap unhappy; a lawyer in Chicago. And I have a housekeeper called Luciana. A widow from the war.' Tony grinned. 'She sees to my needs.'

'Capri really is an island of sin, isn't it?' said Nathan.

'Oh I don't know. She's happy. I'm happy. Life's OK.'

We crossed the River Glass on a wooden bridge right next to a lodge, and entered the estate. Eventually we broke out of the woods and Loch Glass and Ben Wyvis opened up before us. It was a warm day and the heather glowed orange in the August sun. I had always loved the moors in Yorkshire, and this one made my heart sing. If this weather held up, it would be a tremendous few days.

We drove along the edge of the water, a deep royal blue in the sunshine, rounded a curve to the left and arrived at a large Victorian stockbroker's house, squatting at the head of the loch twenty yards back from the water. As we pulled up, a burly young man hurried up to the car to carry my small bag.

The house's decoration mixed Victorian bourgeois and Scottish laird. A magnificent twelve-pointer red deer stag glared at William Morris prints and Chinese vases in the hallway. There was dark wood and heavy curtains, and a few haphazard portraits of people who weren't called Trickett-Smith. It was very comfortable: more than that it was luxurious, especially for somewhere so isolated.

Madeleine, Sophie and Stephen were waiting for me in the drawing room. Madeleine had put on a little more weight every time I had seen her, but she was still a beautiful woman. Unlike Madeleine, Sophie had given birth to children – three of them – yet she was not matronly at all; in fact her figure was just as I remembered it. Her face was lined, but her eyes were still large and blue and wistful. The freckles were still there. And she was very pleased to see me.

As was Stephen, who shook my hand and clapped me on the back. He was probably the one who had changed most: jowls had appeared around his neck, and wrinkles pointed downwards from his impressive nose, lengthening his face. Sadness and anger combined to produce a sort of melancholy bitterness. He was still good-looking, there was no doubt about that, but if you were a cinema-goer, you would want the heroine to fall for the other chap.

'I read *Trail of the Scorpion*,' he said to me. 'We both did. It was in all the bookstores in America. I never realized you had been in so many tight scrapes during the war! I really didn't think you were going to make it through the desert.'

'Neither did I,' I said. 'And poor Binns never did, remember.'

Corporal Binns had collapsed on the third day of our trek away from Gazala. The other soldier, Sergeant Gill, and I had tried to carry him, but had been unable to. So we had left him to die. There had been no choice. Or there had been a choice: die with him, or live without him. Gill and I had decided to live.

Four days later we had bumped into a Rhodesian Long Range Desert Group patrol and been driven back to the Allied lines. But Corporal Binns's body remained in the desert. It was that choice, that decision, that had sat with me two years later when I was in the German prison camp. It was why I had eventually written a book. And it was probably why the book had sold so well. The reader couldn't help asking himself, what would I have done?

'Why did you call it a novel?' asked Nathan. 'Is it fiction?'

'Not really. I made up some of the conversations, where I couldn't remember what people actually said, or even some of the details of what happened. But I now realize that almost everyone who writes a memoir does that.'

'And they are making a movie, I hear?' said Stephen.

'Yes. They've written the script and they are planning to start filming in November. I think they are going to do the desert scenes in Morocco.'

'Who is going to play you?' asked Nathan.

'They plan to ask Richard Crowther,' I said. Richard Crowther was a big British actor who had just starred in a film about the Malta convoys. But as I spoke, the obvious question arose. 'Would you do it, Stephen? I can always ask.'

'That would be swell!' said Nathan. 'Imagine Stephen playing Angus!'

'He'd probably be better at it than me,' I said. Actually, I found the thought of Stephen playing me on the screen a bit creepy. But the producer would probably say no anyway, and if he said yes, that was his problem. I was uncomfortable with the whole idea of seeing myself portrayed on film, and had almost turned down the studio's offer. I had no intention of watching it.

'I'd give it a go,' said Stephen. 'It would be fun.'

'I'll ask them then,' I said.

'So what's it like being famous?' said Sophie.

'I'm not really famous,' I said. 'I'm not like Stephen – no one knows what I look like. The patients like it, those of them that know. And the money was useful. I invested some of it in Wakefield Oil, which was a good idea.'

Nathan grinned. 'I hope that's working out well for you?'

'Very well, thank you, Nathan. Keep up the good work.'

'Did you see Nathan's profile in *Fortune* magazine last year?' said Tony. '"The new breed of American oil baron". All these famous people I know!'

No one said anything. Within a couple of seconds, the silence switched from accidental to awkward, as everyone remembered Tony's desire to become a celebrated artist.

Tony laughed. 'I know what you are all thinking. I wanted to be the next Picasso. But Alden was wrong: it was never going to happen. I just don't have the talent. But I'm OK with that. I love painting. I love Capri. And now Elaine's gone, I love my life. I do miss Alden, though. And I still have him to thank for setting me up.'

'As do I,' said Nathan.

'Yeah, but I'm sure Wakefield Oil has done better with you in charge.'

'Much better,' said Madeleine. 'The other stockholders all love him.'

'Are you going to write another book, Angus?'

'Oh, no. One is enough. And I don't plan to have any more experiences like that to merit it. But there was something satisfying about getting it all down on paper. It sort of worked it out of my system. The fact people want to read it is a bonus.'

We ate a light lunch, prepared by the stalker's wife, Mrs Ferguson, and spent the afternoon lazing outside on the lawn in front of the house, reading and chatting. Tony plunged into the loch, but the shock of the cold water had him screaming, and he was out within thirty seconds. He said the water was invigorating, but no one believed him. He just looked in pain.

It was a magnificent spot: the loch with its graceful curve, the ancient woods tumbling down to its shore, and the brown- and red-flanked mountains. There was not another habitation in sight: the isolation was absolute. The heat of the August afternoon settled on the water and created a bluish haze that hung round the tops of Ben Wyvis.

'How high do you think that is?' said Sophie.

'Five thousand feet?' said Tony.

'Three thousand feet?' said Stephen. 'Four? There's nothing in Scotland much higher than four thousand.'

'Ben Nevis is four thousand four hundred,' I said.

'Trust you to know that,' said Stephen.

'I'd like to have a go at it tomorrow,' said Sophie. 'Will anyone join me?'

'We're supposed to be going stalking tomorrow,' said Stephen.

'But not the girls,' said Madeleine. 'Or even if we are, we spent our childhoods avoiding hunting deer. Papa loves killing deer, and Sophie and I don't. But there is no chance that I will climb that mountain either.'

'I'll go with you,' I said.

'Don't you want to come stalking?' said Stephen.

'Maybe another day. I would like to conquer Ben Wyvis. There is a little bit of the Edmund Hillary in me, and he's demanding a challenge.'

Sophie smiled at me. 'Thanks, Angus. Maybe we can ask Mrs Ferguson for a packed lunch.'

Stephen looked at his wife and at me. 'I'll check with the stalker to make sure you don't scare the deer.'

Dinner was a formal affair. Stephen had warned everyone to bring dinner jackets, and he or his father had somehow rustled up a butler, Macpherson, from a neighbouring estate.

The effort was worth it. The dining room was beautiful: silver and polished mahogany glimmering in the candlelight, with the evening light slipping away from the loch outside the large windows. The heather on the higher moorland burned a dramatic orange in the evening sun, while the loch slumbered a serene grey.

The two sisters looked gorgeous: Madeleine wore an expensive gown and serious jewels; Sophie's yellow dress was much simpler. Stephen took his place at the head of the table, and acted as host. Nathan, who was the real host, was happy to let him do it. Sleek and composed, attentive rather than ostentatious, Nathan seemed comfortable with his considerable wealth and power, so comfortable he didn't have the urge to flaunt it, especially among friends. But the butler loved Stephen, who acted the true aristocrat, even if he wasn't quite. The food was good; the drink flowed. It was all rather fun.

Everyone was drinking, but Stephen was drinking fastest. The butler was happy to keep him topped up.

'Is there anyone you should have brought up here with you, Angus?' he asked.

'Not at the moment, no,' I said.

'I'm surprised,' said Stephen. 'I'd have thought a country doctor would be a real catch.'

'I'm probably too set in my ways for anyone to live with me now,' I said, making sure that I didn't look at Sophie as I did so. That wasn't quite correct. There had been a few girlfriends, but I hadn't wanted to share the rest of my life with any of them, and as I and they had got older, fending them off from marriage had become tiresome. These days, in my forties, I didn't even bother to start the process.

'What about you, Tony?'

'Tony has Luciana,' said Nathan.

'She should have come along,' said Madeleine.

Tony grinned. 'I'm not sure she would have liked it. She's quite particular about cooking. I doubt Scottish cuisine is her thing.'

'No, seriously,' said Madeleine. 'You should have brought her with you. Next time, she's definitely invited.'

'Hold on,' said Stephen. 'She's Tony's housekeeper. I'm sure she's a very good cook, but it would hardly be appropriate.'

'What do you mean, not appropriate?' said Madeleine. 'It would be lovely. And besides, who would care all the way up here?'

'The servants, for one,' said Stephen. 'And me. And Sophie.'

'Don't be absurd, Stephen,' said Sophie. 'It would be wonderful to meet her, Tony.'

'I'm not being absurd!' said Stephen. 'She's a bloody house-keeper, for God's sake. It would be all wrong. Sometimes I think you French let standards slip. Or have you been in America too long?'

Madeleine laughed. 'Stephen, you have met Papa. He would never let standards slip. The poor man still hasn't recovered from us marrying foreigners. And commoners at that.'

Stephen glared at his sister-in-law. He did not see himself as a commoner, whatever a minor French aristocrat might think. 'I'm sure he wouldn't have invited Tony's housekeeper to his chateau.'

'Don't be such an ass, Stephen,' I said, allowing my slight Yorkshire accent to broaden. 'If you can all put up with an oik like me, then you can put up with Luciana. What's her pasta like, Tony?'

'Out of this world,' said Tony. 'You should come back to Capri to try some.'

He beamed at Stephen with such bonhomie that Stephen was forced to smile back. 'That's an excellent idea.'

The pudding was cleared, a rhubarb crumble, and Sophie spoke. 'Madeleine and I will leave you alone to enjoy your port.'

'Oh, no you don't,' said Nathan. 'And before you start, Stephen, I have something I want to say to all of you, and I think it would be best said over a glass of port.'

Stephen looked as if he was about to protest, but decided not to. He nodded to the butler, who returned a moment later with a decanter and a humidor. The other three men selected cigars, I pulled out my pipe and Sophie and Madeleine lit cigarettes. The decanter whizzed around the table.

'I have an ulterior motive for bringing you together here,' said Nathan. 'A secondary motive. The first is, it is wonderful to see all of you together. It's been far too long.'

'Hear, hear,' said Stephen, knocking back his port and refilling his glass.

'But something has come up that we need to think about and discuss. It relates to poor Alden's death.'

The table went quiet.

'Elaine has remarried. Her husband is a lawyer called Francis Brockman. Elaine told him what really happened to poor Alden, and he is of the opinion that as a result Alden's will should be challenged.'

'What, so she gets half the money?'

'He claims Alden's share of Wakefield Oil should have been divided equally between all the cousins and shouldn't have gone to me alone.'

'But that's appalling!' said Stephen. 'How can she do that? We all agreed to stick to the same story. Is she going to admit she lied?'

'Yes. And she is going to say that she was only sixteen and we all put pressure on her.'

'But you saved my life, Nathan! I'm convinced Alden was going to cut my throat. Tony, can you speak to her?'

Tony laughed. 'I could. It would just make things worse.'

'Can't you control your wife?'

Tony puffed at his cigar. 'Honestly? No. Never could.'

Stephen snorted in disgust. 'How can we stop her?'

'I've thought about this hard,' said Nathan. 'And I've spoken to lawyers. We can't stop her. If she decides to tell a court that she saw me kill Alden, we can't stop her.'

'Can you buy her off?' said Stephen.

'If it was just Elaine, I could maybe give her a gift of something to keep her sweet. But this guy Brockman would view that as a sign of weakness.' Nathan sipped his port. 'There is something we can do, but that involves your cooperation. All of you.'

'What is it?' I asked.

'Tell whoever asks that Elaine is lying. Say that she was only sixteen and she was drunk. Say she's just making it up. Four adults against one drunk child. They will believe us.'

'I'll do it,' said Stephen right away.

'So will I,' said Tony, much less enthusiastically. He avoided Nathan's eyes, and stared at the ruby liquid in his crystal port glass. I remembered how Tony had initially been reluctant to go along with the plan.

'Angus? It was your idea after all?'

Nathan was right. Having lied once, we would have to lie again. It was an inevitable consequence of taking that decision over twenty years ago. 'And me,' I said.

'Madeleine wasn't there, so it's easy for her to back us up. That leaves Sophie?'

Sophie slumped back in her chair and stared at her glass of port.

'Sophie?'

'I'm not going to lie under oath.'

'Oh, come on, Sophie!' said Stephen. 'That's ridiculous!'

'You won't have to,' said Nathan. 'You'll be lying to a lawyer. A greedy lawyer at that. He doesn't care half as much about Alden as we do. He didn't even know him; he just wants the money.'

'No, I know,' said Sophie. 'It's just that someone's death is serious. It's not the kind of thing you should lie about. We shouldn't have lied in the first place.'

'Sophie, you have to stick with the story,' said Stephen. His voice was commanding. Aggressive. Threatening.

'She doesn't have to,' said Nathan, calmly. 'But I hope she will choose to. There is no one who regrets Alden's death more than me. Every day, I wish I hadn't killed him. Stephen shouldn't have picked up the sword in the first place. Alden shouldn't have taken the "duel" so seriously. There is a lot we got wrong. But not lying. We all know it was an accident. It wasn't murder, and if the French police had arrested me, that would have been wrong. Unjust. Wouldn't it, Sophie?'

'They might have agreed it was an accident,' she said.

'Maybe. Maybe not. Sadly, I don't think you can necessarily trust the police in murder investigations, especially when there are foreigners involved. It would have been too easy for them to solve the crime and lock me up. Or chop off my head.'

'I suppose you're right,' said Sophie, still fiddling with her glass.

'So will you support me? Us?'

'I'm not saying I won't,' said Sophie. 'But I'm not saying I will, either. I need to think about it.'

'Don't worry, Nathan,' said Stephen. 'She'll do what she should.'

Nathan ignored him. 'Have a think about it, Sophie,' he said. 'You've got all week.'

Sophie smiled her thanks. It seemed to me that Nathan's approach was more likely to work than Stephen's. It also seemed that now we all had no choice, even Sophie. But I did admire her attempt to be honest.

CHAPTER X

The Boathouse

IT HAD PROBABLY been a mistake to drink so much port. At least that's what we all thought as we rose early the following morning for a day on the hills. Ferguson, the stalker, was initially put out that he had to change his initial plan to stalk the Wyvis Forest beat, but the beat further up Glen Glass would be almost as good. He lent me an Ordnance Survey map and pointed out a good circular route to climb the mountain via Fiaclach to the east, and then to descend further to the west, avoiding most of the bogs. It was going to be quite a hike. Mrs Ferguson provided us all with packed lunches, and Stephen, Tony and Nathan set off up the glen with Ferguson, his son Iain and two garrons – highland ponies who would carry the deer carcasses back to the game larder. Sophie and I headed the other way down the track along the shore of the loch.

After a couple of hundred yards we came to a wooden boat-house, and a little further beyond that we struck uphill on a narrow path through a wood. We passed a cottage in a clearing, no doubt housing one of the estate workers, and continued climbing, until we were out of the woods and on to the moor.

It was a sunny day and warm, but as we emerged from the wood the beauty of the wide open moor before us injected us both with a burst of energy, and we made rapid progress. Loch Glass opened up beneath us, and the dramatic rocky face of Meall Mòr opposite. The moorland was not the plain smooth lawn of heather it appeared from below, but a series of tussocks, peat bogs, hollows and hillocks, criss-crossed by burns and gullies. Grasses, bog-myrtle, cloudberries, thyme, dwarf birch and juniper battled with the heather for space. The contrasting scents of baked earth, sweet heather and boggy roots jostled our nostrils.

'I've never been to Scotland before,' said Sophie. 'It's magnificent. Stephen came up here once with the boys to go stalking with his father just after his father inherited the estate, but I took Beatrice to France to see my parents. We should have come too.'

'How old are they now?' Angus asked.

'Fabrice is sixteen, Beatrice is fourteen and Rupert's eleven. And they hate the idea of coming back to England.'

'Why is that?'

'They all go to English boarding schools. Stephen insists on that, even though we can't really afford them any more. But they love the vacations in California. They've got masses of friends, and kids in America have so much more fun than English kids. Fabrice's girlfriend drives a T-bird. I suspect that won't happen back here.'

'No. A Vespa maybe,' I admitted. 'Bicycle more likely. What about you? How do you feel about it?'

'We have to leave. Stephen needs to get away from Hollywood. He drinks too much, he takes too many drugs, these days everyone thinks he's a washed-up has-been. I'm hoping if he comes back to England he can start afresh. Frankly, we are running out of money, so there isn't much choice. I thought I might try teaching French at a school somewhere.'

'You'd be good at that,' I said. 'Your English is perfect.'

'I'd like to teach. But let's not talk about Stephen. It's rather nice being up here away from him.'

We continued up a steep incline to the crag of Fiaclach, and followed a long ridge which led up to the summit of Ben Wyvis itself. The sunshine, the views, the air and Sophie instilled a profound sense of euphoria in me. I was happy; I was truly happy.

The ground was flat enough for Sophie to stride along next to me. She was smiling too. She caught my eye and held my hand.

After four hours of hard work, we reached the summit of Ben Wyvis, which the map said was actually 3,400 feet high. This high up, the heather had given way to a soft matting of a kind of woolly moss. Below us to the north was Loch Glass and Wyvis Lodge. To the east was the Cromarty Firth and the Black Isle, with Inverness in the distance. And to the west were mountains, fifty miles of Scottish mountains. Much closer by, below the southern slopes of Ben Wyvis, lay the village of Garve and the road to Ullapool. Exhausted, we sat on some rocks and broke out our lunch. Despite the sunshine, it was pleasantly cool this far up, especially once our heart rates had slowed.

We were hungry, and the roast beef sandwiches tasted really good.

'I don't know what to do about Alden,' Sophie said.

'We don't have a choice.'

'We do have a choice, it's just a difficult one.'

I munched my sandwich. 'Lies are like that, aren't they?'

'What do you mean?'

'Well, you tell one, and that works out fine. But then you have to tell another and another, and pretty soon you have committed yourself to lying for the rest of your life.'

'That's precisely it!' said Sophie. 'That's what I don't want to do.'

'I fear you've done it already,' I said. 'We all have.'

Sophie didn't answer.

'Can I confess something to you?' I said. 'You're a Catholic, you understand confession.'

'I'm not a priest,' said Sophie.

'No,' I said. 'But I have to tell someone. And telling you way up here seems safe.'

'What is it? I'm intrigued.'

'*Trail of the Scorpion* isn't strictly true,' I said. 'In one important respect. That's why I called it a novel.'

'Leaving Corporal Binns in the desert?'

'Yes.' I stared out over the far mountains. 'He couldn't walk any more. So we tried to carry him.'

'That's in the book.'

'Yes. But I say we both tried. The truth is Sergeant Gill gave up after half a mile. He said Binns was too heavy, we were going too slowly, we would soon get tired and all three of us collapse. I said we had to carry Binns. So I tried to carry him by myself.'

'Could you?'

'Not really.'

'And what did Sergeant Gill do?'

'He went on ahead. And it was true, of course, he was much faster.'

'So what did you do?'

I took a swig of ginger beer from a bottle. 'I carried on. Until Gill was almost out of sight.' I paused. 'Then I lost my nerve. I shouted to him to wait. And I hurried after him.'

'Leaving Corporal Binns alone?'

I nodded. 'I made him comfortable against some rocks, so he would be visible from a distance if anyone came that way.'

'Did he say anything?'

'He said: "Please stay, sir. Don't leave me." He could barely speak.'

'And you left him anyway?'

I winced. 'When the LRDG patrol picked us up, I tried to persuade them to drive off and look for him, but they wouldn't. They had their own mission. He was never found, as far as I know. Missing, presumed dead.'

'But in your book, you say that you and Gill agreed what to do?'

'That's right. And that's what I reported back when we reached headquarters. But it was a lie. When I wrote the manuscript, I described things as they really happened, but I decided to show it to Gill. I thought it was all very well for me to make public what I had done, but I would be ruining his reputation as well.'

'And he didn't like it?'

'Not one bit. He works as a foreman in a textile factory in Leeds now. He wanted me not to publish anything, but I refused to do that. So we compromised on the story that you have read. And I called it a novel.'

Sophie reached out and grasped my hand. 'I'm glad you did leave the poor man,' she said. 'Otherwise you wouldn't be here.'

'No,' I said. 'I know I made the right decision. Gill was right – we would never have made it to the patrol if we had both carried him.'

'At least you tried,' said Sophie.

'I tried.' I took another swig of ginger beer. 'But I think my urge to tell people what happened, even if it isn't quite the truth, came from what we did after Alden's death. I will always feel guilty about that: it was my idea.'

'Me too,' said Sophie.

I needed to explain more. I wanted to explain more.

'At first I thought that the pleasure I felt writing the memoir was the joy of the creative process or some such thing. And writing the book while I had been a medical student at Bart's brought me a lot of pleasure. Except it wasn't really pleasure, it was comfort. It was peace.

'I've always thought of myself as a strong character, someone able to deal with disturbing events and not let them damage me. But I had been dishonest about the deaths of two people, Alden and then Corporal Binns, and my dishonesty was something I denied to myself. I didn't erase it, but I locked it up in a cupboard

209

in the corner of my mind where it couldn't get at me. It was still there, though, creating a tension, an anxiety that was always bubbling in the background. I learned to live with it to the point that I almost didn't notice it.

'So when I wrote *Trail of the Scorpion*, it was as if I were taking these difficult decisions I had made, possibly mistaken decisions, out of that cupboard in the corner and examining them. And in doing so I was learning to live with them; for moments, while I was writing, I felt at peace with them. Does that make any sense?'

'I think so,' said Sophie.

'They are still there though. They won't go away.'

We sat in silence for a while, watching the view shimmer in front of us. Then Sophie leaned forward and kissed me. Not hard – very gently.

She broke away, smiled, and got to her feet. 'It's a long way down, we had better get going.'

Neither of us said anything for half an hour or so. The descent was tricky, it was hard to pick a way through the bogs, which were sprouting pale red cloudberries, and it required concentration.

Eventually we came to a flatter stretch by a small loch, where we picked up a stalker's path skirting the summit, and we could walk side by side. Sophie spoke.

'You remember when Stephen went to Hollywood and I was still in Twickenham with the kids?'

'Yes.'

'I thought you would come and see me then.'

'I said I wouldn't.'

'I know you did. And I'm glad you didn't. But I always sort of hoped you would.'

I smiled. 'I almost sort of hoped I would too,' I said. 'It was iron discipline.'

'It would have messed everything up,' Sophie said. 'Everything.'

'I know.'

'Anyway. Turned out I was pregnant with Rupert so that wouldn't have been much fun.'

I walked on.

'Sorry, Angus. Do you mind me talking to you like this?'

'No.' Although the inevitable question was rising in my mind. Had I been right to keep my promise? In a way Sophie was suggesting I hadn't been. But then she was also saying she was glad I had kept away. She was clearly just as torn as me, and that was nice to know.

'Do you mind if I ask you something?' she said. 'Something that is personal and definitely none of my business.'

'No,' I said, intrigued.

'Why haven't you got married?'

'Oh, I don't know. I almost did, right when you were hoping I would nip over to Twickenham to see you. A girl called Gillian – she was nice. It never came to anything.'

'And then afterwards?'

'I just didn't come across the right person.'

'I see. I've just been worried . . . No. It's stupid to say it.'

'Go on,' I said. 'It's too late now.'

'I'm just worried that you didn't get married because of me.'

'No,' I said. 'No, it wasn't that at all. I know you're married and you want to stay that way. And now I'm older and set in my ways, I just don't fancy it. Marriage.'

Sophie stopped and faced me, her face clouded with worry. 'Are you sure?'

'Quite sure,' I said. It was nice just to reassure her. She smiled in relief and happiness.

We stood on the hillside just looking at each other – for how long? I had no idea. Then Sophie reached up and kissed me again, softly. I held her.

'I'm sorry, Angus, I know I shouldn't do this, but I want to. It won't matter, will it? Up here?'

'No,' I whispered. 'It won't matter.'

I felt the desire raging within me, threatening to overwhelm me. I kissed her again, hard.

Eventually she broke away. Her face was shining. 'Do you mind if this is all we do? Kiss.'

'No,' I said, my voice croaking. I did mind, I minded desperately. The memories of the Villa Fersen flooded back to me from twelve years before. But I also wanted to make Sophie happy. And Sophie was very happy. She was so beautiful when she was happy.

The others had had a long and successful day crawling round the bogs and burns of the upper reaches of Glen Glass. They had shot two stags, which we had seen in the distance slung over the back of the garrons as they made their way down the glen back to Wyvis Lodge. The stalker had ensured that both Nathan and Stephen had kills. Tony had missed twice. But they had all enjoyed themselves. They were tired. And thirsty.

My heart was bursting. The hard physical exercise, the clear air, the astounding views and most of all, a day with Sophie, had left me ecstatic. There was no other way of describing it. I might be a middle-aged country doctor, but I didn't feel like one. I felt like the undergraduate who had first set eyes on Sophie in Paris twenty years before. I could tell from her shining eyes and wide smile that she felt the same way too. I hoped that in the general jollity Stephen hadn't noticed anything.

I, though, was very aware of Sophie, observing her every movement. During cocktails in the drawing room before dinner I noticed Nathan having a quiet conversation with her out of Stephen's earshot. Although I couldn't hear the words, I could tell from the apologetic shake of her head what Sophie was saying – she was not going to lie about Alden's death. Although Nathan seemed to take it well while he was talking to Sophie, afterwards he stood apart from the others, staring out over the loch, deep in thought.

Sophie's decision was going to be a problem. But just at that moment, I didn't care.

We drank, copiously and fast. By dinner we were all drunk. The butler was happy to top us up.

Stephen drank more than the rest of us, but for most of the evening, he seemed the most sober. A function of capacity. When the port arrived – no attempt to banish the ladies this time – I slowed my drinking down. I was content just to watch Sophie, her skin glowing in the candlelight, which danced on her fair hair.

I wanted her. I wanted her so badly.

I was wrong when I had told Sophie on the mountain that the reason I was forty-three and unmarried had nothing to do with her. I had misled her, but no more than I had misled myself over the years. I didn't want to admit to myself that I was incapable of loving anyone else. But the truth was obvious: I had never met a woman as good as her, nor was I ever going to.

I wanted her. And I knew she wanted me.

Madeleine, who was sitting next to me, leaned over. 'It's nice to see Sophie so happy, isn't it?'

I turned to see what she meant by that. She knew. I wasn't sure *what* exactly she knew, I wasn't sure what there was to know, but Madeleine knew how much I meant to Sophie and Sophie meant to me. And she approved.

'Yes,' I said. 'It is.'

She smiled and turned to Nathan and Tony, who had become involved in a long and complicated discussion about the race to get the first man in space, something about which Nathan knew a lot and Tony virtually nothing.

'What about Mars?' she asked. 'When will there be a man on Mars?'

There was a thud. Stephen's head had rocked forward and hit the table, somehow missing the plates. It emitted a hissing sub-snore.

'Oh, dear,' said Tony.

'It might be time to go to bed,' said Nathan.

'Can someone give me a hand?' said Sophie.

Tony and I carried Stephen up to his and Sophie's bedroom. As I heaved him on to the mattress and untied his shoelaces, I glanced at Sophie. I had done this before, in Capri. And I remembered very clearly what had happened next.

Sophie gave me a small smile. She was remembering the same thing.

The household went to bed as Macpherson and Mrs Ferguson cleared up, with the help of her burly son.

I lay on my bed, fully clothed. And waited. I could hear the noises in the kitchen. About ten minutes after they had fallen quiet, I slipped downstairs, and out of the front door.

It was silly really. I had no real reason to think that Sophie would be there waiting for me, apart from the smile on her face as we were putting Stephen to bed.

And the memory of the Villa Fersen.

I couldn't see anyone. There was a half moon, and the loch glimmered gently. Meall Mòr rose steep and dark on the left, and black trees swarmed up the hillside on the right. I could see Ben Wyvis, high above, silhouetted against the soft black-blue sky.

I walked down to the loch. And then I heard movement. A figure emerged from beside a rhododendron bush.

It was her.

'I *knew* you'd come,' she said.

'How long were you waiting?'

'Only five minutes. I nipped out after I'd heard the staff finishing in the kitchen.'

We were too close to the house; someone could easily see us. 'Shall we walk along the loch?'

'Good idea,' said Sophie, and she slipped her hand in mine.

We walked down the short drive and along the track that ran beside the loch. We could see quite clearly in the moonlight, reflected off the flat grey water. Sophie was a little drunk, but only a little. I could feel the excitement through her fingers.

'What we really need is a Scottish Villa Fersen,' said Sophie.

'And there it is,' I said, pointing to the wooden boathouse.

'Do you think it has an opium den?'

'Bound to,' I said. 'Let's just hope it isn't locked.'

It wasn't. And if we left the door wide open, just enough light entered the shed for us to see inside. A tall rack rose from the floor to the ceiling, on which we could just make out three rowing boats.

'I think these are cushions!' Sophie said. 'Yes, they are!'

She spread them out on the wooden floor of the boathouse. Then she turned to me. I was desperate to grab her, to tear all her clothes off, but I forced myself just to stand and stare at her. My eyes were adjusting to the greater gloom. I could make out her hair, her chin, her upper lip and a glimmer from one of her eyes. She reached up and kissed me.

The self-control went. From both of us. In seconds we were naked and writhing on the cushions in the floor of the boathouse.

'Whew!' said Sophie, laughing, as I rolled off her. 'That was quick!'

'It was rather,' I said. 'Sorry about that.'

'That's OK,' Sophie laughed. 'As long as you promise not to start snoring in thirty seconds.'

'I promise,' I said, propping myself up on my elbow and running my finger over Sophie's body. There was no chance I was going to sleep and miss this.

'I know it's dark, but I can see your smile,' said Sophie.

'Good,' I said. I started tracing complicated patterns over her skin with my finger. She giggled, and then she gasped.

I felt confident. More than confident. Supreme. 'You have to come with me.'

'Come with you?' said Sophie. 'Where?'

'I don't know. Anywhere. I'm a doctor. I can be a doctor anywhere.'

'You mean leave Stephen?'

'Of course I mean leave Stephen. We have to be together. I know it. You know it. Tell me you don't feel it.'

Sophie sat up on her knees. 'Don't spoil it all, Angus.'

My supreme confidence faltered. 'You don't mean you're going to stay with him? Not after this?'

'Yes. Yes!' she said more loudly. 'We've talked about all this before. I can't leave my husband. I can't destroy my family. It's a sin. I believe it's a sin.'

'Look, I understand that. We don't have to get married. You can remain married to Stephen. But you would live with me.'

'And the children?'

'They would live with me also. Or I with them.'

'You've never met them.'

'I'm sure I will like them.'

'How can you say that?'

'Because they are *your* children. Of course, I will like them. I'll probably grow to love them.'

'No. No, Angus!' I could make out Sophie's head shaking in the darkness. 'We said before, just the once. And you respected that.'

'And now we've done it again! Is this "just the once" again?'

'Yes,' said Sophie. 'No. Oh, I don't know! Can't you just make this easy, Angus?'

I lay on my back. Anger was seeping into my soul, leaking

out of the love that had filled my heart a few minutes before and enveloping it, drowning it.

'You have been part of me my whole adult life, Sophie. Since I first saw you. Or maybe not then, maybe when we spent that afternoon in Honfleur.'

'I was lusting after Stephen then.'

Her comment irritated me, and I ignored it. 'Yes. And that first time we spent in Capri, I behaved badly. That didn't work. So then, the next time, I behaved well. I didn't throw a tantrum. I didn't come and see you in Twickenham. I respected your request to leave your marriage undisturbed.'

'You did. Thank you.'

'But that didn't work either! It might have worked for you, but I'm not convinced of that. I think you wanted me to come and rescue you from Stephen and Twickenham. I don't know. But I know I can't live without you. That sounds corny, but I've tried it, and I know it's true. I can exist, I can have odd moments of happiness, I can make sick people better, but I can't *live*, truly live.'

'Oh, Angus.'

'No. Listen! You were dead right when you feared that the reason I couldn't get married is you. I deny it, but I'm only deceiving myself. It's you. It's always you. It's only you!'

Sophie sat in silence.

'Whew,' she said eventually.

'So will you come with me?'

She took a long, shaky, breath in. 'No. No, I'm sorry, Angus. I won't destroy my marriage. This was a big mistake.'

'It wasn't a big mistake! It was one of the most important nights of my life. And yours! Tell me it wasn't important to you!'

'Yes,' said Sophie. She was beginning to sob now. 'Yes. But you're sounding like Nathan now. Pressurizing me to do something wrong.'

'It's nothing like Nathan!' I said, the fury spilling over. 'And it's not wrong, it's right. That's the whole point. It is the right thing to do.'

'It's not,' said Sophie. 'I would like it to be, but my conscience tells me it's not.'

I jumped to my feet and pulled on my clothes as quickly as I could, ignoring buttons and buckles. 'Then go to Stephen, Sophie! You don't want me to see you again, fine, I won't. But don't try and claim coming with me is wrong, when we both know it's the *only* right thing to do.'

I stumbled out of the boathouse, leaving Sophie sobbing naked behind me. For a moment I thought of turning back towards Wyvis Lodge, but I wanted to get away. Away. So I turned left and strode along the shore of loch, tucking myself in as I went.

Woods tumbled down the slope to the edge of the water. On an impulse I struck uphill along the path through the trees we had followed that morning. An owl mocked my progress. But as I climbed, my anger abated. Perhaps I should go back. Apologize. Work out how I could see Sophie again, without necessarily touching her. See how I could live on her terms. Because I sure as hell couldn't live without her.

I came to the cottage in the clearing, shut up for the night. I stopped at the edge of the woods. A thought wormed its way into my brain, an evil, malicious thought that found purchase and swelled.

Sophie had dominated my life. But more than that, she had ruined it. She had taken advantage of me the whole time. Everything was always done on her terms. Yes, she liked me, that was obvious, but I clearly wasn't as important to her as she was to me. Sometimes her self-control slipped, and she helped herself to me, like a forbidden chocolate, but most of the time she lived a perfectly normal bourgeois life without me. She had a husband and children and she wasn't prepared to give them up for me.

She had taken from me. Taken, taken, taken! And never given, unless you counted giving me a little of what I wanted once every ten years, and that didn't sound to me like giving. She had taken consistent, cynical advantage of me.

I turned on my heel, the anger burning. I would tell her that. If she was in the boathouse, I would tell her. If she had gone back to Stephen's bedroom I would tell her there. I didn't care. I had never felt so angry in my life before. Part of me wondered at the anger: it must have something to do with all that desire repressed for so long. And now she expected me to repress it again. For how long this time? Ten years? Twenty? Until Stephen drank himself to death at the age of seventy-five?

The flames in my heart roared. I couldn't live without her. She shouldn't live without me.

CHAPTER XI

Justice Undone

I OPENED MY EYES. It was light outside, and the birds were yelling at me. My head hurt. I was lying on top of my bed in my trousers and shirt sleeves.

I was going to be sick!

I rolled out of bed and lumbered to the lavatory at the end of the landing, only just making it in time. I heaved and retched. And again. And a third time.

God my head hurt!

I stumbled back to my room, aware of Tony staring at me from an open bedroom door.

'Are you all right, Angus?'

I waved him away, collapsed on the bed and shut my eyes.

I awoke again later. I had no idea how much later. The light through the curtains was fuller, brighter, and the birds were making a little less of a racket. The headache was still there, though.

And I was going to be sick again.

I ran to the lavatory and only just made it; vomit went everywhere.

Christ this was some hangover! The worst I had ever had, and I had had some in my youth with Stephen. I ran my fingers through my hair and felt a large bump on my crown. There was a scab there as well. I examined the sick-spattered lavatory bowl in front of me.

Projectile vomiting.

I was a doctor, I knew the signs, and I recognized them from my rugby career. I was suffering from concussion. But how did I get it?

Then it came flooding back. The climb up Ben Wyvis. The dinner. The walk with Sophie by the side of the loch. The boat-house. The argument. And then . . .

Then what?

I tried to clean up the lavatory as best I could, washed my face, brushed my teeth and put on some fresh clothes. My head felt as if it was floating a couple of feet above my body as I descended the stairs to breakfast.

They were all there, waiting for me. All except Sophie.

'Boy, you look rough!' said Nathan.

'You look so pale!' said Madeleine.

'You didn't seem very well first thing this morning,' said Tony.

'I wasn't,' I said. 'In fact I don't feel too marvellous now. Perhaps just a cup of tea for breakfast.'

'Nonsense!' said Nathan. 'You need food for a hangover.'

'Do you think Macpherson has one of those Jeeves-type hang-over cures?' said Tony. 'I've always wanted to try one of those. You certainly look like you could use it, Angus.'

I blew through my cheeks. Until I could unscramble my brain, it seemed best to go along with the hangover idea.

'All right. Breakfast it is.'

'Kippers, this morning,' Nathan said. 'I must admit I have never understood what you British see in kippers.'

At that moment, I agreed with him.

'Have you seen Sophie?' Stephen asked me. He wasn't looking too good either.

'Er. No,' I said.

'She's not in your room, is she?'

The breakfast table was silent. Tony opened his mouth to protest, but everyone around the table knew it was a fair question.

'No,' I said, answering the question asked and keeping to that.

'Are you sure?'

'Of course I'm sure. You'd think I'd notice if she was, wouldn't I? And believe me, no one would want to have slept in my room last night.' I could tell that sounded credible. 'Go and check, Stephen! I know you want to!'

Stephen left the breakfast table. He reappeared a minute later. 'Not there. I can't think where she has got to.'

'Maybe she got up early and went for a walk along the loch,' said Madeleine.

'I didn't hear her come in last night. I don't think her side of the bed has been slept in.'

'We put you to bed last night, Stephen,' said Nathan. 'You had no idea what was going on.'

'Well, I got up to look for her,' Stephen said. 'The one place I didn't look was Angus's room.'

Madeleine frowned. She glanced at me. 'Was her dress in your room, Stephen? She was wearing the yellow one last night. Perhaps I should check?'

The stalker's Land Rover pulled up outside and I heard the sound of footsteps on the gravel. In a moment Ferguson appeared. He looked grim.

'What is it, Ferguson?' Stephen asked.

Ferguson looked at the assembly, hesitating. Then he decided to speak. 'It's your wife, Mr Trickett-Smith. I've just found her in the loch as I was driving up here. I'm sorry, sir. She's drowned.'

The first on the scene was the local Evanton bobby, PC MacArthur. He asked us all very simple questions about who

Sophie was and when we had last seen her alive. Then he began organizing prodigious amounts of tea for everyone, especially himself, while they waited for CID from Dingwall.

I lied. I told PC MacArthur that I had last seen Sophie when I had helped put Stephen to bed. I had gone to bed myself, and woken up very early the next morning with a bad hangover.

I lied because I couldn't think straight, I could barely think at all. At first my brain had simply been unable to process what Ferguson had said: that Sophie was dead. I couldn't believe it; in my befuddled state I couldn't even understand it.

Stephen could. His face was stricken with horror, horror which crumbled into misery. Madeleine could. Within a couple of seconds of Ferguson telling her, she began to sob. The sob turned into a wail, verging on a scream. Tony looked shocked. Only Nathan kept his wits about him.

But then Sophie's death forced its way into my cranium, like an approaching army, a gentle drumbeat becoming louder and louder, until it reached a crescendo, surrounding my damaged brain, breaking its way in, overwhelming me.

She was dead! Sophie was dead. I would never see her again. I would never touch her, hear her, I would never even know that she was existing on a continent far away with her children and her husband.

My head hurt, really badly. I felt sick. I wanted to cry out, like Madeleine. But Sophie was Stephen's wife; it would be terrible if Stephen found out that the last thing his wife had done before she had died was sleep with one of his oldest friends.

I rushed to the lavatory and vomited. Again. People noticed. They looked at me with either horror or sympathy I couldn't tell. I knew the concussion was bad and I needed sleep in a darkened room, but I wasn't sure whether I would be able to manage it. I excused myself, saying I needed to be alone, crept into my room, closed the curtains and flopped onto the bed. I need not have worried; within moments my brain shut down and I was asleep.

I was woken by banging on my bedroom door. I heard Madeleine calling out my name and then I heard her come in and felt her nudge my shoulder. 'Angus! Wake up! You have to wake up! The police want to talk to you.'

My brain felt cloudy, but the pain had eased off. My stomach was churning but empty – I was glad I hadn't had time to ingest any of the kippers.

I sat up and remembered Sophie was dead.

Stunned, I turned to Madeleine.

'Get up! You have to get up!'

I did as I was told; I was still fully clothed.

'Oh, Angus!' Madeleine said, her eyes red. 'The police say Sophie was murdered! Someone killed her, Angus!'

She grabbed me and hugged me tight. Behind her a uniformed police constable coughed.

I blinked. 'Murdered?'

Madeleine took me downstairs. 'We've all been answering questions. You are the last.'

'Murdered? Murdered?'

Madeleine led me into the little library which looked out over the walled garden at the side of the house. Two detectives in plain clothes waited for me. The smaller of the two, a dapper little man wearing a three-piece tweed suit with a watch chain, held out his hand.

'Dr Culzie? I'm Detective Inspector Dewar, and this is Detective Sergeant Brown. We have some questions for you about Mrs Trickett-Smith's murder.'

They were sitting in armchairs, but they had pulled out the

chair from the writing desk for their interviewees to sit on. I slumped onto it.

'Murder?' I said. 'I thought she drowned.'

'So did the stalker who found her, but her neck showed signs of strangulation. We won't know with a hundred-per-cent certainty until the post-mortem, but for the moment we are treating it as a murder.'

'Where was she found?'

'In the loch, snagged on the branch of a fallen tree, by the woods on the southern side.'

Just beyond the boathouse.

I tried to think. Think quickly. I couldn't remember what had happened the night before. I had already lied about creeping out to see Sophie, and if I told them the truth about that, then I would instantly be their chief suspect. And I knew I hadn't killed Sophie.

So – keep it simple. Keep it consistent.

'Can you tell me when you last saw Mrs Trickett-Smith?'

I kept it simple: I lied again. I told them I had last seen Sophie when we had put Stephen to bed. I told them I had gone to bed myself. I said I was drunk and was suffering from an unusually severe hangover; I had not been woken by anything in the night.

Inspector Dewar listened closely. He had small bright-blue eyes that seemed to dance over my face, taking in everything. I felt wretched, worse than wretched. I was sure I looked it too, but actually, that might help my credibility.

'Now, Dr Culzie. Were you having an affair with Mrs Trickett-Smith?'

A small part of my brain cleared. I needed to tell the truth, the whole truth and nothing but the truth, at least up to the point I had first gone to bed the night before. I had no idea what the others would say, what they knew, what they might speculate. Who knew what Stephen suspected? Or Madeleine for that matter; Sophie might have confided in her.

I took in a deep breath. 'Do you want a short answer or a long answer?'

Inspector Dewar's eyes darted all over my face before he answered. 'Both.'

'Well, the short answer is "no".'

'And the long answer?'

I spent several minutes describing how I had first met Sophie in Paris, about Normandy, about our disastrous meeting in Capri before the war, and about our return there in 1947. I implied, without being specific, that something had happened in the Villa Fersen. I explained how Sophie and I had gone twelve years without seeing each other, until just then. And how, on Ben Wyvis the previous afternoon, I had kissed her.

'Nothing more than a kiss?'

'No,' I said.

'Are you sure?'

'Quite sure.'

'Didn't you want to?'

I nodded. 'I wanted to.'

'But Mrs Trickett-Smith wouldn't let you?'

I felt a flash of irritation at the way the policeman insisted on calling Sophie 'Mrs Trickett-Smith', as if emphasizing the fact she was first and foremost someone else's wife, but I controlled it. I could tell Dewar had noticed, though.

'No, she wouldn't.'

'Did that frustrate you?'

'A little, yes. But I wasn't surprised. Sophie had made me promise not to touch her.'

'And then she touched you?'

'Yes,' I said.

'That must have been frustrating. Didn't you feel like insisting?'

Suddenly I understood what the inspector was suggesting.

'No,' I said. 'I would never harm her. I respected her wishes after Capri. I respected her wishes on the mountain. She was never going to leave Stephen and I understood that.'

'I see,' said Dewar. I watched the policeman study me. I let him. I was telling the truth, at least in everything up to putting Stephen to bed, and I was pretty sure the policeman could see that.

'What about Mr Trickett-Smith?' Dewar asked. 'Did he suspect there was anything going on between you and his wife?'

'No. At least not that I am aware of. He knew how much she meant to me when he took her.'

'Took her?'

'Won her. I don't know, wooed her. But Stephen thought he was the best man and he had won. He was always confident of his effect on women. I think he knew she liked me, but we saw very little of each other.'

'What about here? At Wyvis?'

'He didn't seem too bothered that we climbed the mountain together. So, no, I don't think he did suspect anything.'

'And this morning?'

I glanced at the policeman. I didn't want to drop Stephen into anything unnecessarily, but the others had all heard his accusation at breakfast.

'This morning, Stephen asked whether Sophie was in my room. He said he had checked the whole house in the middle of the night and couldn't find her, so that was the only place he could think of.'

'So that suggests he *was* suspicious?'

I hesitated. 'I suppose it does, doesn't it?' I admitted. 'But that was just this morning.'

'Is there anything that happened between last night and this morning to make Stephen jealous?' Dewar asked.

That was a good question, and one that I was not prepared to answer. 'I can't think of anything,' I said eventually.

The policemen let me go. The others were in the drawing room, and I knew I had to face them. At least my headache felt a bit better.

Stephen and Madeleine looked miserable, in their different ways. Tony was distraught. Only Nathan seemed calm. He remained at his wife's side.

'I'm sorry, old man,' Stephen said to me. 'For accusing you of having Sophie in your room. I don't know what I was thinking.'

'Don't worry about it, Stephen,' I said. 'I'm just so sorry about what happened to her.'

We all looked at each other in silence. I could tell everyone was thinking the same thing, but couldn't say it. We had been in this situation before, over twenty years before. This was so much worse, at least as far as I was concerned, as it was for Stephen and Madeleine. Although Madeleine had lost a husband in Alden, Sophie meant so much more to her.

At least this time the others didn't have to worry about getting their stories straight. I did: I was lying, seriously lying, and I had to decide quickly whether that was a good idea. I could still change my mind. I probably should; the police deserved all the help they could get to find Sophie's murderer. It would be tough for Stephen, who would inevitably find out from the police that I had slept with his wife shortly before she died.

But before I said anything, I needed to think.

'I'm just going to get some air,' I said.

Outside, the sun was glittering off the loch, and a trio of puffy little clouds drifted through the pale-blue sky. It was a beautiful day. I turned away from the loch and the boathouse, away from the police cars and the uniforms, and strode up the broad boulder-strewn glen along the River Glass. My head was clearer than it had been all morning.

Who had killed Sophie?

I had absolutely no idea.

How had I sustained the bump on my head?

Presumably the murderer had hit me.

Where? When?

I didn't know.

I walked along the footpath beside the fast-running stream. Above me, about half a mile up the hillside to the right, just below an old sheep fold, I saw a stag and three hinds. One of the hinds raised her nose and sniffed the wind. Then she turned, spotted me and loped off, followed by the others.

Would the police believe me? That I couldn't remember what had happened? It was the truth, so presumably they would. I could put my faith in the British justice system, surely. Not only could I, it was my duty to.

They might think I did it. That I had killed Sophie: forced myself upon her, perhaps, or lost my temper with her.

Well, if they thought that, so be it. The truth would out, *I* knew I hadn't killed her.

I stopped short. Except I didn't know that, I didn't know that at all. I had no idea whether I had killed Sophie or not. How could I know? The last thing I could remember was striding off to confront her in a burning fury. Perhaps it wasn't the killer who hit me on the head. Perhaps it was Sophie, while we were struggling. I knew that concussion was not necessarily a result of immediate loss of consciousness; it could kick in seconds or minutes after a blow had been sustained.

I sat on a flat stone on the bank of the burn, put my head in my hands, and wept.

When I returned to Wyvis Lodge, Stephen was being questioned in the library. Everyone in the drawing room looked grave.

'What's going on?' I asked Nathan.

'Stephen lied to the cops.'

'What about?'

'The stupid idiot said he didn't go outside last night. He woke up, saw Sophie wasn't there and searched the house. Trouble was, I had told the cops I heard him shouting and saw him on the lawn by the front of the house. And when the Fergusons' son was setting off home on his bike, he saw Stephen in the garden. Then the police found a footprint in the boathouse which matches Stephen's shoe. So now they are asking him some more questions.'

'They can't think he killed Sophie, can they?' I said.

Nathan shrugged. 'Jealous husband. It's been known.'

It was remarkable that the footprint had matched Stephen's shoe and not mine. Lucky. I considered rushing to tell the police that I had been in the boathouse with Sophie. But that would just put me in the frame. And it would hardly help Stephen: only give them a stronger suspicion that Stephen had discovered his wife having an affair with me. I certainly couldn't disprove that Stephen was outside looking for Sophie. In fact, it sounded most likely that it was Stephen who had hit me over the head.

So I just stayed quiet.

They arrested Stephen. In due course there was a trial at the High Court in Edinburgh. Further forensic evidence was produced to show not only that Stephen had been in the boathouse, but also that that was where Sophie had been killed. She had been dumped in the loch a few yards away, and her body had drifted down to the woods. The post-mortem showed that Sophie had been strangled, and that she had had sexual intercourse just before she died. The police accused Stephen of that too.

I had testified at the trial. I had managed to tell the truth the whole time. No one asked me whether I had been in the boathouse with Sophie, which was a big mistake on the part of

Stephen's advocate; I had been unable to decide how I would respond if asked a direct question under oath.

Stephen's story was that he had awoken, found Sophie missing, and had gone to look for her. He saw that the French windows out to the lawn were ajar, and decided she must have gone outside, possibly to meet me. He had blundered around the gardens, before noticing that the door to the boathouse was hanging open. He had found cushions on the floor there, but no sign of Sophie. So he had stumbled back to bed.

He said that he had initially lied to Inspector Dewar to avoid casting suspicion on himself. It had been foolish and he regretted it.

The prosecution had poured scorn on this, although it seemed perfectly plausible to me; it was pretty close to my own thought process after all. What really did for Stephen was his lack of interest in defending himself. Although he denied he had killed Sophie, it was a half-hearted denial. He behaved as if he deserved to be punished for her death.

He convinced me. I was pretty sure that it was Stephen who had killed Sophie, and had hit me over the head either just before or just afterwards. The prosecution alleged that Stephen had effectively raped Sophie before killing her. I knew that wasn't true, but it was for murder Stephen was on trial – marital rape was not a crime – and it was for murder that he deserved to go to prison.

That's what the jury felt. Fortunately, the offence was classified as 'non-capital homicide', and Stephen was sent to gaol for the rest of his life, rather than to the hangman.

Part of being a good GP is being able to listen to your patients and to listen closely. I was normally very good at all that, but two weeks after Stephen had been sentenced I was in my surgery listening to Mrs Watkins, the seventy-year-old lollipop lady at the

231

primary school, explain the mysterious pain in her side, when I realized that I had taken nothing in. I played for time, reaching for my stethoscope and asking her to lift her blouse up for me, but I was as worried about me as about her. Concentration was becoming impossible, my thoughts these days were constantly diverted from my work and my patients to the loch and the trial, to Sophie and Stephen.

Like Stephen, I felt dead inside. Now Sophie was gone, life had lost much of its purpose. Part of me blamed Stephen – I told myself I was convinced that Stephen had killed her – but part of me, a part that I wouldn't recognize even to myself, forgave Stephen. I felt so guilty myself. If Sophie and I had continued to show restraint she would still be alive. Stephen's suspicions had been entirely accurate. Of course Stephen was wrong to kill her, and I would be wrong to forgive Stephen. And yet . . .

There was something else. I was not completely sure that I hadn't killed Sophie.

And, as time went on, I came increasingly to believe that I had.

The dreams started a couple of months after Stephen's trial. Sophie was naked in the boathouse and I was on top of her. But I wasn't making love to her; I had my hands around her throat.

The dreams changed and varied. She struggled. She hit me with an oar. I dropped her into the loch.

Then the dreams appeared during the day. I would be waiting for my next patient in my surgery, and I would suddenly see Sophie beneath me, my fingers around her neck.

These weren't dreams. They were memories. The fragments coalesced, until about a year after Sophie's death, I was convinced that I had killed her.

The knowledge shattered me. The morally courageous thing to do was to tell the police, but my moral courage had long gone.

I tried to continue at my practice in Knaresborough; I was as safe or unsafe there as anywhere else, but I couldn't.

I woke up at five one morning, after a particularly vivid dream. There was a copy of *The Lancet* on my bedside table, open at the classifieds at the back. My eyes fell on an advertisement for British doctors wanted in Western Australia. I got out of bed right then, and sent off the application. Three months later, I found myself aboard RMS *Strathaird*, bound for Fremantle.

But Sophie lingered in her little patch of ground in the de Parzac churchyard in the Loire, and Stephen in his cell in Wormwood Scrubs.

And I knew I had put both of them there.

Afterword

Although this book is closely based on fact, I have decided to call it a novel. Certain details have been changed and omitted, and some dialogue has been invented. But the essential truth remains: Stephen Trickett-Smith did not murder his wife at Wyvis in August 1959. I believe I did.

The years since then have been a nightmare for me. Every day I think of Sophie and my part in her death. Every day I think of Stephen in prison somewhere in Britain. I have built a new life here in Australia, I have married a woman who knows nothing of what is written here, but I have learned that it is impossible to build a new life without recognizing and accepting what happened in the old one.

I don't know if I believe in heaven or not. But I do know that I believe in hell, and I am living in it. As anyone who has read this book will agree, that is exactly where I deserve to be.

Almost two years ago, I wrote a tentative letter to the police in Dingwall, suggesting that there might have been a miscarriage of justice. Their reply gave me the strong impression that they would prefer to let sleeping dogs lie. So I have decided to write this 'novel' in the hope that it might free Stephen from prison, and just possibly free me from hell. I may well end up in a British prison myself, but that is as it should be.

When I first met Sophie de Parzac that afternoon in Paris forty years ago, I felt my life would never be the same again.

I was right.

Angus Culzie, Mundaring, Western Australia, 1973.

PART TWO

12

'I'm so sorry.' The old man's voice was hoarse. Clémence looked up at him. Two tears, one after the other, were running crookedly down the wrinkles etched in his cheek. 'I'm sorry, Clémence. Will you forgive me?'

As she had been reading the last pages of *Death At Wyvis,* Clémence had felt the anger rise within her. She had tried to keep it out of her voice, but she could hear her own repressed fury as the words came out. It was all she could do to finish the afterword at the end. Angus – Alastair – had slept with his best friend's wife, had murdered her and had let that friend go to jail for it. He had lied to the police and to his companions. Not only had he ruined Clémence's grandfather's life, but the consequences had flowed down the generations to her father and herself.

And yet, looking at the crumpled eighty-three-year-old sitting in front of her, a lost man who had just discovered he was a murderer, she couldn't help feeling a flash of sympathy.

She knew she couldn't answer his question. But she could look him in the eye, and she did so. 'Shouldn't you be asking Aunt Madeleine that?'

The old man nodded. 'Yes, of course,' he said. He turned to Madeleine.

The old woman looked stricken by what she had just heard. Until then, her energetic great-aunt had never struck Clémence as frail, but Uncle Nathan's death had taken its toll, sapping her resilience. And now this.

But Madeleine set her shoulders and raised head. 'I don't think I can ever forgive you, Alastair. Sophie was a wonderful girl – and a wonderful woman. Reading that book, you get a sense of the effect she had on you, but she had that effect on everyone she knew. She lit up a room; she lit up a family. She made life better for everyone who knew her, including me. I still miss her; I'll always miss her. Her death was very wrong.'

Madeleine stared hard at the old man. 'But it was a long time ago. I have learned to live with the knowledge, not just that you murdered my sister, but that you were never punished for it.'

'Why wasn't I?' the old man asked. 'Why didn't I go to jail? Why aren't I still in jail?'

'You got a good lawyer,' said Madeleine. 'A top Scottish QC. He advised you to retract what you had written in the novel. He argued that you couldn't remember what had happened, that you were only guessing. He said the book was called a novel for a reason.'

'And I went along with that?'

'No. You insisted on pleading guilty. A trial date was set, but the QC persuaded the prosecution that they had no case, so they dropped it. You were furious, but there was nothing you could do. Legally, you didn't actually know for sure that you were guilty, so your plea was unreliable, and without that the prosecution had no other firm evidence implicating you. In the end, the lawyer persuaded you to accept it.'

'So Stephen stayed in jail?'

'Oh, no. They let him out. He had already served fifteen years.'

'So no one has been found guilty of Sophie's murder?'

'No. But the police have closed the case. They think it was you. We all think it was you.'

'I see,' said the old man.

'I wondered where you had found the money to pay the lawyers' fees. It was only later that I discovered that Nathan had paid them. He said he owed you for getting him out of trouble in Deauville. I was furious with him.'

238

'Did they reopen Alden's death?'

'The French police weren't interested. It was too long ago; there was some kind of statute of limitations for murder under French law, and after everything that went on in my country during the war, the authorities were very reluctant to reopen any cases from before 1945. A British journalist wrote an article in a Sunday newspaper, but Nathan sued him successfully. Since then no one mentions it. And it does come across as an accident in the book.'

'Which it was,' said the old man.

Clémence stared at him.

'I know it means nothing at this stage,' he said. 'But I am truly sorry. To both of you. For what I have done.'

They sat in silence. Clémence knew that he meant it, with all his heart. The confused, vulnerable old man she had met in the hospital a few days before had had no idea he was a murderer. But he was. She could feel sorry for him, but she couldn't forgive him.

'There's something else,' the old man said.

'What?' said Clémence. But she knew immediately what he was thinking. She wished he hadn't realized it, that she hadn't realized it, that she hadn't told Madeleine, that she could just deny it to herself.

'You are my granddaughter. Your father Rupert must be my son. Right after Capri, Sophie became pregnant. That was with Rupert, wasn't it?'

Clémence dropped her eyes and nodded.

'Did you know all along?' The old man's sad eyes held a hint of accusation.

'I only worked it out this morning,' said Clémence. 'Look.'

She picked up the photograph album that she and Madeleine had been looking at when the old man returned from his walk, and opened it at the photographs of Oxford. 'See this photo of you here? Where you are in profile? You look exactly like my dad. Same nose. Same forehead. Doesn't he, Aunt Madeleine? And Dad has a cleft chin, like you.'

Madeleine nodded. 'It's true.'

'Did you remember knowing that you were Dad's father?' Clémence asked.

'No, I guessed it from the timing. And let's just say I'm not surprised that we are related.' The old man smiled at Clémence. 'I am proud you are my granddaughter. Although . . .' He swallowed. 'Although I am ashamed too. Bitterly ashamed. That your grandfather is a murderer.'

'I think I'll stick with Stephen as my grandfather, if you don't mind.' said Clémence, letting the anger harden her voice. 'He was innocent. You might have put him in jail, but you can't take him away from me.'

'Of course,' said the old man. 'I couldn't do that.'

'I knew nothing about any of this!' Clémence protested. 'I didn't even know Grandpa had ever been in prison. I knew he'd been in films a long time ago, and I was vaguely aware there had been some sort of scandal, but I thought that had something to do with drink. And I believed my grandmother had drowned. No one told me *anything*!' Her eyes were alight as she glared at the old man, and at her aunt. 'At least now I know why my family is so fucked up. Why didn't anyone tell me, Aunt Madeleine? Why didn't you tell me?'

'I am so sorry, darling,' Madeleine said. 'I did suggest that your father explain everything to you. But he had spent fifteen years hating his own father because he believed he had murdered his mother. That's why he ran away to Morocco. He had a troubled time in his twenties, you probably knew that.'

Clémence nodded. She did. In her teens she had come to understand that in her family drugs were an issue for the parents and not the child.

'And your mother just wanted to protect you from it all. I can understand why. I think the only reason she let me see you was that I paid for your education.' Madeleine smiled. 'I was worried about you. About your parents' unconventional lives. But you turned out very well.'

A thought struck Clémence. 'Once the book came out, did everyone else realize I was Alastair's granddaughter?'

'Nathan and I knew all along,' said Madeleine. 'But Stephen never suspected. I don't think it was a question of being in denial, I think it never occurred to him. And from what I can tell, Rupert was the same.'

'What about me?' asked the old man. 'Did I know?'

'We never discussed it,' said Madeleine. 'But you were no fool. I bet you knew.'

'So when you visited us in Morocco when I was little, you knew you were my grandfather?' said Clémence.

'Apparently,' said the old man. 'And presumably I thought that your father was my son.'

'That must have been weird.'

'Rupert was furious,' Madeleine said. 'He didn't know you were his father, but he had read the book, so he did know you had killed his mother. He told me you showed up out of the blue. He only let you stay a few hours – the whole thing was terribly awkward.'

'Do you remember any of that?' Clémence asked.

The old man frowned, but shook his head. 'Just the beach. And the camel.' He allowed himself a quick smile. 'And you.' He turned to Madeleine. 'What did I do afterwards? After 1959?'

'You ran away to Australia. You ended up working as a doctor in a small town in the hills above Perth. You married a woman called Helen in 1968, I think. We came to your wedding in Perth.'

'What was she like?'

'Small. Blonde. At least ten years younger than you. Very pretty. A little bossy, Nathan and I thought.'

'And we got divorced?'

'After *Death At Wyvis* was published. I don't think she liked being married to a murderer. I can't blame her, really.'

'No,' said the old man.

'Is Tony still alive?' asked Clémence. 'No one has ever mentioned his name to me.'

'He died five years ago on Capri. A heart attack. He never did marry Luciana, but she was with him at the end. Nathan and I went to his funeral. It seemed like the whole island was there.'

'He sounded like a nice guy,' said Clémence.

'He was,' said Madeleine. 'Elaine wasn't, though. She drank herself to death some time in the seventies. She and her husband tried to make a fuss about Alden's death in 1959 but Nathan's lawyers shut them up. After the book came out, Elaine was quoted in that article in the British Sunday newspaper, but when Nathan sued successfully, she had to keep quiet. She died soon afterwards.'

'How did the book sell?' the old man asked.

'It caused a little bit of a stir when it came out. It was published here but not in the States, nor in Australia, actually. But it's been out of print for years. I don't think the publisher even exists any more.'

'I wonder why I came back to Britain last year,' said the old man. 'Do you know?'

Madeleine closed her eyes. 'I'm sorry, Alastair, this has taken it out of me. I'm beat. Can we talk about something else until Davie gets back? I will tell you what I know, I promise. But maybe tomorrow?'

'Actually, there is someone we need to see in Dingwall,' said Clémence, thinking of Pauline Ferguson, the old stalker's wife. 'So maybe we can drop into your hotel tomorrow morning?'

'Yes, why don't you do that?'

'I'll make you a cup of tea,' said the old man, but just as he was speaking, they heard the sound of a car drawing up outside.

'That'll be your taxi,' said Clémence.

'Good,' said Madeleine, hauling herself out of the sofa with a grunt. 'I'll see you both tomorrow.'

As Clémence saw her great-aunt to the door, the old man escaped to the lavatory. He was dying for a pee, and he also wanted to be by himself, if only for a minute or two. He knew he deserved the contempt and disgust of Madeleine and Clémence, but it was good to get away from it for a minute. He lifted the lid, unzipped his fly, and let go. He raised his eyes to the small window.

Something moved.

It was something long and thin in a bush up the wooded slope about thirty yards from the cottage.

It was the barrel of a rifle.

The old man's sight wasn't too bad at distance. He squinted. The barrel moved again, and he could see a face. A bearded face. Jerry Ranger.

13

The American was staring at the front of the cottage, where the old man could hear Madeleine bidding goodbye to her niece. The old man flinched as Jerry glanced quickly at the cottage, and then back at the taxi outside the front door. The old man was pretty sure that Jerry hadn't spotted him in the tiny window.

He zipped himself up and hurried out of the lavatory. Clémence was shutting the front door in the hallway.

'Clémence!' the old man said in a loud whisper. 'That American is outside with a rifle! I know this sounds silly, but he looks like he's staking out the cottage.'

Clémence frowned. 'That's ridiculous. He must be stalking a deer or something.'

'It really didn't look like it,' said the old man. Although maybe that was what he was doing when he was interrupted by the taxi arriving to pick up Madeleine. No. That didn't seem right.

Uncertainty crossed Clémence's face. 'I had a weird conversation with him this morning. About you. And he had a copy of *Death At Wyvis* on his bookshelf with notes and underlinings in his own hand-writing. Yet he said he'd never read it.'

The old man and Clémence exchanged glances. The uncertainty each felt fed off the other.

'I know we are going to look foolish, but maybe we should sneak out the back. Just in case.'

Clémence hesitated. Then she nodded. 'OK.'

'Lock the front door. And get your coat. In case we are outside for a while.'

Clémence locked the door and then ran up the stairs to her room. The old man pulled on his boots and grabbed his own coat from the hook in the hallway. Clémence joined him and they moved towards the back door.

The doorbell rang.

'Who is it?' Clémence called.

'It's Jerry!'

Clémence hesitated and then shouted. 'I'm in the bath. Wait two minutes and I'll be down!'

Not bad, thought the old man, although Jerry would be able to figure out it was unlikely Clémence could have jumped into the bath that quickly after her aunt left. But it should give them a minute, maybe two. And from his position outside the front door Jerry couldn't see the back of the house.

Quietly the old man opened the back door and they slipped out. They moved as rapidly as the old man could over the scruffy back lawn to the trees at the rear of the garden. They climbed up the slope, and paused at the crest of a small bank, on the other side of which a burn ran down through the woods towards the loch.

'Let's wait here and watch,' said the old man. 'If he goes away, we will know we just imagined it.'

'All right,' said Clémence. 'He probably will.'

They crouched down and watched the cottage. 'Do you think we're being silly?' Clémence said.

'I won't tell anyone if you don't,' said the old man with a grin.

'Clémence!' They heard Jerry's voice ringing out. 'Clémence, are you OK?'

'Of course I'm OK,' muttered Clémence to herself. 'I'm getting out of the bath. Be patient!'

But Jerry wasn't patient. Thirty seconds later he appeared around the side of the house, with the rifle slung over his shoulder. He peered into a couple of windows and then came to the back door. He studied it for a moment and then turned the handle. They had left it unlocked: it opened.

'Let's go!' said the old man. He was damned sure that a man with a rifle entering a house uninvited through the back door was a problem.

They scrambled down the bank to the burn, and Clémence took the old man's hand and led him down the hill towards the track running along the side of the loch.

'No,' said the old man. 'He'll be expecting that. And he'll be faster than us. Let's go uphill. That way we'll lose him.'

'Are you sure?' said Clémence.

The old man nodded. 'He's bound to go down not up. We should have a few minutes before he has checked the house and realized we skipped out the back.'

So they clambered uphill, along the side of the stream. At one point they heard Jerry call Clémence's name again.

After fifteen minutes they were coming to the edge of the wood, and the old man was getting tired.

'What now?' said Clémence.

'Is he following us?'

They both sat still, although the old man's panting made it difficult for him to hear much.

'Can't hear him,' said Clémence. 'We could hide here until dark.'

'And then what?' said the old man.

'Go back to Culzie? Ring the police? Get my car?'

'He'll be expecting that,' said the old man. 'Where are the keys?'

'I've got them,' said Clémence.

'Well he'll disable the car. Let down the tyres or something. And he'll probably cut the telephone wires.'

'Livvie will be furious,' said Clémence.

'Livvie?'

'Friend at uni. It's her car. Wait a moment! Let me try my phone.'

'Your phone?'

'Mobile phone. I grabbed it when we left the cottage. There was no coverage there, but there might be up here.'

She rummaged in her coat pocket and pulled out a mobile phone. The old man realized he knew what it was. How? He didn't think he had ever owned one, but friends had, people he knew. He saw an image of a middle-aged woman outside a shop in Mundaring talking on one. Who was she? How did he know it was Mundaring? When would his brain start working properly?

Clémence jabbed a few buttons and swore. 'The stupid phone is out of battery.' She looked around the desolate moorland above them. 'Who am I kidding? There's no chance of reception up here anyway.'

From somewhere down below they heard the sound of breaking glass.

'What's he doing?' said Clémence.

'Don't know. But that probably comes from the cottage.'

'Or Livvie's car.' Clémence stuffed the phone back in her pocket. 'So what can we do?' she said. 'There's only one way out of Wyvis. Along the track by the loch to the entrance of the estate at the lodge. He'll be watching it.'

She was right. 'It's at least three miles from here to the lodge. It would take us over an hour.'

'What do you think he will do next?' Clémence asked. 'I can't see him.'

'He could wait for us at the cottage. Or hide by the side of the track. Or he might go back to his own cottage to get his car.'

'I'm scared,' said Clémence.

The old man looked at the young woman who was his granddaughter. She looked scared. So she should be.

'So what do we do, Alastair?'

He thought through the options. They could hide. If it was summer, that would have been the best bet; Jerry would never find them unless he was an expert tracker, which seemed unlikely. But in March, a cold night on the mountain might kill them. Or kill him. Clémence would probably be fine, with her youth, her health and that little layer of fat she carried. He was skin, bones and bad circulation. He remembered — how did he remember? —those news stories over the years about badly prepared walkers dying of hypothermia in the Scottish mountains. Or on Snowdon. And they were under eighty.

There was another possibility.

'We could go that way.' The old man pointed to the mountain above them. 'Jerry would never expect that.'

'Are you crazy?' said Clémence.

'Remember the walk described by Angus in the book? They went up to the top of Ben Wyvis and saw a road on the other side. Close by.'

'Yes, but that took them all day. It's going to be dark in an hour or two. And it's a big mountain.'

'We don't go over it, we go around the side. Look.'

They both looked up at the rough moorland above them. To the right of the massive dome that was Ben Wyvis, a path snaked up a shallow valley, perhaps the 'stalker's path' mentioned in the book, and disappeared around the corner of a crag. Although the summit of the mountain was still covered in snow, the path seemed clear.

'That crag is about a mile and a half, two miles away,' the old man continued. 'We could get there in an hour; it will still be light. And once we are going downhill on the other side we will be OK if it gets dark. We just follow the path. Eventually we'll get to that road – the Ullapool road. Then we flag down a car.'

'Are you sure you can make it?' Clémence said.

It would be tough. But the old man was determined. And he didn't want to be shot by Jerry Ranger. More to the point, he didn't want Clémence to be shot. He would do anything to avoid that, push himself to the absolute limit of his endurance if he had to.

'I might be an old bastard, but I'm a fit old bastard.'

Clémence looked again at the mountain, and then at the old man. 'OK,' she said. 'But if we are going to do it, we had better get a move on before it gets dark. Let's go.'

14

Jerry scrambled down the gully, as fast as he could. He rounded a rocky outcrop and the loch opened up before him.

He paused and dug out his field glasses. He scanned the woods beneath him and what he could see of the track. No sign of them.

After searching the cottage he was sure that Alastair Cunningham and the young woman had sneaked out of the back door. The gully had seemed like the most logical route for them to follow. But now he wasn't so certain. Maybe they had hidden before doubling back to get in Clémence's car. If they had done that he had lost them for good.

Cursing to himself, he turned and climbed up the bank out of the gulley and back up the slope towards the cottage, slinging his rifle over his shoulder. In less than two minutes he broke out into the clearing. The car was still there, and the cottage seemed quiet.

He had to disable the car. He remembered from TV that there was something you could remove from a car engine to disable it. What was it? He knew nothing about car engines. The fan belt? Spark plugs? Alternator?

He stared at the hood of the Clio, and fumbled around. There didn't seem to be a way of opening it outside the car. Where were the keys? In the house? Or did the girl have them with her?

He swung the rifle off his shoulder and smashed the window of the car on the driver's side. He unlocked the door and groped for a lever to pop open the hood. He found it and stared at the engine. He yanked a few wires and then started pounding it with the butt of his rifle. Some things cracked, some things twisted. Then he crouched down and let the air out of all the tyres. He thought of shooting them, but a rifle shot would echo around the valley and might alert Trevor MacInnes. The last thing he wanted was the stalker to start driving around looking for poachers. He needed him tucked up inside his cosy lodge with a glass of whisky watching the TV.

So where the hell were they?

You couldn't see anything very clearly from outside the cottage because of the trees. The view would be better from the upstairs windows. Jerry ran into the cottage and up the stairs. The front bedroom had a good view of the loch. He quickly scanned the track and couldn't see anything. He pulled out his binoculars and started a more methodical sweep.

No, nothing.

But there were lots of blind spots, stretches of track which were out of the line of sight of the bedroom window.

Maybe they had gone the other way, up to the head of the loch and the big house. That was empty and there were plenty of places to hide and shelter in there. He would have to check for signs of a break-in and search the house and grounds, and the outhouses.

Wyvis Lodge itself was out of sight, but the approach to it was visible.

Nothing.

This was like a giant game of hide-and-seek. Jerry held most of the cards, but not all of them. His advantage was that there was only one way out of the estate. He had to make sure he had that under observation at all times.

He was in what seemed to be the old man's bedroom. There was another window facing out towards the north side of Ben Wyvis. He moved over there and scanned the mountainside quickly.

There! Two figures bent against the slope following a footpath through the moorland along the north-west side of the mountain.

He fiddled with the focus wheel on the glasses. It was them! It was definitely them.

250

What the hell were they doing up there?

Jerry remembered climbing the mountain himself and seeing a wooded valley and a road on the other side. There wasn't just one way out of the estate!

They were still in open moorland and there was some distance until they reached the crag. They were well out of range of his rifle, but they would be out in the open and in plain sight for a while yet. Jerry would just have to catch them up.

He ran down the stairs and out of the cottage. There was a footpath leading uphill through the woods, and Jerry followed it. In ten minutes he was out on open moorland.

Jerry wasn't a sharpshooter or anything, but he had been taught how to fire a rifle. He bent low in the hope they wouldn't spot him, and jogged up the path. He was breathing heavily and sweating, but he was catching up with them. They hadn't spotted him yet.

Behind the two figures, to the south-west, the sky was a deeper shade of grey, verging on black. They were all about to get wet.

Jerry came to a boulder just off the path. The old man and the girl were getting very close to the crag, when they would be out of his sight. He didn't want to leave it much longer. It was still quite a distance. The shot might alert the stalker, but he would have to take that risk. If he took the old man down that would be worth it.

He rested the rifle on the boulder, and looked through the scope. The image of the two figures jumped around with his heavy breathing. He waited, breathing slowly and steadily.

The images settled down.

He allowed the crosshairs to rest on the old man's back, and squeezed the trigger.

The old man saw a small stone shatter just ahead of him, and a split second later he heard the shot.

He had been shot at before, nearly sixty years before.

'Down!' he shouted to Clémence, and threw himself face first into the heather.

Clémence turned to look at him, and then down the slope.

'Get down, Clémence! He won't be able to see you in the heather.'

There was another shot, and then Clémence dropped to the ground. For a moment the old man thought she had been hit.

'Clémence! Are you OK?'

'Yes. He missed. But I saw where he was. He's not far down there.'

The old man could see the light blue of her coat through the heather.

'What do we do now?' said Clémence.

'I don't know.' They were safe in the heather as long as Jerry stayed where he was. But of course he wouldn't stay there. He would follow them up the hill and flush them out like game birds. Big fat pheasants that couldn't even fly. They didn't stand a chance, unless they somehow could get to the crag and out of sight.

The sky was darkening. Rain might help a bit. Snow a bit more.

'All right,' said the old man. 'You crawl as fast as you can that way,' he pointed to a direction a little to one side of the path. 'I'll distract him. If he hits me, crawl away from where I am and then just lie still. Go!'

He heard Clémence rustle through the heather.

He pulled himself to his feet and tried to run. It was scarcely more than a shuffle. Sixty years ago, even thirty years ago, he could have sprinted. Moving targets were much harder to hit, but he was barely moving. He tried a change of direction but tripped over some heather and fell, as another shot rang out.

He waited a few seconds, and then started off again. The crag really wasn't very far away. There was another report, and then another. This chap wasn't much of a shot. So the old man carried on running, or stumbling, at any moment expecting to feel the bullet tearing up his back.

Through his peripheral vision he was aware of something light blue moving beside him. Clémence was on her feet as well.

One more shot and they were behind the crag.

In front of them was a broad shallow saddle, between the summit of Ben Wyvis and a lesser top to its west. A small loch lay in the middle of it. No cover apart from heather, until a cliff face about a mile away. They would never get that far before Jerry reached the crag and a clear shot of them.

The light was draining from the sky, but that was mostly the moisture-heavy cloud in front of them rather than darkness. Somewhere beyond that, the sun was sinking behind the mountains.

The old man bent down to catch his breath. 'You run on ahead, Clémence. I'll catch you up.'

'You mean you will distract him?'

The old man smiled weakly. 'Maybe.'

'No,' said Clémence. 'We stick together.'

'Go!'

'No!'

The old man concluded that his granddaughter was very stubborn indeed.

He looked at the sky. 'That's going to be snow, isn't it?'

'I think so,' said Clémence.

He scanned the moorland. About thirty yards off the path a short distance ahead of them was a bump in the heather, no more than a ripple. Perhaps they could hide there. Until it started to snow.

'All right,' said the old man. 'Follow me!'

He led Clémence at a shuffling run to the spot. It wasn't much but, most importantly, it put them just out of sight of a man standing on the path by the crag. 'Down here!'

They pressed themselves to the ground. Through the stem of a twisted heather bush, the old man could keep watch on the crag.

In less than a minute, Jerry appeared, holding his rifle ahead of him. He stopped and looked ahead towards the cliffs in the distance.

The old man followed Jerry's eyes. The cliffs had disappeared. A thick white blanket was moving rapidly towards them; the black sky had turned white.

Jerry hesitated and then jogged slowly along the path for about twenty yards. He was close.

He stopped, and looked around.

He turned off the path and began walking slowly their way.

A snowflake landed on the old man's nose. Then another on the heather an inch in front of his eyes.

Jerry was moving right towards them. He must have identified the ripple in the landscape as a likely hiding place. Damn.

More snowflakes, falling more steadily. But the old man could still see Jerry clearly. He tensed. If he was younger, he could have tried to jump Jerry, take him by surprise. That was still probably his best bet, but who was he kidding? What chance would an eighty-three-year-old man have against a fit fifty-year-old with a rifle?

Maybe he would give Clémence a chance to get away before he was shot.

He was about to whisper his instruction to Clémence to that effect, when Jerry stopped. Looked around him. Stared at the crag.

There was a fold in the rock there, barely big enough to hide a man, but it caught Jerry's attention. He turned and jogged back towards it, his gun held in front of him, ready to fire. Clearly he had decided that's where they were hiding.

The snowflakes fell faster, soft but persistent. The wind got up and the trajectory of the snow flattened below forty-five degrees. The brown heather was now spattered with white. The old man could still see Jerry and the crag, but he was becoming more indistinct by the minute.

When Jerry reached the crag, he was little more than a blurred dab of darkness in the white. And then he was gone.

'What do we do now?' hissed Clémence.

'We move.'

15

Callum O'Neill hoisted his bike off the train onto the platform, and followed the dozen or so other passengers through the barrier. He paused outside the station to check his route from Dingwall to Loch Glass avoiding the busy A9, and set off. It was twelve miles to the foot of Loch Glass, but Callum was raring to go and looking forward to the ride.

When Clemmie had asked him to join her at the crazy old man's place he had desperately wanted to say yes. But he had just started at The Feathers and he was nervous about requesting time off right away. Then one of the other barmen had asked Callum if he could switch Tuesday night for Friday, and Callum had spotted his opportunity. He had agreed, provided the other guy would do Wednesday as well, and so had bought himself two nights away. He would have to be back in Glasgow for Thursday lunchtime, but that was just possible if he got up early and caught the first train from Dingwall.

Callum's immediate instinct was to phone Clemmie and tell her he was coming; she could pick him up from the station in Livvie's Clio. But then he decided to take up her suggestion of bringing his bike and surprise her. Callum was a keen cyclist, and his dad had an excellent library of maps of the Highlands, so he had worked out that it would be a nice ride from the nearest station.

And it was. It was cool, and the sky was grey, but Callum worked up a sweat. He was soon out of Dingwall, and speeding north parallel to the A-road, with the Cromarty Firth and the Black Isle beyond it. He swooped down into the village of Evanton and turned left up a narrow lane signposted to Loch Glass.

This was harder work, but Callum was fit and his legs pumped, spurred on by the excitement of seeing Clemmie. He really liked her; she was attractive, she was funny and she seemed to like him. Their backgrounds were very different: she was part of the English public school contingent with their gap years and their instilled sense of superiority, and he was younger, Scottish and from a comprehensive. But he didn't care about that and neither did she.

Besides, both of them were skint.

He was beginning to learn that her outward confidence and sophistication hid a screwed-up, lonely childhood. Callum liked his parents, he liked his younger sister and he still saw all his pals from school, all of which gave him a feeling of security that Clemmie envied.

That was fine with him. Frankly, he couldn't believe his luck.

He attacked the hill that rose high above the River Glass, and then he was drifting down through the woods to the lodge marked on his map. There he came to a metal gate, with a sign: *Wyvis Estate. Private.*

He hesitated, wondering whether he should knock on the lodge's door for permission to pass through. But then he decided he had been invited to the old man's house by Clemmie, so he had a right to enter the estate. He opened the gate, crossed the river on the wooden bridge, and pedalled through the pine woods to the loch. No one inside the lodge seemed to have noticed him.

As he emerged from the woods, Loch Glass and Ben Wyvis opened up ahead. And an ugly black cloud loomed over both. He put on some speed as the cloud swallowed up the mountain. In a few more minutes snow started to fall.

He reached a turn-off to the left with a sign pointing up the hill into the trees to Culzie, and in another minute he was at a clearing in the woods. There was Livvie's yellow Clio, with the snow already accumulating on its roof. The snow was falling thickly, as was the visibility. A couple of lights glowed in the cottage, so Callum rested his bike against the wall and, unable to suppress his smile, rang the doorbell.

There was no reply.

Rang again. Nothing.

Damn!

It was snowing hard and there was nowhere else to go, so Callum tried the door handle; it was unlocked and he let himself in.

'Hello!' he called. 'Hello? Clemmie!'

No sign of her, nor of the old man. Livvie's car was still there, and they had left some lights on in the house, so they might be out somewhere nearby on foot, in which case they would be back soon with the falling snow. Or, more likely, they had gone somewhere in the old man's car, assuming he had one.

He went through to the kitchen, spotted the kettle and filled it from the tap. That's what he needed: a cup of tea while he waited.

Jerry stood by the rocks and turned his face into the snow and wind. He couldn't see more than ten feet ahead of him.

They couldn't be far away from him. Before the snowstorm had hit, he had had a good view of at least a mile in all directions, and he had seen no sign of them. They had certainly not been on the footpath ahead of him. Which meant they had either disappeared or they were hiding. They weren't in the rocks by the crag. Perhaps they were in that dip in the ground after all.

He set off into the white, stumbling through heather. After about a minute, he realized he had no idea where that hollow was. He stood still and looked all around him. White silence.

He could get lost in this.

He retraced his footsteps in the snow that was already lying on the heather, until he returned to the footpath. He remembered that there was a small loch ahead and that the path ran around the left edge of it, between the water and the steep slope up to the Ben Wyvis summit. If the old man and the girl were heading for the Ullapool road, then they would have to go along that path.

Head down, Jerry followed the path himself, at a jog. He had no idea how fit Clémence was, but he knew he must be travelling faster than the old man. If he kept up the pace, he should overtake them, probably quite soon.

It was hard work, running through the snow, and he had to keep his head down to avoid twisting an ankle. The flakes driven by the wind bit into his face, but he wasn't cold, in fact he was building up a sweat. After ten minutes or so, he could just make out black water to his right. He stopped to catch his breath. Jerry was fifty-six himself: no youngster.

What now?

He was pretty sure that his quarry wasn't just following the path, or he would have caught up with them by now. Which meant they could be anywhere out there in the whiteness. Or the greyness. The light was leaching out of the sky, behind all that snow. It would be dark soon. Jerry would never find them on the mountain.

He thought of continuing on down to the Ullapool road himself. But that was quite a distance. Also, there was a stretch of a mile or two where the old man and the girl might meet it, especially if they weren't following the paths. Impossible to be sure of intercepting them before they flagged down a car.

No, he was better heading back and regrouping.

So he turned around and trudged down the mountain the way he had come.

The old man led Clémence in what he hoped was a straight line parallel to the mountain path. His plan was to continue until they hit the loch, and then try and work their way around it. The trouble was that in the whiteout it was impossible to be sure that they were, in fact, travelling in a straight line. They had no compass; there was no sun to check. The wind was blowing into his face from a direction just a little right of straight ahead. But the wind could change subtly without him noticing.

It was hard work. Not only was the heather rough, but it was interspersed with mud and peat bog. They both had good coats, with hoods, but neither of them had hats or gloves. The old man had had time to put on his boots, but Clémence was wearing trainers which were soaked through. Worse than that, it would be easy for her to twist an ankle on the uneven ground. They weren't cold, the going was too tough for that, but the old man was aware he was running low on energy. Also, his stiff knee was beginning to hurt. There was water all around them to drink if they had to, but they had no food.

And somewhere very close to them was a man with a rifle, who was intending to use it on them.

They had a problem.

'Where is this loch, then?' Clémence said.

'Ahead,' grunted the old man.

'Are you sure?'

The old man didn't answer. Of course he wasn't sure.

Suddenly the old man felt a tug on his sleeve. He turned to see Clémence holding a finger to her lips. She pointed.

Ahead of them, through the snow, they could make out the darkness of a hunched figure crossing in front of them. And a rifle.

The old man crouched low, and Clémence did the same. The figure disappeared to their left.

They waited a minute. 'I think he must be heading back down the mountain,' whispered the old man. 'He's probably on the path. Let's take a look.'

They stumbled ahead twenty yards until they came to the footpath. Jerry's footprints were already disappearing under newly fallen snow.

'What now?' said Clémence.

'He went left, so we go right,' said the old man.

'What if he doubles back?' said Clémence.

'We're in trouble,' said the old man. 'But the only way we are going to get down the other side of the mountain in this visibility is by following the path.'

'All right,' said Clémence. 'Let's go.'

The old man looked ahead at the snow. He was exhausted. He was finding it difficult to force one creaky leg in front of another, and his knee was giving him trouble. He had no idea how far it was to the road, or what the terrain would be like, but he knew it must be miles.

'Are you OK?' said Clémence. 'Can you go on?'

'Yes.' The old man nodded. 'Come on!'

He tried to hurry, but he couldn't. The best he could manage was to force one foot in front of the other in a shuffling limp. The snow let up a bit, so that the visibility was more like thirty yards than five, but it was getting dark. The black waters of the small loch brooded to their right.

They battled on until the cliffs they had seen earlier emerged in front of them.

'You need a rest,' said Clémence.

'No. Let's keep going,' said the old man.

'Just ten minutes,' said Clémence. 'Here. It's out of the wind.'

She found a boulder in the lee of the cliff, and brushed off some snow. The old man let himself down heavily on to it and Clémence sat next to him.

It felt so good to be still.

'Who the hell is Jerry?' said Clémence. 'And why does he want to shoot us?'

'No idea,' said the old man. 'He's American, isn't he? Do you think he is something to do with Nathan? His son, maybe?'

'Uncle Nathan and Aunt Madeleine didn't have any children,' Clémence said. 'I'm pretty sure about that.'

'Well God knows who he is. But he seems determined to kill us.'

'I'm sure Jerry Ranger isn't his real name.'

'I'm sorry I got you into this,' said the old man. 'If it wasn't for me, you would be safely back at St Andrews, wouldn't you? I am very bad news.'

'You are.' Clémence turned to him. She reached out her hand and squeezed his. 'You're freezing!' she said.

'Only my hands,' said the old man. 'Poor circulation.' The truth was that sitting still, he was rapidly getting colder.

'Come on then,' said Clémence.

'All right,' said the old man. But it was all he could do to straighten his stiffened joints and stand up. He stumbled forward.

'Can you do this?' said Clémence. 'I'm exhausted. You must be too.'

'We can't stay here,' said the old man.

They followed the path, which, much to their relief, soon began to head downhill. And then it climbed again. At a couple of points it seemed to fade away under the snow, especially when the heather thinned out. After a few more minutes, they arrived at what seemed to be a fork.

'Which way?' said Clémence.

'I don't know,' said the old man. The fork to the left seemed to head downhill. 'Let's go that way.'

The path descended gently, and then steeply, down towards a stream. It was flowing away from them, which meant that they were probably on the far side of the mountain from Loch Glass. The descent jarred his complaining knee. Then the path forked again: one way crossed the stream and the other ran along it. It was still snowing, and it was getting darker.

The old man leaned back against a rock. 'I don't know which way now.'

'Can you go on?'

The old man shook his head. 'Not much further.'

They looked at each other. 'We're going to spend the night on the mountain, aren't we?' said Clémence.

The old man nodded.

'Well let's get back to the cliff. At least there's a little shelter there.'

The old man nodded again. He looked back up the steep slope they had descended.

There was no way he could get up that.

A night on the mountain would probably kill him. A night on the mountain with no shelter would definitely kill him. They couldn't just collapse where they were. They had to get back to that cliff.

There was no choice.

The old man forced himself to put one foot ahead of the other as they climbed the slope. Don't think about how far they had to go, just one foot after the other. And then again. And again. It was hard going, very hard going, for both of them, but eventually they made it back to the fork. Clémence gave the old man her shoulder and dragged him back to the cliff.

The snow had eased off a bit, but it was now completely dark, and the wind was biting. Clémence left the old man for a few minutes. When she returned she dragged him to a hollow in the rocks she had found, with a flat floor of almost dry dead bracken.

She sat on the bracken in the hollow. 'Come here,' she said, and the old man slumped down next to her.

It was going to be a very long night. He shivered. It might well be his last.

16

In the darkness and the snow, Jerry lost sight of the path down towards Culzie. He shouldered his rifle and stumbled downhill, his confidence that he would eventually reach Loch Glass waning. He peered through the snow-streaked gloom for signs of the twisted trees of the wood which surrounded the cottage, but he couldn't see them.

In the end he stumbled into the ditch which ran along the lochside track. He climbed up on to the track and could just make out the boathouse, and the dark waters of the loch beyond. He turned right, and made much better progress along the road, until he came to the turn-off to Culzie. He decided to go back to the cottage, warm up, search it quickly and try to disable the phone connection. He didn't have anything on him to cut the wires, but he could just smash the phones themselves to make them unusable.

Some lights glimmered through the gloom as he approached Culzie. Alastair and Clémence must have left them on. Snow was piled several inches high on the roof of the Renault. He was about to throw open the front door and flop into the cottage, when he caught sight of a bicycle leaning against the wall.

Strange. He was sure that the old man didn't own a bicycle, and neither did Clémence.

He crept around the side of the house. The curtains to the living room were drawn and a line of light slipped out beneath them. Jerry tried to peer through a crack in the curtain, but he couldn't see anyone in the thin strip of room that was revealed.

Someone had drawn those curtains! Someone had ridden to the cottage, had drawn the curtains in the living room, and was probably waiting for the old man and the girl to return.

Who could it be? Jerry had no idea, but he did know there was just one bike, and therefore probably just one person inside. Jerry had a rifle. He had surprise. He could easily overcome whoever it was: tie him up, or even shoot him. Or her.

But that would add complications, complications that were difficult to anticipate. Much better to sneak back to Corravachie, and figure out what to do next.

Jerry was exhausted by the time he got back to his own cottage, but he had a long night ahead of him. There was a chance that both Alastair and Clémence would die on the mountain, but it was not something he could count on. He had to assume that they would find help, and contact the police, who would then search for him. All that would take several hours: it might not be well into the morning before the police came looking. They would certainly come to Corravachie, so he couldn't stay there. It would take them a while, but eventually they would work out which car-hire firm at Glasgow Airport had rented him the blue Peugeot, and what the licence number was.

So he had some time.

He packed. He shaved off his beard. He used his electric trimmer to shear his hair into a rough buzz cut. He ate.

Then he made a phone call and spoke for ten minutes.

He checked a map. He needed somewhere to lie low, somewhere where police or nosy locals wouldn't find him, somewhere from where he could emerge to finish off the job he had started. At this point, he was committed. The police would most likely catch him eventually. The only thing that really mattered was whether he succeeded in killing the old man first.

That was the *only* thing that mattered.

He stuffed his bags into the trunk of the car, together with the rifle and ammunition, and drove slowly through the snow out of the estate. He barely made it sliding down the hill to Evanton, but once he was on the A9, the road was clear. He headed south for the A835 to Ullapool.

Clémence was cold and she was tired. Her feet were wet and freezing. One thing she was grateful for was her coat. Despite her protest, her mother had insisted that they get the warmest parka they could find in Hong Kong. She knew Scotland was cold and she didn't want her student daughter to freeze.

The old man's coat wasn't bad, but it wasn't as warm as hers. Clémence considered switching. The trouble was that a coat required a body generating heat to create warmth and, unlike Clémence, the old man didn't seem to be generating much heat. He was pale and his bare skin was freezing to the touch.

Clémence had read somewhere that in cases of hypothermia, you were supposed to strip yourself and the victim naked, and huddle together in a sleeping bag. Clémence was willing to do that if it would keep the old man alive, but stripping down to their underwear in a snowstorm just seemed a stupid thing to do.

Yet she had to think of some way of transferring her body heat to him.

'Alastair? Take your coat off.'

'Why?'

'We need to share body heat. I have an idea.'

They both took their coats off and Clémence laid the old man's beneath them and hers on top. She hesitated; it seemed weird to cuddle up to this man who had been a total stranger to her only a few days before. Weird or not, it would be so much worse to be lying in a cave with a dead body. She pulled him to her and held him tight. Very soon the warmth built up, at least around their upper bodies.

'Is that better?' she asked.

'Yes,' said the old man. But she could still feel the occasional involuntary shiver from him. She touched his cheek. It was still cold.

They lay there together in silence. For a while. A long while. Clémence could tell from the old man's breathing that he was still awake.

He mumbled something.

'What?' She leaned towards him to hear better.

'I said, atelier is definitely a French word. I was just letting you win.'

'No it's not! Well, it is, but it's English as well. If we had a dictionary I could prove it to you.'

'That's easy for you to say up here.'

She watched the snowflakes dance and scurry in the wind.

'I wonder where Sophie is buried?'

'What do you mean?'

'I don't know where she's buried. I suppose it isn't up here. They lived in California, didn't they?'

'Didn't the book say that she was in the de Parzac graveyard in France?'

'Oh, yes, I had forgotten.'

'Have you ever been there? Sophie's village in France?'

'No. I've been to France a lot, of course. My mother's family is from Rheims and we went there to see my grandparents and cousins on her side. But she wasn't keen on having anything to do with Dad's family. Apart from Madeleine.'

'Because she paid the school fees?'

'That's right.'

Clémence looked out into the night.

'You know I am angry that my biological grandfather murdered my grandmother,' she said. 'And I'm almost angrier that he let his innocent friend take the blame.'

'I know.'

'But somehow I think of that person as being Angus. Not you.'

'But it was me.'

It was, it was true. Clémence just didn't want to accept that. She

266

was growing quite fond of the old man and she hated Angus; she wanted to find a way to square that circle. 'Maybe you didn't really kill Sophie?'

'Of course I did.'

'No, maybe you just *thought* you did.'

'That note at the end of the book was crystal clear,' said the old man. 'I killed her and I knew it. That's why I wrote the damn thing in the first place.'

He pulled himself up on to his elbows, tugging Clémence's coat up to his chin. 'I can't hide from it, Clémence, neither can you. I knew when you were driving me back from the hospital that I wouldn't want to learn who I really was, what I had really done. Well, it was worse than I could have imagined.'

'Why did you call *Death At Wyvis* a novel?'

'I don't know. I suppose I had written *The Trail of the Scorpion* as a novel.'

'Precisely!'

'What do you mean "precisely"?'

'We know why you called that memoir a novel. Because it wasn't true. Because you skated over how and why you and that sergeant left the other guy to die.'

'That's right.'

'So maybe this is a novel for similar reasons?'

'You're clutching at straws, Clémence.'

Clémence was, but she was determined to hold on to them. 'In *Death At Wyvis*, you say that you had shown a first draft of *Trail of the Scorpion* to the sergeant, whatever his name was, in Leeds, and he had made you change it, right?'

'Right.'

'Maybe you did the same thing this time? Showed the handwritten manuscript to someone who insisted that you change it.'

'But I thought you said the manuscript and the published book were identical?'

'They were at the beginning, apart from changing your name to Angus. But who is to say they aren't different later on? Like when Sophie gets killed?'

The old man grunted.

'Admit it's possible.'

'It's possible, I suppose. Barely. But it's wishful thinking. There might be all kinds of other reasons why I changed my name to Angus. Why I called it a novel.'

'If we were back at Culzie it would be easy to check,' Clémence said. 'I wish I had thought to do that!'

'Maybe we will get the chance,' said the old man. 'If we ever get down the mountain alive. And if Jerry Ranger doesn't find us first.'

Clémence sighed. The old man was right, of course. She *was* clutching at straws. 'Oh, well. I may be deluding myself. But choosing to think it's a possibility makes more sense to me than writing you off as a murderer.'

The old man found her hand and squeezed it. His own hand was cold.

'It's a shame you can't remember anything about writing that book,' she said.

'I can remember parts of it. Writing the bit in Capri with Sophie at the Villa Fersen.'

'But nothing more? Nothing about changing the manuscript? About dealing with publishers? Correcting proofs, isn't that what writers do?'

There was silence from the old man. Clémence could almost hear him racking his brains. 'No,' he said eventually. 'But I do remember writing something. Something else.'

'What?' said Clémence.

'I don't know. It was much more recent. It was in that study at Culzie, at the desk with a view of the loch.'

'What were you writing?'

Clémence could feel the old man tense. 'Damn!' he said at last.

'I can't remember. It's like I described before, I can see the pages, I can see my handwriting, but I can't make out the words. I know it's important, though. And it's long.'

'How long?'

The old man shook his head. 'I don't know. Lots of pages.' He paused. 'You can't imagine how frustrating it is not to remember this stuff! And then when I do remember something, it invariably turns out to be something I wish I'd never known.'

Clémence didn't answer. It must be dreadful. But then it was only so dreadful because the old man had so much to be ashamed about.

'Do you think it's stopping?' said the old man, staring out into the night.

'It's slowing,' said Clémence. 'But now we are here, I think we should wait for daylight. Get some sleep.'

'Good idea,' said the old man, and he rolled over on to his side. Clémence pulled herself up to him, in a spoon.

'I'm going to make this right,' said the old man. 'If we ever get down this mountain, I am going to make this right.

'I don't see how you can,' said Clémence. 'Sophie is dead. Grandpa has already spent fifteen years in prison.'

'I know,' said the old man. 'But I'm going to find a way.'

A minute later, his breathing became more regular. Clémence felt the fatigue wash over her. Soon she would be asleep herself. She prayed, just before sleep came, that the old man would still be alive when she woke up.

17

Clémence opened her eyes. In front of her the snow-draped flank of Ben Wyvis glimmered blue in the early dawn. The sky above seemed clear, save for a smattering of pink-lined clouds.

Her shoulders were stiff. Her thigh hurt where a stone had dug into it. She was cold, especially her feet, which were still damp.

With a start she remembered the body next to her. She couldn't hear or feel any breathing. Gingerly, she touched the old man's cheek. It was cool but not cold.

He moved. Groaned.

He was alive!

She moved over and wrapped her arms around him, holding him tight.

'Good morning,' he muttered.

'Are you OK?'

'I'm cold. But that helps.'

'Let's stay here like this for a few minutes. Warm you up.'

Clémence felt the sharp edges of the old man's bones against her chest. He was her grandfather and she didn't want him to die.

'Ow!' said the old man. 'You are crushing me.'

'Sorry.' She loosened her grip. 'Actually, we had better get going.'

They disentangled, and Clémence pulled herself to her feet. The sky was clear, the mountain was white. It was cold, but the wind had died down.

270

She helped the old man to his feet, and eased him into his coat.

'God, my muscles are stiff!' he said. 'And they ache.'

'But you are alive.'

He grinned at her, his brown eyes warm in the frozen landscape. 'I'm alive. Thanks to you.'

'Let's see where we are.'

Clémence strode out into the snow, looking around her for signs of Jerry. She didn't see him, but she did see a stag, sniffing the air on a ridge barely fifty yards away. It turned and was off, scrambling along the ridge and over its crest.

Clémence followed it, trudging through the snow, until she reached a vantage point to the south side of the mountain.

It was a stunning morning. Snow-blanketed mountain tops stretched for perhaps fifty miles ahead of her. Much closer, to the south-west, was a wooded valley, in the midst of which a main road followed a half-hidden river. A smooth carpet of virgin snow led down the slope to the pine forest. If there were any paths, they were submerged. It looked easy, but she was quite sure it wouldn't be.

She returned to the old man and told him what she had seen. 'How are you feeling?'

'Stiff,' he said. 'Tired. Cold. And my knee hurts. But I can make it. Let's go.'

They set off at a slow pace. On this side of the mountain, heather gave way to grass, and there seemed to be fewer bogs. It was also downhill and, with the good visibility, they were able to take a route that avoided sharp descents or rocks.

Clémence threw worried glances at the old man as they trudged downhill. His skin was pale, and he looked so frail that a gust of wind would topple him, yet there was something determined in his step. She was exhausted; it amazed her that he could keep going.

Slowly, ever so slowly, the pine trees drew closer.

*

The morning light woke Jerry. He had shoved the small passenger seat of the Peugeot back as far as it would go, but it still didn't leave enough room for his tall frame to rest comfortably. He had probably managed four hours sleep.

He had driven from Wyvis to the Ullapool road and then patrolled it up and down countless times until midnight. There had been no sign of the old man and the young woman, but he couldn't be sure that they hadn't been picked up by a car before he had seen them. He reasoned it was more likely that they had stopped at nightfall and decided to stay out on the mountain.

So he had taken a detour to a large twenty-four-hour super-market near Inverness, where he had withdrawn as much cash as he could from an ATM and bought some essentials, including a pay-as-you-go phone with a charger that would work in a car. Once the police were on to him, he would avoid using his credit card for as long as possible. Then he drove back to an empty car park beside the Ullapool Road to get a few hours of sleep. Fortunately, the snow had stopped.

He was cutting things a little fine. It was just possible that they might have got down the mountain and alerted the police, but Jerry thought it unlikely that the cops would be able to track down Hertz at Glasgow Airport and get his registration number before at least the morning. They would guess he had rented a car, but they had no way of knowing where from. And having shaved his beard, he didn't match a cursory physical description.

He started the Peugeot and drove up a track marked on his map on the south side of the road, which should give him a good view of the southern slope of Ben Wyvis. And indeed the mountain rose above him: a high ridge with a number of domed tops, the tallest of which was Ben Wyvis itself, stretching out like an enormous whale.

The blue and pink fingers of dawn caressed the snowfield beneath the summit, eventually leaving it a pristine glimmering white.

Jerry pulled out his binoculars and scanned the mountain. Nothing moved. He gave it a second pass, and this time spotted three dark dots high up to the right of the summit.

Deer. No people.

So the old man and Clémence were not up and moving yet. But Jerry was content. If they were going to descend the south side of the mountain, he would get a clear view of them.

Of course, if they decided to double back to Wyvis, he would miss them. On the whole, he thought that unlikely. It was just a chance he would have to take.

He was committed now.

Jerry scanned the mountain patiently every few minutes. After half an hour or so, he spotted two figures very clearly as they made a slow and indirect path down the mountain. He checked their progress against his Ordnance Survey map of the area. Footpaths were marked on the map, but the two people did not seem to be following them – they probably couldn't make them out under the snow. Jerry waited until he could be sure where they would strike the pine forest and hence from which path they would eventually emerge into the main road.

According to the map, the woods stretched for two to three miles, and there were three main paths through them down to the road. The figures moved along a ridge and then descended in a straight line for the woods on what looked like a smooth slope. Checking his map, Jerry was pretty sure that Clémence and the old man were heading directly for one of those footpaths through the woods, just by a kink at the edge of the splash of green.

Jerry jumped into his car and drove down to the point where that path hit the road. There was a lay-by there, and he pulled over. His blue Peugeot was in plain view of the road, but since he now knew his quarry was still on the mountain, he could be sure they hadn't alerted the police.

Pausing to make certain that he couldn't hear any other cars coming, he popped the trunk and eased his rifle out, before jogging into the woods.

It was a good, well-maintained path that was clearly visible even after the snowfall. He was glad to see that there were no footprints; no random early-morning hikers to get in the way. He hurried up the hill, until he was out of sight of the road, and then began to search for a good place for an ambush.

He came upon a small stretch of open ground along the bank of a stream. He ducked off the path, and soon found the ideal spot, in a dense clump of trees, with an unimpeded view of the footpath. He settled down to wait, ears sharpened for the sound of descending footsteps.

The range was only about twenty yards. No chance he would miss. No chance at all.

18

It took Clémence and the old man over an hour to reach the pine forest. As they approached it, Clémence was disappointed to see that it was protected by a high deer fence. No way through.

'Left or right?' Clémence said.

'Left,' said the old man.

And so they set off, walking quite a way along the perimeter, until they reached a stile and a prepared footpath heading downhill.

The wood was quite beautiful, the fresh snow glistened, flakes on the branches of the pine trees sparkled, and some energetic blackbirds proclaimed the glory of the morning. Clémence was exhausted, but it lifted her and gave her the strength to manage the last mile.

But she wasn't sure whether her companion had it in him. He stopped and leaned against a tree.

'Are you going to make it?' said Clémence. He could barely stand. 'I don't think it's too far.'

'Yes, I'll make it,' said the old man. 'Just give me a moment.'

They waited in silence for a couple of minutes as the old man recovered his breath.

'Clémence?' he said.

'Yes?'

'You remember I said last night I was determined to make this right?'

'Yes.' She did remember. She also remembered how she had pointed out that it was too late now, but she didn't mention that.

'When we get down there, I don't want to go to the police.'

'What?'

'We shouldn't go to the police about Jerry. At least not right away. There are things that I need to find out first.'

'There is a nut-job carrying a rifle trying to kill us!' said Clémence. 'Of course we should go to the police.'

'I've been thinking about that,' said the old man. 'I'm sure he's trying to kill me, not you. And I don't want to put you in any danger. So you should leave. Head off somewhere, anywhere. Not St Andrews, but somewhere where Jerry can't find you. Only for a few days until I have discovered whatever I can.'

'You're crazy,' said Clémence. 'We must go to the police. Then they can go looking for him before he kills you or me or anyone else. And when they catch him, they can ask him who he is and why he is after us.'

The old man sighed. 'Once we tell the police, they will take over. And who knows what they will find, what secrets they will uncover? I want to uncover them for myself. I want to speak to Pauline Ferguson. You are right, we should compare the manuscript of *Death At Wyvis* to the final novel. And whatever it was I wrote in the study at Culzie, I need to find it.'

'And you expect to do all that by yourself, with Jerry Ranger after you?'

'Yes,' said the old man. 'I said I wanted to make this right. I will.'

'No,' said Clémence. 'When we get down this mountain I am going straight to the local police station and I am telling them everything.'

'Please, Clémence.'

'No. Now let's get going.'

After another three-quarters of an hour they reached an empty car park and the main road. It was still only eight o'clock.

There was a bench in the car park, and the old man slumped on to it. He winced and rubbed his right knee.

Clémence stood on the roadside and stuck out her thumb. She didn't have long to wait. The fourth car, a dirty black Volvo, pulled over and the driver wound down his window. He was a thin red-haired man in his thirties with loose pouches under his eyes.

'Are you all right?' he said with a concerned smile.

'Not really,' said Clémence. 'We've spent the night on the mountain. I'm with my grandfather. Could you give us a lift to the nearest town?'

'Aye. Go fetch him and hop in.'

Clémence beckoned to the old man and eased him into the back seat as she joined the driver in the front.

Jerry's excitement turned to frustration as the minutes ticked by. He had been worried that he wouldn't be able to find a good ambush spot before they stumbled upon him, and now they hadn't showed. Where the hell were they?

Jerry pulled out the map again and examined the kink in the perimeter of the forest, where the old man and Clémence had been heading. All right, they wouldn't be on the path marked on the map, but they should be able to see the footpath through the woods. It would almost certainly be signposted.

Wouldn't they see it?

He peered at the map closely.

Maybe not. Maybe if they hit the woods just to the east of the path, on the other side of the kink, they wouldn't see anything. Then they would either plunge straight into the woods, which would be hard work in the snow, or walk around the edge until they found a path. Now, if they turned right, they would very soon find the path Jerry was staking out. But if they turned left?

Damn. Goddamn it to hell!

The other path ran through the woods parallel to Jerry's, but to the east. It was only about a quarter of a mile away.

Jerry grabbed his rifle and ran across the path and down into the stream. He clambered up the bank on the other side and plunged into the trees.

It was hard work, but in a few minutes he came across a well-made footpath.

There were two pairs of footprints heading downhill.

Damn!

Jerry ran, jumped and skipped down the slippery path. He fell twice. They couldn't be that far ahead!

He turned a corner and the trees opened out with a view of the road. A black station wagon was pulled over, and a dark-haired woman in a light-blue jacket was helping an old man into the back seat.

Jerry swung the rifle off his shoulder, and aimed.

He was breathing too heavily to keep the sights still.

In the couple of seconds it took to settle the sights, the car was already pulling out into the road.

Jerry had a blind shot at the car's rear window. He almost pulled the trigger anyway, but decided not to.

He would get another chance.

He would make damn sure that somehow he would give himself another chance.

The car was deliciously warm.

It turned out that the red-haired man was a vet named Matt, who had been up half the night delivering a calf. He lived just outside Dingwall and his wife did bed and breakfast. He offered them breakfast and the use of a bed to recover. Clémence explained that they had been walking from Loch Glass, got lost in the snow and their car was abandoned on the Wyvis Estate on the other side of the mountain.

The vet pulled out a phone and called his wife to have breakfast ready for them when they arrived. After twenty minutes or so, they turned off the main road into Dingwall along a short track to a small farm wedged between the road and a railway line. As they walked into the farmhouse, they could smell bacon, and the vet's wife Agnes,

278

a small, thin woman with spiky hair and a quick, friendly smile, greeted them with a massive breakfast and hot coffee.

'Where are you staying?' she asked.

Clémence thought quickly. 'Nowhere. We were planning to find a hotel in Dingwall after our walk, but then we got lost. Matt said you had a room here? I wonder if we could stay here tonight?'

'Aye, of course you can. You'll have to share a room, mind you. What about your car?'

'We can get a taxi back to Loch Glass to pick it up later on,' said Clémence. She wasn't at all sure whether they would actually do that, but she needed to sound credible.

After breakfast, the vet went off to his practice in town and Agnes showed them a small cosy bedroom, with two single beds and an en suite bathroom.

'You don't happen to have a charger I can borrow?' said Clémence, showing Agnes her phone.

Agnes did, and it fitted. Clémence plugged her phone in. 'I'll leave you to it,' Agnes said.

'Are you going to call the police now?' said the old man, when she had left the bedroom. 'We are not in danger. Jerry has no way of knowing where we are.'

It was true. Clémence felt safe and warm. Yet she also knew they should ring the police.

'I will, but not yet. You have a bath. I'll try and dry my socks. And you might need a nap.'

The old man bathed first, and then it was Clémence's turn. It felt glorious, and she wallowed for twenty minutes. As she was getting dressed, she heard her mobile phone go off in the bedroom. She pulled up her jeans and rushed to answer it.

She recognized the number.

'Hi, Callum!' she said, so happy to speak to him.

'Clemmie, are you all right?' He sounded worried.

'Yes,' said Clémence, uncertainly.

'Where are you? I'm with Terry the gamekeeper in his Land Rover looking for you.'

'Are you?' said Clémence, confused. 'What are you doing with him?'

'I got the train to Dingwall yesterday and cycled up to Loch Glass. I wanted to surprise you, but you were out when I got to Culzie. It was snowing and I waited for you, but you never showed up. I thought perhaps you had gone out somewhere for dinner. Then when you didn't come back I thought maybe you couldn't make it back to Wyvis, because of the snow or something. I fell asleep in the lounge. This morning, when you still weren't here, I went to the Stalker's Lodge and spoke to Terry, and he said the old man's car is at his place, so you must have gone out on foot somewhere. We've been looking for you. Terry was just about to call the police and Mountain Rescue.'

Clémence thought quickly. She wasn't sure that she wanted Terry to know what had happened, at least not quite yet.

'Is Terry there with you now?'

'Yes.'

'Well, tell him Alastair and I are fine. We got stuck up Ben Wyvis last night and came down the other side. We are at a hotel now. We're OK.'

'You spent the night on the mountain? Why on earth did you decide to climb it when there was a storm coming?'

'I know, I know, it was stupid,' said Clémence. 'Look, the important thing is that you and Terry know we're OK. But I'd really like to talk to you properly. So as soon as you are alone, give me a call, right?'

Clémence heard Callum talking to Terry, and Terry's Highland rumble in the background.

'Terry says someone tried to break into your car last night. Do you want him to report it to the police?'

'Oh, no. Tell him not to worry. I'll do that myself when I get back there.'

'Are you sure you're OK, Clemmie?'

'Quite sure. I'll tell you all about it when you call me back.'

The old man was sitting on his bed, watching her intently. 'Is that your boyfriend?'

'Yes. He spent the night at Culzie; he wanted to surprise me. He's with Terry now. He's going to ring me back in a minute.'

'You didn't tell him what really happened?'

'No,' said Clémence. 'But I will. When he's alone.'

'I see,' said the old man. 'You know, you could ask him to bring the handwritten manuscript to us. And the published novel. Then we could compare them.'

Clémence knew what the old man was up to. He was playing for time before she called the police. But she did want to know whether her theory was correct: that there was a difference between the two versions of the story. She really wanted to know. And she felt safe at the farm; there was no way that Jerry could know where they were.

'I could,' she said carefully.

The old man smiled.

'All right,' Clémence said. 'But after we've done that, then we call the police.'

The old man didn't answer, but for the first time in a while, he looked happy.

Clémence's phone rang again.

It was Callum, and he was back in Culzie, alone. Clémence told him what had happened. He was shocked and concerned for Clémence's safety. But when she asked him to bring the manuscript and the novel he was happy to comply. She told him to watch out for Jerry and to ride past the vet's farm a couple of times to make sure he wasn't being followed. He reckoned it might take him two hours to get there. Although it was downhill, there was still snow on the road around the loch and the road from Loch Glass down to Evanton would be tricky.

You could rely on Callum. You could always rely on Callum.

'What do we do about Aunt Madeleine?' said Clémence.

'What do you mean?'

'Well, Jerry doesn't know where we are. But he might know where Aunt Madeleine is staying. Or he might find out. She's eighty-five. We can't put her in danger.'

'Oh, I see,' said the old man. 'It would be nice to speak to her, though. She might be able to tell us a lot.'

'We should make her leave,' Clémence said. 'It's too dangerous while Jerry is on the loose. Even if we call the police.'

'OK. How about we tell her to pack and come and meet us here? We can talk to her and then she can go straight to the station or even the airport at Inverness and go to London, or back to America? That should be safe.'

Clémence thought it through. That seemed reasonable.

'Ask her to come in a couple of hours. Maybe three.'

'Why?'

'To give us a bit of time to look at whatever Callum brings. We may want to ask Madeleine about it. And perhaps we should find a quiet café or pub to meet in, rather than here.'

Clémence was doubtful. She thought about just telling Madeleine to leave her hotel immediately and take a taxi to Inverness Airport, but a couple of hours probably wouldn't make any difference. She had no real reason to think that Jerry was after Madeleine as well, nor that he would be able to find out where she was staying.

'All right,' she said. 'But which café?'

'Ask Agnes. She seems helpful.'

Clémence went downstairs, and found the vet's wife in the kitchen. She suggested a small place in Maryburgh, a village a short distance from the farm, in the opposite direction to Dingwall. Clémence went back to their room and phoned Madeleine at her hotel from her mobile. She only just managed to persuade the surprised and sceptical old lady to pack and meet them, promising that all would be revealed when she got to the pub.

'So now what do we do?' said Clémence when she had hung up with her great-aunt. 'Do you want a nap until Callum gets here?'

'I have a little idea,' said the old man, with a grin.

19

Agnes gave them a lift into Dingwall, which was lucky because although it was only a mile or so, Clémence wasn't sure the old man could walk much further. Agnes herself would be out for the rest of the day, but she said that her guests could use her lounge if they wanted, and suggested that if they needed a taxi to pick up their car at Loch Glass, they could find one at the station.

Dingwall was the old county town of Ross and Cromarty, and lay adjacent to the Cromarty Firth. The snow had been much lighter at sea level, and was already melting to a thin slush. Agnes drove around the outskirts of the town and dropped them at the front door of the Ashwood House Nursing Home. Clémence had told her they had promised to visit a friend of a friend while they were in Dingwall.

She was nervous about Jerry Ranger, but willing to play along with the old man for three hours or so. If they got a taxi directly from the nursing home back to the farm, then it was hard to see how Jerry could possibly find them. And once Madeleine was packed off to Inverness, Clémence would speak to the police.

The nursing home was an imposing Victorian house with half a view of the firth, but inside it was tatty and unloved. The staff were friendly and good-humoured, however, and one of them led them up to Pauline Ferguson's room.

She was a sturdy old lady, with bright-blue eyes and curly hair of steel grey. She was in bed, and a wheelchair and walker suggested mobility problems.

'Ah, Dr Cunningham! Sheila said you would be in to see me! How are you after your fall?'

The old man smiled politely. 'Good morning, Mrs Ferguson. As perhaps Mrs MacInnes explained, I seem to have lost almost all my memory, so I have no recollection of you at all. I do hope you will forgive me.'

'Och, of course I will! And who is this lovely wee lassie?'

The old man smiled with what Clémence suspected was pride. 'This is my . . .' he hesitated. With a surge of pleasure, Clémence realized that the old man was about to say 'granddaughter', but had stopped himself. Mrs Ferguson seemed to assume it was a touch of senility — a trait she was no doubt used to.

'My friend,' the old man said. 'Clémence Smith. She's a student at St Andrews University and has kindly agreed to look after me.'

Mrs Ferguson gave Clémence a cheery smile. 'You seem to be doing a good job with that.'

Clémence couldn't help laughing. 'Not that good a job, Mrs Ferguson,' she said.

'Well, I'm glad you came to see me. After Sheila told me about your wee accident, Dr Cunningham, I thought you'd mebbe not be able to mind what we said, and it seemed gey important to you at the time. So I thought mebbe I'd repeat it.'

Excitement shone in the old woman's eyes. This was clearly gossip of a high order, and she was going to enjoy it. Clémence had read to old people at a nursing home herself, and was familiar with residents like Mrs Ferguson: a sharp brain craving stimulation, desperate to break free of a worn-out body.

'Please do, Mrs Ferguson,' said the old man. 'One of the things Clémence has been doing with me is trying to piece together my past.'

'The idea is to jog his memory, and help him recall things himself,' added Clémence. 'The doctors insisted on it.'

'Aye, they're not daft,' said the old lady. She hesitated. 'Now. Tell me what you've jaloused?'

There was a brief silence. 'What's "jaloused"?' asked Clémence. She thought she was used to Scots by now, but this woman was something else.

'Oh, I'm sorry, lassie. What you've suspected, I mean.'

'Well, we know about Sophie Trickett-Smith's murder,' said Clémence. 'We've read *Death At Wyvis*.'

'So we know I killed her,' the old man said. 'And we know you were cooking at Wyvis Lodge that night.'

'We *think* we know he killed her,' Clémence corrected quickly. The moment she said the words she was surprised at them. She was losing objectivity; she realized she was desperate to believe that the old man wasn't a murderer.

Mrs Ferguson's eyes caught Clémence's. She had noted the doubt in her voice.

'It was that night you were asking me about, Dr Cunningham. You were wanting to ken any wee thing I could mind about it. It was a long time ago, but my certes, it was certainly a night to remember!'

'And what did you tell me?'

'Not much you didn't ken already,' said Mrs Ferguson. 'Or that wasn't in *Death At Wyvis*.'

'Oh.' The old man was disappointed, and so was Clémence.

'But then, just as you were leaving, you were speiring me about my son Iain. He was there that night too, helping out in the kitchen, and you wanted to ask him a few questions.'

'And did I?'

'No. Well, at least not then. You see, Iain bides in America now. In New York. He's in property, or "real estate" as he calls it. He has done well for himself, with him leaving the school at fifteen.'

'That's impressive. You must be very proud of him.'

'Och, away you go! You see, I'm not sure our Iain is just the clean potato, if you see what I mean.'

'Oh,' said the old man. 'Do you mean in business, or in other matters too?'

Clémence knew the old man was referring to the night of Sophie's death. And so did Mrs Ferguson.

'You see, Iain was set up in business in New York by an old friend of yours. Nathan Giannelli.'

'Uncle Nathan?' said Clémence.

'Aye. First he got him a junior office job with a real estate developer friend. Then, a few years later, he lent Iain some money to get started. Iain did the rest himself.'

'Why would Nathan do all that?' the old man asked.

'You asked me that question before, and I couldn't answer it. But I could see what you thought. You thought that it was to get Iain not to tell the truth about whatever he had seen that night.'

The old man and Clémence sat in silence as they digested this information.

'Did you speak to your son about this?'

'No,' said Mrs Ferguson. 'At least not at first. I think you must have visited me about September last year. I got a call from Iain a month later saying that you had been to see him in New York. Iain was angry at me for telling you about Mr Giannelli helping him. It was the first time he had called me since Christmas.'

Mrs Ferguson's cheer had left her voice. She seemed upset by her son's reaction, but more sad than angry.

'Did he tell you what I had asked him?'

'No. He wouldn't. But, as I said, he sounded upset. And worried. Can you remember talking to him? Surely you would remember flying to America?'

'You would think so,' said the old man. 'But no, I don't remember anything about that at all. So that would be October last year?'

'That's right.'

'And I didn't visit you again?'

'No,' said the old woman. 'I wish you had; I was fairly wanting to know what you had discovered.'

'Sorry,' said the old man with one of his comforting smiles. 'I will when I find out what's going on this time. I promise.'

'You do that,' said Mrs Ferguson.

'It was a big move from Wyvis to New York,' said Clémence.

'Aye, it was. But it was good for Iain. He was a bright wee laddie at school. I wanted him to stay on, but he was desperate to leave and become a stalker like his dad. At least that's what he thought when he was fifteen. But as he got older I think he wanted to leave the Highlands and go to the big city: Edinburgh or even London. He was wanting to get on in the world, ken? I was pleased about that, but my husband thought he should stay working on the estate as a ghillie. I'm not surprised that he jumped at the chance to go to New York. Nor that he did well once he was there.'

A note of pride had crept into the old lady's voice, but she banished it. 'Mind you, once he got there, it was as if he was wanting to rub out his past life here. We saw him mebbe six times in the last thirty years. I have grandchildren and I've only seen the wee bairns twice! I think he's ashamed.'

'Ashamed?' said the old man. 'Ashamed of what?'

'I don't know,' said Mrs Ferguson. 'And I'm feart to find out. But if you do discover what, you will tell me, won't you?'

'We will, Mrs Ferguson, don't you worry about that,' said the old man, reassuringly. And as he did so, Clémence glimpsed the bedside manner of an experienced GP.

'Do you know what, Dr Cunningham?'

'What?'

'I mind fine that week when poor Mrs Trickett-Smith was murdered. I never really believed Mr Trickett-Smith killed her. But when I read that book, I definitely didn't think you did it. You were aye the gentleman. And you loved her far ower much.'

'Gentlemen can kill people just as easily as anyone else,' said the old man. 'And the world's jails are full of people who killed people they loved.'

*

288

Clémence and the old man left Mrs Ferguson, and rang a taxi from the nursing home manager's office. They crammed together into a small plastic sofa in the hallway waiting the promised ten minutes. They faced a prominent framed notice on the rules visitors should follow to sign in and sign out, rules they had complied with in full.

'At least I can leave this place,' said the old man. 'Imagine being imprisoned in here for the rest of your life.' He turned to Clémence. 'Promise me you will never let them put me away in a place like this.'

Clémence felt a flash of irritation. It wasn't up to her where the old man spent the rest of his days. He wasn't her responsibility. And, thanks to him, her grandfather, one of her grandfathers, had spent fifteen years in a real prison.

She didn't answer him directly, but asked a question of her own. 'What do you think Iain saw?'

'I don't know,' said the old man. 'Probably me killing Sophie. Or coming out of the boathouse, or something that would incriminate me.'

'But would Uncle Nathan help him like that if that's what it was?'

'Possibly. After all, I had helped Nathan in Deauville, and we know he felt in my debt for that. He's supposed to be one of my oldest friends, but I can't remember him since my fall, so you know him better. What do you think?'

Clémence sighed. 'Uncle Nathan could fix anything. And he was always helpful and generous. It's not as though he was a soft touch; he would always get what he wanted. But if he wanted to help you, you would be helped.'

'Well, that's what he did then.'

They sat in silence for a moment. But it didn't quite make sense to Clémence. 'If that's what it was, why do you think you went all the way to America to track Iain down? If he was just covering for you, why bother?'

'I don't know, Clémence. I really don't know.'

'Can't you remember?'

'You know I can't remember anything!' The old man couldn't contain his frustration.

'Yes you can,' said Clémence. 'Sometimes. Sometimes things like this jog your memory. Did this have something to do with whatever you were writing at your desk at Culzie? Perhaps you were writing a letter to Iain? Or Nathan?'

'It wasn't a letter,' said the old man, furrowing his brow. 'It was longer than a letter.'

'A long letter?'

'No. But you're right, it did have something to do with Iain.'

Clémence saw the old man struggling and kept quiet. He nodded his head slowly. 'Yes. It had to do with Iain. And Nathan. Going to see Nathan in America.'

'Anything else?'

The old man smiled to himself. 'Yes. It was for the book. For *Death At Wyvis*. It was an appendix for a second edition.'

'Are you sure?'

The old man's face was screwed-up in concentration. 'Not absolutely sure, no. But I think so.'

Clémence felt a surge of excitement. 'Where is it? Whatever you were writing. Did you give it to someone? A publisher, perhaps? Uncle Nathan? Is it still at Culzie?'

'I don't know. But . . .'

'But what?'

'I know what I wrote it in. An exercise book. A black hard-backed exercise book.'

Clémence's pulse quickened. 'Big? A4? With red binding?'

'Yes. Yes, that's right.'

'I know exactly where it is,' she said.

'Where?' The old man looked at her, his eyes alight.

'It's at Culzie. Your desk, middle drawer. I saw it when I was looking for photographs.'

'Well done!' said the old man, grinning. 'We're getting somewhere after all.'

'I wish I had asked Callum to look for it.'

'I'll go back and get it,' said the old man.

'No you won't. The police will. I'll tell them about it.'

The old man looked disappointed, but he didn't argue. Yet Clémence was pretty sure that he hadn't given up on trying to uncover the truth without the police.

And what was in that black exercise book?

20

Stephen gazed out of the window at the Firth of Forth shimmering in the weak March sunlight. He had forgotten how beautiful this stretch of the line to Edinburgh could be, at least in good weather.

Which wasn't surprising. Now he came to think about it, he hadn't taken this train for forty years. Not since 1959.

He wasn't looking forward to any of this. Seeing Alastair again. Revisiting Wyvis. Thinking about Sophie and her murder and the horrible things that had happened afterwards.

Of course Stephen had known that he hadn't murdered Sophie himself, but he had felt so guilty that he wasn't surprised that the police believed he had. The guilt was an overwhelming burden that crushed him.

He had tried hard when they had first got married to treat her well, and by and large he had succeeded. Even when he had taken on bit roles in films, he had managed to treat them as a nine-to-five job from which he returned to dinner with his wife.

But the movies were beguiling. Even in wartime there was glamour. Sophie was always beautiful, but then so were the actresses. And they were out of bounds and therefore tempting. There were long stretches with nothing to do, and there was alcohol. As he became more famous, there were the fans: the young women who thought he was handsome and dreamed of sleeping with him.

He dreamed of sleeping with them. And then he did.

In Hollywood it all got worse, as Sophie had known it would. He drank. He took drugs. He slept with lots of women. He treated her badly, very badly.

He treated her much worse than Alastair ever would have done.

And somehow he didn't notice any of this until he was sitting in a Scottish jail, waiting for his trial for Sophie's murder.

The truth was he broke down; he couldn't mount a credible defence for Sophie's killing, since he knew he was responsible for it. When he was found guilty of murdering her, it seemed to him that justice had been done. He wasn't innocent.

It was lucky that he didn't have access to alcohol in prison, but even without it, he reached despair that was so deep he couldn't remember it.

It was Maitland who had pulled him out of it. Maitland was a manager in an insurance company who had murdered his wife in a fit of jealousy when he had discovered her with another man. Unlike Stephen he had always treated his wife well, at least according to him, and Stephen believed him. Unlike Stephen he had actually killed her. Like Stephen he regretted her death.

But he had learned to live with the fact. He was different from other people: he was a murderer, and he was in prison, where he should be. His life was going to be shitty, which was as it should be. But since he was still a living organism on this planet, and likely to remain so for many years yet, he would get as much out of those years as he could. The small things. Like the *Telegraph* crossword.

What was the point of Maitland's life? It was a big question, with no big answers, so he had provided a small one. Doing the *Telegraph* crossword.

Stephen was Maitland's disciple. Life was shitty, but it was no longer unbearable. That was despite bloody Alastair Cunningham's repeated attempts to make it so.

First there was the publication of *Death At Wyvis*. It was true the book had got Stephen released a few years early for a crime that he didn't commit. But it had stirred everything up: Sophie's death, the trial, Stephen's responsibility for the whole thing. Oddly, Stephen blamed Alastair for that, more than the fact that it was he who had actually killed Sophie.

The fuss died down eventually, and Maitland was let out on parole and came to live in Shepherd's Bush. He and Stephen began to meet daily at the Windsor Castle for a pint and the crossword. Stephen's days achieved some focus.

Then, for reasons only known to himself, Alastair had returned from Australia to cause trouble, big time. They were both over eighty, for God's sake! Why couldn't Alastair just stay in Australia and rot?

So Alastair felt guilty? He deserved to! Why mess things up for everyone else? Because there was no doubt that Alastair had messed things up for everyone.

And then the stupid bastard had fallen, hit his head and forgotten everything. Excellent! It should all have just stayed forgotten. And it would have done if Madeleine hadn't interfered again and got Clémence involved.

It was really for Clémence's sake that Stephen was on the train going north. It wasn't just that Clémence was an innocent bystander who didn't deserve to be caught up in the mess. Clémence was Stephen's granddaughter, and even though he rarely saw her, every time he did she reminded him of Sophie.

Alastair could get what was coming to him. But Clémence? Clémence he had to protect.

Clémence heard wheels crunch gravel outside the nursing home. Their taxi had arrived.

It took them less than ten minutes to get back to the vet's farm. Clémence didn't see either Jerry or his blue car lurking, although she couldn't remember exactly what make his car was, so it was difficult to identify it in the traffic.

Her heart leaped when she saw Callum waiting by the front door of the farmhouse, next to his bike.

She rushed out of the taxi to give him a hug. 'I'm *so* glad to see you!'

294

He squeezed her. He was reasonably tall, very thin, with dark curly hair and gorgeous blue eyes. There was something very reassuring, very normal about his presence. As though the boy sitting next to her in her French grammar class would banish all the weird stuff that had been happening to her over the previous few days.

She paid the taxi driver and introduced Callum to the old man, who greeted him warmly. They went inside, and Clémence made them all tea while she explained to Callum the gist of what had been happening.

Callum took it all in, asking some questions for clarification. Despite the extraordinary situation Clémence and the old man were in, Callum seemed to take it in his stride.

'So what do we do now?' he said, as Clémence brought the three of them mugs of tea, and they sat around the kitchen table.

'Did you bring the manuscript of *Death At Wyvis*?' asked the old man.

'Yes,' said Callum, opening the bag he had brought in with him. 'And the published book, like you asked.'

'We'll have a look at this,' said Clémence. 'We are meeting my aunt Madeleine for lunch; she knows as much about all this as anyone. And then we are going to the police.'

Callum handed the manuscript to Clémence.

'I'll just check the chapter where Sophie gets killed,' said Clémence. The old man nodded.

He and Callum sipped their tea, as they watched Clémence scan the relevant chapter, 'Chapter X – The Boathouse'. The chapter – the conversation with Sophie on Ben Wyvis, the dinner back at Wyvis Lodge, putting Stephen to bed, having sex with Sophie in the boathouse, the row, stumbling angrily around in the woods – seemed to be identical, with the exception that the narrator's name had been changed from 'Alastair' in the manuscript to 'Angus' in the printed novel.

But Chapter XI was different. Clémence skimmed the first page quickly.

'Here, let me read this,' she said to the other two. 'In the published novel, Chapter XI starts with Angus waking up at dawn and throwing up in the loo. But there are a couple of extra paragraphs right at the beginning.'

She cleared her throat and began to read.

CHAPTER XI

Justice Undone

'ARE YOU ALL right?'

I opened my eyes to see Nathan bending over me. I was in a ditch by the side of the track and my head hurt badly.

'What happened? Did you fall?'

'I . . . I don't know.' And I didn't know.

'Here. Let's get you out of this ditch.'

I tried to heave myself to my feet, but it was difficult. Fortunately, the ditch was dry, and with Nathan's help I scrambled out. I saw the boathouse.

'Where's Sophie?'

'I don't know. Let's just get you back to the house.'

Leaning on Nathan's shoulder, I stumbled back to Wyvis Lodge and collapsed on to my bed. I was asleep in seconds.

'Then what happens?' asked the old man.

'It looks pretty similar to the published novel again,' Clémence said, leafing through the handwritten pages. 'Hang on, let me check.' She turned to the open book and checked the paragraphs afterwards. 'Yes, it's pretty much the same, but there are a couple of sentences missed out in the novel, about Angus remembering Nathan finding him in the ditch.'

She leafed through the pages. 'Here we go. This is different. Sophie has been found in the loch, the police have come and Angus hasn't told the whole truth to them about going to the boathouse with Sophie. He's gone for a walk and comes back to speak to Nathan. In the book, Nathan tells him that the police now suspect Stephen of being in the boathouse.' She began to read:

'They can't think he killed Sophie, can they?' I said.

Nathan shrugged. 'Jealous husband. It's been known.'

'I didn't tell them about you finding me,' I said. 'I just said I turned in after putting Stephen to bed. I assume you didn't say anything, or they would have questioned me more closely.'

'No, I didn't,' said Nathan. 'I didn't think it would help you very much.'

'I didn't kill her!' I protested.

'Of course not,' said Nathan. 'But who knows what the police would have made of it?'

'But if they suspect Stephen, shouldn't I admit that I was in the boathouse with her? And shouldn't you admit you found me unconscious?'

Nathan pondered this. 'I'm not so sure. I don't think it would really help Stephen very much: it would just make his motive much stronger. And they do have his footprint at the boathouse, so he must have been there too.'

'I don't know.' I hesitated.

'Somebody hit you over the head,' said Nathan. 'It was most probably Stephen. You've got to think of your own position. I'll stick by you, just like you stuck by me in Deauville.'

My head still hurt and I was struggling to think clearly. But I trusted Nathan: he seemed to have things in hand. He was good in a crisis. It was true; he was playing the same role I had in Deauville.

'All right,' I said. 'We stay quiet.'

'So. Nathan helped me cover it up,' said the old man.

'That's not entirely surprising, is it?' said Clémence.

'Is there anything else?'

'Let me look.' Clémence read on to the end of the chapter. The two texts were more or less identical until the very end. 'Here's something. Stephen has gone to jail and Angus is having dreams that it was he who actually killed Sophie.' She read:

These weren't dreams. They were memories. The fragments coalesced, until about a year after Sophie's death, I was convinced that I had killed her.

The knowledge shattered me. The morally courageous thing to do was to tell the police, but my moral courage had long gone. I tried to continue at my practice in Knaresborough; I was as safe or unsafe there as anywhere else, but I couldn't.

One day, about nine months after Sophie's death, I travelled down to London to meet Nathan for lunch at the Savoy on one of his business trips to Britain. I told him about the dreams and the memories. He listened to me with a painful expression on his face.

'I thought so,' he said.

'What do you mean, "I thought so"?'

'That morning. When it turned out that Sophie had been killed. I thought you must have done it. She must have struggled and given you some kind of head injury, maybe hit you with an oar or something, which had a delayed effect. Stephen was blundering around dead drunk; he could barely stand, let alone kill anyone and dispose of their body.'

'If you thought that, why didn't you tell the police?'

Nathan paused. 'Because I wasn't sure. If you had killed her, it was clear to me that you genuinely couldn't remember it. And . . .'

'And what?'

'I thought Stephen was responsible. Just like he was responsible for Alden's death: he was the one who started playing with swords. If you had killed her it was in a moment of madness, just like I lost control when I killed Alden. So I decided to stay quiet.'

So Nathan confirmed what I already knew. I had murdered Sophie.

'Whew,' said the old man. 'What about the rest of it? The afterword?'

Clémence scanned it quickly. 'The first sentence is different. Nothing about it being called a novel. Otherwise the same.'

'Can I read that?' asked Callum.

Clémence glanced at the old man. He nodded. Clémence passed Callum the book. 'Read it from Chapter X. That will tell you why we are where we are.'

Callum opened the book, found Chapter X, and started reading.

'It looks like you were right,' said the old man. 'The manuscript was a draft. I must have shown it to Nathan who suggested some changes, basically leaving him out. And so I decided to call the book a novel.'

'I thought so.'

'But it still looks like I killed Sophie. Even more than it did before. Nathan corroborates that.'

Clémence sighed. She had really hoped that she would find evidence that the old man was innocent, but she hadn't. 'What about Iain?'

'There was no difference in the passages about him?'

'No. I checked.'

'Maybe he saw Nathan carrying me back. That would explain why Nathan wanted to keep him quiet.'

'I suppose so,' said Clémence. The excitement had gone. The old man sitting in front of her who was probably her grandfather, was also almost certainly a murderer after all. Then a thought struck her.

'Do you think Jerry Ranger might actually be Iain Ferguson?'

The old man frowned. 'He does sound American. It's quite possible that Iain might sound American after forty years in the States.'

'And if Iain was eighteen, say, in 1959, that would mean he was born in 1941—'

'And he would be fifty-eight now.'

'That's possible, isn't it?' Clémence said. 'Jerry could be fifty-eight?'

'Possible,' said the old man. 'He looks a bit younger than that to me. But why would he want to kill us? Or kill me?'

'Maybe it has something to do with what he saw that night?' said Clémence.

'What?'

Clémence's mind was a blank. What indeed?

She had an idea. 'Maybe he killed Sophie?'

The old man frowned. 'Why would he do that? An eighteen-year-old kid who had only just met her.'

'I don't know. Maybe he raped her?'

The old man winced.

'I know it's a nasty thought, but people do that. Men do that,' Clémence said.

'They do. But in that case why would Nathan go to the trouble of setting Iain up in New York? Why would Nathan help anyone who had raped Sophie? You are clutching at straws, Clémence. Face it.'

Clémence nodded. 'I know. I wonder what that black exercise book says.' It was her only hope left, although she guessed it would just provide further evidence to support the idea, or the fact, that the old man had killed Sophie.

Who Jerry Ranger was remained a genuine mystery.

21

The walk from the vet's farm to the pub in the next-door village was short, less than half a mile, but it was slow, painfully slow. The old man limped along – his knee was giving him trouble. He was also worryingly pale. Clémence was beginning to wonder whether she should just dial 999 and get an ambulance to take him to hospital.

Their route was along the main road into Dingwall, and around a major roundabout where one road branched off towards Inverness and the other towards Ullapool. Clémence felt terribly exposed along that stretch; if Jerry happened to drive past he would spot them immediately. Callum was lingering in the kitchen reading the end of *Death At Wyvis*, and he would join them on his bike when he had finished.

The pub was along a row of houses up a hill from the centre of the village of Maryburgh. It was empty, apart from the barmaid and Madeleine, sitting alone with her walking stick and a glass of wine, looking very out of place next to a slot machine muttering to itself in disjointed jangles.

Clémence rushed up to her and gave her a hug.

'Clémence! What is wrong?' Madeleine said in French.

'Oh, Aunt Madeleine, we have had a terrible time!' Clémence replied in English. 'A man with a gun was chasing us over the mountains. We spent last night on the top of Ben Wyvis. It was lucky we didn't die of hypothermia!'

'*Ah, mon Dieu!*' Madeleine glanced at the old man for confirmation, and found it in his grim expression. Clémence saw the accusing look Madeleine shot him: *it's your fault my niece was in danger.*

'Who? Who was chasing you over the mountain?'

'It's an American who calls himself Jerry Ranger. He says he's a song writer, but we don't know who he really is. He has been staying in a cottage on the estate for the last few weeks.'

'And why was he chasing you?' Madeleine focused the question on the old man, her eyes accusing.

'We don't know,' said the old man.

'But it must have something to do with *Death At Wyvis*,' said Clémence. 'With Alastair killing Sophie.'

'Must it?' asked Madeleine, doubtfully.

'I think so,' said the old man. 'Our guess is he came to Wyvis to befriend me. Find out what I knew. And then kill me. But we have no idea who he really is, or why he cares.'

'Have you been to the police?' Madeleine asked.

'Not yet,' said Clémence. 'But we will,' she added quickly. 'Oh, here's Callum.'

Callum joined them at their table, bearing the novel. Clémence introduced him to her aunt. The barmaid came over and they ordered lunch.

'We've been finding out a bit more about Sophie's death,' Clémence said.

'Are you sure that's wise?' said Madeleine.

Clémence ignored her and explained what Mrs Ferguson had told them at the nursing home, and the discrepancies they had identified between the handwritten manuscript and the published novel of *Death At Wyvis*. The old lady listened closely, taking everything in.

'So you now know for sure you killed my sister?' said Madeleine to the old man.

He nodded. 'But I have had a partial memory. I believe that very recently I wrote down everything I had discovered in a black exercise book. I think I was planning to produce a second edition of *Death At Wyvis*. Have you seen it? Have you heard anything about a possible second edition, maybe from Nathan before he died?'

Madeleine shook her head. 'Not about a second edition, no. But you are quite right. You have been asking questions about the murder.

You came over to see us in New York last October. You spoke to Nathan about it. You upset him.'

'What did I say?' the old man asked.

'I don't know; Nathan wouldn't say. He did tell me you had just been to see the stalker's son, who lives in Long Island. But I never knew Nathan set him up in the real estate business until you told me just now. You arrived for lunch at our apartment. Then you spoke to Nathan alone for a couple of hours. You were supposed to be staying the night, but you left. Nathan threw you out.'

'Why?'

'He refused to tell me,' Madeleine said. 'I knew it had something to do with that vile book.' She nodded at the volume in front of Callum.

Their food came and they began to eat.

'Then Nathan died a couple of months later?' the old man said.

'That's right,' said Madeleine, flatly.

'What happened?'

'It was at our place in Scottsdale. In Arizona. Nathan used to like to go for a walk in the evening with a cigar. One evening a couple of weeks before Christmas, he went out, and he didn't come back. I waited. I got worried. After an hour and a half, I went out to look for him with the maid. We had just gotten to the front gate when the police arrived. He had been found dead on the road a hundred metres from our house. Hit-and-run.'

'I'm sorry,' said Clémence.

Madeleine's face was impassive, but it was clear she was struggling to contain her emotions. 'It happens,' she said, with a French shrug.

'Madeleine?' The old man sounded nervous.

'Yes?'

'Is there any chance it wasn't an accident?'

'What do you mean?'

'I mean, could someone have killed your husband on purpose?'

'No.' Madeleine hesitated. 'That is, I don't think so.'

'But it was a hit-and-run, you say? Someone ran him over and then drove away. That could have been intentional.'

'I suppose so,' said Madeleine, frowning. 'But who would have killed him? And why?'

Clémence did not like the way the old man had steered the conversation. It seemed to her that he was upsetting her aunt unnecessarily. 'Yes, who?' she said.

'Me?' said the old man quietly.

'You! Why?' asked Madeleine.

The old man shrugged. 'A number of people have died over the years. Alden. Sophie. Now Nathan. And I always seem to be involved.'

'That's ridiculous!' said Clémence. 'You have no reason to think that! None at all!' Somehow the idea that the old man had killed her uncle as well as her grandmother made her furious. She so badly wanted him to be innocent, not a mass murderer.

'Do you know whether I was in Arizona then?'

'No,' said Madeleine. 'You didn't get in touch with us.'

'But I might not have done. If I wanted to kill Nathan.'

The four of them sat around the table contemplating the thought.

Then Callum cleared his throat. 'Dr Cunningham?'

'Yes,' said the old man.

'You don't know that you killed Nathan, do you? It's not as though you remember it. And there is no evidence from what you have been saying that you did. It's just speculation.'

'Callum is right!' Clémence said.

'Forgive me,' Callum said. 'But you . . . we . . . seem to be in some difficulties here with a nutter looking for you armed with a rifle. I think we should stick to the facts, or what we can reasonably take to be the facts.'

The old man smiled at Callum. 'You are quite right. I am assuming the worst. But we should entertain the possibility that Nathan was killed. And it might have been by me.'

'Or by Jerry Ranger,' said Clémence.

'Or Jerry Ranger,' the old man conceded. He turned to Madeleine.

'Do you remember if I sent the original manuscript of *Death At Wyvis* to Nathan back in the seventies?'

'Yes, I do, although Nathan never let me read it. He told me later that he tried to get you to stop publishing it. You see, he was worried about my reaction, and he was dead right to be. When I eventually read the book, I was furious. Until then I had no idea that you had killed Sophie, nor that Nathan had helped you cover it up. I was angry with you, but I was very angry with Nathan. Very angry.'

Madeleine's eyes were glinting, and her accent had become especially thick. Clémence could see why Nathan might have been anxious to hide everything from Madeleine. It was clear that Madeleine was as deeply involved as any of them; possibly more deeply.

'I've said it before, and I have a nasty feeling I will be saying it for what's left of my life, but I'm sorry, Madeleine.'

Madeleine glanced at the old man and shrugged.

'Anyway. You should leave here now,' said the old man. 'We have no idea where this Jerry Ranger is. He may be after you too.'

'Perhaps I should,' said Madeleine. 'I came here to look after you, but I am not sure I can do that now. And I certainly don't want to help you jog your memory any more. You can look after yourself, can't you, Alastair?'

'No he can't!' said Clémence. 'The poor man is exhausted! There is a madman chasing him with a rifle, he lives all alone, and he still doesn't know who he really is.'

'Clémence, *chérie*, you are coming with me!' said Madeleine. 'Leave Alastair. I know old men, and this one is a tough old bird. He'll be all right, and if he isn't, it's his own fault. He knows all that. But for you it's different. I should never have gotten you involved in all this. I would never forgive myself if you were hurt.'

'Your aunt is absolutely right, Clémence,' said the old man. 'You should go with her.'

'No!' said Clémence.

'Yes,' said the old man.

'But what are you going to do?' Clémence asked him.

'I am going to go back to Culzie and find that exercise book. And then I will probably call the police.'

'We should call the police now!' said Clémence.

The old man glanced at Madeleine. 'If you call the police now, you will have to stay here to talk to them. Get yourself to safety. I'll be much happier then, and so will your aunt. If Jerry Ranger shoots me, so be it. I probably don't have many years left in me and as we have all agreed, my life is pretty worthless anyway. What do you think, Madeleine?'

'On this, Alastair is absolutely correct, *chérie*.'

Clémence glanced at Callum, who was listening closely. After all they had been through together, she couldn't bear to abandon the old man — her grandfather. And she, too, wanted to know what was in that black exercise book. Alastair had found something out before he fell and hit his head. Something that propelled him all the way to America to confront Iain and Nathan. Possibly something that had led to Nathan's death. Now that something was causing Jerry whoever-he-was to want to kill.

Something bigger than anything they had discovered so far.

Callum was looking at her oddly. As if he was trying to pass a thought onto her. An idea. And she believed she knew what it was.

'All right,' she said. 'I'll leave too. How shall we do this? Are you packed, Aunt Madeleine?'

'My suitcase is in Davie's taxi,' said Madeleine. 'He's waiting for me.'

'You should go directly to the airport,' Clémence said. 'I need to talk to Callum and to pack up, but I'll follow you. I'll take the train, maybe from Inverness. We probably shouldn't travel together.'

'Let's meet in London, then,' said Madeleine. 'I'll be staying at the Connaught. I'll book you a room for you there. Do you need some cash for the ticket?'

Madeleine gave Clémence six fifty-pound notes from her purse.

'I'm not sure I'll get all the way to London by tonight,' Clémence said. 'I might have to stop over somewhere on the way. Or get the sleeper.'

'What about Callum?' said Madeleine. 'Do you want to come with Clémence?'

'That's all right, Mrs Giannelli,' said Callum. 'I think I'll go straight back to Glasgow. I've got a shift in the pub tomorrow lunchtime.'

They all looked at the old man. His face was still pale, but his cleft chin was jutting out proudly. Clémence realized that this was what he wanted. To be left to face his past alone, even if he might die for it.

22

The train pulled into Dingwall station, and Stephen stepped onto the platform with his small bag. It had been an early start and a long journey, but he knew the day was not over yet.

He checked into the hotel over the road, dumped his bag and asked directions to Madeleine's hotel. He took a taxi up a hill behind the town, through a housing estate to a castle. It was now one of those fancy country-house hotels that Stephen read about in the Sunday papers, but in which he could never afford to stay. Besides, he had no intention of sharing a hotel with Madeleine.

She had checked out.

Which left Stephen only one option.

So, when he returned to his waiting taxi, he had a question for the driver.

'How much is it to go to Loch Glass?'

Madeleine dropped Clémence and the old man at the vet's farmhouse; Callum was following on his bike. Madeleine instructed Davie to take her on to the airport, making Clémence promise to call her at the Connaught as soon as she arrived at King's Cross, whether it was that night, or, more likely, the following day.

'What now?' said the old man. Clémence's heart went out to him. He looked both desolate and determined at the same time, and so frail.

He straightened up. 'I know what you are thinking. But you promised Madeleine you would leave and leave you must.'

'All right,' said Clémence. 'Let me just have a quick word with Callum, and I'll see you upstairs.'

The old man went into the house as Callum freewheeled down the farm track. Clémence trusted Callum to see things more objectively than her, and she needed to check that she had read his thoughts correctly.

She had.

She went up to the room. The old man was sitting on his bed, staring into space. Clémence picked up the telephone and dialled the number from the card that Davie had given her.

'Yes, I'd like a taxi please . . .'

She watched the old man watch her.

'Yes. That's for three people . . . the Wyvis Estate by Loch Glass . . . as soon as possible.' She hung up.

The old man frowned. 'The Wyvis Estate?'

She smiled at him. 'As soon as we've found and read that exercise book, we call the police, OK? Just don't tell Aunt Madeleine.'

He raised his eyebrows and then grinned. 'All right, Clémence. We'll do it your way.'

Jerry was seated at a table in the corner of the Inverness Public Library, poring over a map of Scotland and scribbling in the notebook he had bought that morning from WH Smith. Smith's was one of the few things in this country that hadn't changed since his childhood.

His initial thought had been to find a remote spot off a minor road in which to lie low. But the more he thought about it, the more he felt he was vulnerable in the countryside if the police launched a major search operation. Wherever he was hiding, there was the chance that a local shepherd, or ghillie, or forester would find his car and wonder what it was doing there. And, unlike the countryside of southern England which was criss-crossed with a network of minor roads, the Highlands were traversed by a limited number of through routes, all of which could be easily monitored by the police.

But in a city, he could blend in. No one would know that he was a stranger, and now he had shaved his beard and his hair, there was no description or photograph that the police could issue that would enable him to be recognized. He could easily lose his American accent and resurrect his old one. The Peugeot was parked on a residential street not far from the centre of town, where no one would remark on it. Also, a city gave easier and more anonymous access to public transport.

Inverness was a city, but a small one. It wasn't quite anonymous enough for Jerry's purposes; after wandering around its few main streets for an hour or so, he realized that people might begin to recognize him. He considered fleeing to Glasgow, where they would never find him, but he might be spotted on the way. Besides, he wanted to remain within striking distance of Wyvis or Dingwall, in case he had an opportunity to finish what he had started.

He had spent as long as he decently could in a coffee shop, and then wandered the streets again. As he passed the public library, he ducked inside. It didn't seem the natural place for the police to look for a suspect on the run.

He was thinking through an escape plan. He needed a new vehicle; he would have to assume that his Peugeot had been identified. There were two difficulties: he didn't know how to hot-wire a stolen car, so he would need keys, and he had to be sure that the theft wouldn't be discovered for a few hours. Maybe break into an unoccupied house, steal the keys and then the vehicle? That way he should have an hour or two before the theft was reported. But he would need to find the right house.

The phone he had bought from the supermarket buzzed in his pocket. He answered it, ignoring the filthy glance of a prim woman reading the racing pages a couple of tables away.

The murmured conversation only took a minute.

Jerry stuffed the phone into his pocket, left the library and strode rapidly to the residential street just outside the centre of town where he had parked his car. He opened the trunk, and checked that the rifle was where it should be.

He switched on the engine, and headed out of town and north towards Wyvis, grinning to himself. The job would soon be done. Now he knew the police were not on his trail, he should have enough time to get away, maybe even as far as Glasgow, before they discovered the crime, let alone figured out which car he was driving.

Once he got to Glasgow, he should be able to disappear. It would be impossible to leave the country on his passport. But he had help and access to funds. Between them, they would figure something out.

Things were looking good.

Madeleine hung up the phone in the booth and surveyed the small departure lounge of Inverness Airport. The porter stood a short distance away with her two bags, looking discreetly in the other direction as she made her call.

She didn't like what she had just done, but she had had little choice. This was just like Alden's murder, just like Sophie's. Their deaths set in motion treacherous eddies and undercurrents which dragged down everyone near them for years afterwards.

She wished she hadn't gotten Clémence involved. At the time it had seemed necessary – Clémence was the only person Madeleine could think of to look after Alastair and get him out of the hospital until Madeleine could get to Scotland herself. She had wanted to make sure that Alastair was out of the clutches of any physical therapists or psychiatrists if he did start remembering things; much better if he was in a lonely cottage with only Madeleine there to listen to him, once she had sent Clémence back to university. If the old man really had forgotten everything permanently, Jerry could have let him live.

She had still thought of Clémence as a pliable schoolgirl. She should have anticipated that Clémence would ask questions about the old man's life and get answers, especially since it was quite likely that

Death At Wyvis would be lying around his house. A couple of years ago, Madeleine would have foreseen all that. Age was slowing her down, blunting her mind which had been so sharp. She *hated* that.

She would do what she could for Jerry, as he now called himself. Although Bill Paxton, the family lawyer, would never involve himself with false identities and safe hiding places, she was hopeful that he would put her in touch with someone else who would, for the right amount of money. Bill would know not to ask questions. Like his father before him, from whom he had inherited his practice, he knew never to underestimate Madeleine.

23

Clémence, the old man and Callum rode to Wyvis in silence. The taxi driver tried to make cheery conversation, but soon gave up. The old man sat in the front passenger seat, staring out at the snow-streaked Glen Glass. Clémence sat in the back with Callum, her fingers curled around his. She had interpreted his glance correctly at lunch with Madeleine; he had thought that they should go to Wyvis with the old man before calling the police. She felt bad that she had dragged him into such a dangerous situation, but so relieved that he was there. He was a year younger than her, yet he exuded a calm competence that she and the old man lacked.

But he was no match for a man armed with a rifle who was willing to use it. None of them was.

Callum leaped out of the taxi to open the gate at the entrance to the estate. As the taxi drove through, Sheila MacInnes rushed out, arms folded against the cold.

Clémence wound down her window.

'Clémence, pet, are you OK? Did you really spend the night on the mountain?'

'We did,' said Clémence. 'And it wasn't much fun.'

'You radge! You could have killed yourselves. Are you all right, Alastair?'

'I'm fine, now, Mrs MacInnes,' said the old man. 'I had a hot bath in Dingwall. I can't wait to get home.'

'Shouldn't you be in hospital?' said Sheila.

'Alastair's much too tough for that,' said Clémence.

'Someone vandalized your car yesterday,' Sheila said. 'Callum probably told you. Broke a window and let down the tyres. Terry has pumped them up again. Did you leave anything valuable in there? Terry said they didn't take the radio.'

'No, nothing,' said Clémence.

'It's worrying,' said Sheila. 'We haven't seen any strangers about, apart from this young man, of course. You gave him a scare. And us.'

'I'm sorry, Sheila,' said Clémence. 'Did Jerry see anyone?'

'Jerry's off somewhere. His car is gone.'

That was good to know.

'You will report it to the police, won't you?'

'I will,' said Clémence. 'See you later, Sheila.'

The taxi drove on through the woods towards the loch.

'Callum? Can I ask you something?' the old man said.

'Sure.'

'Do you know what atelier means?'

'It's French, isn't it? I should know, but I don't.'

'Hah! Hear that, Clémence? He says it's French. Smart lad, your boyfriend.'

'No he's not, he's ignorant,' said Clémence, jabbing Callum in the shoulder. 'We've got to find that dictionary!'

It was a sunny day and the snow was melting, at least down by the loch. They passed Corravachie, and Clémence was pleased to see that Jerry's car had indeed gone. The cottage looked shut up: no smoke from the chimney.

Culzie appeared to be empty too. Clémence glanced at the Clio and noted the smashed window on the driver's side. She paid the taxi driver and opened the front door.

'Let me, Clemmie,' said Callum.

Although Jerry was in theory away from the estate, Clémence was happy to let Callum go first.

'Hello?' he shouted. No reply. The house creaked as Callum stepped on ancient floorboards, but there was no sound in response. It felt empty. He put his head into the kitchen and the sitting room, before climbing the stairs. Clémence followed him, and paused halfway up as he checked the bedrooms.

'There's no one here,' he said.

Clémence hurried up the steps and into the study. The desk stood waiting for her in front of the view of the loch. She remembered exactly where she had seen the black exercise book with the red binding.

She ripped open the drawer and there it was!

Carefully, she lifted it out on to the desk, noticing as she did so that underneath it was a second exercise book, identical to the first.

She flicked open the cover.

A blank page.

She riffled through the exercise book. Blank pages. She seized the second book. Same. Empty. They were both empty!

'They must be spares. The one Alastair wrote in must be gone.'

'Let me see!' said the old man who had arrived at the top of the steep staircase panting. 'Yes, that's the right type of exercise book,' he said. He, too, leafed through the empty pages.

'I'm sorry,' said Clémence. 'I was sure it was here. We've wasted our journey!'

The disappointment rested heavily on the old man, adding a further burden on to an already exhausted body.

'Where can it be?' said Clémence. 'Any memory of what you did with it?'

The old man shook his head. 'I can remember writing it just here. And I did keep it in that drawer on top of those two others. But what I did with it? No idea.'

Clémence fought to control her frustration. She knew it wasn't true, but sometimes she felt the old man chose what to remember and what to forget just to exasperate her.

'What are these?' said Callum. He was holding two opened envelopes. 'One was on the desk, and I found the other under that bottom exercise book.'

Clémence looked at them. 'That's from Madeleine,' she said, pointing to the one with the United States stamp, which she had noticed on the desk before.

'And that's from Stephen,' said the old man. 'And yes, I do remember his handwriting somehow.'

Callum handed them to the old man. He stared at the two envelopes, and then passed them on to Clémence. 'You read them,' he said.

'Are you sure?' said Clémence. 'They might be private.'

'They will certainly be private,' said the old man with a rueful smile. 'And there will be things in them that are humiliating. But I've got used to you reading that kind of thing to me.' He gave Callum a wry smile. 'You can listen too. The more the merrier.'

The old man pulled back the desk chair and collapsed into it. Clémence rested against the desk. She hesitated, and picked out the letter from Stephen first. She began to read.

Talbot Road
W11

3 December 1998

Dear Alastair,

I got your letter. I suppose I should thank you for discovering who did kill Sophie. I am sure that now we finally have the answer.

As to your questions, no, I do not want you to go to the police. And I certainly don't want you to publish another edition of that damned book. It's caused enough trouble already.

Drop it, Alastair, you interfering old bugger. Do you understand me? Drop it! Just let me live the rest of my shitty life in some peace, will you?

Stephen

'Well that's pretty clear,' said the old man. 'Poor chap.'

'It implies you told him the name of Sophie's killer,' said Clémence. 'I wonder who it was? That means it wasn't you, doesn't it?' She badly hoped the old man wasn't a killer after all. 'You're innocent! Don't you see?'

'Maybe Madeleine's letter will say,' said Callum.

'Read it,' said the old man.

Clémence thought he was very calm, given he had just discovered he was not a murderer. 'Aren't you pleased?'

'I'm not taking anything for granted until I am absolutely sure. Now, tell me what Madeleine has to say.'

Clémence slid a couple of thin blue sheets of paper out of the second envelope, the one with the US stamps.

> *610 Park Avenue*
> *NY*
>
> *January 10*

Dear Alastair,

Thank you for your sweet letter about Nathan's death. Despite your last meeting, I know how much Nathan treasured your letters over the years. You were a good friend to him in a life, which although so successful on the surface, encompassed a series of such dreadful tragedies.

I am still in shock from what you told Nathan and me when you last saw us. I suppose it must be true, but I cannot accept it.

As you can imagine, the last couple of months have been very trying for me. The double shock of your visit and Nathan's death has been difficult for someone of my age – yes, I must admit that I am eighty-five! And although Nathan retired from the board eight years ago, he and I are still the major stockholders in Wakefield Oil, and there is a lot to attend to there. I suppose money helps – we have so much money – but now I come toward the end of my life, it doesn't seem to matter. Sophie matters still, as do you and Stephen and Nathan.

So please, for my sake, do not republish "Death At Wyvis". I understood that when the book first came out you wanted to set the record straight. But then Stephen was in prison for a crime he did not commit, and Sophie's murder was still part of the lives of the rest of us. But now Tony, Elaine and poor Nathan have gone, it's just you, me and Stephen. My understanding is that Stephen wants to forget the whole thing. I would much rather leave it buried. Sophie's children never wanted to know, and I don't think her grandchildren even know she was murdered.

So it's just you, Alastair, who would like to see the book republished. Please, I beg of you, don't do it.

Amitiés

Madeleine

'They are both pretty clear about not wanting to see a second edition,' said Clémence.

'I bet I didn't listen to them,' said the old man.

'Maybe you sent the exercise book to a publisher, after all?' said Clémence. 'Who published the original book?'

'Woodrow and Shippe,' said Callum. 'I've never heard of them.'

'Perhaps they don't exist any more,' said Clémence. 'What is it, Alastair?'

The old man was thinking. Deeply. Had he remembered something?

'Madeleine wrote that I spoke to Nathan *and* her about something that shocked them both in New York last year. Didn't she?'

'She did.'

'Yet at lunch in the pub she said she didn't know what I had told Nathan.'

'That's right,' said Clémence. 'And it sounds as if you told both of them who had killed Sophie. And it wasn't you.'

'I hope it wasn't me,' said the old man. 'It looks that way, but we can't be absolutely sure of that yet. What I want to know is, if Madeleine was with Nathan when I told him who killed Sophie last year, why hasn't she told us any of this? Why did she pretend she knew nothing about it?'

Clémence and the old man exchanged glances. Why indeed? Clémence thought it was pretty clear now that the old man was innocent of her grandmother's death, but she could understand his reluctance to take anything for granted after the confusion of the last forty years.

They heard a car climbing the hill up to the cottage.

'God, is that Jerry?' cried Clémence as she dashed to the window.

It was a taxi. And inside Clémence could dimly make out the figure of a man. An old man. Another old man.

'It's Grandpa! What's he doing here?'

'Is that Stephen?' said the old man.

Stephen pulled himself out of the taxi and paid the driver. He was tall with white hair and a stoop, but nevertheless he had presence. He turned to the cottage and then for some reason looked up and saw Clémence and the old man at the window. He had a strong rectangular face, doughty chin and long nose. His forehead and cheeks were ravaged by a warren of wrinkles, like a trench system abandoned after a long war. He held their eyes for a moment, his face expressionless, before turning to the front door as his taxi drove away.

Clémence ran downstairs and opened the door. She wanted to hug him, but his tall, stooping presence was forbidding. She jumped on him anyway, and kissed his leathery cheek.

'Goodness me,' he said gruffly. 'Is the old bugger here? I thought I saw him with you upstairs?'

'The "old bugger" is here, Grandpa. Come in. Can I get you some tea?'

'Got any whisky?' said Stephen, following Clémence into the sitting room.

'And this is my boyfriend, Callum,' said Clémence. Callum was hovering on the bottom step.

'Hello, Mr Smith,' said Callum, holding out his hand.

Stephen looked at it, and for a moment it seemed as if he wasn't going to shake it, but then he clasped it briefly. 'Trickett-Smith,' he growled.

Clémence found Stephen a seat. There was a bottle of Famous Grouse on a little table by the door and she fetched a couple of glasses from the kitchen, and put on the kettle.

Alastair shuffled into the living room. 'Hello, Stephen.'

Stephen ignored him but collapsed into a chair. Alastair sat down opposite him. Clémence watched as the two old men stared at each other under impressive eyebrows.

24

Alastair examined the old man opposite, his former friend, former rival, former enemy. He didn't recognize the features in front of him, the unkempt white hair, the ravaged face, the wayward bristles sprouting from nostrils and ears. But he recalled the fair-haired, handsome airman with the Roman nose, grinning at him in black and white from a wartime cinema screen. And then he remembered the picnic in Capri with Sophie and Stephen and Elaine. And the tall, immensely charming undergraduate working his way through a bottle of hock in an ancient wood-panelled room that must have been Alastair's at their college at Oxford.

Clémence handed Stephen his whisky.

'I'll have one of those,' said Alastair.

As she poured a second glass, Stephen spoke. 'And where is the interfering old bat?'

'Do you mean Aunt Madeleine?' said Clémence.

'Of course, I mean Madeleine. Who else is an interfering old bat?'

Clémence handed Alastair his whisky. 'Can you make me a cup of tea, Callum?' she asked.

'Sure thing,' said Callum.

'We had lunch with her in Dingwall,' Clémence said. 'She's at the airport now, probably, waiting for a flight to London.'

'Good,' said Stephen. He sipped his whisky. 'So you fell down the stairs? Those stairs, presumably?'

'Yes,' said Alastair.

'Hit your head? Can't remember anything, Clémence tells me.'

'Virtually nothing. Some things come back eventually, hazily.'

'Didn't it occur to you that that was a good thing?' Stephen said. 'That you should bugger off back to Australia and leave things best forgotten forgotten?'

'It doesn't work like that,' said Alastair, calmly. 'I didn't know what I had forgotten. I didn't even know who I was. That's what Clémence did, help me find out who I was.'

Stephen snorted. 'That must have been an unpleasant discovery.'

'Yes,' said Alastair, holding Stephen's eyes, refusing to be provoked. 'Yes, it was.'

'What are you doing here, Grandpa?' Clémence asked.

Stephen looked away from Alastair and up to his granddaughter, who was still standing. 'When I realized what you and Alastair were up to, reading that bloody book and everything, I thought it would be easier all round if I came up here and told you all you want to know. Then you'll go back to St Andrews, and he will piss off back to Australia.'

'Thank you,' said Alastair. He felt his hopes rising. It sounded as if he was at last going to get to the truth, or close to the truth. And whereas previously the truth had frightened him, now, with Clémence's support, he felt braver about facing it, even hopeful.

Stephen's glare switched back to him.

'I mean it. Thank you, Stephen. You have come a long way. I appreciate it. I suspect we both do, don't we, Clémence?'

'Yes,' said Clémence. 'Thanks, Grandpa.'

'All right,' said Stephen. 'Let's get on with it. What can I tell you?'

Alastair took a deep breath. It was time, time to discover who he truly was.

'Who killed Sophie?'

'You've read all of that damned book, I take it?' said Stephen.

'Yes.'

'Well, it's all wrong. You got completely the wrong end of the stick, old lad.'

'So Alastair didn't kill her?' Clémence asked, her eyes shining.

Stephen seemed a little disconcerted by her excitement. 'No. And neither did I. It was Nathan.'

'Nathan?' said Alastair. A wave of relief was poised to burst over him. Relief that he was not a murderer after all. Relief that he was not quite the evil person he thought he was. But he held it in check. He wanted to listen; he wanted to learn. 'What happened?'

'That night, Nathan saw you and Sophie sneak off to the boat-house. He followed you and waited while you made love to my wife. Then, when you left, he went inside. He killed Sophie. He heard you coming back and he whacked you over the head with an oar, without you seeing him. You were out cold; apparently he thought you were dead. He dumped Sophie in the loch and returned to check on you. But you had come round.'

The old man listened closely. 'Had I seen him kill Sophie?'

'No, or else he would have finished you off. You had no idea she was dead until the stalker found her the next day — the book is correct about that, at least.'

'So what were you doing at the time?'

'Stumbling around looking for Sophie. When I saw the French windows in the drawing room were open, I went outside to search the garden. Then I noticed the boathouse door was open too, so I had a look in there, which is how I left my footprint. I didn't notice anything wrong, but then I was too pissed. Nathan watched me stag-gering around, but left me to it. He just wanted to get you into bed and out of the way. Then, when the police decided I was a suspect, he was willing to go along with that. And so were you, apparently.'

'Yes,' said Clémence. 'We found the original manuscript of *Death At Wyvis*, and that says Nathan found Angus unconscious.'

'I haven't seen that,' said Stephen. 'But you sent it to Nathan from Australia. He put a lot of pressure on you not to publish it, but you insisted. So then he got you to change it. By that stage he had persuaded you that you had killed Sophie yourself and just forgotten it.'

'So that's why Alastair called it a novel?' said Clémence.

'I suppose so,' said Stephen.

'Presumably I told you all this?' said Alastair.

'That's right. You said you'd come back here from Australia to see if you could find out more about Sophie's death. You had read an article in a medical journal about false memories: apparently people with amnesia have a tendency to fill in the gaps with what makes sense, and then begin to believe it's real. You thought you might have done that yourself. Turns out you had.'

'It certainly sounds like it.'

'I think I saw that article upstairs in the study,' said Clémence. 'Something about "confabulation".'

'And then when I got here I spoke to Pauline Ferguson?' said the old man.

'She the old stalker's wife?'

'That's her. We saw her this morning.'

'Well, she told you there was something fishy about her son that night. He was helping out with serving dinner and clearing up; now he lives in New York. You tracked him down over there, and got him to spill the beans. He told you that on his way home on his bike he saw Nathan whacking you over the head with the oar. But Nathan gave him two hundred pounds on the spot to shut him up, and then set him up in business in America to keep him shut up.'

'This was last October?' said Alastair.

'I think so. Then you went to see Nathan. You confronted him. He admitted it was he who had killed Sophie.'

'Was Madeleine there?'

'You saw Nathan alone in his study.'

'So Aunt Madeleine was telling the truth!' said Clémence. 'She didn't know Nathan killed Sophie after all.'

Stephen shook his head. 'After you had spoken to Nathan, you insisted on telling Madeleine. You said she had a right to know who had killed her sister.'

'How did she take that?' Alastair said.

'She didn't like it one bit. She was furious with Nathan. There was an almighty row and you were thrown out of the house. I'm surprised you can't remember that.'

'Why?' asked Alastair. 'Did Nathan say why he killed Sophie?'

'Not exactly. But you seem to have pieced it together. Sophie had told him earlier that evening that she had made up her mind to go to the police about how Alden had really died in 1935 or whenever it was. Nathan tried to blackmail Sophie, threatening to tell me about you and the boathouse if she went to the police about Alden.' Stephen shook his head. 'That was never going to work.'

He paused and swallowed. Clémence and Alastair watched him, gave him time.

'Nathan said when she refused he lost his temper and killed Sophie in a rage. An impulsive murder, just like Alden's.'

'Did I believe him?'

'No. You said it was opportunistic rather than impulsive. You seemed to think that in Deauville Nathan had spotted the opportunity to kill Alden under the guise of the mock swordfight. He knew all along that he would inherit a lot. Nathan was very ambitious then; I remember he wanted to be one of the men with money in college. "Swells" he used to call us. So quaint.'

'People like you?'

'Like me.' Stephen laughed. 'It's extraordinary to think now that I ever had that much money. Not you though. You never had two shillings to rub together.'

'So Nathan killed Sophie to keep her quiet?'

'That's about the size of it.'

The old man thought through what Stephen had said. It all made sense, it all fitted. It injected some logic into what had seemed an illogical life.

'How do you know all this?' Alastair asked. 'I wrote to you, didn't I? We saw your reply.'

'Yes, you did. You wrote saying you were going to publish everything you had found out. I told you not to be so damned stupid. Then you came down to London, oh a month ago, maybe. You had written everything down in an exercise book. Everything I've just told you. I read it through. I told you I still didn't want you to publish, and neither did Madeleine. You insisted. We had quite an argument. Are you sure you don't remember? It was only a few weeks ago.'

'It seems to be the most recent stuff that is hardest to get back,' said Clémence.

Alastair nodded. 'I don't remember the argument at all. But I do remember I needed to give you something. Show you something. It must have been the exercise book. Do you know where it is now?'

'Isn't it here?' said Stephen.

'No,' said Clémence.

'Well, I don't know where it is. Look.' Stephen leaned forward, staring at Alastair. 'I've told you everything. You know it all now. There's nothing to find out. It's done. So you can go back to Australia, Madeleine can go back to New York, Clémence can go back to St Andrews and I can go home. And none of us need talk about this again.'

'It's not that easy,' said Alastair.

'Why not? Why the hell not?' Stephen glared. 'Now you know what you've forgotten, can't you just forget it again?'

Alastair listened to his old friend, the man whose life he and Nathan had ruined. His brain was tumbling, trying to comprehend the rearranged jigsaw of his life. He wasn't a murderer. But he had let down his friends, Stephen above all.

'I'm sorry,' he said. He wouldn't ask for forgiveness this time. He knew he wouldn't get it.

Stephen didn't answer. His handsome face was ravaged with sadness. Anger. Bitterness. Alastair knew he had betrayed this man, and he was truly sorry. Although he barely remembered him, Stephen seemed very familiar, not a stranger at all.

'We used to be good friends,' he said.

Stephen spluttered in impatience. 'And now we're not,' he said. 'Don't talk to me about the past.'

'Why not?' said the old man. 'At our age, what else is there?'

'The past is nothing,' Stephen said. 'Do you know, I actually feel jealous of you? I wish I could forget my past. Erase it.'

Alastair listened. He understood, or at least he thought he did.

'And don't start pitying me either,' Stephen said, recognizing something in Alastair's eyes. 'My life is pretty good. I get up. I do the crossword. I have a pint with a mate. I put something on a nag; sometimes I win, sometimes I don't. Life's all right. Until you bring all this bullshit back into it.'

Alastair wasn't going to apologize again. Nor was he going to back down.

'Do you know who Jerry Ranger is, Grandpa?' Clémence asked.

Stephen tore his eyes away from Alastair. 'Jerry Ranger? No. Sounds like a cowboy.'

'He's a singer. More of a song writer really. He's American. And he chased us over Ben Wyvis last night with a rifle.'

'Really?' Stephen's eyes narrowed. 'Where is he now?'

'We have no idea. He may have assumed we have called the police and disappeared. Or he may still be after us.'

'All the more reason for us all to go home. He won't follow us. Not if we stay quiet.'

'How do you know?' said Alastair.

'I know,' said Stephen.

Jerry made good time to Evanton. Although Madeleine had said he should still be safe, he kept his eyes open for police cars, but didn't spot any.

At Evanton, he turned up the glen and was soon at the gates to the estate. He jumped out of the car to open them, and as he slowly drove through, Terry MacInnes appeared.

Jerry wound down the window. Stay calm.

'Did you have a good trip?' Terry asked.

'Yes, I've been over to Loch Maree. I stayed overnight there at a hotel. I hoped to go walking, but couldn't with the weather. Mind you, it's awesome in the snow.'

'It can be very dangerous up on the hills in this weather. Alastair and the wee lassie who's looking after him went up Ben Wyvis yesterday. Can you believe it? They ended up staying the night up there. They were lucky they didn't die of hypothermia, if you see what I mean.'

'Really?' said Jerry. 'That's awful. Are they OK?'

'Aye. Sheila saw them an hour or so ago. They ended up going down the mountain on the southern side and getting a taxi.'

'Well, I'm glad they're all right,' said Jerry.

'I see you've been to the barber's,' Terry said.

'Yes,' said Jerry, rubbing his smooth chin. 'The beard was only ever temporary.'

Terry glanced up doubtfully at Jerry's poorly cropped scalp. 'Aye, well, I can recommend Tommy in Dingwall next time you need a wee trim.'

'I'll remember that,' said Jerry, reaching for the switch to close the window.

'Afore you go, there's been some vandals on the estate.'

'Oh?' said Jerry, halting the window.

'Aye. They broke in to the lassie's car and let down her tyres. They didn't take anything. But you should check no one has broken into Corravachie. I'm a wee thing worried about the rifle in the gun cupboard there. And if you see any strangers about, let me know, will you?'

'I will,' said Jerry, forcing a grin.

Finally he could pull away. He had no intention of checking the gun cupboard at Corravachie. He knew the rifle was safe in the trunk together with some garden loppers he had bought in Dingwall on the way from Inverness. They should do the trick.

25

'Yes, but how do you know Jerry won't come after us if we leave?' the old man asked.

Clémence was wondering the same thing.

'Look.' Stephen's voice was rising. 'I came hundreds of miles up here to give you what you want. The truth. I've done that. You know who killed Sophie. It wasn't me and it wasn't you; it was Nathan. So it's over. Let's go back to our miserable lives.'

'I need to call the police,' said Clémence. She was beginning to wish she had done it earlier. Much earlier.

'No!' said Stephen.

'But, Grandpa, I must. We were shot at last night! There is a nutcase running around somewhere out there with a rifle!'

'I forbid it.'

Clémence glanced at Alastair for support, but didn't find any. Of course *he* didn't want to call the police.

'I'm afraid we have to, Mr Trickett-Smith,' said Callum. And before Stephen could stop him, he was in the hallway picking up the phone.

Clémence saw him frown and stare at the receiver. He pressed the cradle rapidly. 'Does this phone work, Clemmie?'

'It should do,' said Clémence. 'Here, let me try.' She took the receiver from him. 'You're right, it's dead.'

'Jerry has cut the line,' said the old man.

Fear clutched at Clémence's chest. 'That means he's out there,' she said. 'Maybe right outside now.'

'He could have cut the telephone wire further down the loch,' said Callum.

'I don't care what you two say, we need help,' said Clémence.

'I'll go,' said Callum. 'It's about three miles to the Stalker's Lodge. I can run that.'

'But what about Jerry?'

'I'll keep my eyes peeled. You had better hide out the back somewhere. In the woods.'

'OK,' said Clémence. 'But go out the back door yourself. He might be here already.'

Callum slipped out the back. A moment later, he knocked on the front door. 'It's me!' he called.

Clémence opened up.

'He's definitely not here,' Callum said. 'Which means he must have cut the wires back at the bottom of the loch.'

'Be careful, Callum,' said Clémence, biting her lip.

'And you,' said Callum.

Callum was fit. But he needed to pace himself just right. He had done 5K in nineteen minutes back in November, but that was in running kit. The surface wasn't too bad — the previous night's snow had melted off the track — but it was getting dark.

He was having second thoughts about abandoning Clémence. Someone had to get help, and he was clearly the best person to do it, but he had left her in a much more dangerous situation than his own. Too late now, he was committed and they were relying on him.

He had gone barely five minutes when he heard a car approaching. He darted off the road and threw himself in the bracken behind a scruffy tree, ready to jump out and wave if it turned out to be Terry MacInnes's Land Rover.

It wasn't. Even in the evening gloom, Callum could tell from the headlights that it was a smaller car. As it passed him, he could see there was one driver.

That must be Jerry.

For a moment he hesitated. Jerry was armed. If Callum returned to the house he might get killed. He could quite legitimately press on to the Stalker's Lodge to get help.

Only for a moment. He couldn't leave Clemmie to be shot dead, he just couldn't.

He scrambled to his feet and hit the track running. Back to Culzie.

Clémence put on her coat and grabbed the two old men's. They were showing no sign of moving.

Alastair was looking at Stephen steadily. Clémence knew him well enough by now to see that he was thinking, thinking hard.

'I know who Jerry Ranger is,' he said.

'You do?' said Clémence.

'He's Fabrice, isn't he, Stephen? Your son, Fabrice?'

Stephen raised his bushy eyebrows. 'That's absurd. Didn't you say this man is an American? Fabrice is English! Half-French maybe. But not American.'

'Where is Fabrice now, Stephen?' the old man asked.

'I've got no idea,' said Stephen. 'I haven't seen him for years.'

'Where did he go, last time you heard?'

Stephen spluttered. 'How should I know? That's ridiculous!'

'You must know where he went. You must have some inkling.'

'Well . . . Morocco. Yes, that's right, he went to Morocco.'

'My father went to Morocco,' said Clémence. 'Not Fabrice. I thought Fabrice went to America somewhere?'

'No. I'm sure that's not right.'

'It seems to me most likely that Nathan was run down on purpose in Arizona,' said the old man. 'It's just too much of a coincidence that he should have died that soon after I discovered it was him who killed Sophie.'

'Didn't the American police say it was an accident?' Stephen said.

Alastair ignored him. 'At first I thought I might have killed him, in

331

some kind of revenge. But then it seemed at least possible that Jerry Ranger had killed Nathan and was trying to kill me. Who would want to do that?'

'I don't bloody know,' said Stephen. 'And I doubt you do either.'

'Someone who wanted to avenge Sophie's death. And someone who didn't like me either. You are a possibility, but that doesn't seem likely.'

'Of course it's not likely, you stupid bugger.'

'So then there's your children, Sophie's children. Clémence's father, Rupert perhaps? But Clémence would have known if Jerry was her father, obviously. There was a daughter, Beatrix, was it? And then there was the eldest son, Fabrice, if I remember the book correctly. He would have been born in the early forties, which would make him mid-fifties. Jerry's age now.'

'You're guessing,' Stephen said, but Clémence could see the doubt in his eyes.

'I've never met Uncle Fabrice,' said Clémence. 'But I'm sure Maman told me once he lived in America.'

'No one told me that,' said Stephen.

'You see, the thing is, Stephen, I remember.'

'You remember?'

'I remember figuring this out before.'

The old men stared at each other. Stephen was visibly trying to maintain his angry denial, but Clémence could see it crumble. Finally, he lowered his eyes.

'You're right,' he said. 'When I was sent to prison, Fabrice was seventeen. He was at boarding school and being shuttled between my parents and Sophie's. Then, at the beginning of term, he got on the train to school at Euston Station and was never seen again. Madeleine tracked him down years later and discovered he had changed his name to Jerry Ranger and become a hippie. Wrote songs. Apparently, he went to jail himself.' Stephen smiled ruefully. 'Killed his own wife, just like his dad.'

'You didn't kill anyone, Grandpa.'

'Perhaps not,' said Stephen. 'But we both did time for it. So, you are right. Jerry Ranger *is* Fabrice.'

'And Fabrice killed Nathan?' the old man said.

Stephen shrugged. 'I don't know.'

'But why would Fabrice want to kill Alastair?' Clémence asked.

'Why wouldn't he?' said Stephen. He sighed. 'When you came down to London and showed me that damned exercise book, you had written at the end that Fabrice had killed Nathan. You wanted me to confirm it. I refused to, after all I didn't know for sure myself, and I was pretty certain you were just guessing. You didn't seem to know that Fabrice had changed his name, or what his new name was.'

'And you told Fabrice this?' said Clémence.

'I didn't tell Fabrice, no,' said Stephen. 'I really have only seen him once in the last forty years. He came to visit me in London about ten years ago after he had been let out of jail. I told him not to see me again.'

'So who did you tell?' the old man asked.

'Madeleine. I told her that you suspected Fabrice killed Nathan.'

'You don't think Aunt Madeleine told Fabrice?'

Stephen shrugged. Shrugged in a way that suggested yes, he did think that.

Although Clémence was desperate to find out more, Jerry – or her Uncle Fabrice – was on his way. 'Come on, you two, we've got to get out of here now. Get your coats on!'

'No,' said the old man.

'No? Don't be silly! Come on!'

'I can't face another night out there,' said the old man. 'I want to talk to this man Fabrice.'

'But he wants to kill you!'

'I'll stay too,' said Stephen. 'I'd like to see my son.'

'You're both crazy,' said Clémence. It was possible Stephen might be safe, but it seemed to her highly likely that if Alastair stayed in the cottage, he wouldn't live long. She grabbed hold of his arm, dragging him up out of the chair.

'Leave me alone!' the old man snapped. 'I have a right to stay here if I want to. But you should go. Go now! Go!'

Clémence hesitated. Maybe he did have the right to stay and get shot. But she didn't want to be murdered by her lunatic uncle.

'All right,' she said. 'Good luck, both of you.'

On an impulse, she kissed Alastair on the cheek, and then Stephen, and then she rushed to the back door and opened it.

There, pointing a rifle directly at her chest, was Jerry Ranger.

26

'Hi, Clémence.'

Jerry was smiling. He had lost his beard, his grey hair had been clipped short, and his eyes were red with fatigue. But he was wired; he looked ready to pull the trigger at any second.

Clémence opened her mouth, but no sound came out.

'Step back. Slowly,' said Jerry. 'And go back into the living room.'

'OK,' said Clémence. It was little more than a squeak.

She raised her hands above her head and backed into the sitting room. Stephen was on his feet, but Alastair was still rooted to his chair.

Jerry was surprised to see Stephen. 'What the hell are you doing here?'

'Just visiting,' said Stephen. 'Trying to straighten things out.'

'Hello, Fabrice,' the old man said.

Jerry frowned. 'How does he know who I am, Dad?' Jerry, or Fabrice, asked Stephen.

'I've never heard you call me "Dad" before,' said Stephen.

'How does he know?' Fabrice repeated.

'He remembered. Just earlier, when we were talking. He remembered figuring it out before.'

'Actually, I was guessing,' said the old man. To Clémence's amazement, he was smiling. 'Claiming I remembered just gave it more credibility.'

'Why didn't you deny it?' Fabrice demanded.

Stephen glared at his son. 'Because the more we know and accept the truth, the more we can move on with our lives, and that would be a very good thing.'

'But now *she* knows who I really am,' said Fabrice, letting his gun swing towards Clémence. 'That means I have to kill her too.'

At those words, shock became fear. Clémence didn't want to die. She felt panic explode in her chest; she wanted to scream, to collapse on the floor and sob. She fought to control it. Keep a clear head. Her only chance was to keep a clear head.

'But she's my granddaughter!' protested Stephen. 'Your niece. You can't kill her!'

'She's not your granddaughter,' Fabrice sneered. 'I've read the novel. And I've read that exercise book. She's *his* granddaughter.' Fabrice nodded contemptuously towards the old man. 'Rupert was *his* son, not yours.'

'I don't accept that, Fabrice! That's just not true!' Stephen's voice was rising in anger.

'Clémence is your mother's granddaughter,' said the old man. 'That still makes her your niece.'

Fabrice turned to him. 'I don't care who she is! If she knows who I really am, she will tell the police. She has to die too.'

'Madeleine won't like that, will she?' said the old man.

'What's Madeleine got to do with it?' said Fabrice.

'Madeleine told you Nathan killed Sophie. Madeleine helped set up Nathan's death.' He paused. Clémence could see an idea coming to him. 'Madeleine told you we were here.'

'You don't remember that,' said Fabrice. 'You're just guessing again.'

'But I'm right, aren't I?' said the old man. 'Madeleine was quite happy to see me dead, but not her favourite great-niece. She forbade you to harm her.'

For a moment, hope flickered. Clémence could see the old man was trying to negotiate for her life. He knew he was going to die soon, but he was trying to keep her alive. And not doing a bad job of it.

But Fabrice was right. If he let Clémence live, she would tell the police who he was. She could try promising to stay quiet, but her promise would mean nothing, and Fabrice wouldn't trust it.

'I'll just have to tell Madeleine I'm sorry,' said Fabrice. 'That I had no choice. She won't like it, but she'll have to live with it.' He stared hard at the old man. 'I've come a long way to do this, and I'm going to do it. You and Nathan, you destroyed our family. If my father hadn't gone to prison for a crime he didn't commit, all our lives would be different. My life wouldn't have been the total fuck-up that it is, I wouldn't have done the drugs. I wouldn't have killed Wendy, wouldn't have gone to jail . . .' He paused. 'The shrinks had a field day with all that, said I never stood a chance. And they were right. Nathan did all that. And you, you did it too. I didn't let him escape the consequences, and I'm not going to let you.'

'I understand why you want to kill me,' said the old man. 'And Nathan. But not Clémence.'

'That's your fault, Alastair. You brought her into this. You bear the responsibility.'

Clémence wanted to protest, to point out that it was Madeleine who had sent her to see Alastair, that none of this was the old man's fault, but she found she couldn't speak. And she knew Fabrice wouldn't listen.

'So you have my black exercise book?' said the old man. 'Did you steal it from here?'

'Yes. After I knocked you down the stairs. In fact, that's why I knocked you down the stairs; I meant to kill you then. Madeleine had told me what was in the book, that you had figured out I had run down Nathan Giannelli, and so I had to destroy it, and destroy you.'

'What about me?' said Stephen. 'What are you going to do with me? Your own father?'

For a moment, Fabrice looked confused. The barrel of the rifle was wavering. Clémence thought of trying to jump him. Then she heard a soft click coming from the hallway. Fabrice hadn't noticed.

'I'll hit you over the head,' he said to his father. 'You can pretend to have been unconscious. Say that you didn't know who I was. Better than that, you didn't even see me. You can do that, can't you, Dad? To stay alive.'

Clémence looked at her grandfather. Would he abandon her after all? He might, to stay alive.

That thought seemed to have occurred to Stephen as well. He nodded. 'All right, Fabrice. With any luck I will forget everything, just like this old fool.'

Clémence spotted movement behind Fabrice, who was standing with his back to the doorway, covering the three of them with his rifle. It was Callum!

He raised something above his head with both hands. It was a silver toaster he had grabbed from the kitchen, not much of a weapon, but it should stun Fabrice at the very least.

Too late, Clémence noticed Fabrice's own eyes narrow as they caught where hers were focusing. He ducked, twisted and swung the butt of his rifle, just as the toaster arced downwards. The toaster glanced off Fabrice's shoulder, but the rifle butt hit Callum hard in the ribs, and he doubled over.

Clémence rushed forwards, as Fabrice brought the butt down on Callum's skull. He crumpled.

Clémence threw herself at Fabrice, and they both careered into the wall. But Fabrice didn't fall. He writhed and twisted and shook her off. He took a couple of paces back and pointed his weapon at the two of them. Callum was on all fours on the floor, groaning, and Clémence slowly pulled herself to her feet.

She moved towards Callum.

'Leave him!' Fabrice shouted. 'Stand back and put your hands up. And you, whoever you are, you crawl over to Alastair and stay on the floor.'

Callum looked up, rubbing the back of his head, and did as he was ordered.

Fabrice stared at them, the barrel of his rifle skipping from one to the other. 'All right, who's first?' He glanced at Clémence and then his eyes fell on the old man. 'You, I think, Alastair. Definitely you.'

The old man stared back, defiant. Brave.

Clémence didn't feel brave, she was terrified. She didn't want to die, but the terror paralysed her. What should she do? Scream? Pray? Hold Callum's hand?

'Do it outside, Fabrice,' said Stephen.

'Why?'

'Less mess. Less forensic evidence. If you take them out and shoot them, we can dump them in the woods. It might be quite a while until anyone finds them. No one will even know they are dead for a bit. Shoot them here and there will be blood everywhere.'

Fabrice glanced at his father.

'Trust me. I'm a convicted murderer. I know of what I speak.'

The old bastard was making a joke of it! Clémence was glad that he wasn't her real grandfather after all.

'All right,' said Fabrice, after a moment's thought. 'Line up together in the hallway. If one of you runs, I will shoot the others and then you.'

He glared at Alastair. 'You go first out the back. Then the kid. Then Clémence.'

With an effort the old man hauled himself out of his chair and shuffled out to the hallway. Callum followed, still holding his head, and Clémence came last. She could hear Fabrice behind her. It was as if she could feel the gun pointed at her back.

Then she heard a crash, and swung around. Stephen was holding the toaster in both hands, watching as Fabrice staggered, the barrel of the rifle swaying.

'Callum!' Clémence shouted and grabbed the barrel. There was a flash and a deafening explosion in the narrow hallway. Plaster cracked inches away.

Fabrice straightened up and tried to yank the rifle away from her. Stephen rammed the toaster on his son's skull again, and Callum grabbed the stock of the rifle.

Clémence's ears were ringing, but she saw her opportunity and dug her teeth into Fabrice's hand. He let out a yell, and loosened his grip on the gun. The toaster crashed on his head again. Callum ripped the rifle away from him and then smashed the butt into his face.

Fabrice was on the floor.

'Give me that! I know how to use it,' said the old man. Callum handed him the rifle. The old man chambered the next round and pointed the gun at Fabrice's head. 'Move, and I'll blow your head off,' he growled. 'In fact, I might just blow it off anyway.'

The old man glanced at Stephen, who was straightening himself up, the toaster still in his hands, a lopsided grin of triumph on his face.

The old man smiled gruffly. 'Imaginative use of kitchen appliances, Stephen. When we've tidied up here, can I buy you a pint?'

'A pint? Tight-fisted old bastard. I'd say that deserves two at least.'

27

Madeleine watched as the uniformed British Airways attendant poured her tea.

'Would you like some cake, Mrs Giannelli? Some shortbread?'

'Oh, shortbread, please,' said Madeleine. She liked shortbread, even more than she liked chocolate digestive biscuits, Britain's two greatest contributions to world culture, as far as she was concerned.

She sipped her tea. The first-class lounge at Heathrow's Terminal Four was almost empty. A young man whom she thought she recognized from the television was reading a tabloid newspaper in a seat not far away. Young? He was probably fifty.

She was worried. She hadn't heard from Clémence at all. There were no messages from her at the Connaught when Madeleine had checked out a couple of hours earlier. Madeleine didn't own a cell phone, so she was effectively out of touch until she got back to her apartment on Park Avenue later that night.

Also nothing from Jerry.

Actually, although she was worried, it was nice to be out of touch for a few hours. Up in the sky, there was nothing she could do that would have any impact on the disaster that was unfolding in Scotland.

At times like this, she missed Nathan. They had been such a good team. Both of them capable, both of them ambitious, both of them respected each other. They had achieved a lot together, she and Nathan.

But it was all built on one massive, horrible lie. Nathan had killed her little sister Sophie and then kept quiet about it, despite all the

341

havoc it had caused in so many people's lives. Actually two lies. Nathan had killed her first husband as well. For their entire marriage Madeleine had been happy to go along with the others that it was all some ghastly accident, but now she wasn't so sure.

Her fury, which was never dormant for long these days, reignited.

Nathan had deserved to die. She didn't regret her part in that for one moment.

All along she had done what she could for Sophie's family. She had tried to keep in touch with her sister's three children. She had helped with Clémence's education, and with Beatrice's children's. She had even bought a small flat for Stephen to live in when he had been let out of jail. But she hadn't made it right. Only Nathan's death would make it right.

But the rest? She was too tired for all the rest. Like Alden's death, and Sophie's, Nathan's killing was giving birth to a whole series of unintended consequences, to at least one unintended death. Because Alastair Cunningham would probably now be dead.

And Madeleine regretted that now. Sophie had loved Alastair, of that she was sure. Alastair would have made a much better husband for her than Stephen. And she had felt some sympathy for the courageous old man she had met over the last couple of days, trying to do his best to sort out the chaos he had created.

Fabrice had insisted that Alastair had had to die, and Madeleine felt that she owed Fabrice her help and protection for killing her husband. When she had learned from Stephen that Nathan had really killed Sophie, she had felt it her duty to get in touch with all Sophie's children: Rupert, Beatrice and Fabrice. Beatrice and Rupert had not wanted to know, but Jerry, as he now was, had flown to Phoenix from LA immediately.

They had met in secret at a hotel in Scottsdale. She wasn't sure whose idea it was to kill Nathan; they both seemed to think of it at the same time. Jerry had already killed once before. Madeleine had been involved wittingly or unwittingly in the cover up of at least two deaths.

Nathan had had to die, and Jerry had run him down in a hit-and-run, using precise information from Madeleine about where and when Nathan went for his evening strolls at their house in Scottsdale.

But Alastair, rather than just shutting up, had kept asking questions, to the point where he had guessed or discovered what Fabrice had done, and was threatening to make it public. Although Alastair hadn't made the connection between Fabrice Trickett-Smith and Jerry Ranger, the police would once they started looking through their databases. Madeleine had felt duty-bound to tell Jerry, and having aided in his actions, didn't feel she had the right to stop him from protecting himself, even if that meant killing Alastair.

And, of course, once Jerry had killed Alastair, he would need to lie low. Probably get a new identity. All with Madeleine's help.

And so it would go on. And on. Who knew who else might end up dead in the future? Not Clémence, please not Clémence.

Actually, now Nathan was dead, Madeleine wanted to finish it all. Tell the truth, all of it. And face the consequences.

She bit into her shortbread.

'Mrs Giannelli?'

She looked up to see a polite young man in a suit holding out a warrant card. Two uniformed airport policemen armed with machine guns stood behind him. The other inhabitants of the first-class lounge were silent, staring.

'Yes?'

'My name is Detective Constable Ford. Will you accompany me to the police station? We have some questions to ask you in connection with the murder of your husband.'

Madeleine closed her eyes. Opened them. Smiled. It was over.

'With pleasure.'

28

Clémence slipped out of her French New Wave film studies lecture and hurried down the Scores to the hotel. She saw the old man alone at a table in a corner of the dining room, examining the menu.

'Alastair!' she shouted and rushed over to him. He scrambled to his feet and accepted her hug with a grin. 'It's so nice to see you!' she gabbled. 'Thanks for coming all this way to take me to lunch. You look very well.'

'Not at all,' said the old man. 'I feel very well.'

Clémence sat opposite him. The world-weary confusion had been replaced by sprightliness. His brown eyes twinkled. He was still thin, and very old, but there was steel in the way that he sat, in his jaw, in the way he held his menu. Steel that glinted.

Clémence was almost overwhelmed by a surge of emotion, which it took her a moment to identify as happiness. She was just so pleased to see him alive and well and eager to see her. It was too much of a stretch to say that he was the only family that she had, yet with her mother entwined with her banker boyfriend in Hong Kong, her father in a Vietnamese school and her fairy great-aunt in jail, that's what it felt like.

'Nice smile,' said the old man.

For some reason, Clémence felt her face reddening.

'And nice blush.'

'Oh, shut up,' she said. She pulled a thick hardback book from her bag and dropped it with a thud on the table. 'The Oxford English Dictionary,' she said.

The old man glanced at her under his bushy eyebrows. 'I know. I've looked it up.'

'Read it out loud to me,' Clémence ordered.

The old man flicked to the relevant page. He cleared his throat. '"Atelier. Noun. A workshop or studio. Origin seventeenth century, from French."'

'I think that's pretty clear, don't you?' said Clémence, in triumph. She replaced the dictionary in her bag. 'How did you get here?'

'Train. I drove myself to the station. I'm driving now. I own an old Rover, you know. The MacInneses were looking after it.'

Clémence raised her eyebrows.

'I'm perfectly safe.'

'Is Sheila looking after you as well as your car?'

'She keeps an eye on me. But I can do everything myself now. I even went down to London last week to buy Stephen those two pints I owed him.'

'How was that?'

'He only drank one of them,' said the old man. 'He is a miserable old git. But we're going to stay in touch.'

They ordered. With only a moment's hesitation, Clémence opted for the steak and chips. As an experienced student, she knew meals out were opportunities not to be missed. The old man joined her, and they each ordered a glass of red wine.

'How's your memory?'

'It's improving,' the old man said. 'Jigsaw pieces keep on turning up and I slot them into place. I've remembered a lot about Australia, and some of living in Yorkshire after the war. Oddly, still very little about the last year since I decided to come back to Britain.'

'Will the rest come back?'

'They don't know. It may.'

'You certainly look a lot better.'

'I *feel* a lot better. I can feel that a burden that has been weighing on me for most of my life has been lifted. It's strange, I couldn't remember or identify exactly what that burden was, but that didn't make it any less heavy. And it's gone now.'

'What are you going to do now?' Clémence asked. 'Will they let you stay on at Culzie?'

'Until September.'

'And after that?'

'I've been talking to people in Australia. Turns out I have friends there. And an accountant and a lawyer. I didn't sell my house in Mundaring, I rented it out, but the tenants are moving out in August. It sounds as if I was a pretty good doctor. People seem to have liked me. Still like me.'

'That's wonderful!' said Clémence. 'So are you going back there?'

'Yes,' said the old man. 'In September. It's like starting up a new life.' He frowned. 'Unfortunately, the one neighbour I do remember as a good friend, Mike, died last year. The eagle man. But that's what happens when you get to my age.'

'I'll miss you,' Clémence said.

The old man smiled. 'Perth isn't that far from Hong Kong, is it?'

'It's thousands of miles,' said Clémence.

'I'm sure it's on the way to Scotland. You should drop by. You're a student. You've got a backpack.'

Clémence laughed. 'Yes, of course it is. I'd like that.'

Their steaks came, and Clémence tucked into hers with gusto.

'How's Callum?' the old man asked.

'He's fine,' she said. She felt herself blushing again, but this time the old man didn't say anything. 'He says hello.'

'I thought of giving him my toaster. You know, if he needs a weapon to protect his house. You don't need a licence for it.'

'I'll tell him. He'll be thrilled.'

'Have you heard anything more from the police?'

The legal situation had turned out to be very complicated. The police in Arizona naturally wanted Fabrice and Madeleine extradited, but the Scots wanted to charge Fabrice with attempted

346

murder, or some other legal definition which encompassed running around the Highlands with a gun trying to shoot people. There was also the question of the death penalty. Fabrice had a prior conviction for murder, which made Nathan's homicide a capital crime in Arizona. But it also made extradition from Scotland much more difficult.

'Nothing recently,' said Clémence. 'Madeleine's lawyer came to see me on Monday. He told me she plans to plead guilty to everything. She's going to Arizona next week. Bail is unlikely, even at her age, so she's probably going straight to jail. But at least with a guilty plea there is no chance of the death penalty.'

'I'm glad of that,' said the old man. 'Did he tell you anything else?'

'She has set up a fund to pay for the rest of my education. Apparently she owns Grandpa's flat in Notting Hill and she's giving it to him. The lawyer said she was planning to leave me something in her will. I said I didn't want it.'

The old man raised his eyebrows. 'That might be a lot of money. Wakefield Oil is a big company.'

'I know. But I really don't want it. It's all Alden's, isn't it, originally? It's tainted. Bad karma. Very bad karma.'

'I'm not entirely sure what bad karma is, but you are probably right.' The old man reached into a canvas bag by his feet. 'I've brought something too.' He pulled out a black exercise book. With a red binding.

'Is that what I think it is?' asked Clémence.

'The police found it in Fabrice's car. He hadn't destroyed it.'

'Can I read it?'

'Of course,' said the old man.

Clémence hesitated. She wanted to reach out and grab it, but that seemed rude.

'What are you going to do with it? Are you going to try to publish a second edition of *Death At Wyvis*?'

'Actually, I have another idea, but it requires your help.'

The old man's eyes were twinkling. He was excited.

'Oh, yes. What is it?'

'I thought you and I could write a book together. A new book. Incorporating *Death At Wyvis* and adding your story to mine. After all these years, I finally know what really happened, and I need to set the record straight.'

'And you want my help? You're the one who has written all the books before.'

'I think it would be fun to write it together. And to give your point of view. We could have a crack at it over the summer before I go back to Australia. You could come and stay at Culzie. Bring Callum. We could play Scrabble. I'll let you win again.' The old man smiled slyly. 'Of course if you have to go back to Hong Kong, I would understand.'

The idea grabbed Clémence. She was dreading going home; she wasn't even sure whether her mother would let her back in the house. This sounded fun. She really liked the idea of spending the summer with Callum, and Madeleine's money would fund it.

Then a thought struck her. 'We wouldn't mention Patrick jumping on me, would we?'

'Oh, I think we should, don't you? I think your side of the story will be very convincing. And it would serve him right.'

Clémence hesitated. The old man was looking at her steadily. She trusted him. 'OK,' she said. 'Patrick is in the book. I assume we'd say it was a novel?'

'Of course. Why break with tradition?'

'And what would we call it? *Death At Wyvis Two*?'

'I thought *Amnesia*.'

'So you get star billing?'

'We could be joint authors.'

'You mean ditch Angus Culzie?'

'Yes. That was just me.'

Clémence hesitated. 'Wouldn't one name be better? Another pseudonym?'

'Maybe,' said the old man. 'But what?'

Clémence's mind was blank. 'I don't know.'

'I do,' said the old man, after a moment's thought. 'We can use Mike's name. You know, my friend with the eagles.'

'OK,' said Clémence. 'What was that?'

'Michael Ridpath.'

Clémence thought it over. She liked the idea. She liked it a lot.

'All right,' she said. 'Let's do it.'

AUTHOR'S NOTE

There is a Wyvis Estate on the shores of Loch Glass in Easter Ross, although I have rearranged some of the dwellings there. The various owners of the estate over the years and their families are entirely fictional, with the exception of the nineteenth-century proprietor. The bed and breakfast outside Dingwall run by a vet and his wife is entirely real. The name is Kildun Cottage, and I warmly recommend it.

I should like to thank a number of people who have helped me with this book: Andrew Botterill, Kevin Anderson, Alasdair and Gill Macnab, Aline Templeton, Kate Penrose, Julia Ridpath and Richenda Todd. Also Louise Cullen and Sara O'Keeffe at Atlantic Books, Nicky Lovick, Liz Hatherell, my agent Oli Munson and, as always, Barbara.